HIGHLANDER
Taken

**Also available from
Juliette Miller
and Harlequin HQN**

Highlander Claimed

**And watch for more fiery tales of Clan Mackenzie,
coming soon!**

JULIETTE MILLER

HIGHLANDER
Taken

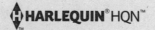

If you purchased this book without a cover you should be aware that this book is stolen property. It was reported as "unsold and destroyed" to the publisher, and neither the author nor the publisher has received any payment for this "stripped book."

Recycling programs
for this product may
not exist in your area.

ISBN-13: 978-0-373-77767-9

HIGHLANDER TAKEN

Copyright © 2013 by Juliette Miller

All rights reserved. Except for use in any review, the reproduction or utilization of this work in whole or in part in any form by any electronic, mechanical or other means, now known or hereafter invented, including xerography, photocopying and recording, or in any information storage or retrieval system, is forbidden without the written permission of the publisher, Harlequin HQN, 225 Duncan Mill Road, Don Mills, Ontario M3B 3K9, Canada.

This is a work of fiction. Names, characters, places and incidents are either the product of the author's imagination or are used fictitiously, and any resemblance to actual persons, living or dead, business establishments, events or locales is entirely coincidental.

This edition published by arrangement with Harlequin Books S.A.

For questions and comments about the quality of this book, please contact us at CustomerService@Harlequin.com.

® and TM are trademarks of Harlequin Enterprises Limited or its corporate affiliates. Trademarks indicated with ® are registered in the United States Patent and Trademark Office, the Canadian Trade Marks Office and in other countries.

Printed in U.S.A.

For M, as always

ACKNOWLEDGMENTS

Thanks to Mel Berger, for saying yes.
Thanks to Tara Parsons,
and especially Leonore Waldrip, for her hard work
and enthusiasm. Thanks to DS, my ideal first reader.
Thanks to H and L, for being beautiful people.
Thanks to SC for her unwavering support.
And most of all, thanks to Miles, my husband, my
resident historian, my kilt-wearing, sword-wielding
muse, my best friend, my true love. For everything.

CHAPTER ONE

I FELT THE TINGLING, heated sensation of someone watching me.

Turning to see who it was, my heart skipped an uneasy beat as our eyes met across the crowded room. I quickly looked away, shaken by the unnerving connection. With some difficulty, I could name the emotions he stirred in me with that one, brief glance. Fascination, caution and, more than any other: fear.

He was standing at the entrance of the grand hallway of his family's manor, flanked by his two brothers. Every pair of eyes at the well-attended gathering couldn't help but stare. They were big, imposing men. With their brazen silhouettes dramatically backlit by torchlight, they commanded attention. Laird Knox Mackenzie, the largest of the three, was known for his well-trained army and his formidable leadership. Wilkie Mackenzie was said to be more lighthearted in nature, and possessed a near-legendary handsomeness that found many women gasping at his sudden appearance now.

But it was this third brother—Kade Mackenzie—who captured my attention most of all. He was equally as tall as his black-haired brothers, but slimmer, and

somehow more lithe—almost catlike—in his movements. His long hair was a deep shade of dark brown
that caught the gold light of the dancing fire he stood
next to, giving him a subtle halo and the aura of a dangerous rogue angel.

All three men looked wholly in control of the scene,
a confidence that might have stemmed from their skills
with the sword as well as their ownership of some of
the richest, most bountiful agricultural lands in all the
Highlands. And while Laird Mackenzie and Wilkie gave
a distinct impression of being at ease in their own skin,
there was a wandering restlessness to Kade that not only
entranced me, but also raised the tiny hairs on my arms
in silent, spellbound alarm.

I took comfort from the close presence and inces-
sant gossip of my four sisters and two cousins. "There
he is," said my sister Maisie, clutching my arm. "It's
Wilkie. Lord above, he's magnificent. None of you are
even to speak to him. Not until our marriage is secured
beyond doubt. Even then, you're to keep your distance.
He's mine."

Maisie had claimed Wilkie for herself months ago,
after he had once visited our manor. Whether he agreed
to the match or not was yet to be determined.

"Aye, Maisie," responded Clementine, my eldest sister. "We're all aware of your designs on him. You speak
of nothing else."

"You can help yourselves to his brothers," Maisie
allowed.

"Who would dare approach them?" said Bonnie, my

younger cousin, eyeing the Mackenzies with trepidation and something akin to awe. "They're so intimidating. Laird Mackenzie is displeasingly gruff, I've heard it said. Look at the size of him. And Kade, well, his reputation speaks for itself. He's as wild as they come."

"Luckily for you, then," Maisie replied, "there are many *other* men in attendance tonight."

It was true. The Mackenzie clan was hosting, among others, the Macintoshes and Munros, whose highest-ranking family was pleasingly populated by a number of rowdy, good-looking bachelors. My sisters and cousins were pink-cheeked, primped and plumped into their best and most revealingly cut gowns, and more than ready for the occasion.

I, on the other hand, wanted nothing more than to return to our guest chambers and retire for the night. Or to flee, or do something completely unexpected of me. I willed myself not to let my thoughts return, once again, to Caleb, the only boy who had ever shown me kindness, lost to me now. It had been a fortnight since Caleb had asked for my hand in marriage, only to be promptly banished to Edinburgh by my father, Laird Morrison. Caleb's status was low—not fit for the daughter of the laird himself—and his occupation as an apprentice blacksmith gave my father reason to have him trained by experts farther afield. Urgently. I had not even been allowed to bid him farewell.

The injustice of that hard-hearted act filled me with a sadness that was outlined by what felt remarkably like anger. It wasn't fair that my father could pluck my beloved out of my life so callously, and with such finality. Gone, just like that. The suddenness of Caleb's absence consumed me to such an extent that I had spent several days heartbroken and bedridden. I'd felt weakened and empty from all the tears I'd wept, as though my spirit had dripped away along with them. And then the heartbreak had turned, uprooting a long-buried resentment that was far less accepting. Our upbringing of abuse and tyranny had conditioned us to submit to the cruel whims of our father, but lately my usual obedience had become disrupted. I was tired of the beatings and the belittlement. A part of me wanted to rise up and break free like never before. I wanted nothing more than to be alone with my thoughts so I could let that seedling of empowerment grow, and lead me where it may.

"Evening, ladies," said one of the Munro men, sidling up between me and Bonnie, standing so close that a long strand of his hair brushed against my cheek. "My name is Tadgh," he said, tilting his head low in a bid to draw my eyes up, to his. "And you must be Stella."

I wasn't sure why he was singling me out, or even how he knew my name. It would have been rude to ignore him blatantly, but in my current state, the last thing I felt like doing was engaging one of these Munros, with their reputations as devout merry-makers and instigators of occasional debauchery. I wildly wished that one of my family members would speak to him instead.

Thankfully, one did. "A pleasure, Tadgh," said Bonnie. "'Tis a fine affair, is it not? The manor is so nicely presented. The Mackenzies are hospitable, and do such a splendid job of decorating, don't you agree?" Bonnie had a flirtatious nature, though she had already selected a husband. It wasn't time for her to ask for permission yet; she knew, as her hopeful conquest did, that my father would not allow either of his nieces to be married until at least one of his daughters had made a suitable match.

"To be sure," Tadgh answered blithely, as though he couldn't care less about the decorating but had his mind on darker, more playful endeavors. And he was still watching me. "So, Stella, what do *you* think of the decorations? Do the finely woven tapestries please *you?*"

I didn't have much experience with the conversations of men, so I couldn't be entirely sure, but I had the feeling he was teasing me. A month ago, I would have been too timid to respond to Tadgh Munro; conversing with the wrong man would lead to punishment: this I knew only too well. Two weeks ago, I would have been too heartbroken. Tonight, however, my emotions were unruly. A newfound internal rebellion seemed to be gaining momentum.

In fact, they *were* beautiful tapestries. The sight of their rich colors and masterful workmanship made me realize I hadn't noticed details of this type—of beauty and depth—for too long. I had a sudden unfamiliar urge to experience and appreciate more of life, and be allowed to do so, on my own terms. But I did not mention any of this to Tadgh. Instead, I said quietly, "Aye, they do."

Two more Munro men joined us, armed with a tray of

goblets and pitchers of ale, and were introduced as Tosh and Angus. "Ladies, may I pour you a goblet of ale?" Angus asked. "The Mackenzies make a fine drop." He poured ale into a cup and handed it to me, which Tadgh intercepted, completing the exchange. I took the cup from Tadgh's hand and almost dropped it when his fingers slid audaciously over mine. I pulled back quickly, spilling a drop of the ale. My father and his men would be watching me, as always. Tadgh, perhaps unaware of this, smiled at my reaction. Dressed as he was in his bright red Munro tartan, the fiery shades in his hair were all the more illuminated. Each of the Munros, in fact, glowed with their red-hued aura and their festive, unreserved manner. The Mackenzies, I couldn't help contrasting, in their navy blues and forest-greens and with their dark night-lit hair, offered a much more formidable presence.

"The lovely Stella is a mite skittish," Tadgh commented to his cousins, "although I've heard that under that exquisite, demure facade there's a feisty wee rebel who steals carriages and takes to men with their own weapons. Captivating indeed."

"Aye," Tosh Munro responded, chuckling. "Hugh Morrison still wears the bandages. On his right hand, no less. His sword-carrying hand." As his eyes roved my face and my body, he said, "Already she is famed for her beauty, and now she presents a dangerous challenge all the sweeter to any man who gets past her defenses."

That the Munros were both entertained and intrigued by my run-in with my father's men was disturbing enough. Much more worrisome, however, was that news of my actions had spread. My father would only be further enraged if my marriage prospects were tainted by a reputation for defiance. The Munros, however, didn't seem at all deterred. Several of them stood close to me, and Tadgh in particular was eagerly attentive. They, as all the men at the gathering, wore their kilts and their ceremonial garb, including swords and knife belts. They were big men, warriors each one. I thought again of Caleb, who was gentle and kind in a way that these men could never be, and I missed him greatly in that moment.

It was true, after all. I had rebelled. Not more than an hour after Caleb's banishment, I had run to the stables. I knew that my father's men would follow me and return me home, disgraced. Even so, I asked one of the stable boys to prepare a small carriage for me. Before he had even secured the horses in their harnesses, my father and his men had found me.

Lash her again, my father had commanded his officers, *so she'll remember that my orders are not to be disobeyed. Again. Let her carry the bruises to remind her of her place.* A task that the men had been all too willing to carry out, and with particular dedication. And I had fought back, as I had done before, but with more strategy this time. I'd grabbed one of the soldier's knives and swiped it at him, cutting his hand. Even so, I'd been outnumbered and easy enough for them to constrain and punish.

The pain seemed to echo through me even now, with

an ache both searing and deep. My outward signs of bruising had faded, but those inflicted on my heart and on my soul remained, as always. And my father's words lingered.

If you carry on with such foolery, you'll not be eligible to marry a nobleman. You'll be forevermore seen as a ruined woman. Your lowly blacksmith has neither the resources nor the disposition to fight off my men. He has no means to support you. You'll be doomed to a life of exile and poverty.

As much as the memory humiliated me, I knew my father's warnings had been accurate enough. Caleb was as young as I was, inexperienced in the ways of fighting and weaponry. He was skilled at making swords, but not at using them. Still, I yearned for him. His mildness. His sensitivity. He was the only man I had ever met who did not make me feel utterly defenseless.

Tadgh, whose bold insistence only seemed to emphasize the divide between these lusty warriors and my gentle lost love, leaned closer, pushing a strand of my long hair back behind my shoulder to gain better access to my ear, then proceeded to whisper to me, "You're far more beautiful than your sisters. Positively stunning, you are, lass."

I moved away from him, staring at his face in mute shock. What an outrageously rude thing to say! With my sisters capable of overhearing. But Tadgh appeared amused by my expression and continued, getting closer despite my attempts to distance myself. "I'd heard you spoken of, but the descriptions hardly do you justice.

The combined effects of your beauty and your feisty spirit have gained you some repute, you know. There are men who have come here tonight, some from great distances, for the sole purpose of laying their eyes on the mysterious Stella Morrison."

I could feel that my cheeks were burning in embarrassment. Was it true? Had I been spoken about in this way?

I wished I could take my leave and return to the guest chambers. But my father would be furious, and the last thing I wanted to do was provoke more of his outrage. I knew I had little choice but to accept the consequences of my privileged position and do as I was told. This gathering, after all, had been planned with that specific goal in mind: securing at least one match for Clementine, me, Maisie, Ann or Agnes. My father was ailing now, and getting old. I had even heard it said that he fought off the beginnings of madness, which I believed to be true. His accusations were becoming laced with nonsensical edges. The fact that he had five daughters and two nieces, but no brothers, sons or nephews, did little to ease his state of mind. To make matters worse, his brother-in-law, my uncle, who had been groomed to take over the lairdship, had been killed in battle during the Campbell uprising over a year ago.

So it was up to one of us to marry well and secure a new laird for our moderately prosperous keep and our large but somewhat-flagging army. Marriage to a Mackenzie would secure an alliance that would unite our forces to theirs; this was crucial to my father, now more than ever since the Campbell rebellion was threatening to reignite.

Maisie was as feverish as my father about her potential match to Wilkie, which she hoped would be arranged officially this night. She felt fortunate that her conquest was not only noble, wealthy and talented, but also exceedingly good-looking. All three Mackenzie brothers were celebrated for their bravery, their swordsmanship, their military prowess and—it had to be said—their looks. Looks that would, in my father's words, produce a handsome heir. So my father was anxious to secure the engagement. He had already begun arrangements with Laird Mackenzie regarding Maisie's marriage to Wilkie.

The rest of us, too, were obliged to seek out men with credentials: lands, wealth and military alliances were to be at the top of the list of our considerations. Only with one or more of these attributes would the suitor in question gain my father's approval. A Munro would please my father, I knew that. Preferably the one in line to accept the lairdship. If I recalled correctly, the name associated with that privilege was Magnus, not Tadgh. Either way, I couldn't quite bring myself to care.

"Would you like to go for a stroll with me, Stella, to the drawing room?" Tadgh suggested. "I've heard the tapestries in there are even more spectacular."

I knew he was mocking me. We were both well aware that there was not the tiniest likelihood that I would—or *could,* for the sake of my reputation—agree to a private stroll to an unattended drawing room with the likes of Tadgh Munro.

"Thank you, but I must decline," I replied, perhaps overly shortly.

Bonnie attempted to smooth over my rudeness with a suitably charming comment. I scarcely heard what it was, or Tadgh's response to it. I was allowing myself a small, delicious reprieve. I thought of Caleb and the stolen moments we'd shared in the blacksmith's hut, where he worked. Once I'd watched him bang a still-molten sword with a hammer, honing its blade. Another day he'd been making chains, linked together while hot, forged solid and unbreakable once they were cooled. *I'm to install these in the dungeons,* he'd said, and I'd marveled at the thought. Such a task would require considerable bravery, and skill, I had thought at the time. Although Caleb and I hadn't spent much time together, these brief memories were some of the sweetest I had ever known.

Such was the extent of my distraction that I didn't notice, after a time, the accumulating crowd enveloping us. I turned to see Kade Mackenzie talking casually to Tadgh, just a few feet from where I stood. I was, I had to admit, riveted by the sight of him. Kade Mackenzie was even taller up close. His shoulders were squared and solid. The white tunic he wore emphasized the dark hues of his hair and his tawny, sun-bronzed skin. He looked every inch the savage warrior he was reputed to be. His eyes were a memorable shade of clear, light blue, a detail I couldn't help but notice as he watched my finger absentmindedly twirl itself through a ringlet of my long hair. An expression of relaxed arrogance played across his bold features, softened only by the glimmer of subdued fascination that lurked behind it. It was true I was somewhat different-looking from my sisters. My hair was darker and I wore it longer. My eyes were a lighter hue than my sisters', almost amber in color, with unusual flecks of yellow. I thought of Tadgh's unsettling comment. And of a description my sisters liked to tease me with. *Stella, you've the eyes of a frightened wildcat and the face of a fallen angel.* My clan members often commented that I was the child who looked most like our mother, though I myself could not remember her. She died when I was three.

Against the backdrop of my lingering thoughts of Caleb, and even amid the jaunty camaraderie of the Munros, the sudden looming countenance of Kade Mackenzie was even more daunting and dramatic than it had been from afar. His presence seemed to close in around me and cause an inexplicable tightening of my throat, as if he were somehow stealing light and air. Sequestered and restricted to the company of my sisters and cousins for most of my life, I was entirely out of my element in the company of men. I knew this was why I preferred the nonthreatening gentleness of Caleb to the overt masculinity of men like Kade Mackenzie. His swarthy charisma leaped into the space all around him, and provided a sharp juxtaposition to the shadow of Caleb's mild, soothing memory. There was nothing soothing or mild about Kade Mackenzie. Which was precisely why I wanted to put as much distance between us as I could.

But I was held in place by my younger sister Ann and my cousin Bonnie, who strung their arms through mine, as though sensing my thoughts and preempting any attempts I might make to leave.

"Ladies," Angus Munro was saying, "may I top up your drinks? 'Tis a night for frivolity, after all."

Ann, my sweetest of sisters, accepted her drink from Angus with a shy smile. Angus, all easy laughter and bright red-lit hair, was clearly enjoying himself as he served our ale. He topped up Kade's cup, then replenished his own with a generous serving that threatened to overflow. Angus watched Ann take a tiny sip from her goblet, and, as much as I would have liked to retreat to the quiet of my chambers, I resolved then to stay and make sure she was well chaperoned. The combination of free-flowing ale, Angus's overeager manner and his hawk-eyed attention of my vulnerable sister were enough to keep me in place, firmly at her side.

And all the while, as colorful conversation filled the large yet still-cozy hall, as people drifted and mingled, Kade Mackenzie's cool predatory stare seemed to fix itself on me all too often, making me feel uneasy and restless. The ale did nothing to calm my nerves and seemed to stretch the minutes into long, hazy hours.

After drinking almost a full goblet of the sweet ale, in fact, I began to feel woozy and decided to avail myself of the inviting courtyard at the far end of the hall. Leaving Ann in Clementine's care, I walked the long length of the hall, feeling heated and flushed, and reveling in the cool touch of the night air as soon as I reached it. I closed the door behind me to distance myself, just for a few minutes, from the noisy gathering.

No one had followed me. I had, for once, escaped the notice of my father's guards. At this realization, I followed a lit pathway that led beckoningly into a tiny rose garden, enclosed by small trees and trellises. Intrigued and invigorated by my momentary freedom, I wandered just a few steps farther—and a few more—to find a secluded bench. Delighted with my find, I sat. I knew I shouldn't be alone in a dark, isolated place such as this, but my newfound despair—and anger—had undermined the forced habits of my upbringing. Just for a few minutes, I wanted to pretend I was free to make my own choices, to fantasize about being treated with respect, or even love. And to appreciate the very simple pleasure of being alone.

The late-summer perfume of the roses filled the air with their heady scent, and I savored the peaceful moment. The past few weeks had been filled with turmoil and sadness, and I was grateful for the window of solace this little haven provided.

But then, without warning, a brisk, high gust of wind blew all the candles out.

The darkness was sudden and startling.

Flickering stars overhead were shadowed by bulky black clouds, and the moon was hidden. I had only the distant torchlight of the manor to guide me back. I stood, feeling unsteady not only from the lingering effects of the ale but also the stark isolation.

As my eyes adjusted infinitesimally to the darkness, I guessed at my return route along the meandering path back to the manor. I took a step, holding my hands out in front of me and feeling somewhat ridiculous. I laughed lightly at my predicament, wondering at my own impetuousness. The sound of my own laughter lingered with me briefly; it was a sound I hadn't heard in some time. If I'd once been prone to bouts of adventurousness as a child, that tendency had been decisively eradicated from my nature by my father's tyranny. If he could have seen me now, I had no doubt I'd be beaten yet again. So there was a small, defiant satisfaction to this seclusion.

But some subtle intuition brought my laughter to an abrupt end. A chill raised the hairs on the back of my neck in a sudden realization: someone was here with me. My senses instantly sharpened.

The fall of a heavy footstep.

The dark outline of a tall figure.

A man, certainly.

A very large one, at that.

My heart thumped edgily and I took a step in an unintentional direction, as though my legs meant to flee whether I wanted to or not. But the darkness, the uneven surface of the ground and my own layered imbalance caught me off guard and I almost stumbled but for the hand that reached out to steady me.

The ironlike bonds of that grasp were dizzying in the promise of strength that lurked underneath the gentle, guiding touch. And the scent of him, like wood and leather and smoke, so foreign to me. So very, entirely masculine.

"I'll not hurt you," he said softly, and in the tones of his voice I detected truth, a sense of honor, a genuine attempt to reassure. His words dampened my fear. I wasn't at all sure why, but I believed them.

He steadied me completely, and I was surprised to find that his protective hold felt more inviting than threatening, especially in this total darkness. An anchor, sure and steady, in the tumultuous night.

I could acknowledge that a small part of me was *enjoying* this wild, illicit encounter. I was not afraid, reassured as I had been by his voice. And I was drawn, inexplicably, to that spiced, enticing scent of him.

Still holding my arm, he drew me closer, until I was pressed up against the hard warmth of his body. He was so dark, this phantom, so utterly unseeable. Yet the solidity of him fed me an encouraging comfort. It was a mercurial comfort, the kind that might only be found in a hidden, clandestine garden, void of light and sound, save the faraway beacon of an untouchable reality. We were frozen in an unexpected and timeless moment.

His other arm wrapped silently around me and I could feel the silky graze of his hair against my neck. I gasped at the intimacy of it, the caressing softness that stirred me in ways I had never known.

Then, under the dark cover of a moonless sky, the stranger's parted lips touched mine, brushing slowly before settling in with gentle, deliberate pressure. My mind went blank and my knees gave out, but his strong-hold was such that it mattered not. The soft exploration of his tongue sent channels of warmth into my body, lingering and curling, reaching deep. The taste of his kiss, so unexpected, so sweet, invited me to open to his supple demands, to take more of him, to let him in.

I had been kissed only once before by my shy and boyish Caleb: a very brief, barely-there touch. This was something else altogether. There was nothing shy or boyish about *this* kiss. This kiss pulled me in directions I, in a saner moment, would never have dared. Wild, re-lentless sensation spooled into me darkly as the strang-er's kiss deepened. His hand held my jaw with infinite care. A vague internal warning was swept away by the billowing, immediate urge my body had become. The effects of his tongue's touch traveled lightly to the tips of my breasts and the softening secreted place between my legs, which piqued and moistened with an awaken-ing want. I wanted his mouth on my skin, everywhere, and his hands to grip me and hold me down with all the promise of their brutal-gentle strength. I wanted to lose myself in this stranger completely, to drink him in, such was the intoxication of him.

From somewhere outside our tumbling, succulent connection, a voice called.

My name. And again.

It was Ann's voice, and it was enough to shock me back into a shadowed awareness.

Slowly, reluctantly, the stranger pulled back.

Into this small distance between us, my regrets

spilled. Regrets, I was amazed to realize, that were not about what I had done with this phantom lover, but what I had *not* done. The potency of him had wholly captivated me, and even now I wanted more of him. I wanted him to kiss me again, to soothe and stoke the burning need he had lit within me.

Here, under an overcast night and still in the dark stranger's enveloping embrace, I had the disconcerting feeling that I had changed. That this place and this kiss would forever haunt me. That nothing would ever satisfy me until I could feel an approximation of this, of him. Again, and always, I would seek the beauty of this sudden and forbidden intimacy.

If this was what rebellion felt like, then I wanted more of it.

The distant calls continued.

My conscious mind insisted I disengage from him, and make a hasty retreat toward the manor. Yet I couldn't move. Who was he? Would I ever find him again, to be touched and tasted and held close to his elusive, sheltering heat?

The stranger moved, and spoke. The roughened notes of his soft, deep voice sent quickening warmth to my secret places, which had become swollen with a sweet ache that caused me to gasp lightly. I would have done anything that voice asked me to do. Anything.

"Hold on to me," he said. "Let me take you."

For a tiny moment, a wicked excitement lurked in the cravings of my body that were new to me, but then I realized what he meant: he would take me back to the manor.

His muscled arm was looped around me, encompassing me in his male-spiced scent. I grasped onto his clothing, and further, reaching my arms around his waist. I could feel the hardness and warmth of his body even through the layers of fabric, and I imagined what his skin might feel like under my fingertips. My fingers curled around the leather of his belt, and I could feel the bone handle of a large knife strung to it.

He began to lead me, supporting my weight easily. He was surefooted, even in the darkness, and he navigated our path without difficulty. And then he stopped. We were still some distance from the lit outskirts of the courtyard, but the path was faintly visible now, straight and smooth. He withdrew his embrace carefully, as though to ensure that I wouldn't topple over without his support. And the air felt cool and stark at the sudden removal of his body against mine.

He stood against the darkness and I could see no more of him than I had until now, just his solid and very black silhouette. He leaned his mouth close to my ear and whispered, "I will taste more of you, Stella. I have not had nearly enough. I want you as my own."

And then he was gone.

CHAPTER TWO

SHAKEN AS MUCH by the stranger's sudden departure as I had been by all that had taken place before it, I walked unsteadily back to the courtyard. Ann, Agnes and Bonnie were there, and they rushed up to me as soon as I stepped into the light.

"Stella!" Ann exclaimed. "What's happened? We've been calling you. Where have you been?"

I smoothed my hair with my hands, hoping I didn't look as wild and wanton as I felt. "'Twas nothing," I said lightly, laughing it off. "I went for a stroll in the gardens."

The three of them stared at me, knowing full well we weren't allowed such larkish pursuits, especially alone and in the dark of night. I watched their eyes register my flushed cheeks, my curled and windblown hair, my wide eyes. I was fervently thankful they couldn't detect the more profound changes in me, or at least I hoped it.

"Whatever for?" asked Agnes.

"I needed some air," I said. "I wandered too far and the wind blew out the candles. It took me some time to find my way back, is all. I'm fine."

"You look like you've seen a ghost," commented

Bonnie, leading me back inside, where the noise and light was very nearly overwhelming.

Not a ghost, nay. A phantom.

A phantom, I only now realized, who knew me. He'd called me by my name. This detail felt significant. Had he known who I was, even before my sisters called out to me? He'd said he wanted to see me, to find me—nay, to *taste* me—once again. I hoped desperately that he would succeed in his pursuit.

But even now, in my sisters' familiar company, surrounded by people's chatter and full-on brightness, my encounter with the hidden stranger felt unreal. Had he merely been a figment of my ever-hopeful romantic mind? Maybe I'd dreamed him in response to the heartbreak of recent days. I could justify my revelation as such, even if I could still taste him on my tongue and feel the effects of his touch to my very core. I knew, too, that this memory—real or not—had nothing to do with Caleb. The phantom lover had been too different, in every way. Already, Caleb's face had faded by the slightest degree. More forcefully, the phantom's looming outline dominated all thoughts. His tamed strength, his intoxicating scent: these details alone were enough to inspire a lush craving deep within me that very nearly made me moan aloud.

What was happening to me? Had I finally had enough of being put down and held back by my overbearing father, and was reacting with bold, bizarre belligerence? Already, I yearned for more of the stranger, as I had known I would. I felt like running back outside to the secluded garden and calling him back to me.

Instead, I took a deep breath and attempted to calm myself. Passionate, temperamental behavior was punished in our family. The only exceptions to this rule were specific indiscretions that might succeed in landing one of us a wealthy and well-bred husband. Aside from that one allowance, obedience, compliance and reserve were the order of the day. And I had carried out my role with suitable deference, for the most part. My life was predictable and comfortable enough, as these things went. I acted as I was expected to act—as I was forced to act—even if my heart questioned the orders. Why I felt the urge to wander, to run, to shout and to kiss mysterious strangers now, I didn't know. The steady ground of my world, of late, seemed to be taking on a new inconsistency that possessed all the solidity of quicksand.

With effort, I took my place in my sisters' circle as we reentered the grand hall. I sipped a cool drink of water and felt better for it. Still, I felt removed somehow. My eyes restlessly surveyed the crowd, measuring, hoping. Was he here in this room? Quite possibly. I studied one man, then the next. But none of them seemed the perfect fit. And, disappointingly, I noticed that almost every single man in attendance wore a belt with a knife strapped to it. These men were warriors. Knives and swords weren't just their tools; they were their fashion accessories. They were their comfort, their necessity and their way of life. If I was to find my phantom, I would need more helpful clues than a belt with a knife, and a physique that was tall and broad-shouldered. So I was not to get off so lightly.

Still, my eyes roved.

I was distracted then by Maisie as she returned to our group, accompanied by Wilkie, her pale arm weaved decisively through his brown, brawny one. I had not met Wilkie before. And although I didn't know much about him, I could detect that he seemed tense. His expression appeared agitated, as if his concentration was elsewhere. Maisie's insistent attention did little to engage him, but Maisie was nothing if not persistent. Admirably so, I thought. She fawned and flirted, softly touching his hair and his face until he relented somewhat, an exhibition I found mildly fascinating. In fact, I was so immersed in watching the exchange that I didn't immediately notice that someone was speaking to me. I very nearly jumped out of my skin when I saw who it was.

"Are you enjoying your evening, Miss Morrison?" Kade Mackenzie's voice was deep and inflected with raw, dark energy. Of course I couldn't help considering the shape and height of him, to compare it against the fresh memory of my hidden stranger. But he was too tall, I thought. And something about his movements seemed too quick.

He couldn't be the one, I felt certain. The scent wasn't quite right, mingled and subdued by the pressing crowd. And he hadn't used my first name. He probably had no idea which Morrison I was.

Instead of the enveloping calm I'd experienced in

the stranger's embrace, and despite the relaxed, festive mood of the scene, the air between us felt charged, as though laced with a barely restrained warning. I could sense even more strongly at this close proximity that Kade was a man with an unpredictable nature. The glint in his eyes seemed to confirm my estimations while also suggesting he was having no difficulty reading every nuance of my tangled unease. Again I thought about fleeing somewhere, anywhere, as quickly as I could. But it was this almost-teasing edge to his manner that held me in place. I felt mildly irked by the nudging humor in him, as though the obvious fact that he was making me nervous was entertaining to him.

He had asked me a question, and was waiting for my reply. I had to concentrate for a moment to recall it. A simple, meaningless pleasantry. *Are you enjoying your evening, Miss Morrison?* The polite thing to do would have been to lie, especially considering it was his family that was hosting the event. Instead, I heard myself saying, "Not particularly."

It was then that Kade Mackenzie smiled, just slightly, at my response. And it occurred to me at that moment that, while Wilkie was the famously good-looking brother, Kade was equally striking but somehow too complicated in expression to be conventionally handsome. His looks were dominated by reckless layers of the unknown. "She has a seraphic face," he commented, "a body that could reduce a grown man to tears, a corralled feistiness that shines through nonetheless, lightning-quick reflexes—if what is heard is to be believed—yet her manners leave something to be desired. How very interesting. I'll admit, you're not quite what I was expecting."

Despite my layered reservations, I almost smiled, simultaneously miffed and flattered by his offhand description. I couldn't help asking it: "And what *were* you expecting?" The admission that he had been expecting anything at all seemed to confirm that Kade Mackenzie had gone out of his way to approach me. I wasn't sure how I felt about this. Apprehensive, certainly. The thought of being conquered by *this* specimen of virile ferocity was more than I could grasp in my current state.

He took a moment to respond, and when he did, I noticed the deep, distinctive huskiness of his voice as he spoke. Oddly, there was a comforting edge to the rough, quiet timbre of it that was not dissimilar, I couldn't help but consider, to the hushed murmur of my hidden stranger. *Let me take you.* "What I was expecting was a quaint, moderately pleasing heiress with a penchant for insolence. The insolence is true enough. Heiress, aye, although the wealth on offer is somewhat overstated, we have reason to believe. As for the other details of the expectation, trust me when I assure you they were entirely inaccurate. Absurdly so."

I could only stare at him, agog at his confessions. I thought he might have just given me a very solicitous compliment even as he also might have insulted me, but, in fact, I couldn't be entirely sure either way. Whatever his meaning, it was clear enough that he was taking pleasure in his attempt to confuse me. And he was coming quite close to succeeding. But I was already riled enough by the recent difficulties of the life I was being forced to lead. So I decided not to give him the satisfaction. "If you find me quaint and insolent, then perhaps you should seek out the conversation of someone more pleasing to you."

At this, he smiled widely, his white teeth gleaming against the bronze glow of his face and his hair. He folded his arms across his broad chest and leaned a shoulder against the stone wall in a languid, insouciant movement that brought to light his sparked arrogance and his easy confidence. He possessed an odd combination of wicked appeal and pronounced, daring impulsiveness that infused me with an unusual anxious thrill. His eyes never left me. "On the contrary, I find insolence in women very intriguing—it happens to be an affliction that I'm able to cure almost entirely under the right circumstances. And if you'd been paying attention, you would understand that I find you quite the opposite of quaint. I can think of several other words I might use to describe you, aye, but even those seem lacking. Give me a minute to think of something more precise."

I wanted to ask him what those words were, of course, but I could see that he was playing with me, and expecting my curiosity to get the better of me, so I waited, watching him study my face. Disconcertingly, the effects of his comments and his smile burrowed into me, touching the shadowy, sensual effects of my encounter with the garden stranger. I tried desperately to distract myself, to tone down or ignore the light swell and the heat of my most private vulnerabilities, but my body had other ideas. I felt my cheeks flush and my breath quicken, and I looked away from him. I was surely going mad. I took a deep breath, willing myself not to burn under the heat of his blazing attentions.

"Am I making you nervous?" he asked softly, his lingering smile irritatingly perceptive.

"Nay," I said somewhat indignantly, albeit breathless, although he clearly was.

I met his eyes with cautious curiosity. I wanted to disengage myself from his arresting countenance but could not. Inexplicably, he was devastating me with a tumult of crashing, unknowable regrets and empty wishes. The search of his focus seemed to illuminate everything I had ever aspired to but had never, either through circumstance or from fear, been able to attain. Freedom. Choice. Love. Real happiness. I could not explain how this rugged stranger was able to expose such deep, suppressed feelings in me, as though he held the key to hidden recesses of my psyche that even *I* had not explored. Kade Mackenzie frightened me, aye, but there was more to it than that; his *effect* on me was acute, as though his own reckless tendencies were impacting me, and guiding me. Under the animated weight of his attentions, I felt I was losing control.

"Or am I affecting you in some other way?" he said, leaning closer. "Some wholly unexpected, visceral inclination that has you, in this very moment, questioning all your powers of resistance?"

How did he know that?

It wasn't *him* I felt the need to resist, I assured myself. I was overcome by my encounter in the secluded garden. I was suffering under the effects of the ale perhaps, or I was flushed and disoriented from the night air.

Kade continued, his voice low, his words meant exclusively for me. I watched his enigmatic, seraphic face as he spoke, with undue absorption. "And that's not the extent of it, I'm guessing. There's more to it, is there not? A wandering, restless hunger newly inspired, as it just so happens, here and now. As soon as you saw me, it would appear."

"You flatter yourself," I said quickly, hoping to break this connection in any way I could. Through rudeness, or any other means—it didn't matter, as long as I could somehow contain my composure and stop myself from doing something entirely inappropriate, like taking his hand and leading him into a quiet alcove. To let his influence arrest me and free me in any way it would. But I would only have been trying to recreate my illicit encounter with the garden phantom, I knew. Either way, I clasped my hands together behind me and made a point of neither reaching for nor even appreciating the invitingly thick locks of his richly colored dark hair that hung almost to his shoulders in shiny disarray.

He was toying with me, overflowing with charm, assured as he was of his own allure. An allure, to be sure, I wanted nothing to do with.

Kade's flashing eyes, as though reading my thoughts and finding reason to believe *he* was responsible for them, gave the impression that he was similarly affected, as though he might strike out at any moment, or indulge a wicked temper or start a fight. Each prospect, to me, was more daunting than the last. And even if I had seen a glimmer of amusement in him that I might not have expected and was undeniably drawn to, I couldn't shake the desire to distance myself from him, and quickly. He was too intense, too fiery, too confident, too masculine, *too everything*.

Fortunately, a commotion caused our circle to disperse. It was Wilkie who was causing a scene. He had, at some point during my distraction, removed himself from Maisie's grasp. Now he was some distance away, and holding the arm of Angus Munro in a viselike grip, pure fury written on his face. And Wilkie's other arm was slung possessively around a young woman I did not recognize. She had white-blond hair and eyes that were green even from a distance, attributes that made it clear that she hailed neither from the Mackenzie clan nor Munro. Her look was decidedly foreign, exotic even, and she was—it had to be said—devastatingly beautiful. I couldn't help but marvel at the shimmery fair colors of her, emphasized further not only by the pastel-pink shades of her dress, but also by Wilkie's black-haired and stormy-eyed counterpoint. Her slender body was pushed up scandalously close to Wilkie's, and her face, as she gazed up at him, clearly shone with a complete and unwavering adoration.

Angus was released and dismissed by Wilkie, and took his leave, retreating to the buffet table, still rubbing his wrist. And any questions the crowd might have had about the fair-haired girl were written most painfully across Maisie's face. Who was she? And why was Wilkie embracing her in this way and with a look on his face as though he was not only enraged and somehow anguished, but also utterly love-struck?

Before any such questions could even be asked and without so much as a backward glance, Wilkie disappeared with his willing captive up the grand staircase of the Mackenzie manor.

Maisie wasn't the only one who was distraught at this unexpected turn of events. The gravity of Wilkie's connection to the mysterious young woman had been apparent to all of us. And, while none of us knew quite what to make of the scene we had just witnessed, I had a distinct feeling that the consequences of that scene would extend beyond Wilkie, beyond Maisie and somehow to me. As though to confirm my anxious suspicion, Kade Mackenzie's narrowed and unyielding stare speared me with its thoughtful, wicked intensity, and I could read there my worst fears.

CHAPTER THREE

I WAS DREAMING. I knew this even as I drifted willingly into the sweet, comforting fantasy. Caleb's cool hand reached for mine, the touch light and welcoming. He helped me from the carriage, taking me close to his slim, warm body, ushering me into a back-alley stables. Sounds of the city filled the rain-soaked night—men's voices, the sharp, rhythmic clopping strikes of a horse's feet on cobblestones, a woman's distant laughter, drifting piano notes—and there was relief in the warmth of the enclosed hay-strewn haven, even if it smelled of burning coal and damp wool. Caleb smoothed the wet strands of my hair from my face. "'Tis not much," he said, "but we're out of the rain. I've some bread and water. And we're together. 'Tis all that matters."

Yet looming wide-shouldered shapes were emerging from the limitless shadows, swallowing Caleb, closing in. I recognized one of them from the distinctive lithe, predatory countenance of him and the glinting devil-blue glow of his eyes. His gold-and-silver weapons were strung across his restless body, bright splintered shards that cut the night. A twisting, edgy appeal to this danger held me and touched my body in a light, sultry caress, but the promise of pleasure was laced with unknowable darkness.

I fled, hiding, seeking refuge in a secluded garden that grew out of the gloom. I was comforted by the country air, the warm, rose-scented breeze. I knew he was there. I could feel him before I could see him. He had returned to me, my garden phantom, as I knew he would, to hold me and lead me to safety. He drew me to his body, enveloping me in his night-fevered embrace until there was nothing but the bold, rising sensation of his touch. His long fingers cupped my jaw. His mouth took mine in a gently demanding kiss and I was transformed. I had become a vessel to be filled, quivering with primal, aching need. His strong, masculine hands roamed my body, lighting the fire I had become. The waves rose, the beauty licked wherever his touch caressed me, I was falling, dying with pleasure, almost reaching the ecstatic peak of my every desire…

"Stella."

…so close…

"Stella."

Bonnie's voice. And Ann's. They were shaking me gently.

I opened my eyes to find them gathered around me, both regarding me with a look of amused concern. "Stella. Wake up."

As my dream faded, I noticed that my sheets were wrapped around my legs in a twisted coil. My skin was covered in a light dewy sweat. My shift had bunched up and was barely concealing my body. The warm, dream-laced throb was dissipating and I was left wanting and bereft in its aftermath.

"Whatever were you dreaming about?" asked Ann, her eyes glimmering with curiosity.

"You were moaning and pleading," commented Bonnie with equal fascination. "He must have been some dream."

I sat up.

"Are you all right, Stella?" Ann smoothed my unruly hair. It was Ann, more than any of the others, with her rich brown eyes and kind heart, who understood my sorrow most of all; she'd always been more attuned with her own compassion than anyone else I knew. Ann's hair was the fairest of all of us and curled around her face in loose ringlets. The light splashes of pink that colored her cheeks gave her a fresh, youthful appearance. Her character was prone to innocence and naiveté, traits that made her seem even younger than her eighteen years. The glint of her understanding almost brought me to tears now, after the rush of my entangled dreams. I held her offered hand for a moment before straightening my shift and rising from the bed.

"I'm fine. It was just a dream. Where are the others?" I asked, noticing fully only then that they were the only two in attendance.

"They've gone to watch the men. There's some sort of swordplay competition going on."

"Why aren't you with them?" I knew Bonnie's secret lover, Jamie, was among our visiting troops, as he had recently been made a junior officer. Bonnie, although a year younger than I, had an adventurous nature and an outlook that made her seem more worldly than the rest of us. Being the niece rather than the daughter of our clan's laird had given her and her sister, Lottie, a freedom that we lacked. Although they were not allowed to marry until at least one of us had secured a favorable match, they escaped much of the tyranny of our father. That, he reserved for us. And Bonnie, especially, took full advantage of her position. She took risks that the rest of us found forbidding. I knew, for one, that she often crept out the window of our chambers at night, climbing down a rickety ivy trellis, to spend secret hours with Jamie in the stable loft.

"We were waiting for you to wake," said Bonnie.

Bonnie and Ann helped me dress, brushing my hair back into some semblance of order after my fitful sleep. I wore a bright jewel-green dress and the gold chain necklace that was as much a part of me as the strands of my hair or the light amber color of my eyes. In a spirit of generosity I had not personally witnessed in my father, he had given my mother a gift of jewelry at the birth of each one of her five daughters. She died when we were very young children, and each of us inherited the individual pieces that corresponded with our own births. The year of my birth must have been a prosperous one, and my sisters agreed that my gift was the most prized of all. It was made of hammered rose gold, small and simple oval rings strung together in a long chain I could slip over my head if I choose to. But I rarely took it off and wore it as a much now as a talisman as I did as a tribute to my mother's memory. The necklace also served as a reminder that my father had once possessed love, and enough of it to bestow lavish, thoughtful gifts; I wondered if he'd loved her so much that he'd used all his love up. He certainly didn't seem to have much of it left for us. If anything, my mother's death had twisted my father's love into something resembling bitterness, as though he blamed us. And I, the daughter most like her in looks and in character, seemed to inspire the most fervent of this vengeful ire. He was angry at her for leaving him. He was angry at us for somehow stealing the life from her. I embodied all of his resentment, which had festered with each passing year.

We walked through the halls of the Mackenzie manor and it was clear by the cleanliness and vibrant artistry of the decorating that diligent care was commonplace at Kinloch. I admired the attention to detail that was obviously practiced in all areas of upkeep.

Our own keep, it had to be said, was not nearly so meticulously and lovingly cared for. I doubted many were. Mackenzie workers of all stations appeared to be not only dedicated to their tasks but also enjoying themselves. We passed several servants who were laughing as they paid particular attention to the correct placement of a flower arrangement, clearly enjoying each other's company as they worked, and allowed to do so.

Then, as we strolled through a picturesque garden on our way to the training grounds, we stopped to watch one of the gardeners give a demonstration. He was explaining the mechanics of a clever new watering device, and each of us was as engrossed by his enthusiasm as the other gardeners were.

I rarely saw that kind of camaraderie among our own staff, and wondered at the difference. My father's ruling overseers took care of all the duties of our keep, including the grounds and the upkeep of the manor itself. He had not thought to pass those duties on to his daughters—something I hadn't paused to consider before now. My father had sequestered us too much, maybe, or thought us not up to the task of managing the manor and all its labor. In fact, we had few duties to perform and found ourselves idle much of the time. As I watched this inventive, engaging gardener and his audience, I thought it might be nice to find such satisfaction in work and in having something truly useful to offer.

After recent events, I wouldn't have dared to bring up any subject other than marriage to a nobleman to my father, but it occurred to me that I could perhaps discuss it with Maisie; if her bid to marry to Wilkie was successful, Maisie would, in time, become the new Lady of Glenlochie. She would have some say in the workings of the clan, and would therefore be able to—if Wilkie agreed—allow us certain leniencies. Perhaps more than we'd ever had. The thought lent a nimble note of optimism to the day.

We neared the training grounds, and we could hear the shouts and commotion of the men's activity. Dust rose in the sun-drenched light.

Reaching the place where a small crowd had converged to watch the sparring, we found Clementine,

Agnes, Lottie and Maisie. My light mood faded slightly at the sight of Maisie's troubled expression, and I recalled Wilkie's disappearance with the exotic blonde stranger last night. I went to my sister, who I'd always been close to despite her high-strung nature, and linked my arm through hers, reading her thoughts. "Laird Mackenzie is as dedicated to sealing the alliance between our clans as Father is," I said, reading her concerns.

"I know," she agreed with some despondency, adding quietly, "Wilkie hasn't appeared yet this morning." Nor had *she*—the blonde stranger—this was clear from my sister's expression. My eyes scanned the crowd in a silent confirmation.

At the far end of the sparring arena, Laird Mackenzie and our father were deep in discussion. I thought that a good sign.

"The negotiations for your wedding to Wilkie are already well under way," I said in an attempt to console her. "You know that. They're likely discussing it now. 'Tis why we're here, after all. We've all heard Father say it often enough—the Mackenzie alliance is crucial to our military position and can only be secured irrevocably by the bonds of marriage."

"'Tis true," agreed Agnes, overhearing and adjusting a curl of Maisie's hair. "They're probably finalizing the arrangement. You might even be wed as soon as tomorrow."

Bonnie's eyes followed Jamie, her betrothed. He entered the ring to face off against one of the lower-ranked

Mackenzie officers. Without taking her eyes from Jamie, Bonnie prodded Maisie gently. "When Wilkie becomes laird, our new lady will have only the best interests of her sisters and cousins in mind, to be sure."

We watched Jamie take his place, and I couldn't help reflecting on Jamie's similarities to his younger brother. His hair was a slightly darker shade than Caleb's. And in his soldier's stance I could see he was taller and broader; Jamie's was a more imposing stature. The distinct family resemblance only succeeded in reminding me of my lingering heartbreak, which had faded by the mildest degree. Maybe it was the bright sunlight or the bustling, charged activity of the scene, but I felt less sorrowful than I had in several weeks—since Caleb's hasty departure, in fact.

"Aye," Clementine, my eldest sister, whose tone was laced with an edge of resigned woe, added. "Eventually, our new laird might even allow us to marry whoever we choose to."

Poor Clementine. True to his character, our father had forced Clementine to make the choices she had made, regarding the men who had humiliated her. Twice she'd been engaged and twice she'd been shunted at the altar, a series of events that had finally convinced her that her true path was to join a convent. She was due to leave soon after the harvest. It occurred to me then that maybe the men had deserted her because they'd been forced into marriage against their will, and had been unable to follow through at the crucial moment. I knew Clementine would never have complained in the face of my father's decisions; we'd been trained all our lives to treat our father's decisions as gospel. And if we ever protested, he had no reservations about using the back of his hand—or his whip, less frequently—to quiet our insolence. He was laird, after all: all-powerful, and with the larger needs of the clan to consider, rather than the only selfish desires of his children. But with all that had recently transpired, my blood boiled at the injustice of it.

I hadn't thought of it before, but my sisters were right. Once Wilkie wed Maisie, he would be in line to take over the title of Laird Morrison, after the passing of my father. As much as I feared my father, I didn't wish him dead, yet I knew his illness to be worsening. And I couldn't help thinking past his reign. Wilkie might not be averse to letting us choose our own husbands. Caleb might be allowed to return, though I knew better than to hope for such a thing.

"Aye." I barely heard Maisie's reply through the haze of my thoughts. "And I also have my own interests to consider. Of that I'm afraid I'll need to be most definite. My first order of business, as Wilkie's wife, will be to make sure he has no visiting…distractions." She didn't need to name her concern to be understood: the blonde distraction she was referring to would not be welcomed by the impending Lady of Glenlochie.

"I'm sure that's a reasonable request," Agnes said. Agnes, so unlike her twin, spoke with an ingrained authority on every subject. While Ann possessed a gentle, elegant beauty, Agnes was more petite, with pale skin and knowing brown eyes. She made up for her lack of physicality by ensuring that her opinion was always heard. "Wilkie will no doubt agree."

I hoped, for Maisie's sake, that he would.

Jamie's small battle came to an abrupt end when his sword was knocked from his hands by his opponent's decisive swipe. There was some laughter from the men as the young Mackenzie warrior jeered.

Clementine tried to reassure Bonnie. "I've heard it said that the Mackenzies are particularly well trained. They compete well against even the strongest of men."

As though to punctuate the remark, a murmur rippled through the crowd as a commanding helmeted Mackenzie warrior walked into the ring. He was challenging not one but two of the more experienced Morrison soldiers, and he looked more than up to the task. Even before he removed his helmet to reveal his identity, I knew who he was. The crisscrossing strapped holsters that dripped with weaponry. The untouchable confidence. Kade Mackenzie, the very menace who had haunted my sleep, overpowering my more-peaceful dreams of Caleb and weaving through my shockingly sensual reveries of the garden phantom.

He was a captivating figure, to be sure, not only for his size and dynamic presence but for the immanent spectacle his very manner seemed to suggest; whatever drama was about to unfold was sure to be perilously theatrical, at very least. He held the riveted attention of every spectator in attendance, myself included.

Kade took his position, clutching a huge, lethal-looking sword, and in his left hand he held a shield that was cleverly armed with small, razor-sharp spears. A second sword was strapped to his back, where he could easily access it, and a large knife hung at his hip. He wore a leather sleeveless vest that exposed his tanned, muscular arms. His eyes caught mine for a long, fortified moment, causing a jolt of awareness to seep into every anxiety I possessed, and deeper still. Then he fitted his helmet back into place and took his position. His concentration honed in on his opponents and he began to circle, like a hungry wolf might circle newborn lambs. He was undoubtedly the most threatening aggressor I had ever laid eyes on. I feared for our own Morrison soldiers and hoped they would not be maimed, or killed.

Bonnie breathed a light sigh, perhaps of relief, now that Jamie was already bested. She muttered an unsteady sentiment we might all have been thinking: "Good Lord."

The spar began and the Morrison soldiers attacked as one. Kade deflected easily, his movements so deft, so cuttingly concise, that the first defender was relieved of his weapons within the minute, and limped from the ring with a bloodied cut to the leg without bothering to defend his teammate. The second opponent didn't last much longer. His strikes against Kade's sword barely registered and were so skillfully countered that they appeared mere child's play. With a circular slice, Kade succeeded in flinging the defending soldier's sword with such force that several people in the audience had to flee from its flying path.

Kade kneeled over the felled Morrison warrior, staunch aggression radiating from him, and he held the point of his spear to the man's throat. Then, after a loaded moment, Kade stepped back, allowing the man to surrender and make his way unsteadily to the sidelines. That he was able to best two of the largest, most battle-hardened Morrison warriors so easily only added to his clinging ferocity.

Again the crowd murmured, and several people backed up.

Kade stood, surveying our assembled Morrison warriors. "Is this the best you can give me?" he growled, issuing a defiant challenge.

"'Tis unnerving," commented Ann quietly.

"He's *brutally* strong," observed Lottie.

"And so *wild*," exclaimed Agnes in quieted tones. "To bloody the man was hardly necessary. He nearly speared Hugh right through the throat."

I allowed that perhaps Hugh was still suffering from the effects of my futile attack on him with his own knife. He'd be wearing more than one bandage tomorrow, a truth that did not vex me in the slightest.

Lottie whispered her agreement. "He's beastly."

"Wilkie's equally skilled but so much more *civilized*," Maisie said.

I could only concur with my sisters as I watched Kade Mackenzie with a mixture of mild horror and accumulating awe. Maybe it was the entwined nature of my morning dream and the way Kade had appeared alongside not only Caleb but also the enchanting garden phantom, but I felt my skin grow warm and flushed from the spectacle of this display, from the effects of his raw, merciless energy. As aggressive as his attack might have been, there was no denying the athletic grace of him, and the articulate control with which he held himself.

My unease—or whatever this was—only intensified when I noticed that the exchange between my father and Laird Mackenzie seemed to be somewhat heated and complex; the way they were articulating with their hands, the grave concern etched onto Laird Mackenzie's features, and my father's, too: what were they discussing? Surely a straightforward negotiation about a marriage that had already been discussed and agreed to wouldn't be so fraught.

Before I could dwell further on what the lairds' angst might be about, a Morrison warrior stepped into the ring to challenge Kade, cheered on by his ranks and his clan members. It was Aleck, one of my father's first officers. He was a massive ruffian who was better known for his brute strength than his tactical intelligence. He could throw a boulder the farthest, drink ale the fastest and had once killed a man with his bare hands. He was also one of the officers who had beaten me, at the orders of my father, when I had attempted to follow Caleb to Edinburgh.

In fact, Aleck and I had known each other as children. We were the same age and he had once, when we were fourteen, given me a thistle flower. At that age, he'd been a gangly boy with long limbs, knobby knees and a clumsiness that was likely a result of his ungainly adolescence. He'd eventually grown into his frame, towering over most of his peers and gaining a reputation not only as the strongest but also the most ambitious. He had been born of a lowly status and would therefore never be eligible to marry one of the laird's daughters, as stated by my father himself. Nor would he amount to much; he might have aspired to be a small landholder, and a soldier of some ranking in the laird's army. But Aleck had not been deterred by any obstacles of class or breeding. He had spent the past six years training endlessly, besting the blue bloods and proving his loyalty so thoroughly that he had recently gained the position of first officer. Twice he had asked for my hand, and twice he had been refused. I believe my father thought Aleck's proposals to be in jest, a joke shared over ale in the late hours of strategic discussions. My father had only mentioned this to me recently, an offhand comment to prove that I could do better than Caleb, that I was sought after by soldiers and nobles alike and that I should not set my sights so low: a reference to both Caleb and Aleck, I knew.

As Aleck had beaten me, more than once, I couldn't help feeling that the whip's bite was laced with sweet revenge. I had not accepted the thistle flower Aleck had offered me those many years ago; my sisters had laughed and I had followed their lead.

Now, as he faced off against Kade, I thought they looked evenly matched. Aleck was bulkier than Kade and clearly outweighed him by a fair amount, but

Kade was quicker and wilier. The crowd watched as the dueling men circled, swords raised. Aleck struck first, swinging his weapon with such force that it made a thrumming whirr as it cut through the air. Kade met the slice with his own sword. The clash of metal was deafening. I couldn't imagine how it would feel to be on the receiving end of such a heavy, solid blow. I found myself wondering in that moment if it hurt, if the jolt would surge up Kade Mackenzie's arms and into his body, if the jarring impact was as intense as it looked. The turn of my thoughts surprised me, that I might feel an unmistakable note of concern for him, that I hoped, somewhere in the periphery of my own emotions, that he would not be harmed.

Kade faltered only slightly but shook it off and quickly retaliated with his own strike. The spar continued and I watched with undue fascination. It was as skilled a fight as I had ever witnessed: pure brawn versus trained, intricate strategy. Kade deflected and sidestepped. He jabbed and sliced. Aleck had only one move. He was strong but predictable, and Kade took his advantage, making impact, once and again, until his sword was stained with Aleck's blood. Aleck, enraged, struck again. Kade ducked and raised his decorated shield. The sharp points on its surface sliced across Aleck's arm and he howled in pain, dropping his sword. Kade leaped on Aleck, catching him off guard and upsetting his balance, until Kade sat astride Aleck, his sword held to Aleck's neck in a very decisive win.

"I would *not* want to be alone with that man," whispered Bonnie.

"Nay," agreed Agnes, her eyes wide. "Either one of them. Have you ever seen such a savage display in all your life?"

Kade was slow to withdraw his sword from Aleck's throat. There seemed to be some kind of continued challenge between the two men, and only when Laird Mackenzie and my father approached them did Kade leave off. He stepped away and removed his helmet to reveal his long, disheveled hair, making him appear all the more wild.

Even from this distance, though, I could detect that Laird Mackenzie's discussion with Kade had nothing to do with the fight. My father spoke, gesturing in our general direction. Both Laird Mackenzie and Kade, to my utter dismay, looked directly at me. My heart clutched in my chest at the visceral impact of their scrutiny. My father took his leave of them, ordering Aleck to rise and follow him, along with several of his other officers. He walked over to where my sisters and I were standing, and he said gruffly, "Stella. Come with me."

Without intending to, I grasped Ann's sleeve. "Just me?"

"Just you. Now. I have something urgent I must discuss with you. The rest of you may return to your chambers where Stella will join you shortly."

I had a bad feeling about this. And so did Maisie. Our eyes met briefly, but I was being summoned, surrounded, flanked and escorted at the insistence of the blood-smeared Aleck and others of my father's ranks.

Dutifully and with no other choice, I followed.

"BUT, FATHER, I CANNOT! Please. Please don't force me." I tried to stop the tears but could not hold them back. The room blurred and I was glad of it. I wanted to block out every glint of this distressing reality.

My father was irate, as always, that I was not accepting his decree with blind obedience. "Do not defy me, lass," he seethed. "I have had *enough* of your pathetic excuses and your ill-fated yearnings. Your pleading will not be indulged."

"But I don't love him. I don't even *know* him." I could acknowledge a certain draw to Kade Mackenzie, but my curiosity was fraught with dark chasms of the unknown. A cutting wit, a glinting eye, a masculine radiance: it was not enough. These were superficial details that did nothing to tone down the certainty of his proven, volatile aggression that was much too fresh in my mind.

My father contemplated me with undisguised contempt. Then he turned from me and chuckled quietly, the sound entirely devoid of humor. He took a long swig from the silver flask he held.

"You prefer the simpering blacksmith to a proven warrior of one of the highest-ranking noble families in the Highlands?" my father hissed.

Aleck contemplated my despair with his dark, suggestive eyes. He was entirely untroubled by the fact that he was smeared with sweat and dirt, or that his wounds, although not life-threatening, still ran with fresh blood. He stood by the door with his arms folded across his massive chest, as though to ensure that I didn't attempt a sudden getaway. To be sure, he was an effective deterrent; his filthy, bloodied bulk would ensure that I kept as much distance between us as I possibly could have.

"Your feelings for him, I'm afraid," my father continued, "are entirely inconsequential. Laird Mackenzie is as dedicated to this alliance as I am. Wilkie Mackenzie, however, has all but refused to marry your sister. He favors another. A fair-haired foreigner, apparently. I know not where she hails from, nor do I care. It matters not. What does matter is that a wedding *will* take place, and soon. It has been decided, therefore, that you will wed the third brother."

My father's suggestion was unthinkable. My worst fears were being realized. If I could remind him of Kade Mackenzie's famously wild, unpredictable character, surely my father would reconsider. "His reputation—"

"Is that of an accomplished, extremely well-armed soldier, which Aleck here can only attest to," my father said with some disapproval; he was less than pleased by Aleck's earlier performance in the training grounds. "He is also brother to a highly successful laird and warrior. You are fortunate that Kade Mackenzie has offered to step up and fulfill his duty where Wilkie has failed."

"But he's as brutal and stormy as he could possibly be!" My voice sounded high with desperation and I made an effort to calm it unsuccessfully. "You witnessed his reckless behavior in the sparring ring. I cannot marry a man like that."

"What I witnessed was a man so skilled in the art of warfare that he bested one of my strongest men and walked away without so much as a scratch. His brother believes he might learn how to teach his skills wielding weapons and also designing them, and in that regard he would be a valuable military leader."

"*Please,* Father. There is more to this than military considerations, surely. 'Tis my *life* we're discussing! He's quick-tempered. Dangerous, even. I—I don't want to be his wife." More specifically: I didn't want to share his bed. To be forever bound to his tempestuous energy, no matter how curious I might have been about the undeniably enticing effect that energy infused me with the few times I had made his brief acquaintance. Any allure he might have possessed was ominously overshadowed by the more immediate and fearsome image of his untamed power in the sparring ring. I knew only too well the kind of damage such manly strength could inflict.

A desperate thought occurred to me, possibly my very last lifeline. I would never have mentioned such a thing unless I thought my sister willing, and I knew her well enough to know that she very likely was. "Why don't you allow Maisie to be the one to marry him? She may very well *want* to wed Kade if Wilkie has refused her. I know she would. She's desperate—"

"I made allowances for Maisie's request to marry Wilkie only because I thought it was a certainty…for reasons I won't expound upon now. Your elder sister is retreating to a nunnery. She has no further interest in marriage. Therefore, you, as second oldest, must be the one to secure the new laird-in-waiting. Complications are wont to arise when the protocol of birth order and marriages is not followed. Besides, Maisie's desperation has undermined her allure. He wants you."

My father paused to take another swig from his flask. In the ensuing silence the words hung in the tense space between us. *He wants you.* What could Kade Mackenzie possibly have *wanted* of me? And why? To be sure, the very thought was enough to inflame all my reservations. "But—"

My father would hear none of it and interrupted me curtly. "The decision is made. The marriage will take place in two weeks, so I suggest you come to terms with your fate and prepare yourself accordingly."

It was foolish of me, aye, but I had to try. *"Father—"*

My father lashed out at me, hitting the side of my face with the back of his hand, causing me to stumble backward. I caught myself and held my own hand to my cheekbone, which throbbed with the heat of the impact and my own humiliation. I had known to expect this; my father's temper was nothing new. I should not have continued to defy him, yet I never seemed to learn. I did not have freedom of choice, yet I craved that one particular luxury, always, and enough to question his caustic authority.

But his wrath now seemed to almost undo him. He was feeling the effects of his age and his illness. In the past, his hits had been much more forceful. His strength

was failing him. He coughed violently and uncontrollably for a few moments, spitting the blood that rose
from his lungs onto the stone floor, where it made a
gruesome blotch.

I knew my father was ill. But I had not known the
extent of it. And, God help me, in that moment I was
almost glad of it. I was glad that he could not hurt me as
much as he once would have done. I could understand,
too, why he was so fervent about securing a laird-in-
waiting, to take his place when he could no longer lead.
And the smallest glimmer of hope clung to the periphery
of this realization. If I did marry Kade Mackenzie, and
if my father became too ill to lead, Kade would step up
to the position. Which meant that my husband would
outrank my father.

And so would I.

"You will do your duty, Stella, and that is the end of
it! Now go. Get out of my sight. I will call for you later."
To his first officer, he said, "Aleck, take whatever measures are necessary to ensure my daughter's obedience
in this matter, lest she dream up another futile attempt
to flee or some other equally daft scheme."

"I am at your service, Laird Morrison," came Aleck's reply.

With a sick feeling in my stomach, I followed Aleck
from my father's chambers out into the wide hallway.
The door closed, and Aleck fell into step beside me; at
his normal pace his stride might have been twice that
of my own. As we walked, he surprised me by looping

his burly arm around my waist. I attempted to remove myself from his grasp, but he was not to be dissuaded.

"You heard your father's orders as clearly as I did, Stella. I must take *whatever measures necessary* to ensure your obedience. Has your father mentioned to you that I asked for your hand before your marriage to Mackenzie was arranged? But you know that already, do you not? If you do refuse Mackenzie, I have every reason to believe the laird will favor my request. I am, after all, one of his most trusted officers."

I couldn't help blanching at his words. I knew this to be untrue; it was unlikely my father would wed me to a man of Aleck's bloodline. But I looked up at him, aghast. The thought of marrying Aleck was even more off-putting than that of marrying Kade Mackenzie. I could remember even now the hurt I inflicted when I had refused Aleck's long-ago gift. His face had fallen and I later regretted the cruel childishness of my reply. Ever since, Aleck had gone out of his way, when our paths occasionally crossed, to ridicule me with threatening intention. Because of this, I thought him an ill-mannered lout who caused more than a ripple of unease every time he flicked me a glance. I knew well that his animosity toward me was laced with desire and revenge.

And the disquieting thought could not be suppressed: if I attempted to mutiny from the Mackenzie marriage, a match to Aleck would likely be considered as an apt, severe punishment. At the age of fourteen, Aleck had been a shy, gangly boy. Now, he was a massive, seasoned warrior with thick black hair, irises so dark it was difficult to distinguish them from the inky hue of his pupils—a detail which only added to his somewhat sinister demeanor—and a face that could have, if I didn't know the history of all the thoughts behind it, been called noticeable if not handsome. He was far too rough to be attractive, and far too coarse to be likable.

"Perchance your father might allow one of your younger sisters to secure the Mackenzie alliance," he said, pulling me closer. In fact, I was growing increasingly uncomfortable with the way this was progressing; there was no one about and we were still some ways from the guest chambers I shared with my sisters. "You and I could get to know each other better, Stella, while we have the opportunity. You know I've always had my eye on you."

I struggled against his advances, pushing my hands against his barrel-like chest. "Aleck. Unhand me. I must return to my sisters."

But Aleck only smiled and pulled me closer. "Don't defy your father again, lass. He'll be most displeased by your continued disobedience when I was given strict instructions."

"To return me to my chambers. Nothing more."

His lips curled in a lewd grin. "I'm sure he wouldn't mind." Holding me in his hard grasp, he tilted his head slightly, leaning toward me as though he might kiss me. The scent of him, of fresh blood and salty musk, filled my senses and I feared I might wretch.

Shocked and distressed, I slapped his face. He was

stunned enough to loosen his grip, and I managed to disengage and run from him.

I held my skirts as I bolted as fast as my gown would allow, turning once to see him running after me, his face thunderous with rage.

And as I turned the corner, I ran right into the solid form of a very large man, who was so surprised by the sudden collision that he held me in a decisive embrace, to corral me or to steady me.

It was none other than Kade Mackenzie.

With my father's declaration fresh in my mind, I couldn't suppress a blush that rose to my face as Kade held me. His hands were clasped on my shoulders, and my body was pushed up against his. The contact caused him to utter a low, strangled gasp, as though this rugged, self-assured soldier was shaken by our sudden and unexpected closeness. The textures of him, I couldn't help noticing as my breasts rose and fell from my exertions, were stunningly hard and unyielding. The scent and feel of him overwhelmed my senses. Sun and fresh air and earthy, spice-touched masculinity. *"Stella."* His muttered exhale, laced with genuine surprise, was a statement of recognition more than a greeting. And it was too familiar, this address: a detail that hardly mattered now, if my father's plans were a certainty. A fluttery memory was kicked up by his utterance. He knew my name. *I will taste more of you, Stella. I have not had nearly enough. I want you as my own.* But I suppressed the thought, which was very nearly painful with its sweetness. Of course Kade would now know my name, if the news that I was to become his wife had reached him, which was more than likely. He, no doubt, would have been given more say in the decision, to be sure, than I had.

After a brief shocked moment, Kade set me on my feet and took a step back. And as Aleck appeared, scruffy and enraged, Kade studied the situation with some consternation. I could see that my reddened, tearstained cheek did not escape his notice, and the observation caused his eyes to darken.

Only moments before, I had been lamenting Kade Mackenzie's very existence, but now, as I gasped for breath, I felt overwhelmingly glad to see him.

Still dressed in his training garb and fresh from the strenuous masculine activity of sparring, and winning, Kade looked rougher and more intimidating than ever. The dramatic vitality of him drew—nay, *commanded*— my attention, as it had before, and I felt uneasy about this power he seemed to hold over me, as though his very presence controlled not only the direction of my eyes, but also the entirety of my thoughts. His too-long hair was windblown and the sleeveless leather training vest he wore showed off the scarred and sculpted definition of his arms. Slung across his body with a mesh of straps, belts and holsters was his ever-present arsenal of weaponry, making him look all the more dramatic. I was thankful I had not been speared by something on impact.

I had noticed an innate confidence in the Mackenzie men at the recent formal gatherings. But now, dressed in his training gear, with the sun and air still radiating from the dirt-dusted set of his shoulders, it was easy to see that this was the more natural, native state of Kade Mackenzie than the clean white shirt and smart attire. Here, clad in his leather trews, combat vest, tall boots and enough swords and knives to equip a small army, he looked wholly at ease, as though he'd not only had all his greatest successes in this outfit but also regularly slept in it. The rugged vigor of him was practically a visible force. The knowledge that I would be forced to marry him—unless I could indeed either escape or somehow talk my father out of the arrangement (either scenario I knew to be highly unlikely)—fed a squirmy, fluttery sensation into the low pit of my stomach. My anxiety—and my fascination—was manifesting itself in unusual ways, it seemed.

Kade, too, seemed oddly ruffled. His breathing was uneven, his mouth opened slightly from the force of his exhalations.

But then I was reminded of Aleck, whose large palm reached for my bare arm. Before his touch was even upon me, Kade's knife was drawn and held decisively between us. Aleck stopped all movement, and his stare in Kade's direction promised death. But Kade did not appear at all intimidated. His own steady blue-tinted threat was as cold and volatile as I had ever seen it.

"There's no need to manhandle the lady," Kade said, fully regaining whatever composure he had temporarily misplaced.

"The lady is my charge and I'll handle her however I see fit," countered Aleck.

"You are within the confines of the Kinloch walls, soldier, and you will follow our rules. Women are not harmed, nor treated with disrespect. Keep your hands to yourself."

Aleck eyed Kade, exhaling what might have been a chuckle of disbelief. Such a rule was not practiced, we both knew only too well, at Glenlochie.

In the wake of their recent duel, conflict sparked in the air.

"I fear I am lost," I said to Kade, hoping to break their stalemate before violence broke out. "Could you be so kind as to show me the way to the guest chambers of my sisters? My guard here cannot remember the way."

"I remember the way," Aleck growled. "Follow me now, lass, and I'll lead you."

"Nay!" I said, perhaps too loudly. "I mean…what I mean to say is, we would be honored by your assistance. To make sure we know the way of it."

"We don't need—" Aleck began, but Kade interrupted him.

"I'll escort you," said Kade gruffly to my intense relief. I knew he could read my predicament; what I didn't know was if he would care. Yet I supposed Kade's irritation was somewhat warranted. After all, I was his betrothed, almost. He would surely be aware of the proceedings by now, and the proposed change to the marriage plans: his, to me. The sight of another brute manhandling me might have been enough to provoke any husband-to-be. I had little doubt Kade would be manhandling me himself, and as soon as he got the opportunity. But he appeared to be miffed by the thought of someone else encroaching on his potential territory. And at that moment, I was almost glad of his outrage.

Aleck did not argue further. I wondered if it occurred to him that if and when my marriage to Kade Mackenzie took place, Kade would, in fact, become Aleck's new laird-in-waiting. He would take the role as first officer and outrank Aleck. Aleck did not appear to be at all pleased by this possibility. His face twisted into a loaded grimace, and he followed along, resentment radiating in waves from the wide set of his shoulders. I could not help thinking this animosity did not bode well.

Kade Mackenzie led us to my chambers, where Aleck took up his post outside the door.

I murmured my thanks to Kade and hastily retreated into the safety of my sisters' company, closing the door securely behind me. And as I was welcomed into my sisters' questioning circle, a detail of my earlier heated exchange with my father lingered with me. I had taken only brief note of it at the time, but it echoed insistently now. I looked at Maisie's grief-stricken face and thought of my pleas to let *her* be the one to wed Kade, if Wilkie had refused her.

Her desperation has undermined her allure, my father had said.

He wants you.

CHAPTER FOUR

Two weeks later

"HE'S ONLY MARRYING you because he's duty-bound. 'Tis the unfortunate truth of it."

"We'll be there for you all the while, Stella."

"Not *all* the while, but as much as we can."

"Whenever he leaves you we'll come to you."

"As long as he allows it, of course."

"He might want you all to himself."

"He'll likely allow us to visit with you during the day, at least."

"Aye. You'll need comforting, after what you'll be subjected to at night."

"Maisie! Don't bring up *that* particular topic. She's already pale as a ghost."

My sisters were gathered around me in the warm confines of our horse-drawn carriage, offering a litany of advice and condolences. A procession of carriages carried the privileged few who would attend my wedding. The cold autumn wind bit and blustered at the windows as we made our way across the Highlands to the Mackenzie keep, where I would wed Kade Mackenzie in less than two days. My arguments had fallen on my father's selectively deaf ears.

At night, I continued to dream of exile with a slim, young pauper, of forbidden kisses in a secret garden, of stalking, glittering shadows that lurked at the fringes, growing ever closer.

The weather matched my mood: chilled and bleak.

I could not have felt any more dread if I was being transported to my own execution, which at this moment sounded like an equally appealing option to that of an undesired marriage to the very figure that loomed ever larger, not only in my dreams but in my nightmares. If I could have jumped from the carriage and fled across the Highlands, I might have attempted to do so, but I knew Aleck was stationed alongside the carriage driver, and for that very reason.

It was Maisie who brought up the subject—yet again— and I could hardly blame her for being more than a little incensed on the entire topic of marriage. Especially to a Mackenzie. After all, this wedding should have been hers, if Wilkie hadn't chosen Roses, his exotic-looking kitchen servant to wed, only to later find out that she was the daughter of King William himself. Such was his devotion, he hadn't cared that she was of lowly status; even before he had learned of her royal bloodline he'd been willing to forsake his own lairdship to have her. Now he would be laird of an altogether different clan, that of King's Stuart clan, presiding over the grand Ossian Lochs.

It was a romantic notion indeed that a man would

dedicate his heart so completely to a woman. And Wilkie's bride's newly discovered lineage presented them with an unlikely and entirely favorable future, even beyond their love.

My own future would be less favorable. My own husband-to-be, I was sure, would be dedicated only to ensuring that my life would be an exercise of intimidation and subservience. On the strength of his reputation as a ruthless aggressor on the battlefield and from the brutality he had demonstrated in the sparring ring, it seemed to be his nature, as estimated by my sisters, and I could hardly disagree. Less discussed but still hinted at was Kade Mackenzie's dominating and lusty escapades behind more intimate closed doors, a topic that had been mostly skirted so far. But it was only a matter of time. My sisters were putting real effort into trying to be sensitive to my impending doom, I knew, but it simply wasn't in their nature to hold back.

Maisie commented further, bemused, "'Tis inconceivable how two brothers can be so entirely different in nature, is it not? Wilkie's so quick to laugh, so vibrant. Kade, on the other hand, seems unpredictable, to say the least. He was civil enough at the gathering, but did you see him fight? He lives, I would guess from that performance, only to fight, and to win, at whatever cost."

I hoped Maisie was wrong, of course, but two weeks of discussion on this very topic had left me feeling hopeless and certain that my new husband would be as ruthless and impulsive as he seemed. Ann, as always, remained optimistic. My gentlest of sisters, the one whom

I could always count on to at least try to find brightness in any dark situation, argued in my favor: "You hardly *know,* Maisie—" Then, in response to Maisie's glower: "I'm sorry but it's true. You spent a fleeting moment with Wilkie, two days at the very most, regardless of how intimate you might have been with him. And you don't know Kade Mackenzie from the King of Spain. You've seen him in passing and spoken to him only a handful of words. You're upsetting Stella with half-truths."

"'Tis just a feeling," Maisie countered, sulky at the accuracy of Ann's reprimand. "A *very strong* feeling." The announcement of my betrothal to Kade Mackenzie had been a crushing loss for Maisie and one she still had not fully recovered from. She was only now, two weeks after the fiasco, coming out of her despondency. My wedding, however, would present an opportunity for her to seek out new conquests. Scouting for potential husbands was an agenda shared by the rest of my family as well, aside from Bonnie and Clementine, and my sisters were bright-eyed even as they attempted to calm my unease. But their words only stoked my apprehension.

"Either way," commented Clementine, "there can be little doubt about his…energy. We all witnessed it in the sparring ring. He's unlikely to be gentle with you, Stella—and we say this, of course, with only your best interests at heart. You must be forewarned. Kade Mackenzie is marrying you to claim our clan's laird-ship, and not for reasons of affection. You must go into this marriage with your eyes open to the grim reality of the situation."

This was hardly news, yet they continued. And it was not the first time I wished they might change the subject, that we might be able to discuss the weather, a favorite song, a new fashion—anything but my troubling future. I knew they were trying to comfort me as best they could, under the circumstances. They were merely excitable at the drama of my predicament and entirely preoccupied with discussing it relentlessly. I wished I could daydream of faraway places. Of Edinburgh, and beyond. But it was not to be.

"I'm sorry to say it, dear sister," said Maisie, "but you have no choice but to expect the worst. He appears charming enough, but it's clear enough he has a *wicked* temper. You saw him in the heat of battle. I dread to think what he'll bring to the marriage bed."

"Aye," said Clementine, still gazing out the window, lost as she often was in her own disappointment in the subject at hand. "He's bound to be an absolute tyrant both in and out of your private chambers."

Agnes and Ann agreed, nodding silently with wide eyes. Since they were the youngest of us, the very mention of a marriage bed was enough to stun them into speechlessness. To be sure, it did similar things to me. In only a few short days, I would be at the mercy of my new husband. The thought of Kade Mackenzie—his size, his flashing light eyes and the contained strength of him that radiated from his movements like an aura—

filled me with dread. My sisters spoke the truth. There was no telling what I might be subjected to.

"He might have redeeming qualities," ventured Ann. "He seemed rather amiable, I thought, even if it was forced. He spoke politely. And he certainly seemed to have eyes for you, Stella."

I considered Ann's words, and could find some truth in them. Kade had appeared relaxed and somewhat amused by the lush attentions of the women at the festive gathering. And as I thought of it now, I couldn't help considering that my sisters and cousins hadn't thought him quite so tyrannical at the time. In fact, once Wilkie was clearly otherwise engaged, they had all turned their attentions quite convincingly to my brutish husband-to-be, and not without some enthusiasm.

And now I could reflect that there had been more to Kade Mackenzie's scrutiny than light, speculative appreciation. He tolerated the attentions patiently enough, engaging in conversation that clearly was not particularly interesting to him. He'd allowed the fluttery touches on his arms and his hair, the tittering responses to his every word. Having so many to choose from, I wasn't sure why his eyes had followed me more than any of the others. In fact, I'd thought I'd imagined his preference for me—which, unlike my sisters, I had quietly attempted to discourage.

I remembered the glint in Kade's eye. *On the contrary, I find insolence in women intriguing—it happens to be an affliction that I'm usually able to cure almost entirely under the right circumstances.* Not malicious, as such. But playfully intimidating nonetheless. I had been indisputably drawn to him, aye, in ways that had confounded me with their glittery insistence. But always, behind his appeal had lurked turbulent layers of the unknown. The rocky landscape of my abusive upbringing had instilled within me a very real fear of all things unknown, especially those bestowed by such a vital, well-armed soldier.

The arrangements had been made, the agreement secured. No more protests would be made.

"At least he's something to look at," Ann continued. "Those blue eyes are striking."

"'Tis true, Stella," said Agnes. "Kade Mackenzie might be fierce, daunting and unruly—"

"And huge," added Clementine.

"And rather unnecessarily cruel," Agnes said.

"And *freakishly* strong," agreed Maisie.

"But he is, in fact, quite handsome," Ann continued. "*Quite* handsome."

"In a very rough, aggressive kind of way," Agnes said. But I could detect from her tone that she wasn't entirely convinced.

And neither was I.

Was Kade Mackenzie handsome? I considered this. *Striking,* aye. His hair was a dark, sable-brown—as opposed to his black-haired brothers: that was the first thing I had noticed about him. His eyes, too, with their ice-blue clarity, spearing and direct. And the jaunt of his movement, quick and athletic; more than once he had reminded me of a predator whose unpredictability would give him every advantage. A man who might either save you or strike you down when you least expected it.

Maybe I just wasn't used to him. Maybe he wasn't as intimidating as I was imagining. Perhaps I just wasn't used to his abruptness, his size and power. My father had little time to spare with all the leadership of the keep resting entirely on his shoulders. He dined with his men and rarely visited our wing. No other men were permitted into our quarters, and those that we mingled with throughout our days were strictly supervised. My one private moment with Caleb—resulting in a rushed, featherlight kiss—had been a result of a bold excursion with Bonnie, for which I had later been severely punished.

I could acknowledge that there was a certain magnetism to Kade Mackenzie, somewhere in the complexity of him. Those teasing hints of his appeal might shine through over time, and overtake the shadowy depths of his personality that I could not interpret. In an attempt to ease my billowing anxiety, I tried to assure myself that my fear was unfounded. But my hope was quickly eroded by my sisters' continued discussion.

"At any rate," Maisie began, and there was sympathy and a note of jealousy in her tone, if I was reading her correctly, "with him, I have a feeling you need to be prepared for the unexpected. No doubt about it, Stella. You're in for a time of it."

Agnes leaned forward, whispering, even though there

was no one to overhear us. "Did I tell you what happened to Claire Buchanan's cousin?" she said.

I hesitated, sensing that I might not want to hear what Agnes was about to share. Ann answered for me. "Nay, Agnes. What happened to Claire Buchanan's cousin?"

"Well. I'm afraid it's somewhat distressing, Stella. But I think you should hear it."

"You never mentioned *this* before, Agnes," said Maisie, her eagerness clearly detectable. "Do tell."

Agnes paused, as though reconsidering. But then she continued. "I wasn't sure if I should bring it up, but I think Stella should prepare herself."

"For what?" asked Clementine.

"Well," continued Agnes, with the undivided attention of all, "Kade Mackenzie attended a gathering at the Buchanan manor—this was half a year or so ago. Lottie told me all about it last time she visited their keep."

We all knew that our cousin Lottie, in fact, had been issued not only an invitation to the Buchanan manor, but also a proposal by a lower-ranking nobleman of the Buchanan clan. My father, predictably, had denied the match outright.

"Claire's cousin invited him to her private chambers— *why* I'll never know. She allowed him…well, whatever he wanted. Claire's cousin said he did *unspeakable* things. It took her several days to recover."

"What do you mean 'unspeakable'?" asked Maisie.

Agnes continued in hushed tones. "Apparently, she was completely overcome."

"In what way?" It was my own hesitant question that lingered in the confined space.

Agnes took a moment to answer. "She said it was the most intense experience of her life."

I couldn't help asking it: *"Intense?"*

Agnes nodded. "She spent the whole night in a state of terrified ecstasy, according to Lottie. Those are the words she used, too, I remember it clearly—'terrified ecstasy.' She didn't know what he was going to do from one moment to the next, but in the end, she begged him to do it all over again the very next night."

This was met with momentary silence.

"She begged him to do it *again?*" Ann asked, as though she was unsure if she'd heard it correctly.

"Aye," said Agnes. "But he wouldn't. She was so eager she even asked him to propose to her. But he refused, and he made his leave the next day."

More silence, as we absorbed this disquieting information.

"What did he *do* to her?" asked Maisie, wildly intrigued as we all were. Me, perhaps most of all, as the carriage continued on its way, swallowing distance and divides, taking me ever closer to my fate.

"Claire's cousin wouldn't tell Lottie everything," Agnes said, "but she did say this—he bound her to the bed."

"*Bound* her?" I asked, my voice doing nothing to disguise my distress. "Why?"

"To constrain her. She was entirely at his mercy."

"Good Lord," whispered Ann.

"So he's as domineering in the bedchambers as he is in the sparring ring," said Maisie. "I guessed as much."

Ann, who was sitting to my right, gave me a sudden hug, holding my head against her shoulder. "Stella, 'tis worse than we feared. He's as cruel as the worst rumors indicate. We *cannot* let you go through with this. Between the seven of us, we might overpower the driver and Father's officer. Or you could pretend to be ill. We could ask to stop at the next tavern and escape somehow. I'll come with you. I'll stay with you. You can't marry Kade Mackenzie. He sounds *utterly* horrific. Marriage to such a beast is too much to ask of you, alliance or no alliance."

"Agnes," said Maisie, interrupting Ann's fevered monologue, "are you sure Lottie said she asked him to *propose* to her? Even after he constrained her like that?"

Ann allowed me to sit up a little, but her arms remained strung loosely around me as we both waited for Agnes's answer.

"Aye," Agnes said. "Even though she was terrified of him, she said his lovemaking was akin to a spiritual experience. And then he left and wouldn't return and she ended up marrying a Buchanan soldier. But now she's thoroughly unhappy. Her new husband doesn't satisfy her. Claire's cousin—and you must never breathe a word of this to *anyone*—she even sent a letter to Kade, asking him to return to their keep for a visit, husband or no husband. But he never replied."

I wasn't sure how to take this mixed bag of information. *A spiritual experience?* What did that even mean?

Was it that bad? Or that *good?* Clearly it must have been good if she had wanted him to stay and marry her, and still she wrote to him despite being wed to another. Yet it didn't make sense.

She was entirely at his mercy.

I felt as though I might pass out. Extricating myself gently from Ann's grasp, I pulled the heavy cloth curtain back from the window of the carriage, letting a current of fresh air waft around me, breathing the coolness deeply into my lungs.

"Stella," said Agnes, placing her hand over mine, patting lightly. "I wasn't going to say anything, but I thought, if it was me, I'd want to know what to expect. So I could prepare myself as best I could."

"'Tis fine, Agnes," I said, not feeling at all fine. About any of it.

"Well, it's not exactly bad news, then, is it?" said Clementine. "If she wanted him to do…whatever it was he *did,* and the very next night, then surely it was—"

"But what exactly did she mean by 'spiritual experience'?" interrupted Maisie. "I mean, when Wilkie and I…" She faltered at the memory. We were all well aware of Maisie's tryst with Wilkie, having heard about many of the details repeatedly and in some depth. "Well, I would describe it in similar terms. I felt changed by it, and not just physically. Perhaps they shared something. You should be careful, Stella. And mindful. 'Tis good that you mentioned it, Agnes. Kade might stray with Claire Buchanan's cousin. You might have to go with him to any gatherings at the Buchanan manor. Just in case."

That seemed the very least of my worries. In fact, I wished Kade *had* taken this Buchanan lass's offer to marry her, so I could be done with Kade Mackenzie once and for all. I wanted nothing to do with terrified ecstasy or spiritual experiences, whatever those might be.

"Try not to think about it, Stella," Ann said softly, holding one of my hands. "It'll only upset you." The rest of them seemed to sense this, too, and thankfully fell quiet.

If only I could choose my own lover, and one who didn't intimidate me so. *Or bind and ravage me.*

I nearly gave in to the tears that stung the backs of my eyes as I thought of Caleb's kind voice, his peaceful presence. *That* was the marriage bed I'd hoped for: one that was as nonthreatening as such a thing could be.

Instead, I looked out the window to see, perched on a hill in the shrinking distance, the grand and ominous Kinloch manor.

CHAPTER FIVE

ON THE MORNING of my wedding day, I awoke to the gushing excitement of my sisters and my attendants. For them, the day promised fun, festive possibilities and a brighter future for the entirety of our clan. For me, however, it offered a wholly different view. I pulled the furs over my head to block out the light and relentless activity.

But my attempts to hide were quickly thwarted and I was fawned over, undressed and helped into my bath, which had been brought into the room and filled with perfumed, steaming water. "You've lost weight, Stella," commented Ann. "You're not eating enough."

It was true. My stomach had been too uneasy for food, almost from the moment my father had presented me with the news of my impending marriage. And I was naturally somewhat slimmer than my sisters, although still curvy enough to fill out the fashionable wedding dress I would wear, designed and prepared for me by none other than Kade's sister, Ailie Mackenzie. The dress had been fitted the previous day, and the waist had needed only minor adjustments. After much deliberation, it had been decided that I would wear my hair down for the wedding ceremony, as my many attendants found its dark waving tendrils with their golden tips pleasing against the off-white of the velvet dress.

"You shouldn't lose too much weight, Stella," Maisie scolded me. "Men don't like their women too thin."

The very subject of men in general—and one man in particular—was enough to start my stomach fluttering again. Whatever preferences Kade Mackenzie held for the size and shape of a woman's body were shady, disquieting details that sent my heart racing. I stood up, dripping onto the floor as I made a move to step out of my bath. "I can't do it. I cannot marry him. I don't love him, and I don't want to share his marriage bed."

Hands were on me, stroking my hair and easing me back into the warm water.

"'Tis not about love, sister," said Clementine, soothing in tone but hardly in subject. "'Tis about duty, honor, protection. You'll be lady of the clan one day soon, remember. Your comfort, your bidding, your every wish will be ours to provide you. Your child will be heir of Glenlochie. You'll have a new status to be proud of, and one which you're bound to fulfill with grace, as kind and gentle as you are." After a moment, Clementine added, somewhat grimly, "You can't run from your duty, Stella." And I felt for her then, I truly did. It should have been her, the eldest, to bear the heir: a thought that plagued her, I could see it written on her face. It should not have been me, the second child. Rather than fulfilling all the promise of her status as firstborn, she would see out her childbearing years in the self-imposed isolation of a nunnery, nursing her own heartbreak and defeat. And in the light of this truth that was clearly painful for her, I took her comment to heart. Nay, I could not run from my duty, a duty she coveted, yearned for, cried for and one that had passed her by. And Maisie, too. For all their faults, they were my sisters and I wanted to keep them safe and protected. For my family, I wanted to do right. My clan was depending on me, and I would not fail them, no matter what reservations I had about my soon-to-be husband.

"There are other duties you'll need to carry out, too, Stella," said Maisie. "Wifely duties that a husband will expect."

I had heard some of these wifely duties discussed by my sisters, first when Clementine had been preparing for marriage—twice—and then when Maisie had been expecting a proposal from Wilkie Mackenzie. But I had studiously avoided thinking too closely about what such duties might entail. My sisters, however, liked details. "Firstly," began Maisie, "a husband expects his wife to undress him."

My soft groan was acknowledged with patting hands, but we all knew there was little they could do to help me aside from informing me and doing their best to pick up the pieces after the fact.

"He might not demand that of you on the first night," Clementine offered.

"How would one even go about undressing Kade Mackenzie without getting speared?" asked Agnes.

"Aye, sounds dangerous," agreed Ann. "Getting past all those blades might present a challenge."

"Some husbands, I've heard," continued Maisie, "like their wives to feed them. It makes them feel powerful, I would imagine." Her comment trailed off wistfully, and I had no doubt in that moment that she had planned to serve her own husband—lost to her forevermore—in these ways and any other she could imagine.

"And then, of course," added Clementine, "the marriage bed presents its own…duties."

"The marriage bed is a minor detail to be endured," offered Ann, perhaps noticing my stricken expression. But her words offered no solace; she knew less about what to expect than even I did.

"You don't have to remain faithful," said Maisie quietly. This comment was met with a moment of awkward silence. Maisie didn't have to mention his name for the reference to be brutally clear. "He'll likely be allowed to return to Glenlochie once you're officially married."

"Just wait until your husband strays before you do," advised Agnes. "Ainsley Munro told me that her cousin's husband annulled their marriage when he found out about his wife's affair, and he was legally allowed to. But if he'd strayed first, then there are no legal grounds for an annulment."

"Is that true?" asked Clementine, intrigued.

"Aye, she told me, too," Maisie confirmed. "And it's true that most men do stray. At least that's what I've heard. And I'd wager Kade Mackenzie will be no different, especially if the rumors of his…vigor are true."

"Well, hopefully Kade *will* stray," Ann added softly.

"He can seek his dark pleasures elsewhere. Then Stella can get what she wants."

Their chatter continued somewhere outside my scope and I let my head slip under the bathwater to further distance myself. In just a few short hours I would be wed to and irrevocably bound to a man I had met but a handful of times, whose unholy vibrancy haunted me from afar. At this moment what I felt was fear, but I could acknowledge a curiosity, too, or what might have been better described as a survivalist instinct. I wanted to begin to emotionally prepare myself for what lay ahead. I couldn't help letting my mind tread in disturbing directions. Tonight. The marriage bed. With Kade Mackenzie. Would he be kind? Or brutish? Would he be cold and disinterested, or possessive and demanding? Would he hurt me? Maisie and Bonnie had spoken to me about the very adventurous marriagelike activities they'd both indulged in with men they desired to wed. For Bonnie, the future looked bright. I worried for Maisie, having given herself like that, so fully, to a man who was now someone else's husband; I worried that it would indeed have an impact on her chances for marriage to another man. She regretted nothing, though, she insisted. Those private moments with Wilkie Mackenzie, she'd said, were some of the most pleasurable and treasured of her life.

I wondered if my experiences would be at all pleasurable. Despite Agnes's gossip, or perhaps because of it, I thought that possibility unlikely. Aye, Kade affected me in unusual ways. The rippling, primal awareness that seemed to infuse me whenever he was near: it was a reaction I had attributed to fear, but there was a warmth to my lingering panic that was quite removed from trepidation, which I might have described as wary curiosity. His grip on my shoulders had been so sure, so strong yet in no way painful. His rasped surprise that was laced with the slightest trace of vulnerability. *Stella.*

Nevertheless, I was too accustomed to violence to expect anything less of him, and *this* type of impending violence would be more personal and more damaging than anything I had so far experienced: this I knew.

If I hadn't been pulled up to have my hair washed and attended to, I might have stayed in my underwater haven, to slip away and never know. As it was, I was so lost in my silent, fevered reservations that before I even knew what was happening, I was bathed, dried, dressed, primped, polished and perfumed to within an inch of my life, and ready to attend my own wedding.

IF I HAD been in a better state to appreciate such things, I might have registered through the haze of my distraction that the day was sunny and warm, that the mood was festive, that Kinloch's small chapel was an exquisite, reverential space with its white walls and shards of colored light.

I floated through the proceedings as though watching them from a protective distance.

My gown was beautiful; that much I could appreciate. Its crushed velvet fabric was white yet tinged with pale shades of pink. The fitted bodice was inlaid with white silk ribbons, intricately woven in a seashell pattern. The long skirt fell elegantly to the floor, and the hem was gathered with shiny white pieces of shell. I wore a lace veil that offered me a welcome barrier against the events of the day, for now.

My father was dressed in his best finery: a purple cloak with gold silk trim, befitting his nobility. We did not speak. All that needed to be said had already been spoken. He led me down the aisle to the pulpit, where Kade Mackenzie stood, flanked by his two brothers. Laird Knox Mackenzie watched me approach with his arms folded over his broad chest. I couldn't help noticing that there was a defined melancholy to his countenance, and I recalled hearing that his wife had died some years ago. Maybe the sight of a wedding dress was reminding him of all he had lost. Wilkie Mackenzie sported a much dreamier expression, but he wasn't looking at me. His eyes were fixed on his own bride, the fair-haired Roses, who sat near him in one of the front pews.

And Kade.

I had not seen him for two weeks since I'd nearly collided with him in a corridor; since he'd rescued me from the clutches of Aleck; since my betrothal to him had been decreed. Now, his face was entirely stoic, as impassive as I might have expected of him. His eyes never left me, but I could look at him only briefly, noticing abstractly that his ceremonial garb suited him. He looked tall and noble and at ease in his clan colors. Yet in the aftermath of all the warnings and revelations of late, Kade's subdued power and flagrant masculinity were enough to wither my courage. If I looked at him, I feared I might faint. So I diverted my gaze elsewhere.

As he lifted my veil, he spoke to me, and there was a soft, distinctive gravelly edge to his voice that I already recognized from the few times we had exchanged very brief conversation. "You look as though you're about to be fed to the lions," he commented. "Be assured, I don't plan on eating you alive. Not yet, anyway."

I looked up at him, caught by his cynical, sensual smirk. Was this an attempt at humor? Everything about him was so very undecipherable to me, I could only stare briefly at his face before blushing, dropping my gaze and wishing I was anywhere but here.

The small chapel was full to capacity. My family sat near the front. My father wore a triumphant gloat, clearly relieved that our clan's alliance to the Mackenzies would, at last, be sealed. My sisters and cousins scanned the crowd, making eye contact with possible conquests, reveling in the moment. There were Munros in attendance, Macintoshes, Buchanans, Machardies, Macsorleys, even Stuarts. People had come from far and wide to witness the convergence of two major Highland armies and to take part in the celebrations.

I realized with some alarm that the marriage ceremony was already under way. And the minister's words only succeeded in deepening my despair. "The Scottish marriage vows are not to be taken lightly," he was saying. "The union is an irrevocable bond never to be broken. Sacred vows, sealed with blood and body, forged by the true love between a man and a woman—"

The room seemed to sway slightly and I felt the light touch of Kade's hand at my elbow. "Perhaps," he said to the minister, "we should get straight to the vows."

The minister paused and nodded knowingly, as though he interpreted Kade's urgency to get this marriage secured as quickly as possible. He did as Kade requested.

I listened to Kade's husky voice as he spoke. "I, Kade Mackenzie, take thee, Stella Morrison, to be my wife." He continued, and I could acknowledge that his words had a mellow authority to their timbre that seemed to echo through me. He was calm, and showed no hesitation whatsoever. And it was fitting, I supposed. He was fulfilling his duty, as I was fulfilling mine. Maybe he gained more satisfaction from his fate than I did.

When he had finished, I recited my vows obediently, repeating the words spoken by the Mackenzie minister, listening to the droning sound of his litany that would bind me forevermore to a man I wanted nothing to do with. I thought of my clan, my sisters, their safety and protection under a strengthened army, the security the new alliance would bring, through trade, military might and commerce. I was a pawn to be used for the greater good and must accept my lot with as much courage as I could muster.

The minister requested my hand and I held my palm up as I was told to do. It was Laird Mackenzie who ran the blade of his knife across my palm in a clean, almost-painless slice, then he repeated the motion across Kade's palm. Laird Mackenzie then sealed our palms together, allowing our blood to mingle. Kade's large hand entirely encompassed my own in its hot, rough grasp. I felt unnerved by his proximity and the knowledge that our essences were combining, that his warrior's blood now mixed with my own. But even if I had possessed the nerve to steal my hand away, I could not have done so; Laird Mackenzie wrapped a white linen ribbon around our wrists, tying a tight knot, binding us to each other.

The minister continued loudly with dramatic flair. "I now pronounce you man and wife. Kade Mackenzie, you may seal your vows with a kiss."

A kiss.

I steeled myself, looking up into the eyes of my new husband. And I was struck by the pale, vibrant blue of them: I had never seen eyes that light, that cleanly blue. Like the sky on a cold, clear day.

He bent to kiss me, his lips barely brushing my own. I thought he would draw away, but his mouth settled with more pressure, inciting a brief sense of recognition at the boundary of my memory. But then it was gone.

The ceremony was done. I was led, by my imposing new husband, through throngs of well-wishers to the grand hall of the Mackenzie manor, where the festivities were already well under way.

"CONGRATULATIONS, YOU LUCKY SOD," Tadgh Munro laughingly said to Kade, patting him on the back, "landing the delightful Stella Morrison."

Kade did not reply to him, pulling me toward a table

at the front of the hall. The crowd parted for us as we made our way through.

"Yet she doesn't seem quite as pleased by the match," Tadgh called after us. "She's no doubt heard much of your barbaric reputation, Mackenzie. You'll have to go easy on the poor lass." Several men laughed.

Tadgh Munro's words did nothing to calm my growing apprehension. I was led to the head table and instructed by Kade to sit. I did as I was told, as I always did. The only difference was that the person now dictating to me was not my father but my gruff new husband, who at this moment looked as displeased by the entire scenario as I felt. He glared at me briefly, then sat down next to me and took a large swig from a goblet of ale. He handed me the goblet and said, "Take a drink."

"I—I don't usually drink ale."

"'Tis your wedding day, lass. Take a drink. Besides, you look like you need it."

Thinking that his observation might be bordering on insulting, I frowned at him. But then I realized that I was already frowning. Maybe he was right. Maybe a drink of ale was exactly what I needed. In a matter of hours, this marriage and my fate would be sealed by the very man whose solid thigh now pressed firmly against mine. It was too familiar, this touch, too close—but then, he was now my husband. My body was his for the taking, in whatever capacity he chose.

As Kade watched me, I took a long sip of the sweet ale. And another.

"I realize this is a marriage of convenience," he said.

"But for the sake of our clan members and our guests, for this evening if not beyond, you might at least pretend that there is something in the match worth celebrating."

I was irked by his request. Was it not enough that I had dutifully, selflessly gone through with an arranged wedding to a man I suspected to be a merciless scoundrel, all for the sake of my family and my clan? In fact, I wanted to be anywhere but here, with anyone but him. Did I need to put on an act for him, as well? As though I was overjoyed that I would momentarily be ravaged by this brute who wore his formidable reputation as a badge of honor? I made a small attempt to constrain my reply, yet allowed myself a quiet response. "For *you,* perhaps."

He contemplated me with a look of mild exasperation. "I hardly find your scowling grimace a cause worth rejoicing over."

I stared at him, attempting to control not only my unease but also my temper. How *rude* he was! "I'm sorry if it displeases you, but as used to subservience as I may be, I don't consider a forced union a cause for celebration. I had hoped to marry for love."

"We all do," he commented. "Yet we'd be wise to make the best of our situation, no matter how difficult it may be for either one of us."

I felt a sense of quiet outrage at his statement. Of course that was easy enough for *him* to say. His situation was hardly difficult. He had just entitled himself to the impending lairdship of our growing, prospering clan, giving him total control over not only our army and our resources, but also…well, *me.* If his reputation as a ruthless warrior had any credence whatsoever, I had no doubt he would avail himself of all his new endowments with gusto, me included. It was with a sense of resignation that I quietly asked him, "And how do you propose to do that?"

He paused, sitting back in his chair, as though considering the question thoughtfully. "I had thought to start by drinking some ale with my new wife and discussing the evening's proceedings, yet she wears a sullen expression and appears to be less of a conversationalist than I had hoped."

My new husband was an absolute *ogre!* Any ethereal attraction I might once have felt for Kade Mackenzie abruptly vanished. "I'm so sorry to disappoint," I replied icily.

"I'm experiencing a wide variety of emotions over our nuptials, lass, but I can assure you disappointment is not one of them."

I eyed him warily, noticing the strong stripes of his eyebrows, his straight nose, the hard line of his jaw. The cords of his neck were pronounced and his arms strained the white cloth of his shirt as he, unnervingly, clenched his fist. His eyes were narrowed slightly in casual speculation as though he were having as much difficulty interpreting my thoughts as I was baffled by his. I wanted to ask him what emotions he might be referring to, yet I was restrained by one detail of his phrasing that echoed disconcertingly in my mind: *the evening's proceedings.*

Before I could dare to ask him to elaborate, we were

interrupted by the servers, who brought heaped plates of food to our table and placed them before us.

Laird Mackenzie stood, presenting an eloquent speech, welcoming me into the Mackenzie family and waxing lyrical about the bright future of our allied clans. I tried to adjust my expression to one of gladness, however forced, not to appease my husband—not at all—but out of respect for my clan members. It would hardly do, after all, to sulk through the speeches. There would be plenty of time for that later.

As I listened first to Laird Mackenzie's speech and then my father's, I surveyed the crowd. I hoped my sacrifice would benefit my people. I knew my father's failing health had negatively impacted our clan's general well-being. Glenlochie was looking somewhat unkempt. The army was less organized. Food, of late, was less plentiful than in past years. And there was the ongoing threat of Laird Campbell's rebellion against the King of Scotland. I hoped our alliance would deter the rebellion, and that my new husband would prove to be an effective leader, as his brother was.

If the appearance of Kinloch was anything to go by, the Mackenzie clan was indeed prosperous. The manor was spotless and well equipped. The bounty of food and drink was enviable. There was lamb and beef, duck and pheasant. Bowls of exotic fresh fruits were displayed on the tables, and a wide variety of vegetables, grown in the Mackenzie gardens, were sumptuously flavored with herbs and butter. Fresh-baked breads were abundant and garnished with seeds and nuts. And the staff and servants worked as an amiable, cooperative team.

I hoped Kade Mackenzie could bring order and a new vigor to our keep, and introduce a fresh optimism to our clan. It was worth the sacrifice I was making: my body and my obedience. Maybe I could find happiness outside my marriage. Maybe Maisie was right: Kade might stray, and my life might be bearable outside the bedchambers, when I was away from my coarse husband.

And so my thoughts trod as I ate and talked and smiled and drank the ale that was offered to me, late into the evening. In fact, I found that, at times, when I was briefly separated from my husband and surrounded by the buoyant excitement of my sisters and friends, I was mildly enjoying myself. That is, until I heard the low, distinctive voice whisper in my ear. *"Stella."* Again, I felt a twinge of wishful familiarity. "Wife, I must ask you to accompany me now. 'Tis time for bed."

CHAPTER SIX

ANY BRAVERY I MIGHT have gained from the ale fleetingly evaporated. My blood turned to ice in my veins and my heart skipped a beat.

My hand was grasped in his strong, heated grip, and I was led from the gathering, which at this late hour was becoming loud and loose. "No one will notice if we take our leave. 'Tis expected of us, after all, to acquaint ourselves in a more private setting."

Each word he spoke seemed to steep me further and deeper into a speechless haze. I was guided up the curved staircase of the manor, down a dark hallway and into the private bedchambers of my husband, whose size seemed only to increase as he locked the heavy door with a very decisive thud. The sound of it was solid and final, delivering the reality of my situation: *I am trapped in the lair of the infamous Kade Mackenzie. There will be no escape, now or ever.*

Despite my anxiety, I could acknowledge that the chambers themselves were cozy and inviting. A fire crackled festively, providing a sharp juxtaposition to my own mood. There was a cushioned window seat, and the windows were hung with furs to keep out the chill. The firelight was reflected in the shiny metallic surfaces of Kade's many weapons, which were distributed liberally around the space, scattered everywhere, save the bed, which was large and comfortable-looking, and laid with abundant heavy fur blankets.

The far wall was lined with wooden bookshelves that were filled to capacity with books, rolled scrolls, trinkets and exotic-looking weapons of many varieties. There were foreign swords, bone-handled knives and devices made of metal, chain, leather and other materials; each of them were a mystery to me as far as their uses might be concerned. The sight of them, to be sure, did little to calm me.

Next to the shelves were a number of large, open trunks, and several of the lower shelves near the trunks were noticeably empty. I realized that Kade was packing, and the thought made me recall an earlier comment he'd made as we'd sat down to dinner earlier in the evening. *We'd be wise to make the best of our situation, no matter how difficult it may be for either one of us.* It was the first time it had occurred to me that something about this marriage might be difficult for him, as well as for me. Clearly, these chambers had been Kade Mackenzie's haven for many, many years. The weapons and belongings displayed around the room were not merely utilitarian; this was a collection of valued treasures and possessions, some of which looked old and worn, as though they had been used and stored not just over one lifetime, but several.

An old leather saddle sat on a wooden stand and had been carefully polished with a soft cloth that lay next to it; I could smell the faint mingling earthy scent of the oil and the leather. A man's fur coat was draped over a chair: a hunting coat. A writing table was strewn with paper scrolls and a selection of quills and inkpots.

I noticed, too, that a small painting of a woman was propped on a lone wooden shelf next to the fireplace. Even from a small distance, she bore a startling likeness to Kade's sisters. It felt too soon and too personal to inspect the painting closely now, but I suspected the woman in the painting to be the Mackenzie siblings' mother. The realization softened something in me. It somehow seemed incongruous: this mighty warrior treasuring his mother's memory just so, reserving a special isolated shelf for her miniature portrait. I wasn't sure why, but this comforted me. Maybe my ferocious husband had a softer side. This room, with its inviting aura, seemed to suggest such a possibility.

At the sight of the small painting, it occurred to me, too, to wonder how Kade felt about leaving his home. It was obvious to me over the past days that the Mackenzie siblings were especially loyal to each other. They were a family that valued each other's company above all others. And now Wilkie was due to leave for Ossian Lochs with his new bride, and Kade would accompany us, to Glenlochie, to become laird-in-waiting of our keep, to succeed my father.

Did he *want* to go, to leave his family and the only home he'd ever known? Before this moment, I'd assumed that such an arrangement would be coveted by any man. What warrior didn't aspire to lead his own army, to be in charge of his own clan, to be bestowed with wealth and land, to do with what his own leadership and industriousness would allow? But the warm, comforting space of this room and the care taken with the possessions that surrounded my husband in his own private chambers made me question whether his own distant lairdship truly would have been a conquest Kade Mackenzie would have actively sought for himself. In the end, he had stepped up to take the Morrison clan lairdship because his brother had refused it. Kade, too, had done his duty, as I had been forced to do.

Kade unslung several of his belts, hanging them on a wooden hook. He walked to the fire and crouched down next to it, adding several more logs and blowing on the glowing embers. The cloth of his shirt stretched over the shaped lines of his broad shoulders and muscular back, reminding me once again of his size and his strength. I thought of his stormy attack during his swordplay and the calculated violence of his strike. The image seemed at odds with the peaceful scene here and now.

I stood near the door, making no move to enter into his private space, but I couldn't help looking now at the soft, warm expanse of his large bed. I realized my own exhaustion, after many nights of broken sleep. When I looked again at Kade, he was watching me, noticing the direction of my gaze.

"Take off your gown and get into bed," he said. "I'll make sure the chambers are warm enough."

As mortifying as this suggestion seemed, I had known to expect it, and more. At least he wasn't tear-ing the clothing from my body, or making any move whatsoever to approach me. And I was glad for his offer to heat the room. It was a kindness he wasn't obliged to extend. That he was taking measures to see that I was comfortable was…well, unexpected.

His back was turned to me. I removed my gown quickly, leaving my shift on, and climbed under the many layers of furs. His bed was plush and snug.

I watched him as he fed the fire, and I waited. I thought of the first time I'd seen him, only weeks ago, and that first flush he'd inspired. And I could acknowledge that my alarm, as I lay here in his bed and watched the play of the firelight paint his face and his hair, was laced with a subtle curiosity. Whatever criticisms I held for Kade Mackenzie—of which there were plenty—I could allow that he was lean and perfectly proportioned, as though sculpted by nature with particular care.

He stood and walked to the far side of the bed. He began to unfasten the last of his holsters.

I closed my eyes.

"It would be in the best interest of everyone involved," he said, "if you would keep our marriage bed activities—or lack thereof—to yourself."

I dared to steal a glance at him, and his riveted contemplation caused a tiny lurch in my stomach. If I had hoped wedding vows might soften my own anxious reaction to him, I'd been sorely mistaken. Yet as my eyes met his, I was momentarily dazzled by the depth of some unfathomable whirl of emotion in him. I had first thought his eyes cold in their crystalline clarity, but they were far from impassive now. His face, framed as it was by the thick, lustrous locks of his dark hair streaked by fiery glints of auburn, showed what might have been a ripple of empathetic concern, brief and disarming. But then it was gone, leaving me feeling inexplicably bereft.

As though unsure whether I had understood his suggestion, he said more forcefully, "I forbid you to discuss what goes on behind our private doors with anyone."

"You don't need to command me," I said. "You only need to ask me. I have no intention of discussing anything, now or ever."

"Good. Because I'll not have you defying me."

Brute! So immersed in the angst and upheaval of my quick marriage to Kade Mackenzie, I had not had the time to consider my new status as the laird-in-waiting's wife. If I had, I might have, in different circumstances (or with a different husband attached to it), been pleased with the title. I'd spent a lifetime under the thumb of my father. Every detail of my life, every activity, relationship, task and outing, had been dictated and contained by my father's enforced decisions. Now, as impending lady of the clan, I might have had an opportunity to free myself of such dictatorial constraints. But clearly, I would be as bound and limited by my new husband as I had ever been by my father. Anger and frustration colored my words. "I wasn't defying you. I said I would do as you asked."

"What goes on in our chambers is between you and me, and is not privy to the intelligence of others. Are we agreed?"

"Aye," I replied indignantly. I was used to being punished, and to hiding the evidence. Was this what my new husband had planned for me? Would he beat me into submission and order me to conceal his secret brutality?

"Are you wearing any underclothing under your shift?" he asked.

I froze instantly at the question, but I met his unrelenting stare with an approximation of the same. The moment was upon me, when my husband would use my body as he pleased. The inevitable consummation of this loveless marriage was about to commence. Would he bind me to the bedposts? Beat me? *It took her several days to recover.* My heart thumped frantically in my chest, but, in fact, I felt almost relieved. At this point, I almost wanted him to do what he would do, to get it over and done with.

"Aye," I said, and my voice had a fearful, breathless quality to it I took care to overcome.

"Take them off."

I suppose I should have expected a harsh, overbearing approach. My husband was a loutish devil, I had known this about him all along. If I had ever harbored secret hopes that he might be a skilled, thoughtful, tender lover, I laid them decisively to rest now, and not without anger. Insolently, and perhaps overly dramatically, I did as he asked. I sat up and removed the thin cotton garment I wore under my shift and flung it to the edge of the bed. Even so, my legs returned to their clasped-together state and I pulled the furs even farther over my body. If he would force me, at least I had a few remaining barriers to comfort myself with. For a few moments longer.

Watching my eyes, Kade reached to draw the furs from where they lay, slowly exposing my lightly clad body and bare legs to the cool air. I could read no emotion in his expression now and I wondered if I had imagined the brief flicker of compassion. Distant: that's what he was, as I had suspected all along. A hint of lightness clung to his words. "I remember. I'm to expect insolence. We established that at the start."

It had been our very first conversation.

"And I assured you then," he continued, "that I might be able to persuade you to comply with my requests, as unreasonable as they may seem."

"Which requests?" I asked.

"Open your legs," he said.

I hesitated, defenseless in the face of his promised strength.

"Do it." The quiet command riled me, and I decided then and there that anger might be more productive than fear. The man certainly lacked any hint of a bedside manner. Why couldn't I at least have acquired a husband who wasn't such a complete and utter bully?

"Nay," I dared to whisper to him.

He wasn't at all fazed by my impudence. Patiently, he said, "Do it now or I'll do it for you."

I clung desperately to my fury, but it was losing ground against the apprehension that seemed to dominate all my interaction with this belligerent, perplexing beast of a man.

"What do you mean to do?" It was an entirely daft question, aye. Of course I knew why he wanted me to expose myself to him: so he could ravage me and impregnate me and trap me irrevocably in this horrid marriage.

As it was, I was mildly shocked when he said, "I mean to make it appear as though this marriage has been consummated. There will be certain people who will inquire after the evidence. I would prefer not to be plagued by other people's gossip on the matter."

I realized my fists were digging little crescents into my palms and loosened my grip as I tried to absorb his meaning. *What?*

My voice sounded breathy and frightened even to myself when I asked hopefully, "Will we…*not* consummate this marriage now?"

"Good God, nay. 'Tis clear you believe otherwise, but I would never force a woman to bed me against her will, particularly not my own wife. Truth be told, as outrageously appealing as you are, you're doing little to stoke my desire by continually looking at me that way."

I was doing little to stoke *his* desire? Indignant, I said, "What way?"

"As though I'm about to string you up on a torture rack and flay you to death. 'Tis unnecessary. I'll not force you, nor will I do anything at all that you don't beg me to do."

I was somewhat taken aback by his words. Relieved, to be sure, and also surprised. Could it be that my husband wasn't quite as unfeeling as I'd first predicted?

Again, his severity became laced with an underlying thread of humor, which, at this moment and in my fragile state, I found more irritating than engaging. I thought it unlikely I'd ever beg my husband to do anything except leave.

Nevertheless, I was mildly intrigued. I couldn't help asking, "What was it you imagine I would beg you to do, husband?"

He paused, and the intensity of his skewering gaze was enough to steal away any boldness I might have enjoyed only moments ago. "All manner of things, when the time is right," was his quiet response. "Now open your legs."

My heart thumped in my chest, and the overzealous pulse could be felt elsewhere, curiously, as I moved very slowly to obey him. I moved my knees just slightly apart, thankful that my shift barely covered my most intimate places. The light fabric didn't feel like enough, though, and I placed my hands over myself in a last attempt at modesty.

But my husband would have none of it. "First, by covering yourself you are only succeeding in rousing my curiosity further. I'm more likely to seek out what you hide from me. Remember that. Second, I am your husband, whom you are hereby obliged to obey at all times. You will do well to also remember that. Now remove your hands, Stella. I'll not hurt you." In truth, hearing my name spoken in the rasping tones of his warrior's voice, then followed by his unexpectedly gentle assurance: it touched something in me. It made me feel as if we were in this together somehow, this ruse. Us, fooling them, taking our time, allowing me my hesitations. It made me want to believe him, and obey him. "At least not unless you want me to," he added, to which I had no reply.

Unexpectedly, he pulled a knife from the scabbard strung to his belt. I felt my eyes widen at the sight of it, but my husband wasn't looking at me. Instead, he ran the blade of the knife lightly along the skin of his tanned, hair-dusted forearm. Then he turned his arm over and, to my astonishment, he pressed the blade deeper, drawing a small clean line along a single vein of the finer skin of his inner arm. Blood began to flow freely and trickled from his arm, spilling a drop onto the stone floor.

He raised his eyes to me and he repeated his soft demand. "Now." His tone left no room for argument.

I removed my hands and placed them by my sides and he watched me all the while, waiting for me until I did as he asked.

Then he touched his fingers to the pooling blood of his wound, and, very carefully, he reached those bloodied fingers to slide under the thin film of my shift. His eyes were on my body and I thought I detected a slight quickening of his breath. I gasped before he even touched my skin, at this bold and sudden intimacy, from the startling sensation of localized heat.

I felt his warm touch very lightly paint the blood to my skin of my upper thigh. Shockingly, the hot silken glide of his fingers spread a sudden molten awareness through my veins, suffusing me with an unfamiliar sensation, which gathered warmly in the innermost regions of my body. He withdrew his touch, reapplying his paint. And then, when his fingertips sought my most secret place, I could not move or breathe. I closed my eyes. His fingers stroked softly, prodding lightly, parting my intimate folds to stain me with his blood. He carried out his task with tender, careful deliberation. The smooth glide of his touch shocked me with its gentle potency. His fingers were barely inside me, and his thumb rubbed against the sensitive hooded nub. My mind went blank, overwhelmed by the rush of vibrant sensation and the complete vulnerability. Involuntarily, my legs opened wider, causing my shift to rise. I writhed slightly against him, not entirely sure whether I meant to move with him or away from him. His thumb circled the little peak again, while an agile finger probed deeper, in a silky, languid rhythm, as though ensuring that he was making a proper job of the task at hand.

Vivid, collecting energy warmed me where his wicked fingers touched me, his movement unhurried and sure. I tried to keep quiet, but I couldn't stop a small gasp from climbing in my throat.

And then his touch was removed.

My eyes opened, and my awareness returned to me. My shift was raised and my legs were parted. I thought of adjusting my position, and covering myself, but he was touching his fingers again to the blood on his arm. I kept myself still. Waiting to see what he would do next. My body was tense with a subdued anticipation.

My intimate flesh, revealed to him, was heated with a light throb. Would he touch me again? I found that I was not averse to the thought. Instead, my body seemed to pulse at the possibility. I was afraid of him, aye, afraid of the dark, challenging glimmer in his shadowed eyes. Yet my fear and a cautious expectancy bundled into a glowing ache that I could not name.

Watching my eyes, he reached instead to paint a light stain on the sheet between my legs. A ripple of amusement, which I was now becoming used to, played across his expression fleetingly. Then he pulled the hem of my shift down to cover me.

"There," he said. "That will satisfy anyone who wishes to inquire after the validity of our marriage. And you can lay your terror momentarily to rest." He rose to his feet and walked to a table where a pitcher of water and a bowl sat. He poured some water over his cut to clean it, then wrapped a small thin strip of cloth around it, tucking the end in place. And I, still dazed by the lingering effects of his slick, debauched fingers, pulled the furs to my neck and lay back in the large bed. "Although," he drawled, "for such a timid, hesitant creature, you react to me in a way that suggests that you are not as averse to my attentions as you may think you are. 'Tis something I had already suspected, aye. A very pleasing detail in a wife, to be sure, and one I intend to make the most of."

I had no idea what he was referring to, yet I had the feeling I should perhaps be offended. Or flattered. My confusion frustrated me somewhat. Would I ever understand the complexity of his textured, layered insinuations? "What do you mean?" I asked quietly.

"'Tis a topic we will revisit later," he said enigmatically, then, to my shock: "Avert your gaze now, if you're as chaste and innocent as you act. Or feast your eyes—whatever pleases you. I prefer to sleep in the raw."

"What—" I began. Then, as realization dawned, I whispered, *"Oh."*

I squeezed my eyes closed.

I could hear him begin to unfasten the straps and holsters that held his many weapons, and the clang of metal striking against the stone floor as he gently dropped them.

"But don't worry, lass," he said, to which I dared to barely open one eye. He was shirtless—and for a moment my eye roved the contours of his broad chest, his skin tawny and glowing from the dancing firelight, until he began to pull at the ties of his leather trews, at which point I squeezed my eyes closed once again. "I always keep my weapons within reach and at the ready."

"That's…that's good," I murmured, unsure of what reply he might be expecting.

I heard the rustling sound of his clothing being tossed to land on a nearby chair, then movement as his heavy form settled into bed next to me. He didn't touch me, but I could feel the instant heat of his body as intensely as if I was standing next to a roaring blaze. With the howl of the cool wind rippling the furs at the windows, I could admit that the heat he provided was not unwelcome. The thought, however, of his bulk and his nakedness so close beside me was alarming indeed. He was so big and so outrageously...male.

I lay entirely motionless, afraid to move lest I rubbed up against him or somehow issued an unintentional invitation of some kind.

He suffered no such hesitations and thrashed mildly until he found a position that was comfortable to him, occasionally brushing some part of himself lightly against me, only to quickly withdraw the touch. He turned his head to look at me, although my gaze remained resolutely directed at the ceiling.

After a time, he spoke. "Stella," he said softly.

Tentatively, I looked over at his face. It was so dark in the room that I could only see the outline of his disheveled hair and the gleam of his eyes. "Aye?" I whispered.

He didn't reply immediately, as though he was considering discussing something with me but was unsure how the topic might be received. It was several minutes before he continued. In the end, what he said was, "Good night."

I almost smiled. It was the very last thing I expected him to say. "Good night," I whispered.

With that, his eyes closed and he sighed deeply. Very soon, his breathing deepened. His big body twitched gently several times as he succumbed to sleep.

As soon as I was assured he was deeply asleep, I exhaled with a great sense of relief. This dreaded day had passed less painfully than I had imagined. I had not been forced by him. He had not hurt me or threatened me. As much as I'd been incensed by his manner, I could understand now that he'd merely asked me to comply with a request—somewhat aggressively, aye, when he doubted my agreement. Yet as soon as he was assured that I would honor his—our—privacy, he had shown me kindness. Respect. Compassion. Not only that, but his touch had inspired unexpected sensations that had not been entirely unpleasant. An inexplicable warmth. The soft pull of a new and enticing anticipation—the same manner of anticipation that had once visited me in the night garden far below us.

Still, it was a long time before I could take comfort in my own dreams.

I AWOKE IN the night, startled to find another person in bed with me.

Kade Mackenzie.

My husband.

He lay on his back with one arm slung over his head. His thick hair was in wild disarray. In sleep, his face looked younger. In repose, his aggression was virtually undetectable. His bare chest rose and fell gracefully with his breath. The top of the fur lay low on his stomach. My eyes studied with fascination the unfamiliar lines of his body. I had seen shirtless men before, from a distance, as they worked or fought or swam. But never like this. Never close enough to touch in the silvery moonlight. I was surprised by the light dusting of hair on his chest, the arrow line that ran below his navel down, to where the furs barely covered him, his carved hipbones. Little scars lined his skin in uneven patterns, including a jagged crescent that circled the front of his left shoulder and shone pale against his brownness. His very color was intriguing to me, the darkness of it, the vivid richness of absorbed sun on his skin, as though he retained some of its heat and its light. He was very muscled, each chiseled curve mortared between by smaller oncs that rippled slightly as he breathed. A light pulse played gently under the skin of his neck.

I was surprised at the sight being delivered to my eyes, and at the turn of my own thoughts. My husband, without his weapons and his wrath, was beautiful.

CHAPTER SEVEN

I WAS AWAKENED by a sound I was now becoming accustomed to: the clang of metal against metal, steel against stone. My husband had risen from the bed and was clad only in his leather trews and the low-slung belt from which one of his large knives hung. I watched him, studying more closely the wide span of his shoulders, the defined muscles of his torso, narrowing to the flat plane of his stomach. The blatant power of his body as he moved was obvious. Rising memories of the brutality I'd been subjected to all my life at the hands of powerful men such as this could not be suppressed. Despite the drowsed comfort of his bed and the dreamlike memory of his face as he slept, the sight of him sent a small chill chasing up my spine.

Kade was taking care to put his weapons into place. He sheathed his oversized sword, distinctive for its unusual gold hilt. The hard leather of its scabbard had been etched and stitched with swirling flame-shaped designs.

He added a second belt, reaching then for a sharpening stone, which sat on a cluttered table. He unslung a bone-handled knife from a holster. Before he began to sharpen the knife, he looked in my direction, as though mindful that the scrape of it might wake me.

He noticed my open eyes watching him. "She wakes," he said.

I didn't reply to him. I wasn't sure what kind of answer he might expect.

His fierceness had returned to him, so much so that I wondered if I'd dreamed the peaceful scene in the quiet moonlight. This was a different display entirely to the tranquil sleeping vision of the night before. Kade's long tousled hair framed his face like a lion's mane. *Be assured: I don't plan on eating you alive. Not yet, anyway.*

Yet the spectacle of him didn't spear me with as much anxiety as it had done in days past. I had seen a softer side of him. And I knew he possessed the capacity to allow me my fears. This seemed important. I had no way of knowing when he might choose to consummate our marriage. But the fact that he hadn't forced himself upon me at his very first opportunity gave me a small measure of comfort.

And I had slept surprisingly well, without the agitated dreams that had recently disturbed me.

There was a timid knock on the door. Kade answered it, ushering two servants with trays of covered dishes into our chambers, indicating the table where he wanted them placed. The women were young, and the sight of my brawny, armed husband, shirtless and barefoot, nearly caused them to spill their delivery to the floor. Managing to place their trays, they blushed and stared, huddling together. Noticing me, still reclined in the marriage bed, they giggled nervously and whispered to each other.

"My wife requires a bath to be brought to my chambers once we have eaten," Kade told them, having no time for their tittering embarrassment. "You will attend to her as she requires. Proof that the marriage is now valid, as requested by Laird Morrison, may then be stripped from the bed and taken to his chambers."

The chambermaids went silent, nodding slightly, and backed from the room with wide eyes to obey his command. They glanced at me once more as they made their leave. I could see the thoughts churning behind their eyes, imagining the debauched scenes of what had taken place here during the night.

So my father was the one who wanted evidence that my marriage had been finalized, proof that his coveted alliance was now sealed irrevocably. This did not surprise me. I was used to my father's domination. I could only hope that my husband would not be even more controlling than my father.

"Come and break your fast," Kade said. "We will attend the farewell of my brother and his new wife. They depart for Ossian Lochs later this morning." His tone was neither friendly nor cold, but there was an implication there that I would do as I was told. "And we will prepare to leave for Glenlochie the day after tomorrow."

He would take and I would give. He would speak and I would listen. These were the rules of marriage and I understood them. Yet it irked me that he was so immediate about his dictatorship. Already he was ordering me about. "Whatever you wish, husband." The last word of my reply was colored with a light note of over-done respect that bordered on mockery. And he noticed.

One of his brows lifted, and he regarded me with cool contemplation. As though entertained by my light disrespect, he seemed to be making a point of regaining control. "What*ever* I wish?" he asked softly. "Were that true, wife, you would be naked and weeping with pleasure at this very moment. But I'll give you time to adjust before I take what's mine."

"Wh-what?" I gasped. Oh, God, Agnes's gossip was indeed true. My mind reeled at the thought but my body had a quite different response to his comment; I felt like our chambers had suddenly become quite warm. "What is your meaning?"

"What is my meaning?" he repeated languidly, as though puzzling over the question himself. He put on his tunic and secured another holster across his chest. He did not look at me. Once he was satisfied that his weapons were in place, he removed the lids from the trays of food. He picked up a piece of salted bacon and took a bite, taking his time to study me as though enjoying my shock. "I *mean* that you're very clearly terrified of me." He caught my eye. "And so you should be." I could hear that twang of amusement in him again, the one that never ceased to not only confuse me but also rile me. Why he found every aspect of our hasty, forced marriage entertaining, I did not know.

"I'm not terrified of you," I lied.

"Of course you are." He carried a tray over to the bed, and sat next to where I still lay under the furs.

"Yet I have reason to believe that you're exceptionally responsive to me, and I mean to test that theory now, if you don't object." He picked up a small piece of bread and, with his hunting knife, spread some butter onto it. "Allow me."

Warily, I sat up against the plush pillows and reached for the bread. What did he mean by "responsive"? I didn't dare ask. He withdrew the offering, shaking his head slowly, his eyes never leaving mine. The light blue blaze of Kade's irises was startlingly bright, and contrasted somehow with the swarthy features of his face. There was something entrancingly colorful about him, like his health and vigor were so potent they exaggerated the hues of him beyond the expected.

"I will feed you," he said. Had my sisters been mistaken? Had they misunderstood? I had been told that a wife's duty might extend to feeding her husband, if he commanded it, yet my husband clearly had other ideas. "Open your mouth."

Hesitantly, I did as he asked of me. He placed a small piece of warm bread on my tongue. As he fed me, he spoke.

"I understand that you have led a sheltered, pampered life and that you are not used to the company of men. 'Tis not difficult to see that you have little to no idea what to expect from marriage. Being the first of your sisters to marry, perhaps you do not know the way of it." His expression was softer now, inciting an unfamiliar sense of reassurance. He paused to feed me another small bite of bread. The bread was fresh from the oven and the butter rich and creamy, melting on my tongue. I had never tasted anything quite so good. "I have thought about how I might ease your fear."

He used his knife to cut a slice from an overripe pear, reaching slowly to place it in my mouth. A drop of juice from the sweet fruit ran down my chin. I licked my lips to catch the moisture and found that Kade was watching my mouth with an absorbed, almost glazed expression. With his thumb, he wiped the sticky liquid from my chin, and the contact sent a light dart of awareness, oddly, to the tips of my breasts, which tightened beneath my shift. I noticed then that the furs had dropped to my waist and I made a move to pull them up. But my husband had other ideas. He placed his large hand over mine, preempting my bid for modesty; the warmth of it gave me pause, and I slid my hand from his grasp, letting the furs lie as they were.

"In regards to sealing this marriage, I would prefer not to force you. I am therefore proposing that we wait one month, to allow you to acclimatize to your new status as my wife," Kade said. "I would hope that you might trust me, eventually, and I make this allowance to give you time to come to terms with all that being a wife requires."

Despite the topic being discussed, I found I was enjoying the taste of the food so much, I felt oddly subdued and compliant. Upon his encouragement, I opened my mouth again, as he fed me another slice of the sweet pear. This slice was bigger than the last, so I had to open my mouth slightly wider. His thumb lingered, brushing against my slippery lower lip, sending another twinge of warmth to my nipples, which hardened further against the soft cotton of my shift. A blush warmed my cheeks at the thought that he might detect my unwanted response. His lurking amusement played across his face, calming me further. I ate the fruit slowly, savoring the syrupy flavor, and I felt more relaxed at that moment than I ever had in his presence. "What happens after a month?"

"We will consummate this marriage properly, and with your willing participation. You will give me whatever I ask of you."

I looked at his face, the roguish bristle of his day-old beard, the dangerous aura of his wicked eyes, rimmed by long, dark lashes.

"I will give you my body, in other words," I said, "to do with as you please."

His skewering gaze was, alarmingly, feeding the soft warmth in my breasts, which funneled deeper and lower, settling into the low pit of my stomach. "Aye, and your willingness."

"My willingness," I repeated.

"Aye."

"What would I have to...do?"

"Not a damn thing, lass. I will do everything that needs doing. I ask only that you allow it."

I watched him as he cut another slice of pear. How strange, that my battle-scarred, muscle-bound husband would make such a concession. *I have thought about how I might ease your fear. I would hope that you might trust me.* These were not at all the words I was expecting. He didn't, after all, need my permission. He could do with me as he pleased now, and as often as he liked.

"And if I refuse?"

"Then we might attend to the consummation right now, if you prefer. 'Tis my right, after all, as your husband, to take of you anything I want. And my *want,* I can assure you, at this very moment, is threatening to overtake my well developed practices of both discipline and control."

I glared at him, and my brief sense of composure fled, replaced by stirrings of the recurring fear that crept with featherlike stealth up the tiny hairs on my arms.

"I would prefer, however," he said, "not to force you, which is why I am proposing this month—or more, if absolutely necessary—for you to get used to me. I am confident that I can win your invitation, in time."

Despite my unease, my body continued with its peculiar reaction. *He did unspeakable things.* His words, and all he referred to, had a physical, seeping effect. *I will do everything that needs doing.* Shockingly, my nipples were now painfully beaded and the warm throb in my stomach had spread lower, tingling and aching. My better judgment warred against his controlling, dominating manner, yet an unmistakable excitement glowed deep within me that I neither understood nor wanted there.

"You appear to be warming to the idea," he said.

The fact that he could clearly detect my body's reaction to him only frustrated me further. "I am warming to nothing you have to offer," I said with hesitant defiance.

"Then why is it," he purred, touching his thumb once again to the stickiness on my lips, the light, gliding touch causing another flare of heat deep inside me, "that your body is unfailingly receptive to me, at even the slightest hint of provocation?"

"I—" I was grasping, my face hot with embarrassment.

"When I told you I found you captivating, wife, I meant it. For two weeks, I have thought of nothing else but the sound of your voice, the perfect, bowed shape of your lips, the unusual golden tips of your long hair, your shining, amber eyes, like jewels from an ancient hidden treasure. And this the little furrow between your eyebrows as you look at me with terror in your eyes that I want to ease away." He touched his thumb lightly to my forehead, smoothing away the outward signs of my anxiety, tracing a line down the side of my face with his finger. "Why do you look at me that way?"

His confession, shockingly heartfelt, especially considering the rough rasp of its delivery, astounded me. That there might be more to his intention that duty, and more to this marriage than military considerations, made me feel light-headed with something close to relief. And hope.

And warm, coiling anticipation.

"What do you think would happen…" he said, letting his finger drop lower, to trace the silk cord of my shift, drawing a line that snaked lower. I gasped as his finger lightly circled the outline of my beaded nipple that was clearly jutting against the fabric of my clothing. His long fingers were graceful in their movement, his hands brown and strong-looking. I remembered the touch of those fingers silkily prodding into my most intimate flesh, inspiring blooming sensation that my body was recalling, and reigniting now. "If I touched you…very, very softly…right here." His thumb and finger skimmed the peak of my nipple in a brief, pinching caress. The touch was so vibrantly intense, I tried in vain to lean back, to evade this scalding intimacy—it was too new, too overwhelming. As soon as he sensed my withdrawal, the touch was immediately removed.

My nipple pulsed with echoing heat. I felt as though hot wax had been poured upon the intimate points of my body and the sensation was sinfully exquisite.

Kade was smiling thoughtfully. "Would you like," he said slowly, "for me to do that again?"

"I—I don't know," I managed to say.

His hand once again eased closer, so close I could detect the heat of him through the thin layer of my shift. His eyes held mine with their sultry power. "I'll only touch you if you ask me to," he said softly.

Nay, don't touch me! my mind was screaming. *You'll hurt me and humiliate me. Like they do. You're a brute and a scoundrel, like all the rest of them. Leave me.*

But his hand was not raised in anger. His touch caused no pain. Only hot, delightful promise. And I heard myself whisper, *"Aye."*

A smile quirked at the corner of his mouth and his hand withdrew an inch, as though he was reconsidering. My breasts felt rounded and swollen, the taut tips hot and flushed. My thighs, too, were overheated and my delicate, swollen flesh throbbed lightly. Muddled thoughts flashed through my mind, reminding me of a dark, secluded garden and an uncontrollable yearning. *Don't pull away. Put your hands on me. Touch me. There, there. Anywhere.* My husband, the devil, smiled slowly and his face took on a hint of the rugged beauty that lurked behind his fierceness, when he smiled and when he slept.

As though reading my mind, he said in a low chuckle, "All right, then."

And his fingers began their slow ascent, touching me, rubbing slow circles around the outline of my nipples. His hot touch was viciously potent, painting my body with raw, ripe need. I arched, wanting more pressure, more contact. He was maddeningly restrained, taking his time, lingering with casual deliberation, rubbing and pinching until I was awash with molten desire.

Kade raised his knife, which he still held in his left hand. I felt my eyes round at the sight of it. Had I misread him? Would he hurt me as I was so accustomed to? He moved slowly, slipping the tip of it under the corded tie of my shift. The coolness of the blunt metallic blade against my skin provided a stark relief to the sudden heat of my body. "And what do you think would happen, then, if I cut the cloth from your skin to touch you with my fingers, here?" His thumb pressed gently, swirling, teasing.

He challenged me with his eyes, and I squirmed under his touch, my body lit with melting sensitivity.

"Nay?" he mused lightly, when I did not immediately respond. "You would prefer that I leave it on?"

Through my shift, he squeezed the sensitive tips of my breasts more roughly, sending sharp rivers of desire to my center.

Against my will, I moaned, "Please. Do it." My voice sounded low and hushed.

He needed no further encouragement. With uncanny control of his knife, he sliced through the cord and the cloth, not once, but twice, allowing my shift to open and fall. At the sight of my naked breasts, Kade's eyes grew visibly darker and his breathing caught.

"Holy God," he said after a moment, all trace of amusement gone. My husband, for all his bravado, was momentarily speechless. My nakedness had somehow tampered with his unerring control. "Your *beauty,*" he whispered, "is nothing short of miraculous. I am at your mercy, wife." His words echoed with the earlier warnings of my sisters, now caught in sharp relief with the contradiction. I was at his mercy, aye. But he was also at mine. This equality and the power of the realization only succeeded in feeding my own desire for him to touch me.

He dropped his knife and reached for me with both hands. Rather than teasing, his touch became reverential and affectionate, caressing my nipples with light, squeezing pulls. Each careful tug of his roughened fingers sent a channel of pure heat to the secreted place between my thighs, which softened and pulsed in rhythmic harmony to the play of Kade's fingers. Only once had

I felt this kind of pleasured expectation, in a forbidden garden with an unknown stranger; the memory seemed far away and long ago. I wanted *this,* now, more—more of the excruciating touch of his warm, gifted hands. As the pressure built, the heated inner channel between my core and my breasts grew in intensity, until the moistened entrance to my body throbbed unbearably. I moaned and writhed to get closer to the enchanting feel of him. The furs fell lower with my movement, and the skin of my thighs was cooled by the sudden exposure to the air. I felt the beginnings of an indescribable rush deep within me. When his head lowered as though to take one of my nipples into his mouth, I very nearly begged him to do it. But before I could, a staccato beat of insistent knocks at the door broke through the haze of my stupor. And again.

"Stella!" It was Maisie's voice. "The maids are here with the bath you called for. We've come to attend to you and help you dress."

More knocking.

Kade withdrew his touch, and pulled the furs back up my body to cover me. His color was high, his cheekbones burnished with a light flush. "'Tis just as well," he said with an unmistakable air of smugness. "I might not have lasted an hour, let alone a month."

He rose and, with barely a backward glance, walked to the door. "I will send for you when I'm ready," he said, then with a flash of a smile, "You are indeed an instrument to be played."

It wasn't the first time I was confused as to the slant

of his meaning. Now, as he made his leave, mortification blanketed the heat of my desire. I had responded to him, aye, shamefully so. My body had come alive under his bold touch. I had not meant to react like that, not at all. I was angry with myself, for my wanton compliance. And his comment irked me, that he would see me like that, as an object, a plaything, an overly willing wench to be used and dismissed. I vowed that I would not allow myself to get so carried away when—if—he were to touch me again. Next time I would say nay to him, and keep my distance.

Kade opened the door to a flurry of commotion. The chambermaids and my sisters silenced abruptly at the towering, sudden countenance of my husband. Without a word, he walked past them and down the hall. As soon as he was gone, my sisters burst into the room, full of curiosity and concern. They clutched gowns and adornments of many varieties. The chambermaids rolled the full tub into the room, which steamed and splashed with the movement.

Still mildly stunned by the intensity of what had taken place, and also by its hasty removal, I lay still. My sisters gathered around the bed, and Maisie pulled the fur down over my body. They stared at my shredded shift and the blood smeared across my thighs and the white sheets. There was a collective gasp.

"Lord above, Stella, you've been *ravaged!*"

I COULD DO little to calm my sisters' reaction. After all, I had sworn to Kade that I would discuss nothing of what had taken place, and I was glad I was true to my word. It wasn't five minutes after my sisters arrived that my husband returned to the room, storming in purposefully as though he had forgotten about my presence—and that of my many attendants. I was also glad that I was fully immersed in the deep bath before he made his appearance. My sisters gasped at the intrusion and clutched drying cloths as though to shield me before their whispers began.

It was the first time I had ever seen Kade look mildly uncomfortable. At the far end of his chambers, he was reaching to grab a rolled scroll from a high shelf, which he briefly unrolled to read, as though searching for something specific, or making every effort to concentrate on anything but our feminine circle.

"Add some bubbles," Ann whispered to Agnes.

"It hardly matters if he sees her," muttered Agnes. "He's her *husband*."

"Besides," Maisie added, hushed, "'tis clear enough he's already done much more than *see* her."

"Aye, look at the state of her," Agnes quietly agreed. "Flushed. Bloodied. Utterly traumatized."

There were noises of sympathy before conversation turned to my wardrobe, more loudly now that the subject was no longer that of my plundering.

"What dress, then, Stella?" asked Agnes. "Not the green one. You always wear green."

"That's because it's my favorite color," I replied.

"Which dress do you favor…Kade?" Maisie asked boldly and with a trace of coy pushiness.

Kade looked at Maisie, and his indifference kicked in. He took a moment to consider his answer. "I'm sure Stella will look ravishing in any of the gowns," he said. I thought I might have detected a note of playful sarcasm in his reply, but I couldn't be certain. Either way, my sisters exchanged meaningful glances, as though pleased by his sentiment, before returning to the task at hand.

To us, Maisie said, "Ailie Mackenzie is so talented. I'm going to ask her to make some of these in my size. In pink, and in this light green."

"Aye, her designs are so sophisticated," Ann said.

"Which one, then, Stella?" persisted Agnes.

"I like the white," I said.

"Not white, 'tis too plain. Something regal, since Wilkie's wife is royalty after all." This from Agnes, who, immediately after she spoke, gave an apologetic smile to Maisie.

"Isn't it unlikely?" Maisie replied, jutting her chin upward just slightly. "Who would've thought that the king's child would prove to be a lass? And a *servant* of all people!"

Kade's movement stopped and he looked once again at Maisie, his eyes narrowed and uninterpretable. "She was never meant for servitude," Kade said darkly.

Maisie blanched slightly at his remark but spoke evenly. "Aye, I've heard the story. I admire her, of course."

"You would be wise to admire Roses by speaking only well of her," Kade said, and there was warning in his tone. I got the feeling Kade did not think highly of

Maisie, whether it was from her offhand comment or some other digression—which I might have guessed at. Either way, the animosity clung to him as he returned to his task.

Maisie did not reply but she continued to watch him.

Ann attempted to change the subject. "I think you look beautiful in yellow, Stella. It sets off your eyes."

"I like the pink," said Agnes.

I tried again. "I like the cut of the white one. 'Tis simple yet elegant." I was so used to having my choices overruled that my voice sounded resigned even to myself; this decision, as every other, would be made for me.

"You should wear something more colorful," said Agnes. "How about the blue?"

"Not blue," Maisie replied. "I don't like Stella in blue. It makes her eyes look positively wild."

"The pink, then," Agnes continued.

Kade, who was listening with more intent to the conversation than I might have expected, walked over to where we were gathered. He outsized my sisters by so much, he reminded me of a great bear who might have wandered into our party. My sisters fell entirely silent.

"Stella," he said evenly and with unmistakable authority, "will wear the white dress. And in the future, you will listen to what she says as soon as she says it."

My sisters went silent, staring up at my husband, mutely agog. I couldn't help feeling a sense of gratitude as my eyes met Kade's. His pronouncement afforded me with a small, nourishing power that was all but unfamiliar to me: I felt *supported*. And *listened to*. The depth of feeling caught me off guard. It made me want to reach out to him, to return the favor.

To me, Kade said gently but with that same ingrained authority that left no room for argument, "My guard is awaiting you outside the door. As soon as you are ready, he'll escort you to me. Do not take too long."

And with that, he again took his leave.

WILKIE AND ROSES were ready to depart for Ossian Lochs. Their travel party was not overly large and required only four carriages, along with a number of guards and officers who rode on horseback. Each carriage had been loaded with trunks of supplies and belongings. Despite the fortuitous turn of events surrounding Roses's newly discovered status as the daughter of the King of Scotland, which resulted in her inheritance—and Wilkie's lairdship—of the most coveted estate in all the Highlands, the mood was heavy.

I did not know my husband well at all. But I could detect that he was deeply saddened by the departure of his brother. He stood next to Laird Mackenzie as Wilkie shook the laird's hand. The laird, unexpectedly, embraced his brother in a heartfelt hug, patting him roughly on the back. It was known that these brothers were especially close. Their skills on the battlefield were discussed far and wide; their success as a team in maintaining and growing the wealth of Kinloch was often emulated but rarely equaled. Now their close collaboration was at an end. Wilkie was leaving now for Ossian Lochs, a three-day ride, and Kade would depart for

Glenlochie tomorrow. I could see the sorrow in Knox Mackenzie's eyes, which to me was one of the more pronounced aspects to his character despite his obvious staunchness. He had ruled without a wife since her death several years ago, and now he would rule without his brothers. His sense of loss was palpable in the set of his shoulders and the low light in his unusual pale gray eyes.

Wilkie put his hands on Laird Mackenzie's shoulders. "I'll expect a visit soon," he said. "Perhaps you'll favor one of the Stuart lasses. The time is overdue for you to find another wife, brother."

Laird Mackenzie, in a rare vulnerable moment, kicked the ground, raising a small tuft of dust.

Wilkie turned to Kade. Kade held out his hand for a handshake, but Wilkie grabbed his brother in a bear hug, cursing and disengaging with a flinch when one of Kade's blades poked his muscular bicep. They both laughed as Wilkie rubbed his arm. "Once you're settled at Glenlochie, we'll expect you and your new wife without too much delay."

Wilkie Mackenzie's eyes turned to me, and he contemplated my face, my hair, my dress. It was the closest I had been to him and I could see now more than ever before why he was legendary for his looks. His eyes were an almost royal blue, darker in the middle and lightening at the edges. His features, if studied individually, were perhaps overly bold, but when placed together presented a perfect configuration, a symmetry. He resembled his younger brother strongly but there was an ease to him that Kade lacked. Where Wilkie's inner glow conveyed reassurance and strength, Kade's relayed volatility. It was a volatility, however, I could reflect in the light of all that had so far happened, that intimidated me less than it had even one day ago. Wilkie smiled lightly at my scrutiny and leaned to kiss my cheek. "'Til soon, sister. Do not fear him. He's bullheaded as a mule, but I think you'll tame him easily enough. His bark is worse than his bite."

At this, Roses, who stood next to Wilkie, linked her arm through mine and gently led me from the men. I followed willingly, although somewhat surprised by her closeness. Her long white-blond hair was loose and strands of it brushed against my arm, as soft as feathers. Her scent was of sunshine and youth, floral somehow, and earthbound. "I hope you don't mind if I speak with you," she said. Her speech was inflected with the lightest hint of an accent I could not place, with rounded vowels that caught the ear. Her voice conveyed a strength, I thought, that belied her slender, small shape and the fairness of her hair. And I knew her story, as an outcast—a servant—swept into the arms of a most coveted, handsome nobleman. I couldn't help feeling a touch of admiration for her. To elevate herself through such a vast social divide, from the kitchens of the Ogilvie keep to the private chambers of Wilkie Mackenzie, even before he knew of her bloodline, was inspiring indeed. To undertake such a journey—both social and geographical—on her own and with such apparent poise and honesty, and to *admit* her very humble origins: it stirred something in me. Awe, maybe. Or a yearning to possess courage of that kind. I thought she deserved her good fortune.

"Of course not," I said, and she smiled.

"I do not know him well, your husband. Yet I see the way you look at him, if you'll forgive me. And I know your marriage was arranged by your father." She paused, as though awaiting a confirmation of sorts.

I gave it. "Aye."

"I wanted to tell you that I was very afraid of him at first. His first impression is one of danger, and he does little to assure one otherwise."

Again she paused. I agreed, wondering where she was going with this.

"Yet I have never had anything but kindness from him. He is thoughtful, and honorable, as all the Mackenzies are. I've seen him with his family. He is trusted, and adored, and he gives love as much as he receives it."

I looked at her, struck by her beauty. Her hair caught the sun and glowed white. Her eyes reflected the shade of the grass.

"I've never had a sister before," she said, somewhat shyly. "I know you have many. But I hope you'll think of me as such. We're so looking forward to visits from you, and Wilkie plans for us to visit you as well in the coming months."

I appreciated her kind words. "I would enjoy that very much, Roses. I wish you all the best with your new life at Ossian Lochs with Wilkie. I know you'll have every success."

Unexpectedly, she hugged me to her, holding me close. "Thank you," she whispered.

"Roses," called Wilkie. "'Tis time."

We drew apart, and we walked back to where the men were congregated. Roses smiled and waved as Wilkie helped her into the largest carriage.

"You might see us sooner than you think," Kade said to Wilkie. "If Campbell's rebellion reignites as it threatens to."

Wilkie's half smile was laced with the confidence of a warrior who knew his own strength. "Unlikely," he said.

"Be well, brother," Laird Mackenzie called after him as Wilkie climbed into the carriage after Roses, "and send your messengers at the first sign of trouble."

We watched their carriages grow smaller for a time, the prance of the horses, the clouds of dust that rose then settled in the midday sun. Kade stood next to Laird Mackenzie some distance from me. And as I contemplated my husband, I saw for the first time not only a fierce, brawny warrior but a man who might be capable of sadness, of kindness and, most of all, of love.

CHAPTER EIGHT

MY OPTIMISM WAS short-lived. Immediately after Wilkie and Roses departed for Ossian Lochs, my husband reverted to his most boorish. As though he'd overheard my conversation with Roses and was determined at all costs to disprove it, he was as cold and callous as I had ever expected of him.

Tomorrow we would depart for Glenlochie, and Kade had ordered a brigade of workers to help him prepare for our departure, which would take place early tomorrow morning. That he was less than pleased, in these final hours, at the thought of leaving his beloved Kinloch was more than obvious. He had done his duty, secured a necessary alliance and successfully staged a bonded union. If he may have once found me pleasing during our private moments, that admission seemed now to have escaped his mind. He seemed more preoccupied by thoughts of his new clan, his new laird—at least until he took over the role—and his permanent separation from the only home he'd ever known. Wilkie's fresh absence only appeared to heighten Kade's fuming state of mind, serving as a trigger that reminded him very convincingly that life would never be the same.

I was ordered to accompany him to the evening meal,

which we would take in Laird Mackenzie's private den, with only me, Kade, the laird and their two sisters. Despite the fact that I was now a bona fide member of their clan, the thought of dining with the Mackenzies made me feel wildly out of place, especially at this somewhat fraught time of upheaval in their family.

And my reservations were not unfounded. The laird spoke very little during the meal, which was as sumptuous a spread as any I had seen. I had a feeling, after witnessing for myself the superior quality not only of their supplies but also their preparation and presentation of it, that my husband would be very disappointed when he reached Glenlochie. Our hunters had had some difficulties in recent months. Our cooks were nowhere near as skilled. And our servers were more sullen, slow and disorganized than the smiling, gracious Mackenzie staff.

Kade's youngest sister, Christie, seemed to rise to the challenge of lightening the heavy mood of the evening. Christie was close to my age, I guessed, and had eyes and hair a similar color to Kade's. But the similarities ended there. She had an innocent exuberance that was at the same time engaging and entertaining. "Stella, you wore that wedding dress within an inch of its life, if you don't mind me saying. Your figure is *stunning*. We knew that already, of course. We'd heard the men speak of you, Kade especially—" A withering glare from Kade seemed to stall that particular commentary, but Christie wasn't easily deterred. "Oh, Kade, stop glowering. You of all people know I speak only the truth."

"Christie," Ailie reprimanded quietly, but for Christie, propriety did not appear to be the foremost goal of the evening. I didn't mind her forwardness at all. Her tendency to delve enthusiastically into sensitive topics was hardly something that was new to me—my sisters did so on an hourly basis, after all—and despite her overt curiosity I found myself enjoying her mild chatter. It was better than silence, at least.

"Aye," Kade grumbled. "We know how truthfully, and how often, you like to speak. Maybe you shouldn't *speak* quite so much, little sister." The endearment, tacked on as it was to his complaint, surprised me; clearly, there was great affection between the two, despite his reprimand.

"Someone has to," Christie replied, "otherwise we'd be all mired in a dull, morose silence. Poor Stella, she'll wonder what kind of family she married into. 'Tis not like Wilkie's gone off to war or to foreign territories. He's a laird now, rich beyond belief, and so in love he can barely see straight. We should be celebrating for him rather than mourning his absence. So, Stella, back to your wedding dress. I've asked Ailie to fashion something similar for me—and I'm helping with the details of the design—when the time comes, which might be never at this rate. The pickings are *so* slim! I mean, the Munros are charming enough, but—"

"Christie," Ailie said again.

Christie leaned toward me with a conspiratorial grin, as if no one aside from me understood or could relate to her considerable challenges. "I mean, *charming* might be a slight exaggeration. *Entertaining,* certainly. But Ailie already has her eye on one of *those*—" To Ailie's glare, Christie insisted, "I can tell Stella—she's *family* now, and we have so little time to get to know her before she and Kade depart tomorrow morning—although we do plan on visiting in a month, isn't it so, Kade?"

Kade acknowledged her question with an offhand grunt, and Christie continued, undeterred. "Anyway, Stella, Knox would prefer that I choose someone further afield. 'To expand our holdings and our influence,'" she mimicked in a deep voice to approximate her oldest brother's.

I couldn't help smiling at her impression. Laird Mackenzie narrowed his eyes at her in mock anger, but Christie continued. "But those Macintoshes are *heathens,* of course, and the Buchanans—*so* provincial. I mean, I say that in the nicest possible way, and it's true that several of them *are* quite handsome. I've never been to their keep, though, and I've heard it's in some state of disrepair. You've been, haven't you, Kade?"

A quiet lurch of discomfort stuck in my throat at the reference. Kade had been to the Buchanan keep, aye, a visit that had been nervously—and thoroughly—discussed by my sisters. *Claire's cousin invited him to her private chambers. She allowed him...well, whatever he wanted.* My unease only heightened when Kade's glance fell on me, as though he was reading my thoughts, or recalling long-ago trysts in lurid detail. "Aye," he said disinterestedly.

"What's it like?" Christie asked, taking a small sip of her ale.

"Unimpressive," Kade replied.

"That's exactly what I've heard," said Christie. "And it hardly makes a Buchanan a desirable choice, I'm sorry to say. Not like a…well, a Stuart or a Munro—but of course those choices are no longer available to me, if I'm to follow my brother's, laird of lairds, strict instructions—although Wilkie managed to skirt Knox's imperial dictates, to be sure. If only I was so clever—and so lucky." She said this affectionately, and Laird Mackenzie only rolled his eyes, not rising at all to the gentle impertinence. It was enviable, I thought—this family's obvious ease with one another. The power of a laird over his own clan was absolute, yet she teased him as though they were children. If I'd ever attempted a playful remark like that, I would have felt the back of my father's hand, and likely the lash of his whip, as well.

I considered again the difficulties and sadnesses the forced separation of these siblings would introduce. My husband, for certain, was in as churlish a mood as I had yet seen him.

But before we could tread further into the topics of either Buchanan's keep or imperial dictates, there was a commotion outside the door of the laird's den. Shouts and urgent voices rose above rapid footsteps. Whoever approached was frantic with their news. Laird Mackenzie and Kade rose from the table. The laird opened the door just as the guard was about to knock heavily, causing the agitated man to nearly fall into the room. He was followed by several other soldiers. "Laird Mackenzie!" the man began. "There is urgent news from your brother Wilkie."

"Wilkie?" the laird said. "What's the news? Is he hurt? He's only just departed half a day ago."

"His travel party has come upon a small battalion from the Campbell clan, Laird Campbell among them."

This was distressing news indeed. I knew, as we all did, that Laird Duncan Campbell was the son of King William's sister, and he believed Ossian Lochs to be his own rightful inheritance. The king had no sons, only one illegitimate daughter: Roses. In most instances, illegitimate children were not rightful heirs. Yet the king had decreed that Roses would be heir of his Highlands throne, and had appointed Wilkie as laird. Campbell's father had led the first rebellion less than two years ago, a battle in which Campbell's father and the Mackenzies' father had fought to the death. Duncan Campbell continued to rebel, to avenge his father's death and to claim the land he felt entitled to, and had attempted to recruit ally clans to fight with him. His recent attempts had been unsuccessful. But we all knew he was bound to try again. This, above all, was the reason my father and Laird Mackenzie had been so urgent about securing the alliance between our clans: to ensure that we had the military advantage over Campbell's army and any others he could convince to join him.

"I knew we should have killed him when we had the chance," Kade muttered.

"Have they been threatened?" Laird Mackenzie asked the guard, with abrupt impatience.

"Nay, Laird Mackenzie. The Campbells were in search of Laird Morrison, and were told that he's in residence here at Kinloch, to return to Glenlochie on the morrow. They will arrange to speak with Laird Morrison—and his highest-ranking officers," he added, looking at Kade, "when he returns home."

"What for?" Kade said curtly.

"He wouldn't say," the guard replied. "Wilkie sent this news urgently. He thinks Campbell wants to discuss an alliance with the Morrison clan."

"That's impossible," I said, aghast. "My father would never ally with Campbell."

"Nay," Laird Mackenzie said. "He's as resolute about containing Campbell as I am. We've discussed this in some detail."

"'Tis obvious," said Kade, his anger tinted by incredulity. "We've just publicly sealed the alliance between the Morrison and Mackenzie clans with our own marriage. He knows we would never join him. Why would he even propose such a meeting? It makes no sense. He must be up to something."

"Wilkie expressed the exact same suspicion," the guard offered. "He urges you to send Mackenzie fortifications with the Morrison party when they depart in the morning. In case of trouble."

My heart leaped in my chest. *In case of trouble?* The thought of traversing the Highlands in small carriages while Campbell's warrior troops prowled—possibly with the intention to attack—was unwelcome news indeed.

"We'll answer his question now," growled Kade, furious. "No alliance—not now or ever. Take *that* message to Campbell and be done with it!"

"Campbell and his men are no longer in the vicinity," the messenger said. "They have taken their leave and plan to visit the Morrison keep in the coming days, once your party has returned. There is no way to deliver your message today, unless you'd like us to follow them to try to seek them out."

Laird Mackenzie turned to his brother. "Kade? Would you consult with Morrison? Or send a message of your own with these guards? Or leave it lie 'til Campbell dares show his face at Glenlochie? You have access, of course, to all the troops you need. I'll alert the men now."

Kade considered the question. "Aye. We'll take fifty men. And leave Campbell to his idiocy, wherever he may be. The very next time I see that menace, I'll be more than tempted to spear him through the heart."

"Aye, 'tis what he deserves," agreed Laird Mackenzie. The laird dismissed the messenger and took his leave to alert his contingent of soldiers to their new assignment.

Christie and Ailie bid us good-night.

Kade stood so brusquely that he upset his goblet, which rolled off the table and fell to the floor, spraying liquid and smashing loudly. I shrank away from his quick, aggressive movement in an ingrained reaction. If I was close enough to a man to witness abruptness and anger, it was usually directed at me. My husband didn't notice. Instead, he said, "Stella. Come with me."

I followed him out of the laird's den and down the corridor with trepidation. Had he changed his mind about waiting? Was he so angered and upset that he'd decided to take out his frustrations on me?

As soon as we entered his private chambers, he closed the door firmly. Taking care to get out of his way, I stood near the fire and watched him throw objects from the bookshelves into the remaining trunks, obviously in a state of irate agitation. I had learned that he would only take some of the things he would need. He planned for us to return for a visit to Kinloch in the spring, and this room would be left as it was, for our use whenever we needed it. I'd felt a small sense of relief at this news. I was glad, for my husband's sake, that his haven would remain untouched. It seemed important to him.

I thought I understood why my husband was upset and I could sympathize. His agitation, to be sure, rekindled my fear of his considerable size and his warhardened strength. But I took heart from the few affectionate moments we had shared. I remembered his stunning admission. I savored his careful, inspiring touch. And I resolved to stay well out of his way until his ire cooled.

Several gowns had been left in disarray by my sisters, draped carelessly over a table. "Why you have need of so many garments for such a short stay here is unfathomable to me," Kade said irritably. He grabbed the dresses and walked toward me to fling them onto the bed. Instinctively, I cowered back from him, holding my arm up to shield my face. Terror rose in me in a reflexive surge as I flinched back from the onslaught. *"Please don't—"* I cried, knowing only too well the amount of pain a warrior his size could inflict.

But there was nothing. No impact. No pain.

After a moment, I dared to lower my arm and look up at him.

My husband was frozen in place, contemplating me with a mixture of puzzled alarm and grim understanding. He didn't speak for several seconds. Turning away from me, he began to pace back and forth, as though attempting to control his own temper. This temper, though, was not directed at me, but at something he was considering. He leaned against a far wall, folding his arms across his chest, as though sensing in that moment that the small distance would comfort me.

When he spoke again, his volume was lower, his anger contained. His measured thoughtfulness was tinged with an air of regret. "I saw the red mark on your face the other day," he commented, and there was an icy gravity in his tone that sent a light shiver chasing up the back of my neck. "Is it your father who beats you? Or someone else?"

I didn't want to answer him. I didn't want to infuriate him even more. And it didn't seem prudent to stir animosity between the laird of our clan and his successor.

"Answer me," Kade said quietly, and I shrank back farther from him, afraid of the stark ferocity in his question. "Stella. I asked you a simple question. Does your father beat you?"

"Aye," I whispered, hoping only to calm him by giving him the information he demanded. "Or he orders his guards to do it."

His expression was measured and contemplative. There was a tenderness to him that was new, a quiet compassion that touched his features, softening his fierceness and causing a sudden pang of inexplicable longing that startled me. He was *concerned* for me. He understood that I had suffered and this realization was distressing to him. It was the first time I had ever been on the receiving end of real empathy from a man—especially one so vibrantly masculine as Kade Mackenzie—and the sensation of it felt wildly endearing. I had the unfamiliar urge to go to him, to touch him and to feel more of this extraordinary comfort he was offering me. "Is that why you cower away from every man, too afraid to speak or look anyone in the eye? Is *that* the reason?"

Was that what I did? Now that he described it that way, I suppose one might have had something to do with the other. If I looked at the wrong man, I was punished. And it was always the wrong man.

"I'd wager, too, that he beat you into agreeing to marry me, is that right?"

I couldn't reply, but my silence seemed confirmation enough.

"How long has this been happening?" he asked.

"I—I don't know. A long time."

It was several minutes before he spoke again. "Is that why you always look at me as though you're expecting me to hurt you?" His voice had taken on an entirely different character, and one that reached into me, beyond my fear to some part of myself I barely recognized. Kade Mackenzie, whom I hardly knew beyond these past few days of turbulent intimacy, was genuinely affected by the information I had just given him. Our gazes met, and the connection was disconcertingly visceral. "Let me assure you of this, wife," he said softly. "If any man threatens to lay a hand on you ever again, he will be exceedingly sorry for it. You're my wife now and you have the protection of my body and my sword."

Here he was, this lethal warrior husband of mine, offering not threats, but protection, delivering the most reassuring words I had, quite possibly, ever heard in my life. He looked more dangerous than any man I had ever laid eyes on, even now, as the flickering light of the fire danced in a fluid motion along the gold-tinted strands of his dark hair that he wore loose, without the braids at his temples that most men wore. Yet it was clear by his manner, his expression and the emotion in his wolflike eyes that he *cared* about my confession. Deeply. And he would do anything within his power to stop it from happening again. This stirred something in me. It made me feel closer to him than I ever had before.

"You don't need to feel afraid of me, Stella," he continued. "Or anyone else. I understand now why you would be. But you're not to fear me. I'll never hurt you. I swear this to you on my life."

Along with several degrees of comfort, his reassurances delivered something more. I felt charged with a rising urge to be closer to him, and to feel his protection in a more profound and absolute way. And the look of him touched a base compulsion deep inside me. The hard line of his jaw, his sensuous, arrogant mouth, the coarse stubble of his days-old beard. The unashamed, brazen virility of him was magnetic. I felt his layered beauty to the pit of my stomach.

I took a step forward, holding his fingers very lightly in silent appreciation. I was touched that he would want to defend me in this way. I felt, in a wider sense, safer and more secure than perhaps I ever had. For the first time, his size didn't intimidate me. I found that in this moment I *liked* the way he towered above me. My fingers weaved through his and he leaned to me, barely tilting his head as though he might kiss me. The scent of him, of leather and smoke and vitality, flooded my awareness. His dynamic presence closed around me, cocooning me and taking me back to a recent, shaded memory of a private, forbidden garden: the intoxicating scent, the sultry anticipation. In my mind I could feel the late-summer breeze. The festive sounds of the night-lit manor floated in the rose-scented air. And he was here with me, my phantom guardian, my shrouded guide. I closed my eyes, allowing the impulse to take hold. His arm wrapped around me and pulled me against the hard textures of his body. His hand stole to cup my jaw and he turned my face up to him. My eyes opened to his dark intensity, his stoic appeal. His lips so close and the light, intimate brush of his hair on my skin stoked the mellow glow in the low pit of my stomach, settling and blooming lower to where he had touched me and painted me with his silken caresses. I remembered the sensation, the feverish intimacy of it, and a sweet, innermost warmth began to unfurl.

I reached to curl my hand around his neck, pulling him to me, bridging the divide. As though caught off guard by my fervent invitation, he took the offering with a low groan. His lips eased over mine, parting me to his succulent invasion, flooding me with recognition and undiluted lust. My hands reached to wander his chest, searching for and finding the confirmation of his lean, solid shape. The belt and the knife. The taste of him and the feel of him: I *knew* him, from night after dream-soaked night. I knew who he was. My garden lover, who had stalked my vivid fantasies for weeks. Shocked and overwhelmed, I pulled away, gasping, holding fistfuls of his shirt.

"'Tis *you*," I whispered.

"Of course it is," he replied with a slow smile, understanding my meaning immediately. "Who else would it have been?"

"But *how?*" My mind was muddled by the shocking realization. "Why didn't I realize it before now? Why didn't I *see* it?"

"Because you didn't want to. You were blinded by your fear. My own fault, possibly."

"'Tis you," I repeated, utterly aghast.

He seemed amused by my amazement. And there

was an edge to his voice that was entirely new to me, infused with tenderness, and, if I wasn't imagining it, vulnerability. "Is it really that difficult to believe?" He paused, stroking the wing of my eyebrow with the gentle touch of his thumb. "The first time I saw you, that very first time…I couldn't believe my eyes. I thought I was imagining you."

I remembered the night. That first glance. The fascination, the fear.

"I didn't think such beauty existed," he said. "Yet you looked as though you were being hunted from all sides. You made it clear enough that you wanted nothing to do with me. So I kept my distance as best I could."

I wondered if my husband was somewhat overcome by the events of recent days, as I was, and even more so: tomorrow he would leave his home to disengage from peaceful familiarity and embark on a new life that involved navigating the intricate politics of a new clan and fighting for position within it. He sounded more emotional than I had ever seen him, or had even imagined he could be. His husky voice was shadowed and raw. "And then when I saw you wander out of doors, I followed you. I found you in the dark and all alone. I couldn't stop myself. I had to touch you. I had to taste you. And the way you responded to me…I thought I might go mad with desire for you, lass. It took everything I had to walk away from you."

"I wanted to disappear with you into the night and never return," I whispered to him.

"If you had said one word to me, I would have done

just that. I would have done anything you asked of me," he said. After a long pause, he continued. "I went immediately to my brother, and I spoke to your father that very night. Your father was against it at first. Against me. It was Wilkie he wanted as his successor. But when Wilkie refused, he had no better alternative. He thought me the lesser choice. I'm too unpredictable, less proven, according to the venerable Laird Morrison. It seems I'll have to prove him wrong."

I looked up at him, understanding only now the complexity of the challenges he faced, as my new husband. *We'd be wise to make the best of our situation, no matter how difficult it may be for either one of us.*

He stroked my cheek with the light sweep of his thumb as he spoke. "And the utter terror written across your face on our wedding day…it seems I'll have to prove you wrong, too."

"Prove me wrong now, husband," I said.

His half smile was enough to bring to life his complicated beauty, which seemed to be getting closer to the surface every time I looked at him. But his smile faded almost before it began. "I thought your fear was directed solely at me, but I think I understand it better now. And I'll assure you again that I will fight any man who touches you. 'Tis even more important now for me to give you time to learn to trust me. The very last thing I want is for you to feel obliged or pressured into intimacy with a man you hardly know, and one that you were beaten into marrying. We'll wait until the month has passed, wife. Only then. I'm promising this to you, and I'll not break my vow. And if it takes longer than that before you are ready to give your consent, then so be it. I would not consider myself an honorable man if I felt you were unsure."

Strangely, I had a fleeting urge to trample through his honorableness and find the scoundrel in him, the brute who had shredded my clothing with his hunting knife, or the reckless pursuer who had kissed me feverishly in a secluded garden because he hadn't been able to stop himself. I wanted to find those facets of my husband, to entice them and draw them out now. Shamelessly, my mind began to rove in wicked directions, imagining how I might do just that. I thought of reaching under his shirt, to feel the heated skin of his chest, imagining what he might feel like.

But before I could, he disengaged. "Go to bed now, lass. We've a long day of travel tomorrow and the next day. You'll be riding with your sisters in their carriage. I'll be taking my own horse to ride alongside the guards. Tonight I need to write a letter to my brother."

"Tonight?" I asked, feeling disappointed not only by his abrupt shift from tender and communicative to once again fierce and war-minded. But his manner had changed, as though he was wary of frightening me. Now that he knew of my less-than-idyllic upbringing, he had reason to tread more carefully. And I appreciated this sensitivity greatly, even if I had newfound reasons to challenge it.

"Aye. I have a bad feeling about this run-in with Campbell. That he has it in his mind to seek out commissions so deep into the territories of clans that are clearly against his cause is not only irritating, 'tis dangerous. He wouldn't do such a thing if he didn't have a lead of some kind, or an invitation. I can't help wondering if your Morrison clan might be harboring a rebel."

The thought was disturbing to me, aye, but I had very little exposure to the ways and means of my father's army. If there were traitors within my father's ranks, I would likely be one of the last to know about it. My husband seemed thoroughly aware of this, and didn't ask me for information either way. "I wouldn't know," I said. "But there's discontent in the clan, in general. My father's illness has taken its toll."

"More likely it's his methods that have taken their toll," Kade said. "He's overly harsh in his approach, I've heard it said. Loyalty is not inspired by tyranny. No one wants to be dictated to without some degree of fairness."

"Nay," I agreed. It was true I'd attempted to flee my own clan myself—or more specifically, the dictates of my own father—and for that exact reason. And I was momentarily shaken by my husband's words. I knew that the Mackenzies were known for their honor, the fairness with which their clan was ruled, their military prowess. Before, I had thought these traits, in a husband, would only serve to make my enslavement to such a man even more extreme. Honor might mean my wifely duties—whatever they might be—would be extensive and strictly enforced. Fairness in the training yards had never, I knew, translated to fairness in the bedchambers. And as for military prowess: *that* characteristic had been the most worrisome of all; a man who was skilled in war would likely be one who was so fueled by battle that he would bring all his rough, dirty, violent demands into his marriage bed.

But now, in the wake of his earlier confessions, I could consider my husband's traits in a new light. To him, honor meant patience. *I would not consider myself an honorable man if I felt you were unsure.* His skills with his weapons, too, were now much less threatening to me than they had been only days ago. In fact, the very thought of his knife slashing through the thin veil of my shift, the feel of his fingers on my private skin, the dizzying contours of his war-hardened body as he kissed me as passionately as he had in our forbidden garden…I wanted to experience more of his military prowess right here and now.

But he was already sitting at his desk. He was preparing his quill and his parchment, and his attention was far away from me, focused on travel, tyranny and traitors. I wasn't sure what to do, or how I might show him…whatever it was that I *wanted* to show him.

I ventured closer to him, standing next to the fire. He was absorbed in his writing, his head bent over his work. He wrote quickly, dipping his quill frequently and scribbling prolifically as though struggling to get all his ideas onto the page. I stood by the hearth, holding my hands closer to the flames to warm them, twirling a strand of my hair absentmindedly. My thoughts reverted to the kiss, the soft, demanding exploration of his tongue, the rigid planes of his body beneath his clothes.

"Go to bed, lass."

I looked at him, and noticed that he'd put his quill down and had his arms folded across his chest, watching me.

"Are you…coming to bed?" I asked.

He contemplated me in a lazy inspection. "After I finish this letter."

"All right," I said quietly.

His gaze continued to follow me as I walked to the bed. I paused before untying the laces of my gown, the white one that my husband had insisted I wear once he'd known my preference. Now that he sat back in his chair, with his arms folded and his knees apart, he seemed to have returned to the churlish, staunch warrior I had first taken him for. His hand caressed his knife handle even now. This was a habit of his, I'd noticed. He held his weapons when he was deep in thought, maybe planning attacks in his mind or pondering mysterious manthoughts of one kind or another, so utterly foreign to me.

Turning from him, but painfully aware of his cool scrutiny, I eased the loosened fabric over my shoulders, lowering it and stepping out of it. I draped it over the other gowns that lay on the near table. I didn't dare look at him, knowing full well that my shift was sheer enough to see through. I still felt the warm effects of my inconceivable discovery: that the figment of my secret fantasies was, staggeringly, my own husband. *I thought I might go mad with desire for you, lass. It took everything I had to walk away.* The revelation danced across my skin like an invisible breeze, and swelled in intimate pinpoints across my body. Could he feel that way now, as he watched me in brooding silence?

I poured some water from the porcelain pitcher into the bowl, using a soft cloth to wash my face. I brushed my hair, all the while aware of his acute observation. It felt strange to be observed this way, as I carried out my bedtime rituals. The knowledge that he could see the shape of my body as I slid the comb through the end strands of my hair brought a flush to my cheeks and elsewhere. I wanted him to come to me, to touch his fingers to me as he had once done before. I thought of my sister Maisie, who would have had no compunction about using all of her feminine lures. I'd watched her with fascination upon more than one occasion. I considered enticing my husband now, going to him, touching his hair, kissing his lips. I knew what I might do; the instincts were there and I had no doubt I could be just as creative as Maisie if I put my mind to it. I thought of Kade's vow to me, to give me time and gain his trust. Already, I could feel that his allowance was exactly what I needed. My ability to trust had been damaged by my background more than any of my sisters. What if my husband lashed out at me or refused me? In my heart I knew—almost—that he would do neither of these things. But I would wait, and heal, and learn to trust. I eased back the fur covers and climbed into bed. Only then could I turn again to meet his eyes.

I wondered why he'd stopped writing. Maybe he was thinking about what he wanted to say in his letter.

"Husband?" I whispered after a moment.

"Aye?"

Come to me. Protect me. Touch me. "Good night," I said.

"Good night," he said, and the rough edge to his low voice was more pronounced than usual, quiet yet raw with a tension I could not name.

It was a long time before I heard the scratch of his quill continue in the flickering candlelit night.

CHAPTER NINE

OUR TRIP ACROSS the Highlands was, in the end, entirely uneventful. Duncan Campbell and his men did not make an appearance, and there was no more word of Campbell's intention to meet with my father regarding alliances, disputes, wars or any combination thereof. In fact, the only thing the news of Campbell had succeeded in doing, as far as I could see, was to send my husband into a cold, guarded stoicism. Throughout the two days of our journey, we did not so much as speak. I remained in the carriage with my sisters. Kade led the Kinloch soldiers who flanked our procession of carriages on all sides. My husband's focus on getting us to Glenlochie without incident was absolute. I knew he suspected a traitor was among the Morrison army, and he eyed each of them with blatant suspicion. The Kinloch soldiers were dismissed once we reached our own gates, and their departure did nothing to soothe either his wariness or his mood.

Once we arrived at my home, Kade's view of the Morrison clan only grew increasingly disenchanted. Used to the unparalleled standards of the Mackenzie clan, he was appalled by condition of our keep. In this I could hardly blame him. After the splendor of the refined, well-run and prosperous Kinloch, I saw our own living conditions in a new light.

Upon our return, Kade and I spent our first two nights in my old chambers, which were adjoined to my sisters' rooms. This did not afford us as much privacy as my husband would have preferred. Once other more urgent matters had been attended to, I was told that I would give him a tour of all the empty upper rooms of the manor. We needed something more suitable for the future laird and lady of the clan, he said.

And he had not touched me again. In fact, he'd barely spoken to me. Both nights, he'd come in late from his time in meetings and in the training yards, and had worked until the small hours of the morning, writing in several leather-bound books he kept locked in one of his many trunks, which he showed no interest in unpacking. And then he'd risen early and was gone before I'd even awakened. No wonder he was ornery and therefore distant, I reasoned: he'd hardly had much sleep.

On the third morning, he left well before dawn, only to return a short time later. I heard him rummaging through one of his larger trunks, where he kept yet more knives and swords and other unusual instruments of war.

"Good morning, husband," I ventured, rising from the bed.

He jammed a second sword into place, still holding a knife's handle in his clenched fist. Then he paused, giving me an assessing, critical glance. "There's work to be done, lass. You've recovered from your wedding and your journey. 'Tis time for you to begin."

"Begin what?" I asked, slipping a gown over my head and tying the front laces.

"Work."

Work. Something I'd never been allowed much less invited to do. "Work?"

"You spend far too much time cooped up with your gossiping sisters. This manor is dirty, disorganized and in no fit state to receive visitors, let alone house the nobles of its own clan. Several of my family members arrive in just over a month, and the place is an utter shambles. 'Tis an embarrassment. Much worse than I ever imagined. Why has your family let it get so run-down?"

It was true that Glenlochie was in need of some serious attention. I'd never noticed it quite so much as I had since our return from the wedding, but the manor was messy, shabby and with no real systems in place to improve the current state of our chaotic existence.

Why *had* we let it get so run-down? I'd considered the condition of our home in the past, and the general feeling of malaise among our workers. But I would no more instruct my father about how to run his manor and his keep than I would advise him about how to rule his army; my outspokenness, of course, would only have resulted in more punishment.

"Who is in charge of the manor?" he asked me.

"My father, of course."

"Your father runs the army —and not particularly

effectively. He's too old and too ill. And too swilled a good portion of the time to do much of anything else. There must be someone who handles the day-to-day operations of the manor itself."

"The staff run it," I said.

"Who's *in charge* of the staff?" he repeated.

"I—I'm not sure," I stammered.

Irritated even further by my inarticulate reply, Kade issued my orders. "Well, from now on, *you* are in charge. Go and speak to the workers. Tell them to clean the grand hall by the end of the day. Oversee it yourself. And the kitchen staff can be told we'll have fresh produce, meat and bread this evening. Why is there so little to show for the harvest? And the dried meat should only be used when there's nothing else available, or the stores won't get us through the winter." He continued to jam his weapons into place. I almost asked him to be careful, lest he spear himself, but then thought better of it.

Despite his curt, business-minded tone, the lingering memories of our spare moments of intimacy and tenderness shone through my apprehension. Kade was temperamental, aye, and I could see that he had reason to be. But I felt little of the initial fear of our very first encounters. Instead, what I felt was a residual link to him, forged with his heartfelt words and his beguiling touch. His distance now only succeeded in rousing a budding curiosity in me: could I succeed in drawing out his softer side again? He was gruff and agitated by his many challenges, but I knew of his innermost desires. I knew how his lips felt on mine, and I had seen the look in his eyes when he'd seen me and touched me so very intimately. This connection gave me a small sense not only of power but of equality.

"'Tis not my place to organize the kitchen staff," I said.

"Not your *place*?" he growled. "Then whose place is it? You'll be lady of this keep soon. 'Tis time for you to learn how to lead."

"But—"

My husband was not in the mood for my feeble protests. "I'll be back this evening," he interrupted. "I'm taking some of the men for a hunt. Tell the butcher to expect us by sundown." And with that he strode from my chambers, slamming the door loudly behind him.

Once I would have cursed him for his rudeness, and thought him a boorish brute and all manner of other insults. Now, I forgave him. Almost. He didn't need to rant nor fume at me to get me to obey him. I allowed that he wasn't used to so many frustrations; his life, aside from the challenges of war—which were expected and embraced when one's lifelong purpose was as a noble, educated soldier—had been free from the kind of challenges Glenlochie presented. His family had run Kinloch flawlessly for generations. He had been born into that privilege. This change would take some time to adjust to.

And his observations about the appalling state of our keep were, after all, correct. I could, I supposed, try to help, as he requested. My father would learn of my new occupation; that he would react unfavorably to the news went without question. But my husband would defend me. The new landscape of my life was difficult to grasp. I would need courage, husband or no husband—such was the thoroughness of my conditioning. We both had much to adjust to.

Not more than a minute after he had stormed from our chambers, the door opened and Kade strode in.

"Oh, what luck," I commented, almost under my breath. "My kindly, chivalrous husband has returned to me sooner than promised."

Kade smiled in response to my sarcasm. He walked back over to where I stood. His hand lifted to cradle the side of my face with his palm. His thumb traced lightly along my cheekbone. "So it seems I have been the brutish husband you were expecting all along, and in no small measure. I was on guard against attack on our journey. And I had thought to be welcomed into a somewhat organized, accepting clan. I have found the opposite to be true. I am on edge for a thousand reasons. But I didn't mean to take it out on you. I want to do the right thing, and most of all, to keep you safe. Forgive me."

Aye, I knew that Kade's nature was unpredictable. I had expected my husband, since I knew no other way of it, to act as all other men: rough and overbearing. That he felt the need to appease me after his frustrated outburst was no less than miraculous to me. No man had ever shown me such regard, nor such care. My husband's apology seemed to seep into some unknowable fissure in my heart and widen it by several degrees. I found myself wrapping my arms around his neck and kissing him.

He laughed lightly, drawing in a sharp breath as though deeply affected by my reaction. He pulled back, holding my face between his hands. "Easy, feisty wee wife," he said. Then, after a pause, as though to ensure that his own fervor was under control, he touched his lips to mine in a hot, reassuring supplication. The contact fed my fledgling addiction with ardent force. My lips parted in a sighing plea. But then, abruptly, Kade withdrew. He was almost panting, visibly struggling for self-control. It was a moment before he spoke.

"If I'd known that was all it took to get *this* reaction," he said, "I'd have followed my wedding vows with a litany of apologies."

"Stay with me," I said, suddenly fervent for more of my husband.

"Believe me when I say I would like nothing more than to spend the day sequestered alone in these chambers with you, making amends for my churlish behavior. I will count the minutes 'til I can next do this, and much more." He kissed me again, just a light brush of his lips against mine. Reluctantly, he disengaged, dazzling me in that moment with his glowing appeal. "But I cannot stay. I've ordered some of the men to assemble in the stables. We ride at daybreak."

After one more particularly sweet, soft kiss, Kade left me, and I found myself surprisingly bereaved by his departure. Something had changed. A bond had formed where I'd least expected it: between myself and my fierce warrior husband. We had need of each other. We had already begun to rely on each other's support amid our shared difficulties. And there was more to it than that. A tenderness had crept into our exchanges: a new, intricate sensibility that drew us together. I found this connection remarkably comforting and found that, increasingly, when we were apart, I craved more of him, his inspiring attention and his enriching company.

Dutifully, and with my husband's wishes in mind, I finished dressing in preparation for my day ahead.

And as they had the previous two mornings, one or more of my sisters waited until my husband left, then came to my chamber door, impatient for news or some hint of scandal. When none was to be found, they seemed bitterly disappointed. It was almost as if they *wanted* me to be ravaged again and were irked when they found me in a semirespectable condition, with my shift unshredded and scarcely a hair out of place.

It was only Maisie this morning, carrying a tray with food and tea. Maisie placed the tray on a table and poured some tea as she surveyed my husband's scattered possessions with interest. She brought me a cup of tea and the plate of food. Then she sat on the bed, helping herself to a rough hunk of bread and some hard cheese. "Stella, I heard arguing this morning," she commented. "And yelling. What was your husband so angry about?"

"I told you already, Maisie," I said, mildly annoyed that she'd bring this up yet again—and that she had likely been listening at the door of our chambers. "I'm not to discuss any of that with you. My husband wishes our private affairs to remain exactly that—private." I, too, took a piece of bread. After the fresh-baked and interesting array of breads that had been on offer at the Mackenzie keep, the stale loaf was particularly unappealing, and the cheese had green spots of mold that needed to be scraped with a knife edge. I decided I wasn't as hungry as I'd first thought.

Maisie interpreted my unwillingness to discuss our marital privacy as proof of my husband's failings. "I just *knew* he'd be a tyrant," she said, almost triumphant that her initial assessments had been correct. "Just give me a few tiny details. Do you enjoy *any* of it? Or is he as loutish and severe as he looks?"

"Maisie," I said, mildly exasperated.

"Because when I was with Wilkie—did I tell you about this? There was this transcendent *rush*—"

"You did tell me, aye," I interrupted. "All about it."

"All I'm saying is that it *can* be…well, miraculous. Maybe in time—I mean, if he even takes you into account at *all*. Some men are like that, I've heard—interested only in self-gratification. Kade's so unlike his brother in other ways, it's not surprising. Although the more I see of him, the more I *do* see resemblances. In his less severe moments, he does take on some of his brother's…magnificence. Not entirely, but there's a hint of it, I've noticed. But his personality is so different from Wilkie's, it makes sense that he'd be different in the—"

"Maisie." Something in my tone finally silenced her, very temporarily.

"Oh, all right," she said, flouncing with indignation. But then she leaned in close again. "But I know you well enough, Stella. And I'm almost entirely certain that you *didn't*, otherwise you'd be gushing with it. There's no way any woman can experience that kind of…*satisfaction* and not feel elated about it."

"It was…different from what I was expecting," I said, attempting to quiet her with a reply, even if it was vague and perhaps misleading. But I spoke the truth. All of what had so far taken place behind closed doors between Kade and me *had* been different from what I'd been expecting.

"In what way?" she asked, her curiosity entirely piqued.

"In every way."

She studied my eyes, then burst into laughter. "My dear sister, you *couldn't* have. Simply couldn't have. Oh, you poor thing. Let's just hope he improves over time."

Even if Kade had not asked me to keep our private affairs to ourselves, I had no desire to discuss my husband's techniques in the bedchambers with my curious sister. And her false assumptions were beginning to rile me. "Maisie, you have no idea—"

I was mildly relieved when she interrupted me, and I decided to keep resolutely mum about the entire subject from that moment forward. "There are ways you can make things more…interesting, of course," she was saying. "If you're as timid in bed as you are in every other aspect of your life, 'tis no wonder."

"What things?" I couldn't help asking.

"Well, a man likes it when a woman takes control. Don't wait for him. Tease him. Use your body. Show yourself. Men simply cannot resist once they *see* you. Use your hands." Her eyes glimmered. "And your mouth."

I turned from her, and finished dressing. It all sounded utterly daunting, yet I was imagining all manner of lurid details. A flush of heat rose on my cheeks, which caused my younger but decidedly more worldly sister to smile.

"I'll keep that in mind," I said. "Now, if you'll excuse me, I'm going down to the kitchens."

"Get some more food for me, too, would you? This bread is hardly edible."

"I'm not returning 'til later. I've been told to oversee the kitchen staff. My husband wants the grand hall cleaned and fresh bread baked for the men—they've gone hunting."

Maisie looked at me, slightly aghast. "Since when are *you* bold enough to oversee anything?"

"Since today." I'll admit the comment stung; it was a little too accurate. My sister had always been blunt to a fault, a trait that was only compounding itself in the wake of her recent romantic disappointments. I'd seen a similar affliction affect my older sister, who had become sullen and wistful. Heartbreak, it seemed, had affected Maisie differently, provoking bitterness and sharp-tongued candor. I'd always loved her despite her consistent lack of either boundaries or tact, but I hoped for her sake that she could rebound with some element of grace. "I've been given no choice."

"Just hope Father doesn't find out that you're interfering. The bruises from your last transgression have only just faded."

The thought caused a bolt of unease, but I thought of my husband's vows, and hoped they were true. *If any man threatens to lay a hand on you ever again, he will be exceedingly sorry for it.* "Someone needs to interfere. Father might be grateful that someone's taken an interest, once he sees that it can improve the look of the place. 'Tis ridiculous that we're not allowed to help when it's so obvious that something needs to be done to improve the standards of upkeep in the manor."

"Aye," Maisie agreed disinterestedly.

"I'll see you at dinner," I said.

I made my way down to the grand hall, where there was no one to be found. The single large tapestry looked dirty and dull. The fireplace—long cold—had a pile of ashes that had scattered across the floor from some errant draft. Days-old cups and plates still sat on the many tables, and I wondered why this big room wasn't used for every evening meal, as it was at Kinloch, to unite the clan members over a meal and a drink, with the fire lit and the atmosphere festive and cozy. My husband was right: the place was a shambles.

I thought of Ailie Mackenzie, who judiciously managed the staff of Kinloch. She was not a woman of particularly forceful character, yet the place ran like clockwork. I hoped, in time, I might be able to do the same and resolved to start today.

I collected a few of the dishes and carried them through the swinging doors to the kitchen, where some of the staff were busy. Not cooking, however. They were sitting around one of the larger tables, eating from bowls of soup, talking loudly and laughing at a joke one of them had just finished telling. As soon as they saw me, they fell entirely silent and stared at me with a mixture of surprise and contempt, as though I had just interrupted a private party I wasn't invited to.

"Good morning," I said, setting the dirty dishes down on a long, high table, where many other dirty dishes were piled.

"Good day, milady."

I recognized all the women, but I didn't know all their names. It was Isla who returned my greeting, the head of the kitchen staff. Isla was perhaps twice my age and had been in charge of the kitchens for as long as I could remember.

"What brings you here?" she asked.

"My husband has requested that the hall be cleaned today, and that a meal be prepared for the returning hunting party, by sunset."

Isla turned to her amused audience, raising her eyebrows. Then she contemplated me, my fine gown and the gold necklace I always wore. "Your husband?"

One of the other women tittered, a petite dark-haired woman with a pointy face and a somewhat ragged-looking appearance, as though she hadn't taken notice of her clothing or her hair in some time. "Aye, I believe congratulations are in order, miss. The fierce warrior Kade Mackenzie, no less. We've all heard of *him*."

"Commission *me,* if you please, to deliver his meals," chuckled one of the other women.

"Gladly," retorted another. "Serve his food cold and you'll likely get knifed for your trouble." This comment was followed by uproarious laughter.

Isla attempted to wipe the smile from her face. "'Tis not for you to concern yourself with such matters as the cleaning of the hall, nor the preparation of meals, milady," she said to me, taking my hand and ushering me toward the door. "I will see to it that some meat is provided for the men upon their return."

I held my ground, although her grasp and her persuasion were somewhat insistent. "He wants them to be served fresh meat," I said. "And fresh-baked bread. And vegetables picked from the gardens."

Isla again made a face of mock obedience, entertaining the women to no end. "I'll see what I can find." And with that, she shooed me through the door of the kitchen and returned to her friends. I could hear their laughter as I retreated to the fireplace. How had I never noticed how dirty this hall was? And how mediocre our food was? And how disrespectful the staff was? I suppose we could hardly expect outpourings of respect, however, when we did so very little to earn it. My sisters and I sequestered ourselves behind closed doors most of the time, chatting idly, reading, engaging very little with any of the workers. And my father used threats to enforce his will when necessary, although in truth he appeared to be past caring about the state of his own keep beyond its army, who tended to dine in the barracks.

Something would have to change. And it was clearly up to me to change it. It surprised me slightly to realize that, rather than worrying about his anger, what concerned me more was that I didn't want Kade to be disappointed in me, and he certainly would be if I failed to follow through with the few simple tasks he'd asked of me. I strode back into the kitchen.

Again, the women went silent, this time eyeing me with less amusement and more irritation. "I said I would like the grand hall cleaned," I repeated. "And I would like you to do it. Now."

Isla rose once again from her seat. "Milady—Miss Stella, isn't it?"

I gave a disgruntled nod.

"I've been appointed by your father," Isla continued, "who is more than satisfied with the way the kitchens are run. If you have an issue with the management, why don't you take it to him? And we'll carry on here with our duties."

"It doesn't appear that you're doing any duties, Isla," I commented, somewhat more coolly than I intended.

"We are breaking our fast," said Isla indignantly. "The workers need sustenance in order to work, do they not?" At this, the other women made various noises of support.

"Will you clean the hall when you're finished? And light the fire?"

"Aye."

"Kade requested fresh bread for the men. I'll go out to the gardens now and see if I can find someone to get us some vegetables."

"As you wish," Isla replied with overemphasized deference that bordered on mockery. "Is that all?"

"I— Aye. Thank you, Isla."

She bowed slightly, to the continued amusement of her rapt counterparts, and I took my leave of them.

That hadn't gone too badly after all, I thought, as I made my way out to the gardens to see if I could find one of the gardeners. They had obviously become accustomed to a somewhat lax schedule, as had we all. It wouldn't take much to gently encourage a more strenuous work ethic. My sisters could help me, too, once I discussed my new plans with them. I could now see the logic in my husband's reasoning. It would be nice to have better food to eat, a tidier living environment and higher standards in general. And I could help make that happen. It was energizing to have a purpose, for a change; it felt good to have a goal to aspire to.

I secured my cape more tightly around me as I stepped out of doors, immediately noticing the chill. It was autumn, and wisps of the coming winter weather were beginning to make themselves felt.

It had been a long time since I'd taken a stroll in the Glenlochie gardens. There were vegetables still hanging on vines that had never been picked and were now rotten and unsalvageable. And the place looked abandoned compared to the industrious Mackenzie orchards, where gardeners lovingly tended their plants with an attentiveness I had never witnessed in our own keep. This difference certainly reflected in the taste and size of the produce, too.

I wandered farther to the storage buildings, which were located where the vegetable groves met the edge of the training grounds. In the distance I could see that the soldiers' area was the busiest of Glenlochie. It was in the barracks and their dusty surrounds where the activity of this clan was concentrated, making it clearer than ever that considerations of all but our military might had fallen to the wayside. And even our military might, if my husband was to be believed, was not only weaker than it should be but also harboring traitors.

It was here that I stopped walking. I had no intention of entering the training grounds or even being seen by any of the soldiers. I was out of doors alone, after all: a crime punishable by a beating, certainly. Or at least it would have been just days ago. But I was a married woman now. I didn't require a chaperone everywhere I went. And my husband's oath lingered in my mind. *You're mine now and you have the protection of my body and my sword.* Let my father's men beat me; I almost wanted to see the look on their faces when Kade exacted whatever revenge he would. I was tired of feeling afraid, and my husband's reassurances gave me a tentative peace of mind that my soul seemed to want to run with, like a calm sense of liberation had settled around me and refused to be dislodged no matter how much trouble I was asking for.

The door of the nearest storage building was un-
locked. I entered. After the bright sunlight of the day,
it took my eyes a few seconds to adjust to the dimness.
I had never been in any of these buildings before. The
mingling smells of earth and sweetness and decay hung
strongly in the air. The walls were lined with shelves and
bins, and the middle part of the space was filled with
worktables that were entirely covered with jars, dirt,
vegetables and fruit in various stages of drying, pickling
or preserving. The entire scene was a study in disorganization. Judging from the smell and the appearance, a
good percentage of the food was rotting before it could
reach whatever state of preservation it was destined for.

I noticed then that two men were seated at the far end
of the long table. They were eating from several of the
jars and drinking from large goblets. A clear bottle of
whiskey sat between them and was nearly empty. They
both stood as soon as they saw me. From their expressions, they looked as embarrassed to be caught eating
the clan's rations as they were angry to be interrupted
doing it. It was the anger in their manner that gave me
pause. I decided to state my request and then leave as
quickly as possible. Strolling the gardens unchaperoned
was one thing, but making demands of two swilled, siz-
able men in a sequestered hut was quite another.

"I'm sorry to bother you both," I said, making up a
story that might be as quick and acceptable as possible
on the spot. "My father the laird has requested fresh
vegetables to be served at tonight's meal—enough for
at least a dozen men."

"The laird doesn't eat vegetables," one of the men commented laconically. "Doesn't like 'em."

"But some of his men do."

"I've yet to meet one of 'em," the other man responded, causing both of them to chuckle heartily.

"His new first officer," I said, feeling more and more uncomfortable with the glint of recognition in their eyes.

"The new laird-to-be?" one of the men asked. "Say, aren't you the laird's daughter—the one who just married...what's his name?" he asked his cohort.

"Mackenzie," the second man replied.

Both men regarded me with labored scrutiny, as though having trouble focusing. One of them swayed slightly on his feet. "Aye, that's the one," he said. "Gonna take over once the old man gives up the ghost."

"Aye," I confirmed. "And he likes vegetables."

"Hear that, lad?" one of the men hollered over his shoulder, and it was only then that I noticed a boy sitting on the floor some distance from them. He might have been ten years old, or twelve. He was eating an apple, seeds and all. "Go and tell the laird that one of his lovely daughters has taken an interest in farming."

"Nay," I said. "That won't be necessary. I'll help myself and be on my way."

"Go on, I said," one of the men insisted, to the boy, who jumped up and ran out a back door.

Their reaction to my simple request seemed excessive. Had my father given strict instructions to report to him if one of his daughters was ever spoken to or sighted outside our private chambers? Was my father so obsessed with his own dictatorship that any breach of protocol was to be messengered to him immediately? It occurred to me that the kitchen workers and these men, too, liked the routine of malaise that they'd become accustomed to. They had access to as much food as they could eat. Efficiency beyond their own scope was clearly not a priority.

And now my father would know that I was interfering in a way I never had before.

I reached into a nearby bin and grabbed as many carrots as I could carry. They were still covered in dirt. I thanked the men and backed toward the door, wondering as I did so how I was going to open the door with an armload of carrots. Before I could answer that question, the door opened, spearing the dimness with a sudden flood of light. Squinting, I could see that the young messenger had returned, and he was now feasting on another apple. And as he opened the door wider, I could see he was not alone. Looming as a black silhouette against the bright light of morning was a most unwelcome sight: the warrior Aleck.

"Ah, my favorite of the Morrison daughters," Aleck commented blithely. "Follow me."

"I'll do no such thing," I said defiantly, making a point to mask all signs of my panic. "I've done nothing wrong. All I'm doing is attempting to prepare a meal for a hunting party that's providing food for our clan members. At the request of my husband. 'Tis hardly a crime, and I'm sick to death of being bullied by you. Leave me alone."

Aleck recoiled dramatically, pretending outrage and indignation. He was so large that when his hand reached out to grab my arm, despite my attempt to step back and evade him, he caught hold of me easily. His painful grip caused me to drop the carrots to the ground, where they rolled in all directions. The dirtied green velvet of my dress was the least of my worries.

"Your father is already regretting his choice," Aleck informed me. "Mackenzie has proven to be nothing but an annoyance since the moment he took your…hand. And the laird would like to illustrate a point to his new laird-in-waiting. So I encourage you to follow me now, and without the theatrics this time, if you please." His grasp grew tight enough, I knew, to bruise me, and I had no choice but to walk along with him toward the training yards. "He's thinking of having the marriage annulled, I suspect, and put me in place as his successor, as he nearly did to begin with."

Maybe it was my newly discovered rebellious streak, or the small taste of security I'd been given by my new husband—even if he was, at times, nearly as daunting as the rogue who was practically dragging me to my next scene of humiliation. Other crimes I'd committed had at least possibly warranted a reprimand of some kind. But *this*. This was gratuitous violence. It was violence that would lead to more violence: possibly enough of it to get someone killed. And it angered me to the point where I hardly recognized myself. I'd truly had enough.

I tried to yank my arm from Aleck's grasp, but I was not to get off so easily this time. He might have been expecting my struggle; he gripped me even tighter, and I had no choice but to walk along with him as he practically dragged me toward the barracks. I knew I'd wear the marks of his clenched fingers for days to come. "That little stunt you pulled last time you tried to evade me will not be tolerated again, lass," he growled. "I have plans for you, which you'll learn of soon enough."

"My husband already outranks you, soldier," I said, more frantic now. His ominous threats turned my blood to ice. "And when he becomes laird, so will I. I'll ask you once more—*let me be.*"

"*If* he becomes laird," Aleck countered, and I had no idea what he meant by that. Of course my husband would be laird. It was decreed by my father; that had been the whole point of our arranged marriage. "I don't like him," Aleck announced, taking a moment to survey the stains of dirt on my dress and the writhing of my body. "Not at all. And I have more power over your father than you might expect, lass. If I get my way, he may change his mind about his successor. Mackenzie's served his purpose. The alliance is secure. But that detail doesn't necessarily mean he *must* step up as laird. That point is negotiable. I'm much more loyal to your father's agenda than Mackenzie will ever be. 'Tis me who would carry on his traditions and his leadership."

Aye, traditions of tyranny and decay.

I stared at him, aghast. I knew Aleck loathed my husband; that had been clear enough the minute both men had entered the sparring ring when they'd faced off. But to attempt a coup against him? Did he really think he could pull off such a bold move? "Aleck," I said, "you have no chance of becoming laird. The decision was part of the negotiation of our marriage. The lairdship was promised to him. 'Tis the reason he agreed to it."

"Nay, lass," Aleck replied, and there was a glint of humor in his eyes that hardly seemed appropriate. "*You* are the reason he agreed to it. Any man offered your hand would die a thousand deaths before refusing you."

"What do you mean?" I whispered. The compliment was so overblown, so sincere and yet still so threatening that I was momentarily unsure what to make of it.

"You have no idea what kind of effect you have on men, do you? You're famous across the Highlands for your beauty and your spirited defiance, and you don't even know of it. Your looks, to be sure, are spoken of. Yet it's your feisty rebelliousness that intrigues most of all. You attempt to flee. You fight back. 'Tis only your reserved, aloof manner that kept your admirers at an arm's length. Even the staunchest warrior fears rejection. But I know that only too well, do I not, Stella?"

This was disturbing information indeed. And I knew what Aleck was referring to in his final question. Afraid of the hold he had on me, which was only increasing in pressure and intent, I said, "Aleck. I'm sorry that I refused your gift those many years ago. I never meant to reject you or give you any impression of that kind either way. And you've had your revenge upon me, more times than I can count. Let me go." I tried not to give in to the tears as I thought of all the lashings I'd endured at his hand; but I couldn't hold back my sadness and my dread, knowing I was in for more of it. "Please stop holding that one long-ago refusal against me. We were children, after all."

"Aye," he said. "But we're not children now." He hulked over me, at least twice my size in bulk and weight. There was a distinct resentment in his black eyes that was far more disquieting than mere aggression. My tears had no effect on him. He'd become immune, perhaps.

"I'm married, Aleck," I pointed out to him, wildly relieved by that fact here and now, even if I'd been less than enthused upon many other occasions.

"You don't love him," he said. It was more than odd, discussing love with this dirty, brawny soldier who still held me in a vicious grip.

"Nay," I said. "I—I don't love him. I hardly know him. Now, please. Unhand me."

He gave me a look of light reproach. "You know I can't do that, lass. We both know you'd run." His hold loosened slightly, enough so it was at least no longer painful. I could try to break free of him, but I knew he'd chase me and I doubted I could outrun him over such a distance to the manor. Strung to his belt was a thin, coiled whip, which I eyed uneasily; it was regrettably familiar to me.

"'Tis clear enough he doesn't love you, either," Aleck said. "You were merely a conquest to him. Which he now has conquered."

I remained silent. Of course I would never admit that I hadn't yet been *entirely* conquered.

"I've seen him with one of your sisters," Aleck said offhandedly, watching my reaction. After a pause, he added, "He has already strayed, and you might therefore feel inclined to, as well."

"What do you mean, 'one of my sisters'?"

"Aye. She visited him in one of the weapons sheds, only yesterday."

Of course I knew exactly which sister he was referring to. And as much as I'd fought against a marriage to Kade Mackenzie, the thought of my sister Maisie approaching him in any way whatsoever sent a vexing lurch through my stomach that I could neither name nor recognize. "That can't be true."

"But it *is,* lass," he said with undue compassion. "I saw her with my own eyes. Buttoning up her dress, she was."

I stared at Aleck, desperately attempting to read the lie in his eyes. But there was none to be found. I wanted to run, to find my damn husband and confront him. Could it be true? And why did my throat feel so choked with not only rage but sadness? I'd just admitted I didn't love my husband. I'd known of his tendencies before our marriage, as so thoroughly discussed by the very sister, among others, who had just betrayed me.

Before I could make a move of any kind, Aleck pulled me along with him, more gently now but no less forcibly. His expression had changed from one of aggression to one of conflicted remorse. "'Tis your father who insists that I be the one to enforce your punishments, Stella. It always was. I never wanted to hurt you. I was just following orders. But no longer. Let me show you what kind of influence I have over your father. And over the clan as a whole. 'Tis me who requested for you to be followed. I have asked to be alerted to any and every move you make."

"Why would you do that?" I said, protesting both his pronouncement and his continued hold on me.

"Let's just say I have a vested interest in your well-being," he said, as though this might be favorable news to me.

"Aleck, *nay—please.*"

But he was already leading me into one of the buildings of the barracks, pulling me inside. For a panicked moment, I thought he might be intending more than a reprimand, but I could see that we were in a meeting room and my father was seated on a high-backed chair. The sight of him gave me little comfort, however. His appearance, in fact, instilled me with a distinct sense of foreboding. He looked unkempt, his wrinkled hand wrapped around his ever-present silver flask. Aside from a small, vicious glow in his clouded eyes, he was completely devoid of vitality, shrouded instead by an aura of bitterness and regret.

"Grace," he murmured, so low I couldn't be sure I understood him correctly. My mother's name.

"Look who I found raiding the storage sheds," Aleck said smugly.

I began my defense. "My husband requested—"

But I was promptly interrupted by Aleck. "Your husband's usefulness ends at the tip of his sword. Isn't it so, Laird Morrison?"

"Aye," my father agreed, his voice gravelly with age. "He is a pest rather than the asset we had hoped for." My father's words were slightly slurred at the edges, and I wondered if his illness might be progressing. "He was chosen for his skills with his weapons, and *only* his skills with his weapons. His arrogance will get him nowhere. I'm not interested in his plans to overhaul our army and our keep. Glenlochie is fine the way she is." My father was not only mean, abusive, ill and drunk; he was also deluded. As we might all have been. It seemed my own veil was lifting, and with my new vision I could see that my father was not only wrong but quite possibly half-mad. As though to prove that his state of mind was far worse than I thought, he said to me weakly, "I've never forgiven you for leaving me."

"Father," I whispered, fearful to my bones, "'tis me. Stella."

"Stella," he said, recognition returning somewhere amid the bitterness and the madness. "What is your complaint now? Must you continually taunt me like this, with her memory? Go to your chambers! Leave me in peace." To his men: "Get her out of my sight. Out! I can't bear it. Leave me." He slumped back in his chair, as though fatigue, vengefulness and heartbreak had finally overcome him.

I moved to obey my father, hoping fervently that Aleck would allow me to. His hand still clasped my arm.

So many times, at every turn, every attempt to live or to thrive on my own terms, I had been cut down. By the very whip that hung at his hip. In a reflexive entreaty, I fell to my knees before him, to beg him for mercy. My fingers found the corded rope, holding it, waiting for it to be yanked from my grasp and used upon my in-laid scars. Not on my skin; care had been taken to keep me appealing enough to wed. These scars went deeper.

Aleck waited, as though taking a moment to savor my pathetic subservience. I hated myself for this, for allowing myself to be so thoroughly broken.

For the first time, Aleck did not reach for his whip. Instead, he pulled me to my feet, resting me against his huge, rigid body. I was so defeated, so conditioned to his orchestrated threats that I did not struggle, only pulling back when he allowed it. His black hair was a blurry shape through my tears, which I wiped away with the back of my hand.

"I am capable of mercy and much more," Aleck said close to my ear. "And I intend to show you all that I'm capable of as soon as I've tied up a few loose ends."

I didn't understand his comment, nor did I care to consider his meaning. To my wild relief, he let me go, and I took my first opportunity to escape him.

Watching my retreat, Aleck issued a disconcerting warning. "I've got my eye on you, lass," he said, and his words echoed in my ears as I exited the barracks and walked quickly away.

Instead of returning to my sisters, I headed in a different direction, to a place I hadn't been in a long time. I skirted the withered gardens, finding a back entrance to the manor that I seldom used. I climbed a curved stone staircase, passing two servants, who eyed my distress and dishevelment with mute curiosity. I found the door I was looking for, entering the silent, empty chambers and closing the door securely behind me.

My mother's favorite place: the turret. My father had forbidden anyone to enter these chambers since her death, preferring to keep it as a silent shrine to her memory. As far as I knew, he'd never entered it since. I had, first, as a child.

"I told you never to go in there." The lash of the belt, and again. "Leave your mother's memory in peace."

It was the very first time I'd been beaten.

Even so, it was a place I secretly went to when I most needed solace.

The chambers were eerily silent, the air cold. A dusty, feeble ray of sunlight shone through a diamond-shaped window, painting a perfect replica onto the stone floor. The only furniture in the room was a large four-poster bed whose faded cloth covering was filmed with dust. I walked to the small stone staircase at the far end of the room that led to an upper level: a tiny lookout, a single small elevated room strewn with her old cushions. From the circular windows I could see across the villages of the keep to the gardens and the fields beyond. The dark, glassy surface of the loch, the multihued forests, and the impressive, rising landscape of the Highlands.

I could understand why this had been my mother's favorite place. I felt removed from them all.

And in this cozy enclosure, I could feel her. This place was infused with her, as though the sunlight itself shone from her faraway memory. The warm glide of tears wet my cheeks. I wasn't sure why. I'd been so young when she died. I had only vague, shadowy recollections of her face, which might have been shaped less by actual memory and more by the often-made comment that I was the daughter who looked most like her—so much like her, in fact, that older people of our clan occasionally gasped at the likeness, as though they thought I was a vision or a ghost when I passed by. I cried more for the loss her death had created: a hole and a hatred in my father that had festered and eaten away at our clan like a disease.

My arms were sore from the bruises Aleck had made, and I rubbed at them, glad for the long sleeves of my gown. The salt of my tears dried on my cheeks in the sunlight. I took in the picturesque landscape, following the rolling line of the hills, the smooth surface of the shining loch. The small turret was so warm from the contained rays of the sun, I felt mildly overheated. I removed my cape and unbuttoned the top of my dress. It didn't matter—no one would see me up here, and I was reveling in the sumptuous heat of my haven and my isolation. I never wanted to leave this place.

Lulled by the silence and the warmth, I dozed off for a time.

I awoke with a start, jarred by the sound of heavy footsteps down below, ascending rapidly.

My heart lurched in my chest. Had my father found me once again? Was Aleck on my trail?

But it was Kade who appeared, windblown and wearing an expression of fierce concern. My awareness was still murky at the edges and was difficult to shake off, as though I had slept for many hours. But I was panicked by the possibility of being pursued and also by the suddenness of his arrival. I shrank back from the sight of him, still in his full hunting regalia, bloodied from his kills, almost blinding with gleaming gold and silver light. Like that very first time I'd ever seen him, I remembered well, he caught all the light of a room, whether it was a grand hall or a tiny enclave like this one.

His gaze slid from my face to my breasts, half revealed, rounded and rosy from the heat. He made a small sound, like a strangled sigh that might have been the words *Holy God in heaven.*

I clutched the fabric of my gown together and glared up at him with wide eyes.

"There you are, lass," he finally said. His gentle tone clashed entirely with the spectacle of him. He was invigorated and energized from his hunt, but his immense presence before me gave me a sudden, overwhelming feeling of relief that caught me completely off guard. He looked so unexpectedly magnificent in his protective glory in that moment my tears threatened to spill once more.

But then I remembered Aleck's pronouncement.

My momentary elation seeped away, replaced by

a sad and seething regret. "How did you find me?" I asked coldly.

"A servant saw you walking this way. She said the corridor led to only one room."

Kade watched my face, noticing the dried tears and registering my indifference, my anger. He looked mildly confused by it, squinting his eyes slightly in a measuring study. "What are you doing here, hiding away?"

It wouldn't do to tell him the truth; I had a distinct feeling it would lead to the imminent death of Aleck— or of my husband himself if he were to be bested by my father's officer, although that scenario seemed unlikely. And as much as I hoped to keep as much distance between myself and Aleck as I possibly could, I wasn't sure I wanted to be the cause of his demise. "This was my mother's room," I said, making a point of keeping my voice emotionless.

"It will be perfect for us," he said. "Far removed from the other residence chambers. Our own wing."

I didn't bother telling him my father would never allow such a thing. Kade looked out the window, appreciating the view. "Kinloch is just beyond those hills," he said, clearly cheered by the thought.

It did intrigue me to see him always visibly brighten when he thought of his home and his family. He had sacrificed much to fulfill the duty of marrying me, I knew. A part of me wanted to ease his longing and his homesickness, to make his sacrifice easier to bear. But my sister, it seemed, had already stepped up to do exactly that. I guessed Kade's homesickness wasn't quite so acute as it might have been only a day or two ago.

Drawing back from him, I held my hands low at my throat, where my dress was clenched tightly in my fists, closed now, revealing nothing.

Kade hesitated. Then, carefully, as though wary of spooking me, he climbed into the turret to sit next to me, and the small space became even smaller with his large presence filling it. He looked entirely out of place. His size and his clanging arsenal seemed entirely excessive in the feminine, pink-cushioned enclosure of the turret.

He unbuckled one of his many belts, placing his sword to the side. His eyes traced the line of my tear tracks down one cheek. He fingered a long strand of my hair in a disarmingly affectionate gesture. "Tell me what has you upset. And why you're hiding."

"I tried to do as you asked," I said, a mild defiance coloring my words; I had been too thoroughly reminded of my weaknesses only hours ago. "They wouldn't listen to me. They take orders only from my father."

"Then we will go have a word with them," he said, but he made no move yet to leave.

Kade was sitting close to me—he had no other choice in the confined space. My gaze traveled up his powerful arms and his wide shoulders. His hand rested loosely around the leather strap at his chest: strong brown hands that had killed countless men and seduced willing women. My sister among them. The thought caused my inner chest to tighten. From disappointment perhaps. I'd known he was a reckless brute all along. Of course

I'd hoped otherwise. Glimpses of his humanness over past days only succeeded in making his betrayal all the more disheartening now.

He contemplated me, his eyes as pale as blue quartz crystals in the afternoon sunlight. The glint of his hair caught shards of red, and his lips—I hadn't noticed it before now—were perfectly shaped. As he'd once commented about mine, I remembered. I thought of those full lips on Maisie, kissing her, tasting her. *He did unspeakable things.* Whatever these things might be, I didn't even want to consider.

My husband leaned closer, very slowly. I tried to shrink away from his touch, but there was nowhere to go. His finger teased the strand of my hair he still held, coiled loosely around his finger. His other hand rested on my clenched fist, enclosing it in his own. "I've seen you look at me with profound fear—which lingers in you even now. I've seen you look at me with hopeful defiance, and even with something akin to desire. This look is different, wife. Tell me what it's about."

I remained silent, noticing the length of his eyelashes, dark against the strikingly pale hue of his eyes. His warrior's hands were unclenching my fists, burrowing and loosening my grip.

"Tell me," he repeated, finally succeeding in releasing my hold. I had a fleeting thought, at the bruised edge to his inquisition, that he saw me as his only friend, his only confidante, in this unwelcoming and foreign setting. For someone used to brothers and sisters and a close-knit clan from whom he'd never been separated, it must have been a big change for him. He was alone among our Morrison clan with no companions, save me. And I'd hardly shown him the kind of supportive camaraderie he was used to. If it hadn't been for the news of my sister's recent offers to him, I would have. As it was, I was still reeling from my confrontation with Aleck. And all I could think of when I looked at Kade was his strong hands…on *her*. His warrior's grip on her bountiful body and her plush curves. And I was surprised by the amount of emotional poison the image infused me with.

"All right, I'll tell you, *husband*." The address sounded jeering and sarcastic. "You said to me you wanted my consent and you were prepared to wait for it. Something about…" I recalled his words. "If I'm not mistaken, you said that you wouldn't feel you were an 'honorable' man if you felt I was unsure. Did I get that right? You even said that if it took longer than a month, then 'so be it'—I believe those were your exact words." I paused to glower at him. "What *I* say, husband, is that your definition of honorable is laughable! Not that I'm overly familiar with such a concept to begin with, I'll admit." I was ranting now but I couldn't stop myself. I was too outraged. "I know you've been with my sister. And I want you to know I'll have nothing to do with you, not willingly. *Ever*. A month isn't long enough. Nor a year. A decade! It'll be an entire *century* before you get my consent. You can have your way with my sister—*all* of them, if you please. It bothers me not. Take all the Buchanans, too, while you're at it. Or maybe just the ones you haven't *already* bedded. We always knew this marriage was in name only, and so it is. Now please leave me. Attend to the servants yourself if you're so concerned about the manor's upkeep. Gather your own vegetables."

With that, I tried to turn from him. But he, very gently, held me in place. One of his palms curled over my shoulder, pinning me down and causing my unbuttoned gown to part farther.

I was astounded, after my tirade, to see that he wasn't angry. Nor bitter or vengeful. He was concerned. And unfathomably luminous, in this muted afternoon light.

For a long time, he said nothing, allowing me to seethe and finally to calm, smoothing my hair all the while with his careful fingers.

"If you find her more pleasing, husband, I give you my blessing. You should have chosen her sooner, if that's what you wanted all along."

The now-familiar lurk of beguiled amusement shone in his eyes, and a quirk of a smile played at the corner of his mouth. "If I didn't know better of my enchanting, impassioned little wife, I'd almost say you were jealous." He looked more than a little pleased by this.

"You'd be wrong," I replied, indignant.

His half-cocked grin, I'll admit, made him look ridiculously handsome. But I no longer cared about his handsomeness, I reminded myself. In fact, I never had. Or the potent vigor that clung to him like a glimmering sheen.

"I wouldn't be jealous if you sowed your seed across all the Highlands," I told him. "I simply don't care."

"Is that so?" he asked softly. Still holding me down, Kade moved over me, straddling my hips. Sitting as he was, I could feel the rock-hard pressure of him in a most intimate place, and the contact was maddeningly rife with sensation. He rocked against me in a shrewd, barely there movement that caused a vibrant hum within me.

With a gentleness that belied his obvious insensitivity, he drew the gaping neckline of my dress lower over the tops of my breasts, so that my nipples were barely covered. His fingertips moved across my skin with a slow reverence. He watched me with an awed expression. I made no move to struggle against him. Let him feel my total indifference to him, I thought. Let him know that nothing he could do would touch me, not really. He might touch my body, but never my soul. Never *me*. I willed my body not to rise to his command. My body, however, had a mind of its own and was conducting a mutiny against all my attempts at resistance. My nipples were beading under the near caress of his fingers. I was growing soft and wet where his hardness dug against me.

"Be assured of this—I didn't touch your sister," he said, his bright, aqua eyes still focused on the pale curves of my breasts. His thumbs slid under the velvet of my dress to brush against the distended tips, sending a charged pleasure rush to my deepest depths. "She came to deliver a message."

"A 'message'!" I scoffed, squirming under his body

like a fish on a hook. To escape him, aye. To distance myself. "I'm sure I know exactly what her message was." Of her availability, if I was ever unwilling. Of how much Kade reminded her of his brother. Of her expertise, in the wake of my reticence and my awkward inexperience.

"Aye. A *message* I had no need to receive. Why would I stray from *you?*" he whispered, pushing back the fabric to reveal my breasts fully. "Why would I stray from *this?*" His breath fractured into uneven rasps. "You have no idea what you do to me, lass. I am consumed, in fact, by my desire to prove myself to you. 'Tis all I care to do. You have recited my speech back to me, but you forgot the most important part. Remember this— that I would hope, more now than ever before, that you might learn to trust me." He bent over me, taking a nipple into his mouth, sucking strongly and grazing the sensitive flesh with his teeth, inciting a wash of feeling so intense I moaned aloud.

Despite my body's wild response to him, which it seemed I could do nothing to tone down, my anger still clung to my earlier suspicions. But his words, his mouth and his earnest promises began to allay my resentment, smoothing it. I remembered that part of his speech, aye. *I would hope that you might trust me, eventually. I am confident that I can win your invitation.* I felt in that moment that I *could* trust him. That he didn't want to stray from me. That he wouldn't force me, but inspire me. It was an unspeakable relief to me not to feel threatened by him, and I could acknowledge that it was, in the wake of my abusive upbringing, a new sentiment: the absence of danger. I realized that he had known this about me. It was clever of him, to make his oath and to allow me time to adjust to him. His plan was working. This knowledge lit an unexpected little blaze of curiosity in me. I did believe him. And I felt desperately inclined to invite him, despite my better judgment. Oddly, I felt the urge to test him in some way; in what way, I wasn't entirely sure.

His mouth released my swollen nipple, but he continued to lick at it, to tease my aching flesh with his tongue. He moved lazily to my other breast, feasting on me as if I were a lavish buffet. I arched to him, offering myself to his hunger. Plumping my breast with his hand, he eased the tip into the greedy heat of his mouth.

I moaned again, his name. I twirled my fingers through his thick hair, holding his head as I writhed beneath him.

He chuckled at my feverish reaction, moving his mouth up to kiss my neck, biting gently. "Does this mean my wife is no longer angry at me?" he mused. "Nor terrified of me?"

At that, I couldn't suppress a light smile. Aye, for now. All hesitations had been dulled by the billowing urges of my body under his expert advances.

"Or is this your way of escaping my wrath?" he said, his tone still gentle, teasing. His fingers glided and explored. His face was above mine, and his expression was serious and intent despite his playful tone.

"Which wrath?" I asked quietly. "Are you angry because I could not get my clan members to do as you asked?"

"Aye," he said. "Very angry indeed."

"'Very angry indeed,'" I mimicked in a hushed whisper, my heart beating in an up-tempo.

"How shall I teach you that you no longer need to fear anyone?" he said. "Not them. Not me. I do think you're learning, lass. Already you're gaining confidence."

Aye. Here, with him, I could push all the treachery and abuse at the hands of my father and his henchmen out of my mind. In Kade's presence, I felt safer and more daring than I had in a very long time. I grasped a handful of his hair, tugging gently, pulling him closer, so our lips were almost touching. But he held himself in place.

"I did make a promise to you, wife," he said quietly. "It may very well kill me to keep my word, aye, and I'll soon retreat to the loch to have an exceedingly cold swim." He gave me a wry smile. "But, alas, my word is my law. It seems I have a growing list of reasons to prove to you that I am trustworthy, and *honorable*," he said, repeating the word with emphasis, echoing my earlier reservations. He sat up, still astride me. His roughened fingers idly wandered the low line of my dress where the buttons were still fastened, touching the skin of my stomach. Shamelessly, I wished he would rip the buttons open. I wished he would run his hands lower, and lower still.

Curse his word and his law. I reached up to finger one of the leather straps that crisscrossed his chest, tracing the outline of a leather pouch that carried a sharpened circular blade. The fire he had introduced within me was now having its way with me, and quite insistently. I let my fingers trace lower, to the bone-handled knife that hung at his hip, fingering the smooth, worn surface lightly in swirling circles. Kade watched me do this. And in this relaxed, aroused state of mind, he looked more handsome than I'd ever seen him.

In a daring move, I drew the heavy knife from its scabbard and held it up, where it caught the light with dramatic effect. Without design, I was issuing him an unspoken invitation. To shred my clothing, as he had done before.

He contemplated his knife with cool regard. With careful force, he took the knife from my hands and placed it with the other weapons he had laid to the side.

Kade placed his hands on either side of me, supporting himself with his arms as he laid his body over mine, barely touching me. He was covered in blood and dirt, but I barely noticed; I, too, was dirtied, my dress muddied and my skin covered with a damp mist. His hair fell in a thick, satiny curtain around our faces. The scent of him was as I remembered it from our very first encounter in the secret garden: spiced and sensual, unruly with undiluted masculinity.

I weaved my fingers into his hair, pulling him to me. Reaching up to tentatively touch my mouth to his, I kissed him softly, delicately tasting his lips with my tongue. He let out a low oath, as though surprised by the intensity of his own reaction, and he returned the kiss, so tender and sweet I felt I was melting from the inside out. This big, rugged warrior had the most wicked, inviting mouth. His tongue played my own, searching and tasting. His lips nipped and ate at mine with such beguiling, captivating allure that I succumbed entirely to his unyielding demand, opening to him, wanting anything of him he would give. He deepened the kiss, and I could not help responding to the potent coercion of his tongue, which flicked bolts of flowering warmth to the sensitive tips of my breasts and lower, to the smoldering fire at the innermost points of my body. My body felt alive and hungry. For him and only him.

As Kade kissed me, he increased the pressure and the measured pace of the profound contact between our pressed-together bodies, where the hardness of him rubbed between my legs. Already, I could feel the assuaging effects of his kisses. My body was softening and moistening to cradle the rigidity of him in an astoundingly intimate way. I felt open and flushed. And the sensations that leaped through my being every time he rocked himself against my most sensitive place were relentless, searing me with pleasure. His body was so hard, so big. So persuasive. Yet so gentle. So sensitive to my hesitations that he swept them aside entirely. With each roll of movement, the delicate trigger where he pressed against me spiked with decadent sensuality, gaining momentum. With divine deliberation, he continued this delicious torture, until the melting rush rose to such heights I felt as though I was about to float off an invisible ledge. And I *wanted* to reach this exquisite precipice as I'd never wanted anything in my life.

I moaned into his mouth, arching into him, rocking my body against his in a dueling rhythm. He drew my tongue into his mouth, pinching my nipple between two fingers and driving against me all at once. And there it was. The overload of feeling held for a white-hot moment, riding an excruciating swell. And then, the severe pleasure erupted in a violent surge of ecstasy so extreme that I might have blacked out for a moment, or drifted on a cloud of manic pleasure. The innermost muscles of my core clenched in rolling, sultry bursts that found me crying out with each one. I was a quivering mess, my hands coiled in his hair and his shirt, my body convulsing with rapture.

He continued to kiss me and rock himself against me, coaxing the waves further while he absorbed the sounds I made, until finally I grew limp with the extent of my own release.

After a time, Kade straightened his arms slightly, raising himself off me, holding himself above me. The expression on his face was a mixture of smug amusement and mild agitation. His face was flushed as though from strenuous activity, and his pale irises had been all but consumed by the inner blackness, making his eyes unusually dark. "*Responsive* is hardly an apt description of my lovely wife," he said blithely. "Oh, that I could spend the evening eliciting a dozen more responses from you. But I'm afraid we've other matters to attend to first."

Of the little I knew about such things—I *had* been given somewhat explicit descriptions by Maisie, especially, and also Bonnie, after all—I knew that the final satisfaction in regards to this encounter had been one-sided. Namely: mine. And after learning that Maisie had most likely propositioned my husband—unsuccessfully, if he was to be believed—I felt inspired to rise to the challenge. I was still reeling from the intensity of my throbbing climax, which echoed with a gentle pulse even now. Greedily, I wanted more of my husband's expertise. *His lovemaking was akin to a spiritual experience.* Aye, I was beginning to understand. I was already addicted. With this man, the reticence that had been conditioned into my character seemed a long-forgotten memory.

I had some idea about how to offer him such a thing, but, in fact I was entirely inexperienced. I thought of Maisie's advice to me, before I'd left her this morning. *Tease him. Use your body.*

Clearly, the lack of resolution on his part had implanted a layer of tension into Kade's manner. He climbed off me and reached for the weapons he had discarded. I couldn't help noticing the swollen bulge of his immense, roaring arousal as he hastily refastened his belts.

Show yourself. Men simply cannot resist once they see you. "Husband," I said, sitting up, and making no move to close the sides of my gown. The women of my family had been blessed, as it were, with abundant curves. And I was no exception, despite my slightly slimmer figure. My full breasts still felt ripe and swollen from the play of his mouth and his hands. I touched myself, as he had done, fingering my nipples, teasing them once again into tight buds.

Kade regarded me warily, but his guardedness was undermined by a glazed hunger that he was visibly attempting to control. *"Holy mother of God, lass,"* he said, turning his eyes away with a quick jerk of his head. "I've a vow to keep to you. Cover yourself or you'll find me breaking my word for the very first time in my life. And if that happens, there's no telling what kind of debauchery you're in for."

Instead of instilling fear, as his words might have only days ago, they emboldened me by his obvious— and quite rampant—desire. "I thought I might do something for you," I said.

"Nay," he replied gruffly. "'Tis not about me. When the time is right, you can have your way with me. As it is, we've work to attend to. You're coming with me. Make yourself presentable."

A man likes it when a woman takes control. It was with a sense of competitive spirit that I made my decision; I didn't want Kade to be tempted by my sister's advances, even if he said he wasn't, when *I* should be the one tempting him. I moved closer to him, which he seemed not to notice, so embroiled he was with his own irritability and the task of refitting all his many weapons into their correct placements.

I reached for one of his hands with both of mine. At my touch, he froze. As I moved closer, my beaded nipple brushed against the flat metallic plane of one of his knives, causing me to shiver with a light sigh. If I was afraid that he might try to ward me off or reject me altogether, it was a fleeting concern. The fabric of my dress had fallen off my shoulders. My breasts were pushed up lightly against him. Without intention, I licked my parted lips in a silent invitation, and his eyes watched the movement with a stricken, beguiled glint.

Use your hands. And your mouth.

"'Tis not fair, husband."

"What's not fair?" he said shortly, as though trying to hold off the question and annoyed that curiosity had got the better of him.

I held his hand and gently pulled it to me, placing his palm on my bare breast. He allowed this, but his look had turned stormy. I felt doubly vulnerable half-naked before him, offering myself to his force and his fury. Yet his refusal and the reasons behind it lit something within me, giving me a new resolve. I kissed a line along his bristled jaw toward his mouth, but he turned his face away. He exhaled in a long, tortured breath. His hand curved around the rounded shape of my breast, and I held it there.

He exhaled in a light groan.

"That you inspired in me such a…rush," I replied, "And took nothing for yourself."

"Trust me, wife," he said. "You pleasure me more than you know. Just seeing you is enough. Nothing could equal you. Just…*tasting* you—" The admission seemed to jolt some inner sanctum within him. Abruptly, he curled his hand around mine, removing his touch from my skin.

Undeterred, I placed my unoccupied palm on the solid surface of his upper thigh, resting it on the hard leather of his trews. "I wouldn't have thought you to be such a sweet talker upon our first acquaintance," I said.

He stopped the exploration of my fingers, taking my hand in his own much larger one and removing it from his leg. "Nay, that was obvious by the look on your face. Which is precisely why I made the oath—which I can assure you I'm beginning to severely regret. I told you, one month. Cease this now. I'm a man of discipline and control, but I'm not a saint. Don't start something you can't finish."

"I can finish it," I said softly. The effects of my husband's reverence and desire were inspiring every brazen inclination I might ever have possessed. I hardly recognized myself as I said to him, "Taste more of me, husband. You promised you would." The sultry memory of our first kiss in the night garden and his whispered farewell only fortified my resolve. My fantasy had become my reality: *him*.

His voice was quiet and husky. "I have never wanted anything as much as I want to spend the next week locked away in this turret with my flawless, spirited wife, tasting every inch of your perfection, again and again. And I am reaching the limits of my restraint."

I touched my mouth to his, teasing him with tiny licks and bites, testing the very restraint he spoke of. Kade groaned again, a low, savage sound, and I could sense the brimming surge of his surrender was close at hand. He fought it, allowing me to kiss him while remaining entirely motionless, save the willing parting of his lips. I didn't know how far he would allow me to take him, or what limits he had set upon himself with his promises to ease my fear, but I intended to find out.

But before I could, a commotion shattered our privacy. A cacophony of heavy footsteps could be heard in the chambers below us. Soldiers' footsteps, I guessed, and many of them. The hostile voice of my father yelled, "Where is she?" Behind the familiar flare of fear, I felt a fleeting flash of anger at the interruption. Didn't my father and his soldiers have anything better to do than keep endless tabs on me and my wayward whereabouts?

Kade grabbed all of his weapons, slinging them into place. And I hurriedly buttoned up the front of my gown. My husband gave me an intense, brusque command: "Stay behind me."

With all the poise of a seasoned, confident warrior who had every faith in his own ability, he strapped his sword belt around his waist, securing it. Then he motioned for me to follow him. We descended the small stone spiral staircase to find my father, Aleck, Hugh and two other officers whose names I knew to be Callum and Rupert.

Four against one. My father and I hardly constituted threats to anyone, but I couldn't help cataloging the size, the strength and the combined arsenal of my father's four guards and compare them with my husband's. Kade was legendary for his war skills, aye, but could he outmatch all four of them?

"To what do we owe this honor, Laird Morrison?"

my husband said pleasantly, but his question was underlaid with a contempt I hoped only I could detect; Kade, clearly, had little respect for the man whose leadership he was now in line to inherit. "We were just surveying our new chambers. Is there something you require of us?"

"This room is not available," my father said gruffly. Then, with the barest edge of emotion, he said, "'Tis the chambers of my late wife and is not to be disturbed." He turned to me. "You know this, yet you insist on going out of your way to soil her memory with your disobedience. Yet again."

Always before, in my youth and at my most vulnerable, my father's words had sounded like wisdom that shone a light on all my inadequacies. Now I could see it for the madness it was. "I am not soiling her memory, Father. I'm honoring it. Eighteen years have passed since her death. We will use this room, and restore it to its finest."

"How dare you defy me!" my father bellowed, swaying slightly with the effort. "Men, bring her with us. She will receive her penalty belowstairs, and this time, do it properly, lest she once again forgets her place."

Out of habit, I froze, my blood turning to ice in my veins. It was a familiar feeling and one that renewed all the angst my husband had somehow managed to displace.

But Kade was with me now, standing in all his radiance, between me and my aggressors. In a slow, deliberate challenge, he slid his largest sword from its scabbard and held it up. "At the risk of gaining even more of your disapproval, laird, you must be even further down the road to madness than it appears if you think there is any chance whatsoever of you and your thugs laying so much as a finger on my wife."

"Your wife," countered my father, "is my daughter and my charge. As laird of this keep, I will carry out her punishment as I see fit. Now stand aside, Mackenzie, before you live to regret your defiance."

Kade's low chuckle was not one of humor but of utter malice. He pulled a second sword free of its sheath with his left hand. In answer, Aleck and Hugh raised their own swords.

"I will not be stepping aside, laird," Kade replied. "You will have to kill me to get past me, and I daresay I'll take at least you and several of your men with me. And who will lead your struggling army then?"

"Alternative arrangements have been discussed," Aleck commented, to which my father momentarily gave him a questioning glance. Aleck took no notice. "You are not the only officer who is fit to lead this army into the future, Mackenzie."

"Nay," agreed Kade. "Credentials, skill and discipline aside, I am, however, the only officer who links your clan definitively with the Mackenzie army, an alliance you sorely need. Think on it, Laird Morrison. If you kill me, you will very decisively break your alliance with not only the Mackenzie clan, but also those of the Munro and Stuart clans. Can you afford to be so cavalier about my death? Over a dusty turret that has been unused for eighteen years? 'Tis in the best interests of everyone if you leave me and my wife to our private chambers, and allow me to do as I've promised—assist in the revival of your army and your keep."

The murky hatred in Aleck's eyes as he watched my husband unnerved me. I knew him well enough to see that there was jaunty yet sinister confidence to him that had once been lacking, and something about this realization didn't sit well. I was afraid of the thoughts going on behind his black, shining eyes. "Perhaps we can explore *other* alliances," Aleck said darkly. And there it was. Or was it? An admission? Was *Aleck* the traitor, plotting with Campbell to reignite the rebellion from here within our own walls? Had his ambition driven him to treachery of this magnitude? Aye, I believed him capable of it. I wanted to point this possibility out to Kade, but I knew I had no need to do so: my husband's weapons rose higher, his stance becoming more hostile. He looked as though he might strike at any moment.

My father, however, appeared not to notice either way. He was clearly exhausted by this entire confrontation, too absorbed in his own accumulating ailments to argue further. Perhaps he realized Kade was right. It was also abundantly clear that Kade was not bluffing; if my father followed through on his threat, he and at least several men would very likely be killed, a possibility that seemed to undermine my father's anger. He coughed several times and when he wiped his mouth, bloodstains tinted the back of his hand. "So be it. Do not expect me to bend so easily to all your requests,

Mackenzie." He turned and addressed Aleck and Hugh. "Men, escort me to the barracks so I may take a drink."

With that, and a final combative glare from Aleck, the men took their leave.

WEAK WITH RELIEF, I watched my husband. He sheathed his swords into their scabbards and turned to face me. He reached to finger a golden end strand of my hair. "See?" Kade said. "I swore to you the protection of my body and my sword. 'Tis my duty and my honor. You have nothing to fear now."

Still stunned not only by the reverberating effects of our near conflict but also by the weight of my gratitude, I looked up at Kade's face. The glaze of aggression clung to him, but under it, from the very heart of his emotion, I could read there his sincerity. "Thank you, husband," I said, entwining his fingers with my own.

Just then, my stomach made a little growling sound. Kade grinned lightly. "When's the last time you ate something, wife?"

"This morning. Some stale bread."

"Let's go down to the kitchens and find some supper. While we're at it, we can have a chat with the kitchen staff."

Still holding his hand, I followed him down the corridor to the staircase, along the back entrance and into the kitchen, where the staff were seated in a very similar position to the one I'd found them in earlier this morning. Kade paused for a brief moment, taking in their position, their obvious leisure, the state of the kitchens. The sight of them did nothing to cool the lingering volatility my father and his men had introduced. I remembered, too, that my husband had other reasons perhaps to feel…unfulfilled.

"Ladies," Kade said, approaching them and pulling up a tall stool to half sit on it. Despite the layered turmoil behind his expression, his manner was calm and engaging.

With his long hair dark and windblown yet somehow still glossy, his muscled bulk still stained by the blood of animals he'd killed, and his eyes like a pair of gleaming stolen coins, the women stared at him with a mixture of curiosity and awe. "You know," Kade began, "I asked my wife to give a few simple instructions this morning, just before I went out to the barracks to see if I could find a handful of men to accompany me on a day's hunting trip. If you can believe it, that's all I was able to find, a handful. Five men out of hundreds volunteered. *Five men.* Have you any idea what the rest of the men were so busily engaged with?" he asked them, pausing, awaiting their reaction. They stared at him guardedly. "Nay?" he prodded. "No idea whatsoever?"

Isla obliged with a slow, wide-eyed shake of her head.

"Well," Kade said, "let me *tell* you what they were doing. They were *sleeping,* well past sunrise, despite the fact that they're living in relative squalor, the state of their weapons is disgraceful and there are scarcely enough swords to go around. If we were to get invaded this very day—which is not beyond the realm of possibility—we'd be done for. And if my information on

the momentum of at least one of several Highlands rebellions currently brewing is correct—and I have every
reason to believe it is—we'd have some serious trouble
on our hands.

"So this is the situation I find myself in, if you can
imagine," Kade continued, with overexaggerated pleas-
antness. "Attempting, unsuccessfully, to deploy several
hunting parties. But the men are tired, they say. They
were up late into the night with their revelries. And their
swords are not sharpened, I'm told. In fact, it appears
to me—and I consider myself somewhat of an expert
in this area—not a single sword's been sharpened for
possibly weeks, maybe even *months*."

He speared Isla with a glare of conspiratorial outrage, as though not satisfied by her level of disgust at
his pronouncement. *"Months,"* he repeated. "'Tis inex-
cusable, to be sure. A soldier's pride is his sword, you
see. His honor depends on it. His very *life* depends on
it." He paused again, as though allowing his words to
adequately sink in. He focused on one of the women,
a cook whose name I knew to be Jinty. Her rounded
cheeks had gone pink with the attention. "Tell me, then,"
he said. "When an army of ill-equipped, underskilled
warriors such as these is challenged on the battlefield,
what do you think the chances of actually *winning* that
battle might be?"

Kade waited for their input, and when none came, he
repeated his question. "Come on, give me an answer.
What do you *think?* Do you think they would win?"

A smaller, more timid member of the kitchen staff replied with an earnest "Nay?"

He gave her an intense, congratulatory look. "You're exactly right, lass. They—*we*—would *not* win. There's not a chance in hell that those men out there would last five minutes on a battlefield against the likes of Campbell and his ruffians—ruffians, by the way, who are growing increasingly lethal, because they're highly dedicated to their cause, as unwarranted as that cause may be. And do you know what would happen to likes of such dedicated staff as yourselves if we were, say, to be overrun by Campbell's very big, brutal men, with their lust for revenge and their lack of honor? Have you any idea?" When no reply came from the women, Kade said, more softly, "Aye, it doesn't bear thinking about. 'Tis too disturbing, to be sure, to contemplate."

It was clear that my husband had a long list of frustrations to deal with, and that the accumulation was getting to him. I had never heard him speak so much, or with such careless abandon. It was true, however, that he had the undivided attention of all in attendance. And he seemed to be coming around to his point.

"So," he continued, "what *I* couldn't understand is why all these men were sleeping late on this fine morning when there's clearly plenty of work to be done. And when I explained to them—and why I should *have* to, I've no idea, they're grown men, after all—do you know what their response to this was?"

The women, riveted, gave him multiple encouraging shakes of their head in unison and made small, chorusing noises of empathy, wanting now to know where he was going with all this. "Well, I'm afraid I can't repeat their words in front of respectable ladies such as yourselves, but I can assure you that they weren't jumping up to agree with me. As you can imagine, since their refusal to comply with my requests makes our collective situation even more dire with each passing day, I was less than pleased by their response. I can also tell you that it put me in a bit of a mood—as I'm sure you'll understand."

Kade took a moment to calm himself, and the women allowed him this, waiting patiently for him to continue.

"By this time, however," he said, somewhat more composedly, "the hour was getting later and the deer tend to scatter when the sun warms up, so I and my five—*five*—men took our leave, and managed to kill ourselves a bounty of seven does and two young stags. So we were able to return earlier than I'd originally thought we might, and I've commissioned several of the very same five men—who I plan on rewarding with the choicest selection of cuts from these deer, along with a promotion as soon as I step up—to butcher the meat and bring it to you fine ladies to prepare for the contingent of the army who has agreed to rise early on the morrow and begin dedicating themselves to the considerable amount of work we have cut out for us."

He paused again, looking at the women one by one, as though expecting a protest. None came.

"I mention all this to you for several reasons. First, you must understand that I am occupied with the army and the hunting parties, so I must leave the management of the manor up to my wife, soon to be Lady Morrison. Second, I realize that you may not be used to some of the tasks that will now be asked of you. There will be more meat, and food in general, to store, preserve and prepare. We will be using the hall to dine in on a regular basis. We therefore need a clean, efficient kitchen staffed with people, such as yourselves, no doubt, who are up to the job."

My husband looked around the untidy room, at the dirty dishes, the unorganized shelves and in the direction of the neglected pantry, before continuing. The women exchanged nervous glances. "Your workloads must have indeed have been heavy, since you weren't able to carry out even the beginnings of my explicit directions, as given by my wife. So, what I suggest we do is to work together to complete the tasks. *Now.*" It was this word that, finally, hammered his point very convincingly home. He was highly irritated that he had come in after a long day of arguing, dueling, hunting and riding—as well as attending to somewhat more private pursuits, which had not been entirely…resolved for him—to find that none of his simple requests had been carried out. At all. "We'll need to work later than you might be accustomed to, but you'll be rewarded, of course. You'll be given extra meat for yourselves to share with your families—but that's only if you get the jobs done in a timely manner. 'Tis all or nothing, and it's up to us to work until the work is done." He surveyed the faces of his rapt listeners, with pronounced, assertive cheerfulness. "Are we agreed?"

These nods of agreement were more tentative, and his speech had taken on a decidedly harder edge.

"*And* are we agreed that, in the future, when my wife asks you to complete a task, you will *do* so without questioning it? I am not only extremely observant, but I have every reason to take as gospel every word, every impression and every grievance that my wife presents me with—not that I would expect any of those. We work with our own best interests at heart, after all, and hard work, as I've said, will be rewarded handsomely. Those who choose not to work—well, let's just say I've been told I'm overemphatic about my dismissals, and those who are dismissed or demoted are offered the last of the food rations from that day forward. But I'm sure that's of no consequence here. Now, you will tell me your names, in turn, and I will assign you each an important, necessary job. I will be on hand to assist anyone who needs it."

There were tactics behind Kade's message; we all understood that. Our dedication was as necessary as that of the soldiers and hunters if our keep was to sustain us through the long winter months: that now seemed obvious. That he had taken the time to explain this, I could see, was far more effective than my father's method of leadership: of giving haphazard orders that were then followed up with demeaning punishments if the indiscretions were even noticed. My father was old and had never been fastidious. Hard work was never praised, or even valued.

It had been a challenging day for my husband. His

fierceness—a fierceness I could now recognize that was comprised of spirit, industriousness and honor, not irrational wrath—had returned in full force. The servants saw it, too, and they reacted with a hesitant obedience. In fact, I'd never, ever, seen any of them work like this. Once given their assignments, they launched into their tasks wholeheartedly. Kade helped them, and so did I. As a cooperative, driven team, they cleaned, cooked, set tables, lit fires, baked bread and even attended to their own appearances. Within several hours, the kitchen and the grand hall of Glenlochie had been transformed.

CHAPTER TEN

I woke in the night. A sharply defined ray of purple moonlight illuminated a square of the stone floor. Dull orange embers glowed.

It had been a week since we had claimed the turret as our own, and the space was now filled with our belongings, which were still in a state of disorder.

The room was warm. The fire burned from the logs Kade had stacked it with some time before.

I noticed that my husband was seated in a chair, asleep, slumped over the table he had claimed as his desk, his quill still grasped loosely in his hand. I could hear his deep, even breathing, which was never harsh or loud in his sleep. He looked uncomfortable, with his big body laid heavily across the table, his head resting on his outstretched arm, his hair askew.

I rose, and I went to him. I hoped he wouldn't wake in a state. He'd been so aggravated by the unfolding reality of our clan's appalling disorganization—understandably so—and he'd hardly slept since his arrival. At least when he did, I thought, it could be in the comfort of a warm bed.

I'd asked him once before about what he wrote in his books and letters, to which he'd given me a gruff reply. "Weapons designs, battle plans, tactics. Nothing you need to concern yourself with." I knew he had dispatched at least one letter to each of his brothers in the days since we'd arrived at Glenlochie. Now the unrolled parchment of a letter was displayed, held down by the length of his arm as he slept. The tip of the quill had bled a small black smudge onto the top of the page.

I didn't mean to pry, but the words jumped out at me before I could stop myself. There was much my husband wouldn't discuss with me, about his difficulties during the days, when we were apart. I knew of his conflicts with the men of our army—as illustrated by the confrontation earlier with Aleck and the others. Only the day before, he had returned to our chambers bloodied from a duel; he'd only mentioned this when I'd asked him about it several times. And I knew from his grim expressions whenever I saw him during the days that he spent much of his time seething, or wishing he was anywhere but here. I wanted to learn more about the secret workings of his mind. Justifying my intrusion as a genuine bid to support him, if I could just better understand how I might, I began to read.

Knox,
The situation at Glenlochie has worsened. Though
I have managed over time to convince for y men
to hunt in semiorganized groups, at least half the
men of the Morrison army still dispute my com-
mands. We have, in one week, succeeded in killing
no less than twenty-eight deer, seven pigs, rabbits

aplenty and a wealth of other game that should begin to keep the clan in provisions for some time to come. If we're able to keep up this pace throughout the remaining days before snowfall, we might stand a chance of surviving the winter. The northern lands are indeed rich for hunting, I suspect because no one has bothered to do much of it and the animals have multiplied. The gardeners and farmers arrived—I thank you for sparing them for these winter and spring months—and I have put them to work training the recruits and salvaging what can be pulled from the pitiful gardens and the unkempt storage sheds. The croplands, thankfully, are in a somewhat less dismal state and there is plenty of wheat and barley. If need be, we'll be dining on barley soup and coarse bread through the late-winter months. So I am hopeful we will not starve. I thank you also for your offer to send provisions if necessary. My hope is that we can subsist without depleting your stores. The cooks, alas, are entirely uninspired, but that is the least of my worries.

Morrison has little life left in him, and what remains is bitter, swilled and disoriented, and this appears to be nothing new. I have learned that he has ruled not only his clan but also his family with a mixture of abuse and disregard. For these reasons, he leaves a legacy of fear and complacency, even before his death, that will take some months—if not years—to remedy. His highest-

ranking officers are among those who fight me at every turn and I fear I may have to kill one of them to prove my rights as their laird-in-waiting. I had expected to be accepted as successor, as discussed, but the men appear to regard me as an unwelcome intruder. I had not thought to go entirely uncontested as leader, but there is one officer in particular who would prefer to claim the title of laird-in-waiting for himself. Bloodshed, however, may only serve to divide the clan further, which is why I have refrained as yet. It would be easy enough to do. The men are lazy and lack both will and proficiency. If Father could see the neglected state of their weaponry, he would no doubt be rolling in his grave. Heads would roll, and I am tempted to follow his methods. A mass mutiny, and with one target in mind, would hardly serve to better my position, however, so I must tread carefully.

Continued threats of Campbell's arrival are rife. The men speak of him as though messages have been received, and I have strong suspicions that there is at least one traitor among us, if not a contingent of them. I have my suspicions about one officer in particular. I can only hope that I can succeed in training the few that are loyal and continue to win the regard of the masses before the rebellion reignites, which I feel certain it is bound to do. I dread to consider the outcome if I

*fail on these counts. Be prepared to deploy if you
receive word.*

*Marriage presents brief moments of sweetness
amid a sea of uncertainty. My wife is a vision who,
I'll admit, blinds me with her magnificence. Hers
is a beauty that only seems to compound itself the
more I see of her. She continues to regard me as
a boorish brute of the worst order. I have reason,
however, to believe she may one day believe otherwise. I live in hope and work to prove myself
in every regard.*

*Kinloch is never far from my thoughts. I hope
this letter finds you and our sisters well.*

*I am including a sketch for a high-powered
catapult that may interest you.*
Your loyal brother,
Kade Mackenzie

The letter sent a warm curl of emotion through me,
which took some moments to identify. Awe perhaps.
Compassion. And strangely, a deep and desperate *longing.* I wasn't sure what it was I was longing for. To ease
his burden, maybe. To help him somehow. I'd known his
new life presented him with difficulties and a sense of
displacement. But I'd had no idea how profound those
difficulties were. He was facing a mutinous army, death
threats, the possibility of his new clan going danger-
ously hungry, and a lethal ongoing rebellion whose
reaches could be taking hold even now and within our
very walls.

His words regarding *me* were even more astounding. That he regarded me in this way, and enough to expound the details of his yearning to his brother, was no less than astonishing to me. And I was having a physical reaction to his admission.

As my body reacted undeniably to his presence, my heart, too, was reacting to his words. He was capable of love, as Roses had made a point to explain to me. He strove at all times to live up to his family's ideals of honor, as *he* had made a point to explain to me. These realizations shone from his letter as though the ink itself were lit with truth.

I felt a blooming sense of connection with my tormented, complicated husband like I'd never felt before.

It was true that once I *had* regarded him as a boorish brute of the worst order. I didn't want to admit to him outright that I had read his letter, but I wanted to assure him that I no longer saw him that way. That the day had arrived. *Today* I believed otherwise.

Touching my fingertips to his hair, I smoothed it back from his face, brushing the loose strands from their disarray across his forehead and his neck. His hair was thick and shiny, soft to the touch. I let my thumb trace the stripe of his eyebrow, as he sometimes did to me. I drew my finger gently along the sharp line of his bristly jaw, to the plumped surface of his full lips, parted slightly in his slumber. His eyes blinked open. I continued to stroke his hair, hoping to ease his reaction before he could decide what that reaction might be.

"Husband," I whispered. "Come. You'll be more comfortable in bed than here at your table."

He lifted his head.

"I'll help you," I crooned, hoping desperately he wouldn't rise in anger when he realized that his letter was exposed, that I might have overstepped my boundaries.

He let me help him, allowing me to ease my arm through his, to hold him and guide him to bed. He was clad only in his underclothes, and his lean, muscled body was cool on the surface with a heated warmth under the skin. The dark of his hair and the dazzling light blue of his eyes created a delicious aesthetic contrast that I couldn't help pausing to appreciate. He allowed me this, and seemed lost in a reverie of his own, gazing down at me as if I might have been an apparition. I pulled the furs down for him. When he didn't react at all, still watching me with a glazed tenderness, I crawled under the covers, sliding over the wide expanse of the bed to my side of it. He followed me, covering us with the furs, lying to face me.

We lay like that for some time, just facing each other, with me touching his hair, smoothing it back from his face in a gentle, repetitive line. "'Tis all right," I said softly, and he watched my mouth as I spoke, and my eyes. "You're all right," I said again, feeling somehow that he wanted to hear it. "I'll watch over you."

My fingers traced the line of his collarbone to the uneven surface of the scarred and sun-darkened skin of his chest. I touched the puckered knot of his most pronounced scar, the one that curved in a pale crescent at the front of his left shoulder. It was long healed now but must have been a terrible injury.

"What happened to you?" I whispered.

He didn't respond immediately. "My attention was diverted by the death of my own father," came his low reply. "It was Campbell himself who speared me. Our fathers took each other's lives that day. Campbell the younger is one of the most vicious men I've ever fought. 'Tis the only time I thought I might actually be taken in a fight. But it was not to be. Knox saved my life, right before I saved his."

He spoke matter-of-factly, as though spearing, fighting and saving lives were something he did on a daily basis. Which I suppose it was. I knew him to be one of the most lethal warriors in all the Highlands. But there was sadness in his tone that was unmistakable.

"You miss your brothers."

"Aye," he said simply.

My careful exploration wandered lower, to the coiled muscles of his stomach. His hand reached to grab my wrist in a stronghold, drawing my hand away. "Stella," he said. A low warning.

He released my hand, closing his eyes, as though the matter was now closed.

The night was lit with sound and sensation amid the enclosing darkness. I could hear the soft crackle of the fire. I could feel not just the heat of Kade's body but his brimming restraint. I let my fingers steal again toward him under the furs until my delicate touch again rested on the skin of his stomach.

He withdrew instantly, lying flat on his back, pulling his body farther from my reach so the coolness was starkly defined. "You know the rules, wife. We wait. We wait until you're ready." Then he lay back, again closing his eyes, yet his brow was still furrowed.

We wait.

I understood why, aye. He was using his self-inflicted rules to control himself, to allow me time to adjust. What I realized was that I *had* adjusted. I felt I *was* ready. I wanted to challenge his rules, to push his boundaries.

"I'm cold," I whispered, not entirely untruthfully.

Kade opened one eye, reaching to fit the furs more snugly around my shoulders, but he did not touch me directly. Then he lay back once again. "Good night, lass. Go to sleep," he said.

Silence, for a time.

"I can't sleep," I said.

"'Tis late," he murmured dismissively.

Stillness wrapped around us, embellished by the rustle of the wind outside, the lonely call of a faraway night bird.

Emboldened by the heavy darkness and the lingering epiphany of my husband's writing, I reached again, finding his fingers. I held them in silence and he allowed this, although his breathing caught, as though I'd charged something in him. As though there were only so many times he could refuse me.

I wanted to reassure him, that I no longer regarded him as I once had, as a threat, as yet another man who might use his might in punishing, overbearing ways. "I don't feel afraid anymore, husband. Of you," I whispered. "I wanted you to know that."

His eyes opened and he regarded me silently. Then he said, "I told you I would work to earn your trust, and I will."

Without intent or design, I smoothed one finger along his open palm, curling my fingers around his hand, pulling it closer.

He held his hand firmly in place, and his eyes remained closed. "Stella. Cease this," came his low command. And I heard in his voice his own simmering challenge. *How far will you go?*

I did not cease. My leg twitched forward of its own accord, causing my thighs to part slightly wider and my shift to bunch just higher. I couldn't quite catch my breath, and my breasts rose and fell with my light gasps. I waited for his arm to relax, and I cautiously pulled his hand closer until I could feel the heat of it against my thigh.

His head turned, and his open eyes blazed with blue-lit intensity. "Little wife," he said softly, laughter and promise in equal measure coloring his words. "Be careful, or you will get as much as you ask for."

Aye, my fevered body *was* asking. I knew I was playing with fire. But I was already burning.

Returning his challenge, I drew his large, warm hand higher along the fine upper skin of my thigh, so very close to where I wanted to feel his touch. The anticipation was nearly overwhelming. He might still refuse me, aye, but the mere *nearness* of his fingers to my dewy, intimate folds was almost too much to bear. I was awed by the power he seemed to hold over me, and breathless at the heightened responses of my body to his.

Intent, his fingers touched me, and began their own stealthy caress, guided by desire to rest under my shift, between my legs. I heard his low intake of breath. I could feel the light echo of his pulse beneath the skin of his wrist. The touch of his warrior's fingers against me intensified the low, damp sweetness in my center. All my senses gathered on that singular swelling place.

And then his fingers began to move, rubbing in slow, steady circles. With his other hand he pushed my shift higher, lifting it over the abundant swell of my breasts. He cupped the full, rounded weight, kneading gently, circling my nipple in an identical rhythm, pinching in luring, furtive pulls.

"You want to feel me, lass? Is this what you want? My hands on you?"

"Aye, I want to feel you. I want to *feel*..."

"*Feel,* then, wife," he said, parting my secret swollen petals, sliding his fingers just inside me while simultaneously squeezing my nipple in a tighter clench of all of his fingers, pulling and elongating the hard peak. "I've a mind to restrain you and tempt you with my denial... or by other means. I can be quite creative when I put my mind to it. You'll see."

His mouth took mine, opening me to his unhurried

demand. His desire was aggressive yet controlled, supple yet dominating. He was no longer a phantom but my fierce, tumultuous husband. My body was open to him in any way he chose to take me.

He drew back just slightly, deeply affected by my total compliance. "I'd made up my mind to wait, lass. But it seems I don't have it in me to deny you anything. I'll give you a taste of what this marriage bed has to offer, shall I?" His fingers slid deeper into the slippery core of my body. *"Oh, God Almighty,"* he whispered, "The *feel* of you… I can feel your innocence, right here. The barrier I've yet to break."

"Do it," I whispered, wanting more than anything for him to take my innocence. To take me as his own. As his wife, in every sense.

His voice was agonized. "Nay, lass. I must be true to my word. I can't have you believing me untrustworthy." He spoke the words as though they pained him, yet there was steely resolve behind his meaning.

In this moment, I cared not about his word, nor his resolve. All I could comprehend, in fact, was the rising sensation he drew from my body. His skill in the matter of loving was unmistakable. Kade tantalized me with his expertise. *You are indeed an instrument to be played.* His fingers were barely inside me, prodding into the stretching tightness, exploring deftly to find a profound and excruciating sweet spot, as his thumb skated deliciously across the sensitive nub, swirling and teasing. The sultry pleasure spiraled, glowing from within. His left hand continued its playful torture, rolling my nipple in needy tugs. His mouth found my other breast and he sucked me and bit me, devouring with his tongue and his teeth, delivering a harmonic rhythm of pleasure that spiked avidly, and quickly. The rapture was sharp and bright, erupting in ecstatic bursts through my core, warming my breasts, spilling with an eager beauty that I could feel to the very tips of my fingers and toes. I moaned, digging my fingernails into his skin.

"'Tis a good thing we have our own wing," he said, chuckling softly. He continued to suck languidly on my breasts, one, then the other. The feeling of his mouth on me, softly pulling and demanding, as the echo of my release still pulsed, was indescribable. My body felt molten and alive, more liquid than form and flesh.

"My wife is insatiable. Let me give you a wee bit more *feeling,*" he said against my skin, suckling more gently now. He eased lower, kissing a line down my stomach, licking into my navel, which made me squirm and laugh. I began to turn, to escape his wicked tongue. But my husband held me down, arranging me as he wanted, spreading my legs farther and lying between them. I struggled lightly against him, not to rid myself of him, but because the melted core of my body still throbbed with the lingering waves of my release. I felt flighty, reckless, covetous. I wanted more. I wanted *him.* To give and to take, to rub against him and consume him. I writhed beneath him, gripping the hard muscles of his arms. He was so much stronger than me that I was entirely overpowered by him. My desire for him to do *anything* to me, combined as it was with the knowledge that he *could,* and easily, was stunningly arousing. I was brimming with moisture and heat.

"Husband," I murmured.

"Aye," he answered.

"Do that again."

This made him laugh, and the sound of his laughter seemed to vibrate in the still-pulsing depths of me. "I aim to, lass. Lie still. You're going to like this."

"What are you going to do?"

"Something I've been wanting to do for quite some time. Ever since the very first moment I saw you, in fact, from across the room." He was easing himself down my body, running his tongue along the line of my hip bone, trailing lower. And closer.

I pushed against his head as I realized what he was doing. "Wait," I breathed, propping myself up on my elbows to look at him.

But his fingers were parting me and he was lowering his mouth to me.

"Kade! *Stop.*"

He looked up at me, his hair wild and his eyes twinkling. "Why?"

"Don't do *that.* You can't. 'Tis indecent."

"Good. I like indecent. And so will you." His head began to lower again, but I squirmed more forcefully, attempting to back away from him. I wasn't able to budge even one inch. His hold was absolute.

"*Nay,* I said!" My voice didn't sound as stern as I'd intended.

His crooked smile both irked me and disarmed me.

"And I say *aye*. You should know that about me. I'm *exceedingly* indecent. Depraved, even. Debauched, too, upon occasion. You started this, remember. Now lie back this instant, or I'll be forced to restrain you."

I paused, remembering. *He bound her to the bed.* To be sure, the idea of my husband's domination seemed far less daunting than it once had.

"Lie back, wife. If you deny me the pleasure of tasting you for even one more minute, there's no telling how I might react. I'm feeling somewhat overcome with anticipation. Do as I say." His devilish smirk left no question as to his intent. "Let me pleasure you, lass. Let me take control." The affectionate edge to his voice was enough to see me obeying his command. I was saturated with desire for him, aye. I knew he would get his way and I *wanted* him to have his way with me. And, while I hadn't been expecting *this,* there was no escaping him. So I lay back, my fingers still entwined in his hair, more gently now.

Kade spread my legs wider. Then he licked into the softness of my hot core, nudging deeply with his tongue. The fire was instant, the pleasure all-consuming. His mouth moved to the tiny nerve center, sucking greedily on my furled flesh with sumptuous absorption.

Slowly, his fingers entered me. I could feel a light, compounding thrill as he rubbed against that wildly sensitive place inside me, once, and again. Wanting more, I grasped more tightly the fistfuls of his hair, writhing along to his rhythm. He withdrew his touch abruptly. I whimpered a moan of protest. I tried to relax my quivering, restless body. After a moment, he seemed satisfied by my submission and he fixed his mouth onto me once again, continuing the enchanting suction of his mouth, entering me again, now with two fingers. The starry, prickling ecstasy began deep inside me, spurred by the languid pulls of his mouth and the exquisite pressure of his fingers, feeding a cyclical, liquid bloom of sensation. The pleasure was disabling, maddening, fracturing my consciousness into dreamy shards of light. Mind-numbing bursts of bliss clenched tightly around his slippery fingers. His tongue slid and flicked, prolonging the swell until I lay panting and spent. I felt drowsy and drunk as he continued to kiss my throbbing, most intimate places.

I was barely conscious of his big body lying heavily atop mine. He moved to kiss my face and my hair, smoothing his hand along the long strands. It might have been several minutes later, I wasn't sure, when I felt the weight of him removed. Time was wistful and vague.

The sound of fabric and the clang of his weapons brought me back to a soft-edged awareness.

He was up and getting dressed.

I rolled to one side, to watch him. "Where are you going?"

"A walk. A swim. I'll be back later."

A small stab of panic jabbed against my heart. "Nay," I said immediately. "Kade. Don't go. Come back to bed."

"Sleep now, Stella." He had slung one of his weapons holsters across his chest, and his trews were on but yet unfastened, low on his hips. His arousal was so strained and enlarged that I could see the broad tip of it protruding from the linen of his underclothing. The sight of him did strange things to me. My pulse was a gentle throb in my chest, and elsewhere, exciting a primitive yearning to get closer to him, to his magnificence and his war-scarred beauty. I wanted so much to *touch* him. "I said I'll be back. Get your rest."

I sat up, my feet dangling off the side of the bed. My shift was bunched around my neck, falling to my back, so my body was entirely exposed to him. This thought barely registered, except perhaps as a necessary detail of what I was already planning to do. Somewhat irritated by it, I slipped the garment over my head, letting it fall. I didn't want him to leave me. Especially not in frustration. I knew what the consequences of enticing him, of asking him—or begging him—to stay would be. And I was willing.

"I *beg* of you," I said. *I'll not force you, nor will I do anything at all that you don't beg me to do.* "Come to me."

He looked at me warily, as though *I* were the threat. To his honor and his law.

"You won't be breaking your word to me, husband," I assured him. "I want you to. Please don't leave. Please come to me."

It was the vulnerable edge to this final soft-spoken entreaty that seemed to break down his defenses.

He walked over to me, still barefoot, shirtless, clad only in a leather strap dripping with knives and his un-fastened trews, which revealed more to me, as he drew closer, than I might ever have imagined. His expression bordered on sulky, guarded. Yet he came to me, standing several feet from the edge of the bed.

I rose, bridging the divide. I looked up at him, feeling small yet perhaps bolder than I ever had felt. I reached to unfasten the buckle of the holster draped across his bare chest. He allowed this, and I lifted the weapons from his body, bending to place them on the stone floor. I was entirely unworldly. I had no idea how to go about any play at seduction, yet I could sense from the look in his light, penetrating eyes that my nakedness, my movement and the fumbling insistence of my hands were working in whatever way I might have intended. I slid Kade's bone-handled knife from its scabbard at his hip. It was heavy and solid in my hands. I took a step back, half sitting against the bed, laying the knife on the furs.

"I have but one weapon left to me," he said, his voice gravel-edged with passion.

"Come closer," I whispered, easing myself back up onto to the bed.

He obeyed my request, standing silently at the edge of the bed. I opened my legs so he could move closer, not touching me, yet close enough for me to reach out to him. Tentatively, I pushed at the fabric of his underclothing and his trews, drawing them down lower on his hips to reveal him to me.

I had felt him brush up against me in past nights under the heavy covers and in the total darkness. Now, with the fire casting its gentle light, I could for the first time marvel, aghast, at the full extent of his manhood. I had, of course, never seen anything like this and not even in my wildest dreams could I have imagined such…*impressiveness.* Even in my innocence it was clear that he was gloriously made. The sight of his body, fully revealed to me, imbued me with a sudden pang of longing, like hunger or thirst.

Carefully, I took him in my hands, marveling at the feel of him. Like hot silk over rigid stone. He cursed and closed his eyes as my cool fingers explored his full length. I was fascinated by the surprising textures of him, the softness of his skin, the heat, the generous solidity. The touch of my curious fingers seemed to have a profound effect on him. His eyes opened to watch my beguiled study, and their blue light was fiery yet tinted with something deeper: awe perhaps. Reverence. For the first time, I felt entirely in control. He was mine, completely. I'll admit it pleased me, this small power. It was the first time my femininity felt to me like a strength. This formidable warrior was wholly at my mercy, just from the light caress of my fingers. I wanted to work this power, to see where it might take me. To see what it might *do* to *him.* Would he find that sublime, overwhelming *rush,* as I had? I had no knowledge of such things, and I wanted to find out. I increased the pressure of my grasp, sliding my hand along his length, getting a feel for his reaction. His eyes were heavy-lidded, glazed with lust. His broad chest rose and fell in uneven rasps. And I was intrigued to find that a bead of moisture had gathered at the tip of his shaft, which was so engorged, it did look, to be certain, as if it might burst at any moment.

Using my hands, I guided him closer, so that the broad end of his jutting manhood was level with my mouth. Would he allow this? He had used his mouth on me, so perhaps he would, I reasoned. He made no objection, only growling a loud, exhaling oath as I eased my lips around the tip of him. The taste of him was so compelling to me, so hypnotically absolute, I could only draw more of him into my mouth, seeking more, licking him with soft, devoted strokes of my tongue. I waited for him to draw away. But instead of withdrawing, he weaved his fingers around the base of my skull, under my hair, pushing himself farther into my mouth.

Encouraged, I took as much of him as I could, increasing the light suction, easing him in and out of my mouth, tasting the salty essence of him as my hands continued to stroke and explore.

"Stella," he rasped. "Hellfire and damnation, I can't hold on to this. 'Tis too much."

I wasn't sure what he meant by that. But I was soon to find out. As I took him deeper once again, suckling him in a gentle rhythm, he groaned as though he were being burned by the hellfire he spoke of. Hot liquid filled my mouth in jetting, milky pulses. His rush had overcome him, and here it was. As he had done to me, prolonging my ecstasy with his mouth, so I did to him. I took his essence, swallowing his bliss, licking and kissing and playing him with my lips and my tongue until he was completely spent.

After a time, he pulled himself away, tilting my head up with his hands. In his eyes I saw amazement, and tender revelation. He rid himself of his low-strung trews, kicking them away. He took the knife from where it lay on the bed and placed it on the bedside table. Then he gathered me into his arms, against his skin, laying me back and covering us with the furs. He wrapped his long limbs around me, settling me close to him in a comforting, all-encompassing embrace. My head was tucked against his chest, so I could hear the steady beat of his heart. I could feel his soft kisses against my hair. I was more content than I had ever been, and my eyes closed.

I WAS AWAKENED by the silky touch of Kade's thick hair brushing along my thigh, his wandering fingers playing. I was positioned on my side, my knees bent, with one leg propped up and slung across his brawny shoulder. His head rested on one of my splayed thighs as the soft, nuzzling wetness of his tongue stroked me open, infusing me with restless, awakening rapture.

I tugged on his hair, and my husband chuckled, even as his tongue slid deeper into my body, possessing me as he gripped me with his ironlike hands, pulling me closer to his mouth, feeding on my pleasure. His unholy tongue stroked me open, lapping against my secret petals, parting me to his hungry persistence. He licked a small circle around the sensitive bud, flicking and teasing before his mouth fixed upon it, sucking strongly in cyclical pulls. With each tug, a rising bolt of sweetness rose from within me. *"Kade,"* I moaned, my hands on his head, in his hair. *"Please."* I was sobbing. 'Twas too much. I couldn't contain the overloading tide, which spilled from my core in rushing, clenching bursts that seemed endless in their intensity. I rode the undulating wave, rolling my hips to quell the excesses. Still he wouldn't relent. He pushed his tongue deep inside me, delving along to the rhythm of my body, igniting fresh, torturous ecstasy. My inner muscles clamped voluptuously around his wicked tongue. He kissed my swollen, sated flesh, licking me, whispering against my body.

"Nectar," he murmured. "Heaven on earth."

After many minutes of this attentive, unhurried appreciation, my husband crawled up my body to lie next to me, propping himself up on one crooked elbow. He regarded me with a smug, lazy grin and narrowed eyes. I felt the connectivity of our locked gaze in my heart as a small ache that I could not name.

But then he disengaged, rolling away and rising from the bed. His manhood was no less pronounced that it had been the night before, but he made no move to cover himself. I wondered what it must be like to walk around like that all day. Was it painful? Distracting? He seemed to take little notice of it as he retrieved something from an open trunk. He'd yet to unpack all his belongings. It was just one of the many jobs to do.

He returned to the bed, holding a small leather bundle. "I've made something for you," he said. "I want you to keep this with you at all times."

"What is it?" I asked, sitting up.

"A knife," he said, holding it up. It was a miniature of his large bone-handled knife, with its own fitted holster and small belt. Its blade caught a flicker of light. "I've sharpened it well. It will inflict a fatal wound if used correctly. I'm going to strap it to your leg, where it's hidden from view. No one will know you're armed. Yet you have protection, if you happen to need it."

Kade strapped the small belt to my thigh just above my knee, cinching it and placing the knife securely in its pouch.

It felt strange to be naked like this, with him, my only adornment a small yet lethal weapon. Yet I didn't feel uncomfortable. Already, I was adjusting to this closeness, this familiarity. Because I had been given time to get used to him, and because I knew that he would allow me all my hesitations and respect my limits, he'd effectively banished my reservations. I felt no residual fear. His presence offered me only comfort now, and promise. And I felt touched that my husband had prepared this for me. He'd been thinking of me.

Kade leaned over me, and a tiny surge of excitement pricked my intimate places. He withdrew the knife from its small scabbard. He held its sharpened blade in his closed fist and I almost reminded him to be careful. But it occurred to me, of course, who I was speaking to. He hardly needed reminding of such things. Reaching for my hand, Kade placed the handle of the knife in my grasp, wrapping his own hand around mine. The knife's glinty tip was pointed at him and he placed it against the skin of his side, above his hip and below his ribs.

"Here," he said. "If you are ever threatened in this way, this is where you strike. Gouge deep—and put some effort into it. Muscle is more resilient that you might expect. Up and in. Twist and slice. Like this." He twisted the knife in our collective grasp to show me the motion. "All right? Show me."

He let go of my hand, watching me. I mimicked the movement he'd shown me, twisting, gritting my teeth, giving him what I hoped was a look of ferocious menace.

He smiled widely, flashing white teeth. Then he laughed. I thought it strange that I would feel his laughter in my deepest depths, feeding the small excitement that lurked there at the sight of his blatant, rampant desire.

"That's good," he said, "although you need to concentrate more on your technique than your scowl. Like this," he said, holding my hand and jerking the knife in a more forceful thrust as he twisted it in one fluid motion.

He was more satisfied by my second demonstration, and he rose from the bed as he watched me. "Keep practicing when no one's about." He pulled on his trews, tucking his massive manhood into place with some difficulty before fastening the ties.

"Husband," I said, and I couldn't hide the shyness in my voice, even though, by now, I had little cause for it. "Would you like me to—"

His heated gaze speared me with its intensity, and I paused, not entirely sure how I would articulate my offer. "Aye, wife. I would. But that will have to wait until later. I'm needed below."

"But your—"

"I've been walking around like this since the moment I laid eyes on you, lass. The daily swims, alas, have little effect. I'll be glad when this month is over," he said wryly. Then he pulled his tunic over his head, slid on his boots and secured the three weapons belts he always wore, plus an extra one. "And you'll be well occupied."

CHAPTER ELEVEN

OVER THE NEXT WEEK, Kade kept to his grueling schedule of hunting, working, leading and planning. By the end of the second week he was able to recruit as many as forty-seven men, whom he organized into ten separate hunting parties. Meat was distributed, the choicest cuts going to the men who made the best kills. At least half of each beast was used for drying and salting, to sustain our clan during the winter months. The butcher was a man of importance and would be newly recognized as such. The head gardeners had been relieved of their duties and replaced by younger, keener understudies, led by the Mackenzie gardeners who had come to train them. The Morrison clan, according to Kade, was ridiculously uneducated in the ways of agriculture; our methods were archaic, our equipment lacking.

Late at night, Kade would record the days' events in detail into one of many leather-bound books he had brought with him in his travel trunks. He sent correspondence to both his brothers every third day, letters that were dispatched by messenger—with generous bribes for quick delivery. I wasn't invited to see his writings—aside from the letter I had read while he slept—but I was occasionally given brief informational snippets when I asked him about a particular detail of his work.

Progress, he said, was slow. A growing number of clansmen were warming to his methods, aye, but the majority preferred the lax, hedonistic traditions instilled in the men by my father and encouraged by Aleck.

Kade returned late to our chambers, usually in a state of exhaustion, dirty and with his weapons stained with blood from one or more duels he had either been challenged to or instigated—these, he would not discuss. He took a swim in the loch behind the manor each day, either in the early morning or late at night; it was a ritual that had been instilled in him by his father, he said, before his memories even began. He seemed pleased that the back entrance easily accessible from our new chambers led directly to the loch's edge, and even commented that our loch had cool, clear water and a small beach that was unusually sandy. The comment stuck with me since it was the only one I could recall that was even remotely positive about Glenlochie. He spoke of his beloved Kinloch often, and any comparison between the two keeps—and the two clans—was always heavily in favor of all things Mackenzie.

During the days, while Kade was busy hunting, swimming, dueling and training, I began to tackle managing the refurbishments of the manor. The staff, true to their word, carried out all instructions I gave them, with only the occasional grumble. Kade's very first order of business each morning was to reward any staff member I happened to praise. He asked me to write down the names each day of those who excelled. He gave these workers meat, most of all, but also promised newly cured furs to those who were able to sustain their newfound work ethic. After a week of this routine, the kitchen workers were all but falling over themselves when I made my appearance each morning, awaiting my instructions and dutifully launching into their tasks.

And so, with much work to be done, my husband and I did not revisit the brief, private moments we had so far shared. For this, I felt both a mild sense of relief and a somewhat more pronounced disappointment. With all the stress of his situation, he had, at times, returned to the hardened warrior I had first seen him as. But now I knew better. Instead of recoiling from him in fear, I was drawn to him. I thought often of the dizzyingly pleasurable effects of his hands…and his mouth. I remembered his astonishing responses to *my* touch, the scalding intimacy. But Kade was resolute about keeping his vow to me, seeing his oath as the foundation of trust he was determined to uphold. He knew of my past, that I had been forced into complying with the commands of men under threat and abuse. *I will secure your trust if it kills me,* he'd said to me. *I am nothing like them.*

That the vow was difficult for him was obvious and it occurred to me that he kept this somewhat cold distance between us to ensure his own restraint. I didn't know if he was avoiding me intentionally or if he was merely immersing himself in the work that needed doing. Either way, we did not see much of each other for days on end. Secretly, I counted the hours until our month-long sentence would come to an end.

Nine more days.

I hadn't even been aware of his late arrival in the night and his early predawn departure this morning. I knew he had been here, though, since the fire was lit. It was a detail he never overlooked. Fire, he said, was life. It was warmth, security, fuel, safety. And he would not have his wife getting cold.

So it was that I dressed by the pleasantly blazing flame, readying myself for my day. I heard a knock at the door, recognizing it instantly, since the knock was immediately followed by several more impatient knocks.

My sisters.

I hadn't seen them in more than a week, since Kade had moved us into our new wing and appointed me to oversee the staff. My sisters didn't often venture far from their quarters, and I knew they had been busy preparing for Clementine's journey to the convent. My lingering resentment over Maisie's betrayal, too, had kept me away. I had chosen to believe my husband's assurances. I steeled myself now, however, as she entered my chambers followed closely by Clementine, Lottie and Bonnie.

"Stella!" exclaimed Bonnie. "I have the most outstanding news. You won't believe it when you hear it."

"However did you convince Father to allow you to use Mother's private rooms?" interrupted Maisie. Her eyes were bright with the conflict between us. We both knew of her own treachery and all the sorrowful reasons behind it. Once I might have let the matter go, preferring to keep the peace at all costs to myself. But I had grown too attached to my husband to forgive her so easily now.

Bonnie came to me, studying my face as though she hadn't seen me for some time. "Stella. You look different. You look...more at ease. You look good."

At first I was unsure of her meaning. But then, I think I knew what she meant. I *felt* more at ease. I was no longer plagued by a feeling of uselessness and worthlessness. I was no longer afraid.

"I remember this room so clearly," commented Clementine wistfully as she walked around the chambers, stopping to gaze out the diamond-shaped window. "I remember sitting right here, where you're sitting, Stella. With her." Clementine was the only one of us who had distinct memories of our mother. The rest of us had been too young to remember anything beyond a ghostly, undefined image.

"Are you packed for the nunnery?" I asked her.

Bonnie answered for her. "Clementine will stay a little longer. Your husband has deemed it too dangerous to be transporting her at the moment. He thinks she should wait until Campbell's intentions are better understood."

I was glad of this news. I watched my older sister's face, reading there a relief, and always a compounding sadness that was now a pronounced part of her character. I smiled at her, and she managed to smile back. "I'm relieved, sister," I said. "I never thought you'd be particularly well suited to a nunnery."

Bonnie's hand brushed a strand of my hair behind one

shoulder as she abruptly changed the subject. "Stella, Caleb's back. Jamie told me. Now that you're married, he's no longer considered a threat to the alliance. Jamie said Campbell's men have been sighted prowling around the Highlands—in our near vicinity. 'Tis making everyone uneasy. And all Morrisons have been ordered to return to Glenlochie to bolster the forces, in case we have need of them. He arrived last night."

It was a lot of information to absorb.

Caleb.

With some shock, I realized I hadn't thought of Caleb in some time. Had I thought of him since we'd returned to Glenlochie after my wedding to Kade? I couldn't remember. Taking a moment to measure the time since I'd last seen him, I realized it had been six or seven weeks since his banishment. Now the memory of him, still sweet, was dulled somehow. Instead of gripping my heart as it had done in the days following his exile, the recollection of him brought only a mild twinge of affection, mingled now with a lurch of tumultuousness.

"Isn't it wonderful news, Stella?" Maisie said. "Now you can get what you truly want." Her pink-cheeked face beamed with the pronouncement.

Very nearly losing my temper right then and there, I summoned all my powers of control. I knew my sister very well. And I could read the earnestness in her eyes. She thought, in her heart of hearts, that I wanted nothing to do with Kade Mackenzie. That detail, in itself, was not enough to allow me to forgive her for offering herself to him. I knew how desperately in love with

Wilkie she had been, and still was. It was a love that
would never, ever be realized. He was not only married
but madly in love with his royal wife. It might have been
only natural that Kade would be the next best thing. A
substitute, aye, but still Wilkie's flesh and blood. Easily
accessible. As close to Wilkie as she would ever come,
now that he was sworn to another.

But Kade Mackenzie was *mine*. A wave of zealous
possessiveness undermined my self-control. "What I
want, Maisie, is for you to stay away from my husband," I said, and I had never heard my voice sound so
forceful and direct.

Maisie looked temporarily stricken, but she recovered quickly. She twirled a lock of her hair around one
finger. "Whatever do you mean, Stella?"

I stood, overcome by the image of Maisie, in all her
voluptuousness, revealing herself to my husband. "You
know what I mean! You offered yourself to Kade! How
could you do such a thing? He's not Wilkie, he's Kade!
My husband!"

"You never wanted him!" Maisie countered. "It was
me who was meant to marry a Mackenzie!" Maisie
broke down into impassioned tears. Bonnie went to
her, patting her head, smoothing her hair as she wept.
I felt little empathy for her. "You don't deserve him,"
Maisie blurted out weepily. "*You* can't give a man like
that what he truly wants."

"I didn't want him then, Maisie, but I want him now.
And you're wrong about that. In fact, I can give him
precisely what he wants." Beneath my anger and my

jealousy, I felt the twinge of a new insecurity. *Was* I giving him what he wanted? I thought of his ecstasy under my touch, his revelatory release, and I knew that I had *begun* to give him what he wanted. But there was so much more I could give, if he would only let me.

Maisie wiped at her tears. "But what of Caleb?" She was already feeling remorse for her uncaring outburst. "I was only trying to *help* you, Stella. I thought…if Kade strayed first, then you could be with your beloved Caleb, as you wanted from the start."

"Aye, Stella," urged Bonnie. "Do you still have feelings for Caleb?"

"I don't know," I answered truthfully.

"He wants to see you. Right now."

THE THOUGHT OF what I might say to Caleb, after all that had happened to me since we'd last been together, was unsettling. Two very distinct desires warred in my head. I thought of the fond memories: the soothing effect his presence had once afforded me, the gentleness of his approach, and how novel that had seemed to me at the time, after all the roughness I'd endured at the hands of men.

But much had passed since Caleb had been exiled. Much had changed. *I* had changed. I was a married woman now. Aside from the technicality of the marriage vows themselves, I now understood that I shared a very real and powerful connection with my new husband that only continued to intensify each time I saw him. Aye, Kade's aggression had initially stirred my deepest anxieties. But now, after nearly a month as his wife, I knew there was more to him than aggression. I knew there was compassion. I knew there were wildly appealing layers to his personality and his motivations that I had only barely begun to discover. And I *wanted* to discover them. I wanted to discover *him*. As sweet as my memories of Caleb were, I didn't want his reintroduction into my life to undermine this complex and intriguing quest.

Or did I?

It was this indecision that unnerved me most of all.

"I can't visit him now," I said. "I've work to do. My husband has appointed me in charge of the refurbishments of the manor."

My sisters—aside from Maisie, who already knew of my strange new pastime—stared at me in openmouthed surprise.

"And," I continued, ignoring their shock, "I'd like it very much if you would accompany me. You may choose any area of the keep that you'd like to assist with. You might find you enjoy it, as I have. 'Tis really rather rewarding to watch a room transform from one that's dirty and unkempt to one where you'd actually like to spend your time. There were some difficulties at first, but the staff is working well after my husband talked to them. The food is somewhat improved, although I still think we could do better. And I've a group of young girls I've recruited whose job it is to collect the wildflowers—there are some lovely ones this time of year."

I couldn't help noticing a change in Clementine's

expression. She seemed almost…excited. It was a look I hadn't seen on her face for some time. "Aye, Stella, we'll help you," she said. Then, quietly, as though she feared voicing the question aloud: "But what of Father? Won't he be angry with us for interfering?"

"My husband has promised his…protection." I hoped for a fleeting moment his sworn protection would extend to my sisters. But then, Kade was staunchly dedicated to his own family—his sisters included. I'd witnessed their close family ties firsthand, and I'd been amazed by their camaraderie. I felt entirely certain that Kade would step up if any threat was posed to my sisters. If I hadn't felt this certainty, I would never have suggested they come with me. As it was, they seemed surprisingly eager to help. Only Bonnie and Maisie bowed out, claiming that they had other matters to attend to. Lottie and Clementine followed me down the stairs.

And they were intrigued already, I could see, at the difference. The morning was cold and gray. Outside the windows, winter's promise hung in the cold wind and the steady drizzling rain. The hall, though, as we entered it, was warm and cozily lit, with the fire crackling in the grand stone fireplace. Candles ensconced into inlaid nooks of the stone walls flickered, casting a pleasant glow into the large space. A large bouquet of late-autumn flowers was placed in the middle of the largest table, giving the room an added measure of grandeur and sophistication. It was I who had gathered and arranged the flowers and I was pleased by the way their rich green and gold colors complemented the tapestries, which had been taken out of doors and beaten until all the many years of dust had blown away. Without the dust, the weaved images came to life, depicting scenes of hunts and landscapes. These tapestries had been weaved by my ancestors, my kin, and I was proud that they were being restored and newly appreciated. They gave a magical aura to the room, as though they presented windows into past glories and future possibilities.

And the hall itself was spotlessly clean. Cleaner, in fact, than I had ever seen it. I'd watched and helped in past days as the staff attended to their work with a renewed enthusiasm, but the overall effect, as I viewed it as though with the fresh eyes of my sisters, was quite remarkable.

"Stella," Clementine gasped. The scent of freshly baked bread wafted from the kitchens, and as we entered, all the workers looked up, pausing in their tasks to greet us. Isla seemed especially welcoming and rushed over to me.

"Milady," she said, "we've lit the fire early this morning, since the day is chilled."

"I noticed that, Isla. 'Tis so inviting. I'm going to mention to my husband what a pleasing job you've done."

She clasped her hands together at this pronouncement. "I thank you, milady. My grandson has already grown an inch, I swear it, since I've been feeding him the extra rations of meat your husband has given me. I've been promised a fur if my work pleases you. It would be so nice to have the extra warmth this winter."

"I'm going to tell him as soon as I see him, Isla," I assured her, "that I think you deserve two furs—one for you and one for your grandson."

Isla's face lit up. "Would you? Oh, I'd be so indebted." She seemed almost overcome with the possibility. "I don't know how to thank you. I truly don't."

"There's no need to thank me, Isla. You deserve all the rewards you're given. Your hard work of past days is obvious. This manor is slowly coming back to life. It is I—it is *we*," I said, gesturing to my sisters, "who are indebted to you."

Clementine stepped forward and weaved her arm through mine. "Aye," she agreed. "You've outdone yourself, Isla."

I was deeply touched by the extent of Isla's gratitude. It occurred to me that the workers of our clan had gone unrewarded for many years. It was no wonder they had become lax with their work habits if they'd never reaped the benefits of their labors. My husband's methods of leadership were indeed much more effective than those of my father.

"Would you like to see the menu we've planned for the noon meal, milady?" It was Jinty, one of the cooks, who spoke. "Your husband said he likes herbs with his carrots and fresh bread along with his meat, and butter for his bread and salt on the table. So we've been trying a few new dishes."

"I'm sure he'll be very pleased, Jinty," I said.

"We're a little behind this morning, alas," Jinty lamented, "although we've been up since before dawn.

One of the bakers—Mary—she's taken ill. Nothing serious, I hope, but we told her to stay abed until she's well. We don't want her passing on her illness to your husband, now, do we? We're just a little behind without the extra pair of hands, but we'll be sure to have everything ready by the time your husband returns to us at noontime. He said he's not hunting today, but working in the weapons sheds."

I had no knowledge of my husband's schedule for the day, but I was glad to hear that he was close by and that I might see him during the day. This knowledge, however, was prickled with the new information Bonnie had given me. Caleb was here, also close by. The thought of both my husband and my first love together, in the same keep—or in the same room—brought an uneasy glimmer to the light, which I made a point to ignore.

And I was distracted by my elder sister, who'd taken an unusually keen interest in the goings-on of the kitchen. "If you need help with the bread...I'd be happy to contribute," she said softly.

"I will, too," said Lottie.

Isla welcomed Clementine's help, and I recruited Lottie to help me set the tables in the hall.

"You know," said Clementine. "I've always—my whole life—wanted to learn to cook. I was hoping to ask for that assignment at the convent." After an uneasy pause, as though a thought had occurred to her, she said, "Are you sure that Father will allow this, Stella?"

"I'll handle Father," I said, experiencing a wash of courage that was entirely new to me. I was tired of being afraid of him, of hiding away from his misdirected, useless anger. There was work to be done that was not only highly beneficial for the well-being, success and prosperity of our clan, but also *enjoyable.* For the first time in my life, I felt a sense of purpose, and of strength. In fact, I was overcome by a strong yet inexplicable desire to not only clean up this keep but oust my own father from his reign altogether. My father's power had brought me endless misery—although I hadn't realized the extent of it until my husband had shone a light on all things remiss. Each and every discontentment of Kade's, since he'd arrived within our walls, had been astute and entirely accurate. Through my husband's perspective, I was able to see that the life I had led thus far was not easy, pampered or safe, as my father had always claimed to us. It was riddled with fear, abuse and isolation.

I wanted my husband's reign to start now.

I hadn't known Kade Mackenzie all that long—less than two months—but what I did know of him had enlightened me on every level. I thought of him now. His light eyes and the enticing grip of his strong warrior's hands. The shape of his mouth. His smile. *His wicked, wicked tongue.* As it always did when I was in his presence or remembering his reverberating effect on me, my skin grew warmer, my body stirred with a muted self-awareness that charged me with restless, undirected urgency.

My husband would protect me, if it came to that. With his assurances, I could follow through on the jobs that I needed to do, and that I *wanted* to do. And if

Kade wasn't able to shield me from the consequences of my own actions for one reason or another, well, so be it. I would fight for myself. I would take the hours as they came, and do my best to act honorably and for the greater good, as he did.

Lottie and I chatted idly as we straightened the settings for the tables and lit the many candles placed liberally around the room.

I stopped abruptly as I heard commotion. A number of people were entering the main doors of the manor. There were voices and footsteps.

It was Maisie, Bonnie and Jamie, dressed in his soldier's garb.

Jamie was followed by his brother. None other than the boy I had once cried for and yearned for above all others, who'd given me comfort when before I'd had none, and to whom I had first promised my heart and my hand.

CHAPTER TWELVE

I FROZE AS Caleb approached me, standing only feet from where I stood.

It had been almost two months since I'd seen him, but the change in him was dramatic. He'd lost weight, and his worn clothing hung from his thin frame. His brown eyes were shadowed by the hardship of past weeks, and his fair hair was long and unclean. The trials of his banishment were written across his disheveled appearance. His had been an arduous journey, I could see. And the worry in his eyes brought tears to mine. He knew of my marriage, of course. My unwillingness, my fear. My attempts to flee. I was sure Jamie had been given the full, descriptive version of the story by Bonnie, and that Caleb himself had likely been spared no detail of it. And I could see in his expression that he was, even now, imagining every brutal aspect of my forced marriage bed. I watched the thoughts ripple across his face with transparent emotion, and I could see that the light in his eyes had changed, almost imperceptibly, yet the change was unmistakable. As I had changed, so had he. He had endured much: this was clear and made me wonder what kind of punishment my father had, in fact, subjected him to, beyond merely banishing him to a warm, dry stable somewhere in the heart of Edinburgh, as I had visualized his exile.

He reached for my hand and held my fingers lightly in his own.

The contact felt foreign and strange. There was a distance there. I now belonged to another man. The sweetness of our youth and innocence had taken a turn, and there was a guarded air between us.

"Stella," he said, stepping closer and reaching to touch his cool fingers to the flushed skin of my cheek. "You look lovelier than ever. Are you well?"

The question was cautious, hinting at deeper curiosities. *How badly did he hurt you? Was it a ravishing that has hardened your heart? Do you still love me as you once did?* These and other questions seemed to drift like weaving threads of mist through the air around us.

Once, when Caleb had touched me, the light brush of his fingers had delivered a soft, simple promise that had calmed me. Now the gentle caress felt hollow somehow. I had become accustomed to more immediate, vigorous reactions at a man's touch: a roaring, febrile flame as opposed to this, a wispy, endangered ember.

Before I could speak to him, the very subject of his unspoken thoughts strode into the room. Stunned and speechless as I was, my attention might have been too absorbed to take much notice. But the presence was too large, too glinted with light.

My husband.

Keenly observant at all times, Kade's stormy eyes took in every detail of Caleb's proximity to me with hawklike acuity, and watched with dark alertness as Caleb abruptly removed his touch from my face and my fingers. Kade walked to where we stood, and began to circle us, his gaze taking in Caleb's unthreatening, ragged appearance.

It was impossible not to compare the two of them, given the situation. Caleb was in every way a less imposing figure. He was as boyishly handsome as I remembered him, although his sandy-brown hair had lost its sunny vibrancy, dirty and unkempt as it was. His face looked thinner, his already lean body even more angular beneath his rough-hewn tunic that was threadbare and patched. Caleb's fingers, as I had always known them, were still stained with the charcoal of his work.

And if Caleb was earthy and subdued in appearance, Kade, in contrast, was blindingly...*shiny,* as always. His hair had a sheen to it that was noticeable, and might have been a result of his almost-ritualistic daily swims in the loch. Kade's shoulders were brown and gleaming with strength. The rich leather of his sparring vest and trews clung to him like a second skin. His weaponry glittered with his movement, and the effect was somehow festive even in its warning. And his pale predator's eyes were narrowed with his discovery yet illuminated with the layered emotions of his character that I was beginning to learn. Resilience. Charisma. Power. And, if I wasn't mistaken, searing jealousy.

What surprised me about my own reaction to the very different spectacles of Caleb and Kade was that the solace I used to find in Caleb's company was much less pronounced than it once was. My body had grown warm and aware, aye. My skin was heated and tingly. The secret place between my thighs felt sultry and warm. I was responding, not to Caleb, who I had once found so soothing. Nay, I was *responding,* I realized, to the close proximity of my protective warrior husband, whose fierceness—so frightening to me once—was arousing me beyond belief. I tried to quell the thoughts, but my mind seemed intent on remembering, in some detail, the intensity of pleasure forced upon me by the clever suction of his mouth, pulling, feasting with relentless intention. The methodical thrust of his tongue. The clenching, succulent rapture. I felt almost faint with longing as I watched the razor-sharp blades of my husband's knives catch shards of sunlight, throwing the silver-cast reflections around the room in an iridescent display. The boundaries between safety and danger were distorted. I wondered at my own reaction even as my nipples beaded and the low ache of my most delicate places began to throb with a fervent, ripening desire.

"It does not surprise me," said Kade evenly, without slowing his measured, stalking movements, "that my wife attracts the attention of other men." His tone was calm and direct, laced with a distilled fury that raised the tiny hairs on the back of my neck—and inspired a light quiver in my moistening core. And there was more to Kade's manner than anger; he looked to be genuinely interested in the details of this encounter. I had little doubt that Kade knew of my former youthful attraction to the man he was now on the verge of attacking.

Caleb's banishment and the reason behind it had become somewhat of a discussion point among our clan's people. News of that kind had a way of traveling, and would likely have reached Kade at some point between Caleb's exile and this moment. Kade had probably heard of it before our marriage had even taken place. And now Kade, seeing the object of his wife's onetime affection, appeared vaguely bemused by the sight of him.

"What does surprise me, however," Kade continued, "is that *this,* by all accounts, is my most fearsome competitor for her affections." He was studying Caleb, and it was a scrutiny that was clearly making Caleb wildly uncomfortable. Caleb stared at my husband—and his myriad of gleaming armaments—with a mixture of awe, terror and evident resolve: whatever my husband decided to do about Caleb's mild advances would go uncontested. It was glaringly obvious to all that Kade outmatched Caleb in combative skill by a measure of at least ten to one. My sisters whispered in a huddled group from the periphery, unnerved by the prospect of watching Caleb gutted. As was I.

"I'd challenge you to a duel," my husband said, "but you don't appear to be carrying a weapon." Kade's expression was sardonic, disbelieving. He half smiled, as though he found Caleb's omission not only foolish but entertaining.

When Caleb did not reply to Kade's observation, my husband continued. "I'd offer to lend you one of *my* weapons, but I fear that if you chose to accept a call to arms, your death would come so swiftly and so easily that it would greatly upset my wife. And I can't have my wife upset with me, now, can I? It never pays to upset one's *wife,* so I've heard." He repeated my title with emphasis, as though to reiterate the justification behind his barely corralled wrath.

Still, Caleb remained silent, watching Kade's feet as he circled us.

"What say you, man?" Kade asked pointedly. "What are you doing touching my wife *in any way whatsoever?*" Kade's words were dripping with murderous ire. "You are asking to be challenged, are you not? You've started something, aye, and so you must be prepared to finish it." And then, with a quiet menace that renewed all my original fears of him, even if those fears were inlaid with confounding desire, Kade leaned close to Caleb and said, "Are you imagining that my wife might have lingering feelings for you, even though she is now married?"

"That would be a question for your wife, I imagine," Caleb said, finally meeting Kade's hostile gaze. I could see Caleb was working to keep the panic from showing in his voice and in his manner.

Kade paused for a brief moment, spearing Caleb with a glare so intent that any inkling of courage Caleb might have summoned withered instantly. Kade surprised me then as he appeared to take Caleb's reply to heart. "A very good point," Kade said, turning to me. "Wife," he began, his feral eyes wandering my face, lingering on my parted lips.

Then, in a quick, soldier's movement, he stepped forward, clasping my wrist with brutal, unthinking force before immediately gentling his grasp and weaving his fingers through mine. He was watching my face as he pulled me along with him. I had no choice but to follow, even if I wanted to refuse. My head issued warnings, conjuring protests. But my body wanted nothing more than to obey his every command.

"If you'll excuse us," he said shortly, as though he cared not whether our audience was inclined to allow us our leave. "I have some urgent matters I need to discuss with my wife. Do not expect us until the morrow." Then, as a vicious afterthought, Kade turned to Caleb and uttered a frigid warning. "If you ever so much as brush up against my wife again, I will have no choice but to challenge you on the spot. And I'm not inclined to show even the remotest hint of either mercy or remorse when it comes to matters concerning my wife. Either stay away from her, or be prepared to defend your actions. Consider yourself duly warned."

With that, Kade turned to go, leading me, not unwillingly, along with him.

A sharp stab of anxiety entwined with pure, primal excitement speared me. The seething emotion behind my husband's outrageous, barely contained strength made me wonder what he intended to *do* with me. Would he punish me? Would his rage be enough to see him breaking his vow? The thought brought a flare of heat to my nether regions that caused me to gasp lightly. My sisters and Caleb seemed to interpret the sound I made as one of distress. Their faces showed concern, and pity. There was nothing they could do to stop Kade, or to protect me. I was his. As it was, my husband barely gave them a backward glance as he hauled me through the door, down the corridor, and up the staircase to our private chambers.

CHAPTER THIRTEEN

WE'D BARELY ENTERED the bedchambers, the door decisively slammed—and locked—behind us, before the tirade began. Any control my husband had mastered in the public eye vanished as soon as we were alone.

"That—?" He was so upset he could barely get the words out, and it was the first time I'd seen him so utterly ruffled. "That *boy* is the one you pined for all this time? That mess of inadequacy is the object of your burning desire? The one who you cried for and dreamed about, even so recently as three nights ago? *That—?"*

"What do you mean?" I said. I didn't recall my recent dreams. And I hadn't pined for Caleb in...well, in some time.

"You talk in your sleep, wife. You say his name." He glared at me, wounded accusation in his sky-hued eyes; it looked strange there, the youthful admonishment contrasting with his seasoned hardness.

"I don't," I said, perturbed by this information.

"What do you mean 'I don't'? You *do!* I *hear* you! I'm here with you, as you sleep, am I not? You say his name. I've heard it. Several times."

"'Tis just dreams," I whispered. "I can't remember them. I can't control that."

"Nay, you can't control the deepest desires of your heart. Is *that* what this is? Is it *him* you think of?" He was pacing now, highly agitated. He ran his hand through his hair, grabbing it in a fistful. "I'd heard of your broken heart before we wed, aye. Some stable boy who'd been banished to Edinburgh. I'd heard the story of you father's refusal, your sorrow—all of it. I chose to treat it as the gossip I thought it to be."

My husband approached me, frustration radiating from his big, battle-sculpted body. His hair was in disarray and his strength a visceral presence. But I didn't flinch back from him. I knew by now that he wouldn't hurt me. Over time, as this realization had taken hold, my body seemed to have adjusted to the knowledge with odd effect. As though the little reservoirs where the fear had once lurked were now simmering with understanding. With heat and passion. With soft-edged lust.

Kade stood before me, ferocious and immense, his weapons, his fury and his musculature displayed in full. His intensity only succeeded in stirring my smoldering arousal further. Within the glaring aura of his raging masculinity, I felt more feminine than I ever had. I felt receptive, as though the purpose of my humanness resided here, in this room, with him.

"I haven't thought of him in some time," I said honestly. I wanted to reassure him and, most of all, to calm him down.

"Well, you *dream* of him. Is that not *worse?*"

I realized then that something had changed between us. We were discussing this jealousy as though it was something real to discuss. My husband was, quite obviously, well... *jealous*. Wickedly so. It wasn't just an animal jealousy, either, although that was part of it: a possessive male protecting his own territory. There was more to it than that. There was emotion to this envy that surprised me with its vehemence, and with its complexity.

"I told your stable boy I would challenge him to a fight to the death if he ever touched you again," he said. "And I meant it."

"Aye," I commented. "I heard you."

He strode over to one of his half-emptied trunks, riffling through it until he found what he was looking for. I couldn't see what he held behind his back as he returned to me, the menace of him glimmering in the firelight. "I have other ideas for *you*."

Kade stood close to me, his eyes uncharacteristically dark. "You deserve...a lesson, let's call it. You can ask me for mercy at any time, of course, and I will do my best to honor your request. I have, however, been pushed past my boundaries. You should know this about me—I do not take vows lightly, and I expect you to uphold yours. I happen to be *very* protective of what is mine. You, whether you like it or not, happen to be just that. *Mine*. My *wife*. And I will not tolerate infidelity."

It was true that my body was already responding to his potent virility; I couldn't seem to stop my own deep-seated primal urges whenever my husband so much as entered the room. But I didn't like the sound of his barely concealed threat. Already, I could feel my defiance rising. "I haven't been unfaithful to you. His fingers barely touched mine. I didn't even speak to him."

"I don't care if you spoke to him or not!" he said savagely, startling me with his loud outburst. "I will not tolerate *thoughts* of infidelity!" I almost smiled at this, gently; but I didn't dare, in case he misinterpreted the reason behind it. His emotion touched me and endeared him to me with potent effect. He seemed genuinely hurt by the fact that I called out to Caleb in my sleep. I wanted to explain to him that my dreams were convoluted. Caleb was in them, aye, but so was *he*. My dream lover, my garden phantom. My husband, one and the same.

He paused then, his brow furrowed, his shoulders hunched slightly as if he was expecting a blow. "Do you love him?" he asked quietly.

"I—" Kade's darkened eyes were searching for honesty. I decided to give it to him. "I thought I did, once. Yet it never felt like something that was meant to be. We were doomed from the start."

"We're all doomed from the start," he replied.

"I felt safe with him," I admitted, ignoring his morbid comment. "He was the only man I'd ever met who didn't frighten me."

He snorted lightly at this. "Nay, he is perhaps the least frightening specimen of mankind I've yet to come across." Despite his scoffing, my admission cooled his rage by a single degree. "I understand, with your history, why you might have chosen someone so mild, Stella, but surely by now you realize you have no need for such preferences."

I touched his bare arm, looking up at him. "Husband," I said, "do you hear me call to *you* in my sleep, as well? Have you heard *that* part of my dreams? Because you're in them, too. Those are the ones I remember. I had all but forgotten Caleb."

I had meant to appease him, but my words seemed to have the opposite effect. Any reference to Caleb in my dreams or otherwise was *too* much reference of Caleb; this was clearly written on my husband's face. "*All but* forgotten?" he said, running his hand through his hair, making his appearance all the wilder. "I am going to give you reason now to forget him entirely, wife, once and for all. I will keep my word to you, you need not worry yourself about that. But I'm afraid I'm going to have to make it very clear to you that I expect everything of you."

Without meaning to, I took a small step back from him. But he would have none of it. He snaked his arm around my waist and pulled me roughly to him, so I was arched up against him, my breasts lifted against his chest. I could feel the many hard edges of him, uncomfortably, and I made a small sound of protest. Yet I had never been more hopeful, more receptive or more turned on in all my life.

"Is this dress one of your favorites?" he asked, and the question caught me off guard; it seemed wildly off-topic. He disengaged his hold on me, fingering the front buttons of my gown with both hands.

"N-not especially—"

My husband ripped my gown and my shift open in

one swift yank. My full breasts bounced free of the constraints. I huffed in surprise. "What are you—?"

"I want you completely naked before me. Take off your clothing." He observed my face, challenging me with the garish jewel-like glint of his turquoise eyes and his white teeth, exposed in a half snarl. "No fear," he said. "I'll not hurt you, and you know it."

Did I know it? I contemplated the smoldering vulnerability of him. He looked bigger and more powerfully built than I had ever seen him, carnal and determined in the fire-flicked night. And here I was, half-naked, quivering from the cool air and my feverish responses.

And I decided that I *did* trust him. Not only that, but I *wanted* him. I didn't want to protest whatever it was he was about to do. I wanted to find out exactly what unspeakable things he was capable of. Aroused and with defiant flair—I wanted to show him that it was *me* that was inviting *him* as much as he was making whatever point he had in mind—I did as he commanded, lowering the gown from my shoulders to drop to the ground, and stepping out of my shoes.

He circled me, letting his fingers trail across my skin in an unhurried claim. His hands brushed the taut surface of my nipples, playing lightly. Then his touch feathered down my stomach. He circled me again, lazily tracing the swell of my hips, and lower, delving gently between my legs, where his fingers slid silkily across the dampness. He leaned close to me, supporting some of my weight as I swayed. "You want me," he purred into my ear.

I said nothing, forcing my own silence and unable to do so under the glide of his nudging fingertips. A small moan escaped me.

"Say it to me."

"Aye," I murmured, barely audibly, but he smiled.

"Say it," he growled, pushing his fingers farther into me, stretching the unyielding tightness, finding the sensitive trigger he had already memorized.

"I want you," I gasped unsteadily as the heat of his inspiration darkened and flared within me.

Smugly satisfied by my admission, he withdrew his touch. In a deliberate, contemplative movement, he held his fingers up. I was mortified to see that they were glistening with the effects of my own desire. Watching my eyes, he slowly licked his fingers. "Sweet, sweet Stella," he said.

I was throbbing from my knees to my navel, wondering if I might crumple to the floor.

He surprised me by kneeling down on one knee before me. He looked up at me with an expression of assurance: he would allow me my hesitations, as always, but he would get his way. The humor in him lurked in his eyes, a detail that only succeeded in exciting me and also vexing me further. "Do you trust me?"

"Aye," I whispered. I found that I did. Mostly.

"Good. Surrender to me. 'Tis, in fact, your only option."

Kade placed his hands on me, curling his fingers around my thighs in a gentle yet bold clasp. Then he leaned his head closer, kissing between my thighs, where I was saturated with devastating lust. His teasing mouth kissed lightly, erotically restrained, touching me only once with the slow, carefully placed glide of his tongue.

But then he rose, keeping his hands secure on my body, and he lifted me into his arms in one easy movement. He carried me to the bed, settling me gently upon it. He sat next to me.

"I'm going to blindfold you, lass," he informed me, pulling a length of white fabric from a pocket; it must have been what he retrieved from his trunk. "It will add a certain…*mystique* to the proceedings, don't you agree?"

"Why?" I said, my voice sounding undisguisedly flustered. I no longer feared him, yet the beastly streak in him had risen. My husband's restraint had been tested, his dominating masculinity bruised by a weak, timid interloper—an affront that had riled him to his depths.

"'Tis best if you're kept in the dark, so to speak, at least for now."

"I don't want you to blindfold me. Let me see."

He held up the white cloth, turning it in his hands to fold it into a thick, opaque strip. Holding it at eye level between his fists.

"Nay," I said, reaching to hold the center of the cloth as he held it. "There's no need."

"And *I*," came his low reply, "said *aye*." His words were disconcerting, but his smile calmed me, and when he bared his clenched teeth with a playful growl, I almost laughed.

I could handle whatever he gave to me, I told myself, not entirely convinced of my own hopeful strength even as I steeled the turmoil raging within me. I could handle him, but I wanted to *see* him.

He made a move to affix the blindfold, but I fought against him, climbing on top of him, straddling his hips. I knew there was no way he would allow me to escape him. So I drew closer to him instead of farther away. He held my wrists tightly in his hands, lifting us, laying me back on the furs. He was so much stronger, his manipulations seemed entirely effortless.

"Stop fighting me, wife. You can't win. I'm going to blindfold you, and then I'm going to take you over my knee. For allowing yourself to be touched by another man, no matter how innocent the exchange may have been. I will simply not allow it." Reading the anxiety in my eyes, he said again, "Trust me. I'm not going to beat you, lass. This is a small, inviting pain that only makes the pleasure more intense. I daresay you'll offer no protests once I begin, little wife."

His intentions were to blind me and punish me and control me entirely. And I wanted all of it even as I wanted to lash out at him, to somehow even the imbalance. "You...you *big man!*" I yelled at him.

He did not immediately react. But then his mouth quirked into a slow smile. For a moment, he lost all trace of his warrior's mask. His tough, bold, impenetrable demeanor was temporarily lost, allowing his youth and his beauty to shine through. When the touch of happiness lit his features, he was shockingly, devastatingly handsome. *If only he would smile more,* I thought. Then he began to laugh. It was a real laugh, and I realized I loved the sound of it. "'Big man'?" he said. "Is that the best you can do?"

I contemplated him shyly, somewhat overcome by this new side to him: this beautiful, exuberant side that stole my breath. His laughter was infectious, and I smiled along with him. But then I remembered that I was trapped underneath him, naked, powerless and furious.

"I'll have to teach you some slightly more colorful language, lass. You're too pure for your own good. That, of course, is an issue I plan to remedy once I've made good on my oath."

I was becoming accustomed to his gentle, lurid taunts, laced as they were with the special breed of humor my husband had claimed as his own. "What is it you would *prefer* I called you in the heat of anger?" I asked him sulkily.

He laughed again, and the sound of it fed me a hazy warmth, as if a stray ray of summer sunshine had stolen its way into our chambers. I felt comforted by his laughter in a way that was unfamiliar to me, even as I lay naked underneath him in all his war garb and glory. "Good God," he mused. "*That's* the heat of your anger? We'll have to work on that, too. I'll have to be more clever, and think of a way to really get your sparks flying. A few ideas are coming to me even now." He paused momentarily, as though overwhelmed by anticipation. He brushed the back of his fingers along my cheekbone. "My beautiful, feisty, tantalizing wife."

His eyes held mine at the weighty clarity of the phrase and the affectionate tones of its delivery. *My wife.*

"Tell me what words you *really* use to describe me when you think of me," he said, sitting up slightly to remove one of his weapons belts. And another. His eyes never left my body.

I watched him as he placed his arsenal to the side. "Nay," I said. "I wouldn't want to offend you."

He pulled off his tunic, revealing his carved muscles, his sun-burnished skin. Without his weapons, he was free to lay his warm body more heavily over mine without danger of injury. The long strands of his hair fell in a soft curtain to frame our faces. Even as he held his weight with his arms, I felt unequivocally dominated. With him, I could admit, the feeling wasn't at all unpleasant. "Tell me," he rasped in a lightly menacing tone.

"I'm not afraid of you, husband," I said, attempting a different strategy. "Your scare tactics no longer work on me. Bind me and blind me, but I've seen your softer side." I closed my eyes to him, hoping to annoy him with my indifference.

"I have no softer side."

"Aye," I said, opening my eyes. The vivid hue of his eyes disarmed me momentarily with their vibrancy. He looked almost offended by my comment. "You do."

"Where?"

"Certainly not on the outside," I said. I was irritated to feel a small smile pull at the corner of my lips, which I made a point to banish. It wouldn't do to let him know how easy it was for him to get past my defenses without even intending to.

"Nay," he agreed. "If I get any harder, we're both in for a bit of trouble."

"'Tis inside you." I was disconcerted to find that I wasn't just teasing him now, or testing him. I found that I meant what I said. "In your heart."

A sweet-edged silence comforted us and linked us as never before.

It was a few moments before he spoke again. The connective thoughtfulness in his eyes gave way once again to his mischief-laced power. "Tell me," he repeated.

I paused, waiting. His body was stunningly solid, and heavy. His arousal pressed against a very sensitive place. "Brute," I whispered.

He smiled, biting not so gently on the lobe of my ear, kissing a line down my neck, licking and nipping at my skin. "That one might not be entirely unwarranted, at times."

"Ogre." I could feel his light laughter everywhere. His hands were on my breasts.

"Truly? *Ogre?*" he said, looking up at me with mock offense. His gaze returned to my breasts, which he kissed and fondled with something akin to wonder. Then he took a nipple into his mouth, sucking strongly and biting with his teeth as he pinched my other nipple between two fingers, sending shards of reactive sensation to every inch of my body. "Tell me another."

"Savage," I whispered.

"I'm getting harder with each accusation," he said, lifting me into a sitting position, placing the blindfold over my eyes and tying it securely. This time I offered no protest. The sudden darkness was startling. I was adrift, yet my senses became highly attuned. To him, to his every breath and movement. "Let me see if I can prove you right," he whispered into my ear. "You will no longer distract me from the task at hand, even if you do happen to be outlandishly, achingly, mind-numbingly lovely to such an extent that I am, right at this moment, questioning my powers of resistance. With still eight days and fourteen hours left to go of my idiotic self-induced sentence. Already you possess my whole heart, wife. All that you are is exactly what I didn't even realize I needed. I can see now that you want to trust me, and you're beginning to. I will keep my vow, as I said I would. But I can assure you that doing so is not without intense, *ravaging* difficulty."

He reached for something, then pushed me across his lap so that I lay on my stomach across him. His hands were strong, guiding me, and I didn't protest, but I was not as agreeable as I could have been.

"Do not fear my punishment, lass. You're going to enjoy this."

He positioned me with care, lifting my hips until I was on my knees with my head down, laid against the softness of the furs. Not satisfied, he continued to adjust my body, until my knees were farther apart. With one hand, he began to caress my back, trailing ever lower. Exploring intimately, he reached between my legs, parting my humid petals, dipping and wetting me with my own desire. With his fingers he squeezed my aching flesh gently, tantalizing the sweetness. As he continued to play me, a soft material was dragged across the skin of my backside.

"What is it?" I asked, trying to turn to him, but he held me in place. My voice sounded muffled and husky.

"A leather strap," he said, lashing the strap very lightly against me, not enough to hurt—just a light promise of what was to come.

The leather was drawn lower, across my raised buttocks, to fall between my legs, where it brushed against my saturated core, which was so sensitive that the light contact caused me to squirm. I felt a slight slap on my backside. Not a sting, but a caress that warmed me at the place of impact, and deeper. Again, the leather fell with gentle force, spreading the heat, igniting the center of my body with an exquisite, scorching glow. Again. The fluid ecstasy built within me. He lashed me again, at the same time pushing his fingers gently into the tight constriction of my body. This time the lash *did* sting— a sharp, painful shock that caused me to gasp. The lash licked me with pain, but it was a pain laced with burning, needy pleasure. I thought I might overflow with it. As soon as the leather left my skin, the pain eased to a radiating warmth, funneling strongly to the place where Kade caressed me with his fingers.

The lash fell again, lower this time, closer to the billowing ache that flared with the echo of his strikes. I was breathless, on the verge of begging him to show me mercy. But the pain had turned, mellowing into a deep, luscious craving. His fingers worked that pleasure, enticing it and energizing it.

"You have no need to favor weakness or mildness any longer, lass. You're stronger than that, and you're free now to follow your fiery instincts. To me, and with me. I'm yours and you're mine, do not forget that. I vowed to give you this time to adjust to me, yet you are still mine to do with what I please."

He paused, as though waiting for my answer, but I was blind and mute, it seemed. I was too strung-out, waiting for his whip.

"What say you, wife? Do you want me to do with you what I please?" He struck again, lower across my skin.

"Aye," I cried out, stunned by the blaze of sensation. The glowing burn in the core of my body was feverishly intense, stroked by his fingers and stoked by the sharp sparks of his indulgent punishment. I was moaning—profanities, no less. "Oh, Holy God," I was saying. "Oh, *please.*"

"I *chose* you, Stella. You're mine. *Mine.* Do you understand me?"

The delicious contact of the lash struck again.

"Aye."

And again. The soft pain leached instantly to ecstatic, greedy sweetfire. My body felt alight with the promise of a rapture so extreme I could only lift my hips higher, pushing against his hand, pleading and squirming with need.

"Please, husband," I begged him, and again.

"You *like* your punishment? Or do you beg me to stop?" Again, sharper. The sting funneled instantly to the glow, feeding it, expounding it.

"Nay," I moaned. *"Don't stop. Please don't stop."*

I waited for the sting of pleasure-pain, but he would not give it to me. "Who is it you will think of *now?*" he said. "Who will haunt your dreams, wife, and invade your fantasies? Who?"

"You, husband. Only you."

The lash found its mark fiercely.

Oh, God. There it was. I was on the precipice. The punishment had become the reward.

"You think that *boy* could satisfy you? Think again. You need a man who can fulfill your voracious womanly appetites. Like *this,*" he growled, smacking the whip against the swollen, aching, delicate place where the entirety of my being was centered.

The flare of pain and pleasure consumed me. I lost hold of myself completely, riding the euphoria in an utter haze of bliss, so immersed in the clenching spasms deep within my body that I was aware of nothing else for quite some time. My body bucked gently, my moans undulated along with the waves, my hands gripped fistfuls of the fur blankets. And my husband's hands teased the pleasure further, relentless and so thorough I wanted to hold them, and him, against me, and in me, forevermore.

It occurred to me, with wonder, that this was only

the beginning. We hadn't even fully consummated this marriage. I felt a mild sense of alarm and of awe, somewhere outside the periphery of my clouded, entranced mind. How could it get even *more* intense?

And now his hands were rearranging my supple, supine limbs, turning me and laying me back against the pillows. I wondered for a moment if I had indeed lost consciousness. Why was it so dark? Then I remembered that I was blindfolded.

"I'm going to tie your wrists now," he said.

He took one of my wrists and lifted it to the bedpost, securing it with what felt like a thick silk tie. My reflexes were slowed in the aftermath of my release. I pulled against the restraint. *"Nay,"* I protested weakly. But my husband seemed not to have heard. My body was pinned under his and he was securing my other wrist just as tightly.

It was just as Lottie had warned! I was bound and trapped. As lust-infused and satiated as my body was, I fought against him. Aye, it would take several days for me to recover *already* from what he had done to me. I couldn't take any more. Yet *I wanted more,* as I'd never wanted anything in my life. The intensity of my release had left me dazed and muddled with conflicting urges. I felt replete yet perturbed and restless. My body echoed with starry decadence, the memory of it etched into every part of me. I knew if he touched me again the pleasure would only compound itself. Already I recognized the quiver, the building warmth. I wanted to *touch* him, fervently, to take out my passions and frustrations on him. Strangely, I wanted to bite him, to taste his skin and rub myself against him. *Now.*

My head lolled from side to side. I felt delirious with the aftereffects of my release and the need for more of his erotic expertise. *"Kade—"*

"Hush." The command was unconditional, without even the slightest hint of leniency. And now my ankles were being tied, one, then the other. My feeble struggles were entirely ineffective. Kade waited, not touching me. I tried to calm myself, listening. Where was he? What was he doing now? I couldn't bear to think of how I looked to him, laid out for his pleasure and his domination.

I felt his mouth softly kiss me *there* where I still pulsed with his forcefulness. He licked into me, reminding me, coaxing me. The sweet ache closed in, gathering, divine. But then he pulled away. "That was more for my own gratification than for yours," he said. "I've developed something of an addiction for my wife. But first things first."

I froze as the lightest, softest touch grazed the sole of my foot, tickling me, silencing me. The touch traced languidly, barely a touch at all. All concentration drew to that soft, gliding line as it slid over my ankle, up my calf.

"What is it?" I managed to ask. My voice sounded low and fevered.

"A feather."

It traveled farther, a fluid, sensual path along my

thigh, my hip, circling my navel, to my breast, eliciting sensation, teasing.

Such a light, delicate sensation, focusing upon and circling yet never touching the most intimate points of my body. As the line traced across my skin, its touch seemed to burn me, to brand me with a fiery, penetrating neediness.

Long, torturous moments of anticipation and desperation.

My body was on fire. I thought I might go up in flames, merely from the inspiration of this soft, enticing brush against my sensitive skin. But then the touch was removed. Quickly, without pause, the touch was replaced with a much more solid one. Still soft in texture but unyielding, no longer brushing but tapping.

"What's this?" My voice was sultry, frantic.

"A small whip with a triangular leather tip."

I heard myself cry out as the leather slapped against my nipple, causing a sharp bolt of sensation that shot straight to my center, scalding me with spiky pleasure.

"You thought your punishment was finished?" he said. "Not even close, wife. I'm exceptionally thorough, you should know. I want to ensure that you remember this lesson. So that you're not tempted toward further indiscretions."

I couldn't help myself. Even though I knew it would cost me. "It was hardly an indiscretion! I didn't move, or speak. 'Twas a greeting—of *his,* not mine—nothing more."

"A greeting," he scoffed, pausing for a moment to

circle my nipple with his whip. His mouth found the teased, sensitive peak, closing over it, suckling with surprising warmth considering the topic of conversation. I had a feeling that he was, once again, allowing himself a reprieve that had little to do with either my pleasure or my punishment. After a voracious minute, he disengaged, leaving me maddeningly enflamed. "Nevertheless, I insist that you remain faithful to me from this day forward. And so I must make this as memorable for you as possible. I have reason to believe it won't be memorable for the wrong reasons, however, but for the *right* ones. You can beg me to stop anytime you wish, of course."

I thought of begging him to stop, now, once and for all. I would. Soon. But the soft leather was brushing enticingly against my skin, weaving to my other breast, where the light tap was repeated, heightening the fever, jolting my senses, so I could feel the effects to my fingertips and toes. Again. And again. With each stroke, a rising ache swelled deep within my body, feeding the burn, melting it and stoking it with pleasurable fire.

Then the touch of the soft leather left me. I listened and waited. My breasts rose and fell with my anticipation. My heart thumped heavily in my chest.

"Tell me to stop and I will," he said, his voice raw not with ferocity but with heavy tenderness. "Tell me what you want."

"More," I whispered.

I heard his light chuckle. I wished I could see him.

After a moment, the whip touched my thigh, tracing

upward, circling in ever smaller circles, until it rubbed against my swollen petals, petting me and parting the intimate curls to expose me, tapping lightly. The core of my body began to pulse along to his deliberate, measured pace.

I wished my hands were free, so I could grab him and hold him. I was ravenous to taste him, to take any part of his body into any part of mine. *"Husband,"* I whispered hoarsely. "Come close to me. I need to tell you something."

He paused, as though considering whether to indulge my request. But then I heard movement. He leaned to me and I could feel the heavy placement of his hands on either side of me, and the brush of his hair on my face. He kissed my lips lightly yet with raw, openmouthed hunger; it was a kiss such as I had never experienced: wet, full of his dominance, laden with the promise of more to come. His kisses trailed across my cheek, to my ear. "What?" he whispered.

"Take me now," I said. "As your wife. Irrevocably. I don't want to wait another eight days and fourteen hours."

"Thirteen," he corrected. He bit my earlobe sharply, kissing my neck, moving lower, availing himself to my body freely. "You know I can't do that."

"I don't care about your vow. I want you to break it."

"Nay, lass, I can't. I don't break vows. And we haven't fully established whether or not you trust me unequivocally."

I knew it was irrational even as I said it, but I didn't

care. I was irate with my own deluge of feeling. There were too many emotions, too much sensation, too much need. "Your vows are *foolish!* I didn't ask for you daft vows! *I need you.* Please. *Please.* I want to feel you, husband. Let me touch you and hold you. Let me feel something of you. All of you. Anything. *Anything. Please.*"

"You want to *feel* me, wife?" he murmured, consumed by his own desperation, I could hear it in his voice. And then I felt him. Exactly where I wanted him. Not his hands or his mouth. The heavy, solid bulk of his manhood, pressing against me. The massive, satiny touch parted me but did not enter me. He held himself against me but did not give me the movement or the possession I begged for.

"Not yet, wife. You know you're being punished. You know you have to wait."

"Is that what this is? Part of my punishment? You punish me by withholding yourself from me?"

"Perhaps," he teased, but then his voice took on a more serious tone when he said, "I just want to prove myself to you. That I'm true to my word. That you never, ever have to fear me or doubt me."

At that precise moment, not only my body craved him with a desperation I had never known, but my heart seemed to swell with my desire to keep him and hold him close, forevermore, to love him and believe him. Aye, I would allow him to keep his word to me, as he had allowed me my hesitations.

But my body had other ideas.

When I began to writhe against him, he removed his

touch altogether. I almost wept from the sudden depriva-
tion. But he was rubbing himself against my stomach,
between my breasts. I was astounded by the joy this contact fed me. I wanted him to use my body in any way, in
every way. I could feel his own need and his aggression
in the gliding, thrusting assault. Timeless and sublime.
He was everywhere. His low groan was followed by the
warm beat of his seed raining across my tender petals,
my cool stomach, my swollen breasts.

The light touch was immediately replaced by a more
forceful one. The whip flicked at me in rhythmic bites,
piquing my flesh into an agony of ecstasy. Without
warning, it slapped against the bundle of nerves at the
very heart of me. The sensation was so overwhelming
I thought I might explode. It was too much. If he did it
again, I feared I might lose myself, step over some sort
of edge that I couldn't control or understand. But I had
to have it, I didn't care. My release simmered hotly, so
very close, daunting with its promised magnitude.

"Again. Now. Please," I pleaded, out of my mind.

"Patience, lass," came his devil-edged reply.

The swell began even before the whip touched me. I
knew it was coming and my body responded, blooming
and rising, so that when the strike hit me in that most
sensitive, ready place, it fed an overwhelming torrent
of pleasure. Another tap and I was lost, swept away by
a physical rush that washed through my core with violent, voluptuous bursts. I was crying, writhing, begging. I was blind and bound, my only sensation this
rich, rolling pleasure.

After a long, dreamlike swell, the waves eased and calmed. I didn't know if the blindfold was removed; I couldn't have opened my eyes.

I heard a soft murmur at the edge of my consciousness. "My wife is a goddess."

AFTER THE THIRD—perhaps fourth—climax, I entered a state of physical transcendent enlightenment in which my body existed in its own realm, thoroughly base and primal. My mind went dark and quiet, able only to comprehend the acute, drawn-out rapture. Throughout the night, I was taken beyond any and every limit I had never known existed. After hours of exquisite torture and unimagined bliss, I was vaguely aware that my ankles and wrists were being unbound. A cool cloth washed me. I was covered by the warm weight of the furs. And I awoke with my arms and legs wrapped possessively around my savage warrior husband.

CHAPTER FOURTEEN

KADE WOKE ME, the light trace of his fingers drawing a line along the arch of my eyebrow, down my cheek, across my lips. His expression was softer than I had ever seen it. We lay like that for several minutes, in silence, savoring this nearness and this new, strengthening bond.

There was an inexplicable, thoughtful glow in his eyes. Not sorrow, not awe. Something rare and vast. "You hold my heart with both hands, lass. I have completely fallen. I am forever at your mercy."

His words, so touching and unexpected, fed me a strange warmth. "I will take infinite care with your heart, husband," I whispered to him, sensing that the changes in me, in him, were more profound than I could ever have imagined. I repeated the assurance he had given me, and proven to be true. "You have nothing to fear with me."

Kade continued to draw his soft line, as though committing each nuanced curve of my face to memory. There was a deep fondness in his expression, a gentle amazement. Gone was the heartless savage I had once taken him for, replaced, here in our private haven, by a lover who was becoming so deeply comforting to me I wondered how I ever could have feared him so.

"I must rise now to organize the hunting parties," he said. "I'll stay close to home today to attend to matters here. I might see you in the day."

"I'd like that very much. You don't need to hunt?"

"The hunting parties are able to dispatch without my guidance. There is a growing number of men whose loyalty I trust. I was assured of this yesterday. We ran into a small brigade of Campbell's troops."

This news sent a bolt of foreboding through my heart. "Where?"

"About ten miles from here. In the exact direction that leads to Campbell's keep, if one were to follow the line due northwest. We have reason to believe they were expecting a message from a Morrison soldier. They asked us if we had word, before they realized that I was among the party." The very fact that Kade was sharing this information signaled a change. I thought he might be warning me. To be aware. To be on guard. "We're better prepared than we were only two weeks ago. Many of the soldiers' training is coming along well, Jamie among them. Most of the key weapons have been newly sharpened. And I will remain within close proximity to my wife, who I have sworn to protect above all others."

Of course I was glad to learn that he would be close by if I needed him. If he needed me.

"And so I must take my leave of you, for now," he said, rising from the bed, preparing himself for his day.

Before he left me, he kissed me only once, as though mindful of our effect on each other, and making a point to avoid temptation. "Good day, milady," he said.

A short time later, several of the housemaids arrived at my door. I spent most of the day with them, organizing the rooms that Kade's brother and sisters would sleep in during their visit, along with their entourage of military and other personnel. I was glad that we could greet them with a more welcoming keep than they might have found only weeks ago.

And I couldn't get my husband out of my mind.

I couldn't wait to see him again. I couldn't wait to lie next to him, to feel his hands on my body. In my anticipation, I felt like a different person altogether. I was still glowing with the effects of Kade's erotic torment. My limbs felt loose, relaxed yet strong. My body was fizzing with satisfaction the likes of which I had never experienced. And my mind was sharper than I could ever recall. I felt, in the broader sense of the term, powerful, as though I had swallowed a seed of invincibility. I felt peaceful. Whole. Womanly. Alive. My husband had beaten my weaknesses out of me, apparently. He had soothed me, riled me and awakened me all at once.

And I was pleased with the newfound harmony of the manor in general. We still had mountains of work to do, but the small changes were evident. The hall and the kitchens were noticeably cleaner and more efficient. The staff were more energized as they spoke and worked. Once the new ground rules had been established—and rewards aplenty gifted to those who followed through—real change was detectable, not only in the slowly improving look of the place but in the entire atmosphere of the keep. The changes, it was widely acknowledged, were positive. We were enjoying the tastier, more abundant food. Random clan members commended me on my efforts, and those of my husband, and had begun to offer to assist in any way they could. The manor itself was looking somewhat more polished and proud and was getting close to being ready, Kade said, to host his eldest brother and two sisters, who would visit in two weeks' time.

Knox Mackenzie's visit, I knew, could not come soon enough for Kade. My husband was becoming increasingly anxious about the uprising not only outside our walls, but inside them, as well. About half the men of the army were loyal to Kade, he estimated, or perhaps more. It was the other contingent he was worried about. The timing for an internal uprising couldn't be worse, if the threat of Campbell's return—wherever it might be—was to be believed. I knew my husband took Campbell and his army seriously. I remembered my husband's words about Campbell's vicious nature. The large crescent-shaped scar on Kade's shoulder was proof that there was at least one warrior roaming the Highlands who posed a very physical threat. That the man in question had been spotted repeatedly in these very parts was distressing indeed. And with only half an army's allegiance, Kade was eager to have his brother—and his brother's troops—on hand and at the ready.

I hoped my husband's worries were for naught. I hoped Campbell's men were merely en route to some other conquest. What, after all, would they be seeking here at Glenlochie? We had little to offer them. As improved as our provisions and our living quarters might have been, we hardly seemed worthy of a full-blown takeover. It was Ossian Lochs they wanted—Roses and Wilkie's keep, given to them by her father the king.

I allowed the disquieting thoughts to fade into the background. I wanted instead to savor the effects of the night and to appreciate the momentary harmony of my home. In fact, both the pleasant, beautified state of our keep and the lingering aura of my husband's astounding night-lit attentions were nothing short of miraculous. I had never, in all my twenty-one years, experienced such a profound sense of physical well-being.

It was late afternoon by the time I made my way to the kitchens where several of my sisters and all of the staff were busy at work. I could hear their laughter. The hall, although set for the evening meal, was empty. I took a moment to revel in the quiet scene that bustled at its edges. The fire was lit and I went to stand next to it. The doors to the kitchen had been propped open, and I could hear the busy, productive sounds of pots clanging and cooks' discussions, my sisters' voices among them. Clementine, in particular, had taken to her new pastime with dedication. Her plans for the nunnery had been delayed, at the orders of my husband, since he didn't want to spare the men who would escort her at such uncertain times. She'd offered no protests, I'd noticed, and instead seemed more than content to spend her days in the kitchens. Baking had become her new obsession. I could hear Agnes's and Ann's voices, too. It seemed my sisters were glad of their new opportunities. The minute they'd been allowed to work, they had embraced the employment with something akin to happiness. Just as I had.

At that moment, they came bustling as one out into the hall, noticing me immediately.

"Stella!" Clementine said, beaming, coming to me. In her hands she held a platter. "You have to taste this bread. It's fresh from the oven. And we've just finished churning the butter. I've added walnuts and grains to the dough. 'Tis simply divine."

"It looks it," I said, taking a bite of the piece she held out to me. But before I could compliment her or comment on how fine she looked with the new sparkle in her eye, we were confronted by the sudden presence of our father, Aleck and one of my father's other senior officers, Hugh. The officers themselves strode into the room, while our father hobbled. With each passing day his frailty seemed to be compounding. He looked tired yet agitated, and his eyes were watery with age and the debilitating effects of his accelerating madness. I noticed immediately that my father was not leading his men, but following. This was no small detail. My father was all-powerful laird, no matter what his condition. He had either bestowed a new authority to Aleck, or Aleck had taken it regardless—either scenario spelled trouble, I could feel it to my bones.

My sisters began to retreat to the kitchen, pulling me with them. But I had had enough of running, and hiding. "Go," I said to them, surprised by the authority in my voice. "I'll stay." Something had changed in me, and the small detail had distanced me somewhat from my sisters. I was married now, and they were still hoping. I was spoken for in a way that they had never been, by a man who was not only laird-in-waiting but also as masculine as it was possible for a man to be. My status had given me their respect, I realized. And it was true that I'd hardly seen them of late. I'd make a point to remedy that, I decided. But it wouldn't be now. Reluctantly they backed away, standing near the open doors of the kitchen for a moment before disappearing within.

Aleck walked over, standing close to me. He reached to tuck a wayward strand of my hair behind my ear. The gesture was unsettling. Too familiar. Possessive. I didn't like what it implied, nor the confidence it took to execute it. "So," he drawled, "the women have taken control of the manor, it seems. Isn't it quaint?"

"Aye," agreed Hugh, a thug with long dirty-blond hair that was matted into long strands. His demeanor and size were similarly daunting to Aleck's, but it was Aleck who held my attention. Something in him had changed. His confidence was laced with an aspect I could not name. Malice, perhaps. Achievement. His movements appeared unusually jaunty, as though he was excited about something, smitten with anticipation. Whatever it was he was celebrating, I couldn't help thinking it would affect us—*me,* in particular—badly. I wanted to distance myself from him as quickly as possible, even more than I usually did.

He reached for the bread I still held in my hand, taking it and helping himself to a bite.

And his comment irked me. I didn't want to cower from him any longer. I could feel Kade's support from afar and my own empowerment. Once, only days ago, I might have stood there and taken any insult he might have tossed. But we were entitled to care for our home. Kade had convinced me of that with his disbelief over the fact that we hadn't done so in the past. Ours was a clan that had been ruled by unhealthy rules for many years. Now I could see that it was *normal* to work and to prosper because of it. To ignore this truth any longer seemed downright wasteful. And I wasn't so willing to accept the dictates of selfish, mad or dishonorable men any longer.

"We haven't taken control of it, Aleck," I said. "We've taken an interest in its upkeep. And we're all the better for it. What is it you want?"

He leaned close to my ear, murmuring lecherously, "You know what it is I *want,* lass. Surely you're not that oblivious. When are you going to make good on our… discussion?"

"What discussion?" I asked him, irritated. I tried to lean back from his nearness, but he only moved in closer, looping his arm around my waist. It comforted me to know that a small but extremely sharp knife was strapped to my thigh, hidden and undetectable. And I knew how to use it. I was armed for the first time in my life and I felt wildly comforted by my small weapon. In that moment, I felt not only grateful to my husband but closer to him than I had before, as though my knife provided a link to him, and a shared motivation.

"The one about your straying husband," he said, pulling me against him. "And your freedom to seek satisfaction elsewhere."

"I would hardly refer to it as a 'discussion,'" I seethed, struggling against his grip. "Besides, you're wrong. My husband hasn't strayed. He assured me of that. And I believe him." Aleck's boldness angered me, coupled as it was with unrelenting force and this daft misinterpretation of the situation: he seemed to honestly believe that I was interested in a tryst. With *him*. In the wake of my recent enlightenment, I was irritated enough to lash out at him, unthinkingly. "As for your insinuations, Aleck, forget it! Put it out of your mind altogether. You're the last person I would ever seek out, even if I *had* already—"

I realized my mistake as soon as I uttered it. I attempted to backtrack. But Aleck's eyes narrowed with understanding. "Had already what?"

"Had already felt inclined to seek satisfaction elsewhere," I said quickly. "Which I would never do, by the way. My husband provides more than enough satisfaction." I hoped my indignation and the honest truth to that statement would put Aleck's suspicions to rest.

But the strategic ambition and sudden understanding in his eyes sent bolts of icy fear through my veins. "He won't force himself on you, will he? He's too honorable for such treachery, isn't it so?" Aleck was practically gloating with his dawning realization. He spoke quietly, with a note of gleeful disbelief, as though unintentionally voicing his thoughts aloud. "Those Mackenzies pride themselves on it. Honor." This last word he said with some distaste, clearly not consumed by its premise, as my husband was. Aleck looked at me, studying my face, finding there the regret of my mistake. The turn of his calculating intent played clearly across his face. "Your marriage has not yet been sealed," he said quietly. His hand slid farther, settling on the swell of my hip.

But I jerked away from him and was able to escape him. I ran to the kitchens, taking refuge among my sisters and the kitchen staff. Aleck wouldn't dare abduct me, or whatever it was he might do, so publicly. At least I hoped it.

And my hopes were confirmed, at least for now. Aleck did not follow me.

This was a very bad development indeed: that Aleck even suspected that my marriage to Kade was not yet truly sealed was not only disturbing, it was dangerous. I knew Aleck coveted the lairdship of our clan with every fiber of his being, and had from the time we were children, when he'd sought my affections even then. I'd suspected his betrayal and so had Kade. I'd wondered if Aleck had had a plan all along. And I'd wondered at the lengths he'd go to.

I needed more information from someone inside the ranks of our clan's army. Someone who'd known the inner workings of the clan before Kade's arrival, and before the threats of Campbell's attacks. Someone who might sense a shift, or who might hear rumors from both sides of the divide. I had an idea of who that someone might be.

I found Bonnie, seated at one of the tables, folding

the linens for the evening's place settings. Even Bonnie and Maisie, of late, had taken an interest in the more mundane workings of the manor, when they'd seen how enthusiastic Clementine and I had become. Maisie, it seemed, had a flair for flower arranging. And Bonnie was clever with a needle and thread.

"Bonnie," I said. "Can you lead me to Jamie? I need to speak to him."

Several of my sisters overheard me, and moved closer. And Bonnie looked at me, taking her time to study the difference in me since we'd last had a real, sisterly conversation. I'd been preoccupied and had so far managed to avoid discussions on the more intimate details of marriage, which my sisters asked about at every opportunity. And here was another opportunity, which Bonnie, it appeared, intended to take full advantage of. Her mouth eased into a knowing smile. "Stella, I daresay marriage suits you to the extreme. What they say about Kade Mackenzie must indeed be true, and then some." She lowered her voice. "*Is* it true? Is he as *beastly* as we've heard? You've hardly told us *anything*."

I knew I wouldn't get away with skirting her questions entirely. It was bad enough that Aleck suspected the secret of my marriage's yet-to-be-consummated status. I didn't want my sisters to suspect the same, especially since it was a detail I planned on addressing sooner rather than later. To hell with my husband's oaths and his honor. There were bigger problems to consider than an outdated vow that I'd never even asked him to make in the first place; I intended to convince him of this at my very next opportunity. I needed to make my reply convincing. "Aye," I replied, attempting to match the worldliness of Bonnie's tone, "he's exactly as beastly as a wife would want him to be."

Bonnie's eyebrows shot up. Hoping she was placated enough to allow us to change the course of the conversation, I said, "We'll talk more of that later. But first, I have something urgent I must ask Jamie. Do you know where he might be?"

"Aye," Bonnie said. "He had an idea for a new sword design, and he's taken it to Caleb to see if he could fashion one."

Maisie had come up next to me. She smoothed a wrinkle in the fabric of my dress, in a gesture of hopeful entreaty. "Could *that* have anything to do with the urgency of your question, dear sister?"

I had not forgiven her either for her betrayal or for her hurtful outburst. "Nay, *dear sister.* I asked to speak to Jamie, not Caleb. At present, my hope is to avoid Caleb. My husband has forbidden me to speak to him."

"Of course he has," said Maisie. "He knows of your desire."

"He knows of our history, or lack thereof. That's all there is to know. I'm married now, Maisie. There's no future between Caleb and me. It wasn't meant to be." I realized it then: I meant the words as I spoke them, even though I hadn't realized, fully, how I felt until this moment. I no longer yearned for Caleb. I yearned for only one man. The one I was now married to. The one I would share a bed with tonight. The one whose increasingly infuriating countdown numbered…fewer than eight full days.

I was furious enough—by both the countdown and my unresolved dispute with my sister—to brush her off. I began to follow Bonnie, who had already risen to accompany me to the blacksmith's hut. But Maisie walked along with us. I looked at her as we walked, and she read my gaze but didn't rise to it, nor did she comment on it. The trace of guilt in her was etched with the lingering traces of sorrow that her disappointments had introduced. My own damages, I could now consider, had been tempered just slightly by the security and comfort—among other things—that my husband had now introduced. Maisie wished for what I had: a husband—a Mackenzie, no less—whose growing devotion to me had been convincingly demonstrated. With that thought, I began to forgive her. Whether or not she'd had my interest at heart or her own didn't really matter. This was more about my relationship with Kade than it was about Maisie. My sister couldn't help herself. She was in love with a man she would possibly never see again, let alone have. A man who resembled my husband as only a full-blooded brother could.

But my husband didn't want Maisie. He could have had her. She had been his for the taking, only to be refused.

He wants you, my father had said.

And Kade had confirmed it, more than once. Words spoken in the heat of the night, followed by the sensual, devastating pleasure of his claim and his desire as he confirmed his declaration.

I felt mildly flushed when my thoughts were interrupted. We were being approached by the very men we sought out. Jamie and Caleb. We were out of doors, but had only started on the path toward the tradesmen's village.

I couldn't help looking around the vicinity, to see if Kade might be around. We were near the manor's picturesque rose gardens, at the side entrance. In the distance were the orchards, which sloped down a gentle incline to the loch below. I could see the small, moving figures of several gardeners pruning and tending to the trees, readying them for the winter. Mackenzie gardeners perhaps. Or our own, now newly trained and productive.

It was unlikely Kade would be in the orchards or nearby. His place was in the weapons sheds and the sparring yards, where he bested men one by one and slowly but surely earned their hard-won loyalty. Nevertheless, I wanted to make this quick. It wouldn't do to be caught again in Caleb's company. I could only imagine what punishment a second offense would bring.

Caleb's appearance had improved somewhat after our last brief encounter. He had washed and put on fresh clothing. He didn't appear quite so gaunt. His hair gleamed with strands of gold, and his white shirt suited the lightly browned skin of his face and his neck. His hands, as always, were dirtied with a perpetual film of soot. Once, this image of him, healthy and sunlit, would have clutched at my heart, inspiring me to follow him to the ends of the earth, no matter what the cost.

But now I felt little. Nay, I felt *something*. What I *felt* was the shadowy effects of Kade Mackenzie's fingers in the most intimate place imaginable. I felt his biting teeth. I felt the hard heat of his body next to mine and the fierce, devoted greed of his kiss.

Caleb reached out to me, as though he'd forgotten Kade's warning. Abruptly, I flinched back. Caleb's hand dropped to his side, his expression hurt and confused by my odd response.

"Caleb," I said softly. "Please. You mustn't touch me. My husband is very…possessive. You must take his warning seriously. He meant every word of it." I had a brief, outlandish desire to reach for Caleb's hand, to hold his coal-blackened fingers in my own, not to feel him, but to inspire a repeated punishment at the hands of my jealous husband. But it wouldn't do. Such an act might put Caleb's life at risk. Tempers were too high. Danger lurked and war threatened. So I took a small step back from him.

And Jamie began the very conversation I had been seeking. "Stella," he said, his eyes bright with urgency. "Mackenzie is in danger, and so are you. Aleck and his rebels have allied with Campbell. They plan to storm the keep at Aleck's invitation. I'm loyal to your husband, as are enough of us, we can only hope, to outnumber Aleck within our own ranks. You must tell your husband of this, and quickly. Have him summon his brothers and their armies tonight. Tell him the attack is coming."

CHAPTER FIFTEEN

ALMOST IMMEDIATELY, I began to make my way back to our private chambers. The evening meal was being served in the hall, and I briefly looked for my husband there, but he was nowhere to be found. I made my way to the back corridor—the only one that led to our separate wing. This corridor was always dark and quiet, removed as it was from the central, busier areas of the manor. I thought I might position some candles or some small torches to light the way, but I hadn't yet got to it. The passage was dim, and I ran my fingers along the cold stone wall.

I wondered why Kade had retired early. But then I remembered he'd had maybe an hour of sleep the previous night.

I neared a segment of the passage that veered to the right. And as I turned the corner, I was shockingly confronted by the huge form of Aleck himself. Before I could react to him, he curled his massive arm around me, hugging me to him and simultaneously covering my mouth with his hand. It was a calculated, well-rehearsed move. He'd been thinking of this technique, practicing it, making sure he wouldn't miss. He dragged me back the way I'd come, through a door and into a room, closing the door securely behind us. Then he released his hold. Panic clutched in my throat and I thought of screaming for help, but I knew the sound would barely penetrate through the thick wooden door. I recognized the place immediately as one of the rooms of the healing quarters. The air was thick with the medicinal smells of herbal concoctions, alcohol and the earthy notes of freshly cut roots. Relief washed through me when I saw Fee, one of the Morrison clan healers, standing next to a bed that had been laid with a clean sheet. Her small form was eclipsed by the bulk of Aleck as he hauled me to the bed and ordered me to climb onto it.

"Why?" I asked defiantly. Fee's presence gave me courage; he would hardly, after all, force himself upon me with Fee standing right beside us. Or would he?

"This healer will examine you," Aleck said. "I have doubts now as to the validity of your marriage."

My defiance was punctured by a spear of anxiety. "The evidence was given to my father after our wedding night," I said.

"I saw that evidence, aye. And if it was, in fact, your virginal blood, then you have nothing to worry about. I suspect it was not, and so I mean to find out for certain whether your maidenhood is still unbroken. Healer," he ordered, "do it now."

Fee was one of the older healers, perhaps nearly sixty. She was equally well-known for her expertise and her appalling bedside manner. Perhaps overly jaded by many decades of witnessing illness and often death, she had little time for compassion beyond the pragmatic. Aleck had chosen well. He knew, as I did, that Fee would have no compunction about telling the truth of the matter. She placed her cool, bony hands on me and urged me to lie back onto the bed.

I shook off her hands. "There's no reason to doubt that the marriage has been properly consummated," I insisted, my voice sounding steadier than I felt. "My father was satisfied, and so should you be."

"Yet I am *not* satisfied," Aleck said. "You as much as admitted it, earlier, in the hall. And it makes perfect sense. I've seen the way you've looked at your husband in the past. With revulsion, at times, and most of all with fear. I'm sure this has not escaped his notice. And if the Mackenzies are half as honorable—supposedly— as their reputation seems to suggest, I'm guessing that he hasn't forced himself upon you. Which would mean that the marriage is not, in fact, legally bound."

"'Tis a ridiculous accusation," I protested. "You're wrong."

He took no notice of my protest. "Which would *also* mean that if someone else was to wed you, then *properly* consummate the marriage, then it would be the second marriage that would be, in fact, the valid of the two. The first marriage would be instantly annulled."

"Well, the first marriage *has* been consummated," I lied, desperate. "Yours is a false assumption. You misinterpreted my words entirely, today in the hall. I was not implying that—"

"Do it now," Aleck growled at the healer, undeterred. I was pulled onto the bed by his meaty hands, and my shoulders were held under his firm grasp. "If I don't believe your verdict, I'll examine her myself."

Fee did as she was told. A shiver ran up my spine as her cold, knobby fingers raised the hem of my gown to find the soft skin of my thigh. I closed my legs, but her grip was surprisingly strong and she quickly clasped my ankles into iron rings that had already been attached to the examining table to hold me in place. "Lie still, dear," she said, the pleasantry sounding unnatural in this closed, distressing space.

I struggled again, but I was too tightly held. I cried out, but the old woman's fingers found their goal, sliding into me and prodding gently, searchingly. I closed my eyes against the nimble, snaking assault.

The examination was brief and the violating touch was removed. "Aye, she is still intact," said the old healer, unshackling my ankles.

Aleck smiled, sinister intent sparking in his black eyes. But then, as he took a single step forward, his eyes rolled back in his head and his heavy body fell to the floor with a painful-sounding thud. Shocked, I looked at Fee, who smiled knowingly. "I laced his drink, lassie," she said, indicating an empty goblet that sat next to a bottle of whiskey, perched on a nearby shelf. A large blue glass vial set next to it. "Now I suggest you go attend to the matter at hand at once."

Wasting no time, I offered my deepest thanks to the healer Fee, whose parting words as she ushered me out the door were these: "The thug will sleep for a short time, I cannot say exactly. An hour. Maybe two. Did you happen to know, by the by, that my name at birth was Fiona Mackenzie? I married into this clan at the tender age of seventeen, but once a Mackenzie always a Mackenzie. Now go, and hurry to it. Tie the man up if you have to but for God's sake, lass, get the job done."

Somewhat taken aback by her confession, and by the urgency in her voice, I rushed back to my chambers. I noticed unusual noises coming from the grand hall, and from outside. Clanging, shouting, the voices of men. But I had no time to stop and investigate. I made it back to our bedchambers without seeing anyone. I closed the door quietly behind me, taking a moment to catch my breath from my run.

My husband was deeply asleep in the large leather chair by the fire, one of his leather-bound books open across his chest. He wore his kilt, the sash loosely draped across his chest, with no shirt underneath. His daily training garb was his leather trews and sparring tunic. Generally, men wore their kilts for more formal occasions, and into battle. Kade would wear his, I noticed, in our private chambers, when he was writing his notes and the letters to his family. I'd suspected that he found it comforting, as though having his clan colors wrapped around him gave him the kind of comfort he often lacked in this new and largely inhospitable environment.

He was a quiet sleeper. His beauty to me was no longer confined to the times when he slept and when he laughed. But now, as I watched the rise and fall of his chest, the severe lines of his face softened by the blue light of night, I was overcome by a longing that was immediate and dynamic, a flood of determination. There was a job that needed doing, aye, and I found that I *wanted* to do it, and badly. My heart still beat rapidly from my escape, and the blood of my body warmed me lushly, pooling, it seemed, in selective areas where the pulse lingered and played.

I knew it would take very little provocation for my husband to kill Aleck, and I guessed that if he learned of what had taken place below in the healing quarters, he would have no qualms about acting upon his hatred, possibly immediately. But I had no need to tell him. *The thug will sleep for a short time, I cannot say exactly. An hour. Maybe two.* I didn't have a moment to lose.

Yet my husband might protest. He *would* protest. He was adamant that we would see out his month-long waiting period, to secure an invisible bond of trust he seemed utterly determined to uphold. And I understood his motivations. He didn't want to push me into doing something I didn't wholly consent to. I knew him well enough by now to know that forcing himself on a woman was an act my husband, despite his reputation for reckless violence, would never, ever resort to. Even Aleck had noticed my fear. Fear that had transformed, over past weeks, to a smoldering lust. And, while I was no longer afraid of my husband, I could admit that I had occasional flashes of fear at *what he might do to me*. At his basest, he was dangerous and unpredictable. But now it was the thought of that lust-darkened glance that spurred me. I could feel my own excitement as though it was painted onto my skin, coloring my intimate places. Remembering his touch, his tongue, his lash.

The lengths of silky cloth still sat on the bedside table. I knew I would have to be careful and quick. Kade was a sound sleeper, but he was also a soldier, whose instincts were attuned to any and every threat. I secured the first tie quickly, binding his right wrist to the leg of the chair. His head turned, and he sighed in his sleep. I fumbled with the second tie, securing his arm to a wooden beam that ran from the floor to the ceiling, next to his chair. And as his eyes opened, I pulled tight the knot at the same moment he strained violently against it. He cursed and thrashed against the bindings, so much so that his book fell to the floor.

I stood in front of his chair.

He stared at me warily, his chest heaving from his sudden exertions. "Stella?" he growled softly, his confusion inked to his gruff delivery.

My eyes drank in the hard curves of his sculpted shoulders, the bronzed hue ingrained with the light, puckered imperfections of his many scars.

"Aye, husband. 'Tis me."

He pulled against his restraints again and contemplated me once more, as though bewildered by the scenario. "What—? What are you about? Untie me. Now."

"I will untie you," I responded with coy obedience. "Soon."

"What do you mean 'soon'? Release me, I said."

"I mean to attend to a matter that needs attention."

"What matter? Untie my wrists, Stella." His voice

was forceful and his anger was easy to detect, but I had to admit a part of me was enjoying this. I'd never before wielded any kind of power over my rough, brawny husband. He was always unfailingly in control. Until now. "*Untie me,* Stella. Or I'll make you regret this. I swear it. You won't want to get near me."

But I did want to get near him. *Very* near. Nearer than he'd ever allowed.

My gaze met his as I slowly unbuttoned the top of my gown, making a real effort not to lose my nerve. The thought of what would happen if I failed in my goal emboldened me. I eased the neckline open to frame my breasts. My husband regarded me with a look of incredulity, yet it went deeper than that. His eyes wandered over my skin, and I could feel the intensity of his gaze as a warm, intuitive surge.

"God Almighty, lass," he whispered, his voice softened by a degree. "You burn my eyes with your loveliness. I may go up in flames any minute." But then, as though remembering himself as I moved to approach him, his tone turned aggressive again, quietly hoarse: "Keep your distance."

Distance, however, would not get results.

I placed my hands on his parted knees, pushing them wide so I could kneel between them. Tentatively yet purposefully, I touched my fingers to his thighs, letting them glide against his hair-dusted skin.

He flinched and spread his legs wider, as though to evade my touch. But his movement only succeeded in raising the wool of his kilt a fraction higher, making my task all the easier.

"Don't touch me," he said.

He speared me with a look that sent a jolt a fear through me. But the strain of his muscles and the tension in his body were not about anger, nor the rise of his kilt where it covered him. "I am going to touch you, husband. I'm going to take you as you take me."

"*Nay.* We will wait until I have made good on my word to you."

"I'm tired of waiting. I don't want to wait any longer. I never asked for that oath."

"*Stella,*" he warned. "I said a month, and I meant a month, for good reason. You needed that time. I want you to—"

"I do trust you," I said, leaning closer, letting my hands glide farther up his thighs, pushing his kilt higher. "And I want you."

He groaned, an unmistakable note of agony in the sound. "*Nay,* lass. Not yet. I'll not agree to it!" He writhed, and I pulled away as he strained violently against the bindings at his wrists. But the ties held, and after a moment he calmed, although his breathing was heavy and his eyes were enraged. "Untie me." The words were brittle with authority, but I knew what obeying him would cost me, and us both. But as hurried as I was, I wanted him to agree. I wanted to break down his barriers. I wanted him to forget his vow, for him to beg me instead of resist me.

I let my fingers ease around his manhood, which was

already as large and as engorged as I had ever seen it. "I think you *will* agree to it, husband. I just need to convince you. Let me try this—"

"Damn it all to hell, lass! I said nay! I'll not cooperate—"

He exhaled sharply as I squeezed him and cupped him, letting my fingers work nimbly across his rock-hard length, which gave every indication that he was, in fact, ready to cooperate quite fully.

"Stella," he growled again, yet this growl was laced with the very beginnings of surrender.

Fascinated by the size of him, the hot silken feel of his skin, I played him with my fingers, exploring the heavy weight, the satiny hardness.

"Can I kiss you, husband?" I asked him, more for effect than for actual permission. I intended to do it anyway.

"Absolutely not." His reply sounded deep and strangled.

"Just one. One kiss." I leaned to him.

His breath hissed through his clenched teeth as I kissed the broad tip of his immense shaft, licking a small bead of moisture. *"Nay,"* he snarled. "I can't—"

"Hush, fierce warrior husband," I crooned against his skin, aware of the effect the movement of my mouth was having on his limited composure. "Cease your complaints. I haven't complained nearly so much, and I'm much less experienced."

"Untie me at once," he rasped, sounding less forceful than he had only moments ago.

I took him into my mouth, tasting him with my tongue.

"Christ." He sighed, his head falling back. His body became very still. It was fascinating to me that this big, lethal soldier could be tamed this way. I wanted to use that power, to feed it and explore where it might lead me, and us.

I kissed him and licked him playfully, taking him farther into my mouth. He was too big to take fully, so I used my fingers to stroke the base of his shaft as I continued to suck him more deeply and tease him with my tongue. His breathing was rough and staggered as he again pulled against his ties. He lifted his head in one last attempt as my fingers explored further. *"Stella.* You're too—*ah, God. All right.* I'll give you what you want, I will. Come to me. Release me."

I paused, not sure if I should trust him. But then, that's what this—all this, the wait and the desire *not* to wait—was about. Trust.

I eased him from my mouth, but I continued to hold him, to slide my fingers, to squeeze gently and to wander the beguiling textures of him. "Promise," I commanded him.

"What?"

"Promise me you'll not change your mind."

"Aye, aye," he said quickly, sensing his impending escape. "I promise."

I raised the hem of my gown and crawled up his body, straddling his hips, very aware that his huge, rigid manhood was resting insistently against the bare skin of my thigh. My gown fell to cover us, and the secrecy some-how heightened the thrill of sensation. I looked into his eyes, wriggling slightly, using my body to caress him.

"Holy mother of God, lass," he said, chuckling in an aggrieved moan. "My revenge will be sweet. You will be begging for mercy. Now *untie me*. I'll go easy on you if you release me immediately."

My squirming motion caused the head of his shaft to slide between my thighs, where I was slippery with warmth. He swore again, more loudly. He seemed al-ready on the verge of his release, or of some internal shift or collapse; he was struggling against it, holding back, gritting his teeth with it.

I paused in my movement, searching his eyes. "No more holding out on me. I want you. No more waiting. I didn't ask for you to wait a month. I'm ready *now*. *This* is the vow I want you to honor. *This* is the one I will trust. That you'll take me fully, right now." I was almost moved to tears from the flood of my emotion. The residual terror of Aleck's threat. The relief that I was with Kade here and now. The monumental, wel-come shift that was about to take place.

"All right," he said, reading the weight of my emo-tion even if he couldn't know the reasons for it. "If that's what you truly want, then that's what you'll get, lass. I don't have it in me to deny you any longer."

I reached under my gown to hold him with my hand, touching the tip of him to glide wetly against me, press-ing him gently so his shaft prodded at my snug entrance. There was a taut, stretching burn as I increased the pressure. I had lost my mind, it seemed, with abandon, with the necessity of securing my bond to him. I could take him like this, bound and protesting. Or I could trust him to take me willingly, as I wanted him to. I wanted his arms around me as he took me, finally, as his wife, wholly and completely.

I leaned to kiss his mouth softly, letting my tongue glide across his lips, licking lightly into his mouth. My movement caused his hot, rigid manhood to slide a fraction deeper within the tight constriction of my body. I waited for his protests, but none came. Instead, he rasped, "*Christ Almighty. I* promise you anything, everything. I'll not last this way. Let me pleasure you. In every way I know how. Let me take control. Just this once, for your first time."

I thought about this. He sounded sincere, although I doubted this would be the *only* night he would demand full control; that detail, however, bothered me not at all. He could have his control if I could get what *I* wanted. "As long as you give me your word," I said. "No more waiting."

"*Aye,* I swear it."

I was satisfied by this. He'd told me often enough that the Mackenzies' word was their law. I crawled farther up his body, reaching for the bindings, hesitating. In this position, my breasts were just above his mouth. Not long ago, I would have been far too shy to do such a thing, but now I had a quest. I had to use every weapon in my own arsenal to achieve it. And his eyes were feral, inviting me. I offered a full breast to him, which he accepted hungrily, drawing my nipple into the plush heat, teasing the sensitive bud with his tongue and the soft abrasion of his teeth. Straddling him, with his mouth drawing mad pleasure from my fevered flesh, I began to lose myself. My body seemed to be melting from the inside out.

So it took me a brief moment to realize that our peace had been shattered.

A loud crash drew my attention to the now-open door. In my haste, I had forgotten to lock it. And there stood not only Aleck, fully awake, but also six other men in full war regalia with swords raised, and many more lined up with them, led by—

Campbell.

CHAPTER SIXTEEN

"WELL, WELL," CAMPBELL said, lowering his sword, a smirk of amused triumph rippling across his expression. He was a staunch-looking man with long black hair and a black beard, appearing every bit as dangerous as his reputation suggested. He wore almost as much weaponry as my husband usually armed himself with—weapons that were, at present, well out of reach. "Isn't this well timed?"

In a desperate attempt, I reached for the ties at Kade's wrist before I even made a move to cover myself. But Aleck was there, his arms wrapping themselves around my waist, pulling me away with a strength I could not begin to defy. As my hands were dragged from my husband's body, I was able to pull the wool of his kilt lower over him, covering him. And I fumbled with my own garment, pulling it over my exposed breasts as I was carried some distance from my husband and placed on my feet. Aleck's hold on me did not ease.

"Take me," Kade said, his voice eerily calm. "Leave my wife. This has nothing to do with her."

"In fact," said Aleck, clear glee in his tone. His eyes were bloodshot, perhaps from the effects of the drug he'd been given by the healer. A drug that was regrettably weaker than I had been told. "This has *everything* to do with her. Isn't that right, Stella? Shall I check you for blood? Because it doesn't appear you were able to fully succeed in your quest. It appears, aye, that we arrived just in time."

Kade's expression did not change. His face was a mask of composure, but his eyes were blazing with hatred, with rage and realization. And with regret.

"I'm going to kill you anyway, soldier," Kade said evenly, his eyes locked on Aleck. "How painful your death is will depend on your willingness to take your hands off my wife this instant. And refrain from ever touching her again."

Campbell laughed loudly. "These Mackenzies never fail to amaze. You're as defenseless as you could possibly be, soldier. Yet you insist on tossing out threats that will only succeed in making your predicament all the worse."

Aleck seemed to barely register Campbell's remark. He replied to my husband's words with the confidence of a man whose opponent was at a distinct and pleasing disadvantage. "On the contrary, Mackenzie, this lass no longer belongs to you. Your marriage is a sham. Unsealed and invalid. If I hadn't just witnessed what appeared to be your willingness, I might have suspected that you found the lass displeasing, which is beyond my powers of comprehension. I intend to wed her myself. And to give her what she is clearly crying out for. You might as well witness at least part of the proceedings.

Since you don't appear to have much of a choice." To his soldiers, he commanded, "Bring in Laird Morrison."

My father was dragged into the room by Hugh and another guard. And as I looked at the man who had raised me from a distance with tyranny, abuse and displaced grief, I could feel only pity. His eyes had lost their spark entirely. Perhaps the storming of the keep by Campbell's army had pushed him over the edge of his loosening grip on reality. His madness had taken over. He seemed barely able to comprehend where he was or who he was.

Aleck loomed over his laird menacingly. "I've agreed that Campbell should be the one to kill your laird-in-waiting, Morrison. I'll take the pleasure of securing my title as laird with my own sword." With that, Aleck, without removing his hold on my arm, drew his weapon from its scabbard and drove it into my father's heart with one quick, forceful thrust. "Your time has come, old man. 'Tis something I should have done long ago."

My father's frail body slumped to the floor, blood spilling freely, inky black. He was dead before he even hit the cold stone floor.

I gasped, not with anguish over my father's death—his cruelty had steadily eroded any affection I might once have felt for him—but with shock. Not only was Campbell's army within our walls, but my father was dead and my husband's life would be the next to be taken. Campbell, even now, was approaching Kade, his sword raised and a large knife clenched in his other hand.

Strangely, even amid the dire situation at hand, a

pressing regret echoed insistently in my mind. *I have not yet made love to my husband.* I *wanted* to, before we were both separated, imprisoned or worse. Not because I was being forced to consummate our marriage under threat, but because the time I had spent in his company was the sweetest, most nourishing of my life. I wanted a thousand more moments with him, learning him and treasuring his beauty and his comfort and his love. That was what I wanted from him: love. In that tragic, terror-stricken moment, it was the only thing I could comprehend. That I loved him. The very real possibility that he might be taken from me before I would truly know him, in every sense of the word, felt tragically unjust. I loved him and he might never know it.

"I now pronounce myself laird of the Morrison clan," Aleck said, "since the previously appointed laird-in-waiting's time has just run out. And I am the rightful second in line for the title. If any man present has any reason to dispute this claim, speak your piece now."

My mind was reeling. How could I save him? Fighting them would be foolish. I remembered the small knife strapped to my thigh, but there were at least twelve hostile warriors in this room, every one of them armed to the teeth, and with an endless army huddled outside the door.

Campbell held his sword so the very tip of it hovered near Kade's chest. Right over his heart. "This almost seems too easy," he taunted. "I've been looking forward to this moment for quite some time. Yet I never envisioned it quite like this."

My husband's chest rose slightly with his breath, putting the sword's blade that much closer to contact. "Fight me like a true warrior, Campbell," Kade said. "Wouldn't you rather live out your days knowing you bested me with your skill and not your underhanded deceit? Fight me in a duel and kill me if you will. But do it with honor."

Campbell was not at all conflicted. "Ah, but I've already bested you with cunning and strategy, Mackenzie. I can live with that. Honor, I believe, is overrated. The ends justify the means, so they say, and this end—your death—will be the sweetest revenge of all. 'Tis your own sheer misfortune that the lass was able to assist us so thoroughly with our plan. She could not have been more helpful if she'd been given explicit instructions."

Kade's gaze found mine, and in that flashing, quick intensity I could read there a fleeting question, one that stemmed from our history: my fear of him, my unwillingness to wed him, my long list of hesitations.

It was that question that gave me an idea.

I had just watched one of my father's senior officers kill him in cold blood. And now I was about to watch this ruthless rebel kill my husband. I could see the anticipation and the bloodlust written across Campbell's face as his sword's tip drew ever closer to my husband's heart.

My plan was risky, aye, and would have dire consequences for us both. But it might keep him alive. It was the only priority: I needed him to *live*. So I could tell him and show him how much I had grown to need him.

"*Nay!* You *cannot* kill him," I said too loudly. It took everything I had to steady my voice, but I continued. I directed my gaze at Campbell, avoiding Kade's eyes, knowing the questions there, the hurt and the anger, would very likely cause me to falter. "He's too valuable. If we use him as a hostage, we're safe from attack from both the Mackenzie and the Stuart armies, as well as their allies."

The room fell entirely silent. All eyes were on me, and my skin felt hot and awash with anxiety under the scrutiny. I could practically feel Kade's disappointment, his sorrow and his remorse, piercing into me like a sword of steely despair. But if I was to be at all convincing, I would need to show no fear. I condemned myself as I spoke, and I resolved to spend the rest of my life making it up to him—if we survived. I needed now to be stronger than I ever had been in my life. And so I drew on the memories. The secret garden. My husband's face as he slept in the moonlight. The astounding pleasure of his kiss and his touch. I would hold those memories close to me as I endured what I must to keep him alive.

I squared my shoulders and continued, leaning closer to Aleck, allowing his hold instead of struggling against it. "'Tis true. I've met them, and I believe both his brothers will agree to virtually any request you make of them if they knew Kade's life depended on it. With that in mind, and with the Morrison and Campbell armies newly allied, your rebellion could go far. Further than it ever has."

Aleck, whose hands were somewhat indecently

placed in his eager acceptance of my sudden acquiescence, said, "She's right, Campbell. Consider it. I know your ultimate prize is revenge, and I agreed you could claim his life—but think on it. There's no telling what they'd agree to."

Campbell paused, and his eyes found mine. He was wary and skeptical. "What is this? The lass supports your coup, Aleck, against her own husband?"

"My husband is a brute and savage," I said, impressing myself with the cold brittleness of my delivery. I sounded almost convincing. "'Tis well known this was an arranged marriage I wanted nothing to do with. Aleck here knows it to be true."

"Aye," Aleck gloated, believing me almost instantly; I was thankful in that moment that he was a man led by desire and ambition, and not by powers of intuition. "The marriage is not yet sealed—I confirmed it myself with the assistance of a healer. She remains intact."

Kade had been entirely silent until this point, but at Aleck's pronouncement he let out a low, animal growl. I flinched from the impact of his enraged glare. Even bound and defenseless, he looked fiercer, more malicious, and more foreign to me than he ever had. I was almost glad for his constraints as I pulled my eyes from the icy lock of his accusations.

Campbell chuckled, studying Kade with real interest. "Is this true, Mackenzie?"

When Kade did not answer, Aleck said, "He refuses to force the lass against her will."

As amused by this information as he might have

been, Laird Campbell was not entirely convinced. "What I witnessed with my own eyes was a scene in which this lass did not appear unwilling, not in the slightest."

I felt a light rise of heat at the embarrassment of being discovered as we had been, and I grasped for a persuasive explanation. "I—I had been given reason to suspect that your army's arrival was imminent, Laird Campbell, and I knew I had to keep my husband suitably distracted—and restrained. If he wasn't restrained here and now, all the men in this room would likely be dead. You know it as well as I do."

Campbell was highly offended by the confidence I had in my husband's military skill. "Unlikely," he said, surly at the implication that he and his men could be bested by a single Mackenzie. To Kade, he said, with inflections of sarcasm, "Your precious 'honor' has cost you dearly, Mackenzie. Not only has it cost you your wife and your alliance, but it is the cause of the mutiny of half of Morrison's army. I know your skill, soldier. I know you could have cut them down one by one if you'd chosen to. Aleck here has spared me no detail of your methods. You prefer to coerce them with 'honorable intention' and prizes for valor and loyalty, rather than ruling with an iron fist. Your downfall, in every way, can be blamed wholly on your *honor.* 'Tis a pity."

"Rot in hell, Campbell," growled Kade, "along with your underhanded old man."

With that, Campbell swiped Kade's jaw with his fist and the blunt end of his knife. Kade's head swung to the side with the blow, and his eyes closed for a brief moment. I had to physically restrain myself from crying out, from breaking away and running to him. "Gladly," replied Campbell. "But first, I've some business to attend to, involving you, the dungeon, and my formidable knowledge in the ways and means of torture. For the next few days, you're going to wish *you* were in hell, Mackenzie."

Aleck appeared to be enjoying the proceedings immensely. It mattered little to him whether Campbell chose to kill my husband or not. He had other things on his mind that were far more pressing to him. He pulled me against him, and I could feel his intent in the hard lines of his body. "Your marriage, Mackenzie, is now, therefore, invalid—or at least it will be in a matter of minutes. And you're of no more use to us except as a bargaining tool. Take your revenge as you wish, Campbell. Beat him, torture him, cage him in the dungeons. Break him until he is no longer a threat to us. But keep him alive. It would be in all our best interests if we could hold off the combined force of the Mackenzie and Stuart armies simply by using him as a pawn. 'Tis a brilliant idea and one we should have thought of ourselves. My bride is not as naive as she looks." He gave me a look of proud approval and of menacing promise.

Campbell was circling Kade now, his sword lowered but still at the ready. He appeared to be giving the suggestion, or his methods of torture, some thought. Kade did not seem to notice him; his eyes were fixed on me. Coldly. With all the severing emotion of the doomed.

"Meanwhile," said Aleck, "as you avail yourself of your revenge, Campbell, please excuse me and my bride-to-be as I proceed to finally make an honest, satisfied woman of this lass. And I," he added, tossing a glance at Kade that I could feel as a heavy ache in my heart, even as I turned my eyes away, "will waste no time in consummating *our* marriage, immediately and enthusiastically. Stella, come with me."

With that, Campbell's men surrounded Kade, cutting his silk ties to replace them with their own restraints, made of tight leather and hard metal. He fought them like the savage that he was, but he was vastly outnumbered. They beat him with the bone handles of their knives. They kicked him and cut him. His blood was astoundingly red, accusing me with its bright, gaudy hue. Tainting my soul with his pain.

But the image was blurred by my own terror and the weight of my betrayal, as I was grabbed and carried up the spiral stone steps of my mother's turret. By a very strong and very determined Aleck.

CHAPTER SEVENTEEN

THE SCENE WAS eerie and unreal, and seemed to unfold with extraordinary slowness. My senses took in every detail as I was carried up the familiar steps to the hidden enclosure of the turret. The light was purple, stained with dusk as day gave way to night. We passed the series of diamond-shaped windows as we ascended. His footsteps were quick, heavy but agile with his anticipation. His arms were warm against my back and beneath my knees, and his chest was a solid mass of pinpointed sharpness. I could smell the intensity of his desire, and I knew he would not be gentle or kind. He did not have it in him. Once he might have, but compassion had long ago given way to raw ambition. And I was the pinnacle of all that he had ever worked for, yearned for, fought for. It didn't matter that I would be taken by force. I was the crown upon which he would proclaim his manhood and his victory.

I was laid down onto the ancient pink sun-bleached pillows where my mother had once slept. Aleck straddled my hips, pinning me painfully. I struggled, but he didn't so much as budge. His finger swept down my cheek, touching my lips.

"I am laird of this keep now," Aleck said, "My word is law, and I claim you as my wife. We will make it official before the minister tonight. But first, I'm going to take you as my own, as I have long dreamt of. You know this, lass. You know that you were destined to be mine. Isn't that true?"

I did not answer him, and my silence angered him. His voice was brutally calm: an undisguised order. "Tell me what I want to hear."

"Aye," I whispered, afraid of what he might do, to make this even more gruesome than it would already be, if I did not obey him.

My gown, which had been hastily rebuttoned at the front, was torn open. My breasts were exposed and he took them in his huge, calloused hands, pinching roughly. "I saw you, you little wench. Offer yourself to me, like you did to him."

My sorrow at the reference—to *him*—was profoundly painful. I thought of what they might be doing to him now. I knew Campbell would be creative with his revenge. My only cold comfort was the final agreement. *Keep him alive.*

My task was to make Aleck as mindless as he could be. It would make my plan easier to carry out. Carefully, I took his hands and held them. He allowed this, his dark eyes heavy-lidded, questioning, dull yet hopeful. I slid my own hands over my breasts, plumping and playing them, teasing my nipples between my fingers. "Take me in your mouth," I told him.

He leaned down to obey me. He was too manic and

ungainly to be gentle. There was pain as he sucked and bit at me, and I was glad of it. I wanted to feel pain. Any pain. As though it might link me to the torture my husband was surely experiencing, far below us.

Aleck was thoroughly distracted, and I was able to reach down and unfasten the soft leather of my knife's holster. I removed it entirely from my body, placing it under one of the cushions near my right hand. My heart thudded in my chest so loudly I feared he would sense my panic and the real reason behind it. But terror was only expected in a scenario such as this. And this man had none of the perceptiveness of my husband; he was entirely immersed in his own agenda.

"Take off your tunic," I said. "Let me see what a strong warrior you are." *Gouge deep—and put some effort into it. Muscle is more resilient that you might expect.* I wanted easy access. A clear, unfettered strike.

He followed my request immediately, removing his weapons and his shirt. His chest was huge and barrel-shaped, less lean than Kade's, equally marred by battle scars. His breathing was uneven, his weight crushing me as he laid himself over me. He fumbled with the ties of his trews with one hand. With his other hand, he was clawing at the fabric of my gown at my hips, yanking it up to my waist.

I felt him, hot and rearing, against the skin of my thigh, seeking, finding.

It was then that I struck.

The expertly sharpened blade of the long, thin knife sank easily, more easily than I was expecting. It was embedded to the hilt and I twisted and thrust, digging as deep as I could in one, fluid slice.

Aleck yelled out, pulling away and sitting up. His movement caused the knife to gouge a long, gaping crescent in his torso, just below his ribs along the side of his body. It was a lethal wound. I could sense this immediately. The blood was profuse, gushing in a pulsing, cascading flood. His face registered confusion, a baffled bemusement. And then it turned. To rage. He was dying, but there was still enough life left in him to seek out his weapons. But he was having difficulty coordinating his eyes and his hands.

And I still held my knife.

My attack was more instinctive than calculated. If he reached his sword, I would die. I knew this unconditionally. So I struck again, reaching up to slice the blade of my knife across Aleck's neck, putting as much driving effort into the assault as I had the first time. The knife cut deep and so cleanly that when it emerged there was but a thin red line across his neck. Within a second, the blood bubbled and spat, staining his neck and his chest. I watched the life leave his eyes in a ghostly, horrific shift. I pushed at his body with as much strength as I could, knowing he was about to slump on top of me. The thought of being trapped beneath his big, lifeless, blood-soaked body was horrifying, and I was desperate to escape him. Even more than I had been when he'd been alive and terrorizing me with the most profound threat a woman can face.

With wild relief, I was able to scramble out from under him. I was covered with his blood.

But I was free of him.

And I needed to find my husband.

CHAPTER EIGHTEEN

I WAS SHAKEN to my bones. My face was wet with tears, and I felt sticky and hot with drying blood and the residual sweat of my terror.

I would not be expected; this would work in my favor. If I could keep myself hidden, I might be able to find him, and help him. It occurred to me that I would have to go back up to the turret—even though I was more than halfway down the stairs—to get my knife. But then I looked at my bloodied hand and saw that it was there, still held in my white-knuckled grip. This relieved me to the depths of my soul. To retrace my steps and once again lay eyes on Aleck's corpse was more than I could have handled. I would have done it, but I was glad I didn't have to.

Our private chambers were empty now. The door was still open. The silk strands I had used to bind Kade's wrists lay shredded on the floor like shiny, forlorn reminders. Was he still alive? Aye, I knew he would be. It had cost me dearly, but they'd recognized the value of him for the cause of their rebellion. He would be highly useful. The state of him didn't matter to them, as long as he lived.

He'd be badly beaten, chained, tortured within an

inch of his life. All of it, every degree of his pain, was my fault, but I couldn't berate myself on that count. If I hadn't done what I done, he'd most certainly be as dead as Aleck.

Kade's weapons still lay where he'd left them. I picked up one of his weapons belts—the one with his sword and his bone-handled knife, his two favorite weapons, if the time he spent sharpening them was any indication. It was far too big to strap around my waist, so I slung it across my chest. These weapons were exceptionally heavy, and I doubted I could even have wielded the massive sword. But I didn't intend to use them myself. He would need them, as we made our escape from whoever guarded him. A small stab of dread shot through me as I wondered: would he even believe me enough to allow me to help him? Would he ever trust me again? Would he be so disgusted by me that he'd leave me behind? Or worse, would he kill me?

I made my way down the corridor toward the kitchens. But I was wary. I couldn't be seen. And I had no idea where the dungeons were actually located. All I knew was that they were rarely used and highly guarded. I'd heard it said that they were in underground tunnels, but I didn't know for sure.

But then, aye, I remembered. There was one person I could trust who knew exactly where the dungeons were. He'd made the thick chains and installed them in the prison chambers. The very same chains that probably bound my husband's wrists at this very moment.

I had to find Caleb.

My FIRST STOP was the healers' quarters. Before I entered, I remembered to draw closed the gaping sides of my ripped, bloodied gown. When I pushed the door open, the room was empty. Bubbling pots had been abandoned and several were spilling over. In my distress, I'd almost forgotten that our keep had been invaded by a small but hostile army. The healers had fled, maybe under threat. There were signs that a struggle had taken place: spilled concoctions and broken glass. Without lingering, I went to the shelf where the blue vial of Fee's drug remained untouched. It was more than half-full. The bottle of whiskey was gone. I grabbed the vial and continued on my way.

I followed a hidden back passage to the kitchens, which, I could hear as I neared them, were bustling with activity. The conversation was not hushed as it had been over past years, or boisterous and industrious, as it had been in recent weeks. It was alarmed, hurried and agitated. And there were calls from the hall that I could hear through the wall: men, demanding food and drink, clanging their cups and their plates. Campbell's army's ranks, I guessed, wanting their every appetite satisfied. I prayed silently for my sisters' safety at the same time I peered around the corner into the crowded kitchens.

It was then that I saw Ann.

She gasped at the sight of me, rushing over to me but at the same time hesitant. Her expression startled me with the horror it registered and for the first time, I considered what I must look like. My gown was ripped and almost saturated with Aleck's drying blood. Across my shoulders hung a holster strung with swords. And still I held the bloodstained murder weapon in my hand.

Several of my sisters and cousins were there, and I felt a surge of relief for their safety. "Bonnie," I said, clinging to her. She drew back from me, from the gore and the weapons, but I was too out of my mind with my mission to take much notice of her reaction. "Where's Jamie? Where's Caleb? I need to find Caleb. I need to get to the dungeons."

"Stella," Ann gasped. "Why?"

"They've taken him there. I need to get to him," I said urgently.

"Who, Stella?" Bonnie asked. Her voice sounded odd, as though she were speaking to a spooked animal.

"Kade! They've taken Kade. They're going to beat him. 'Tis already done, I'm sure they're hurting him. I need to help him. 'Tis my fault, all of it!"

"But, Stella," said Ann, "what's happened to *you?* Have you hurt yourself? Whose blood—?"

"It was Aleck," I replied quickly. "He's dead. I killed him."

There a communal gasp of horror. "You did *what?*" Clementine asked. "Oh, God, Stella, *how? Why?*"

"Isn't it obvious?" I yelled, frantic with my quest. Each second seemed to compound the distance and the channeling effects of Kade's agony in me. "I had to. He tried to force me, and Campbell and his men took Kade. I need to find Jamie and Caleb. He knows the way to the dungeons. Tell me where they are. *Please!*" I was holding Bonnie's shoulders, and her eyes were not on me but on the blade of the knife I still held, which ran through the strands of her long dark hair, cutting a loch, causing it to fall to the floor.

"Aye, Stella!" Bonnie said.

"I'm not asking you to come with me. Just tell me where he is. And Caleb, where's Caleb? I'll find the way myself."

"I don't know, Stella. *I don't know*," she repeated. "They're using him as a messenger. He could be anywhere."

This was unwelcome news, to be sure. I didn't have time to wander the keep in search of him.

I knew it was a futile question, but I asked it anyway. "You don't know where the dungeons are, do you? Any of you?"

Bonnie answered as I expected. "Nay. They keep its location secret, even from the men. Only senior officers are privy to that information." Bonnie was wide-eyed and shaken. As were we all. "Would you have me... come with you, Stella?"

"I'll go alone. I can keep myself hidden more easily that way."

"Nay, Stella!" cried Ann. "'Tis too dangerous! I'm coming with you. You need someone with you in case something happens. In case you need help."

"Nay," I said, surprised by the raw authority of my own voice. "Clementine. Bonnie. Take some food and go to your chambers. Find the others. Keep yourselves safe." My father had fortified the locks of our private chambers long ago. I knew them to be virtually unbreakable. "Lock the doors well. Stay there and do not come out until the Mackenzie army has not only arrived but also driven the Campbells either back to their keep or to the fiery depths of hell itself."

My sisters seemed taken aback not only by the tone of my command but also by its somewhat colorful delivery. I couldn't help being secretly pleased by the thought that my husband would have appreciated that line. I was picturing his face and the tiny quirk at the corner of his mouth when I amused him. The image made me more determined than ever to save him. The ache in my chest was very nearly overwhelming. His agony and mine felt like one and the same.

And my sisters obeyed me.

Except one.

She had been quiet until now, but her eyes were lit with the singular feminine tenacity and also the willfulness that were among the strongest threads of her character. It might have been the mention of the Mackenzies that made her decision. If the Mackenzie army was alerted to our dire situation, that meant that the Stuart army would also inevitably learn of it. And *that* meant that Wilkie Mackenzie might, very soon, be on his way to Glenlochie. There was no way Maisie would allow herself to be holed up and hidden if even the slightest likelihood of his arrival was upon us. And there, amid her stubbornness and her hope, I could see a realization in her eyes, too. "You love him," she said.

"Aye," I told her with utter sincerity. "I'll do whatever it takes to free him."

She understood, and against every impulse I knew my sister to possess, there were tears in her eyes as she said, "I didn't mean what I said, Stella. Of course you deserve each other. You and Kade are a perfect match, 'tis obvious to all of us. I'm sorry for what I said to you. I was jealous and heartbroken. And now I'm going to make amends for my horrid behavior." My sister was a ball of feminine wiles and urges. But she had a good heart. This, I had to—and did—believe. She continued, her eyes shiny with tears. "I didn't know, Stella. He just looks so much like…and I thought—"

"It doesn't matter, sister. I knew why you did it. 'Tis of no consequence now."

Ann was draping a cape over my shoulders and securing it tightly at my neck. "To hide the weapons and the…evidence," she said, her voice choked from emotion. "Come back safe to us."

And so Maisie and I took our leave of our sisters in search of the dungeons.

CHAPTER NINETEEN

THE NIGHT WAS eerily dark. Thin black clouds veiled the feeble light of a slivered crescent moon. The keep was far from quiet. The sound of men's restlessness punctuated the darkness. Metal and leather. Footsteps and shouted commands.

I was glad of the darkness and the noise. We could keep ourselves hidden and stay well clear of the gathered clusters of soldiers, whose raucous activity seemed to suggest that they were well stocked in whiskey and were ready to partake now that the sun had gone down. If we were seen, the consequences were too dire to consider. Women didn't wander alone, out of doors, and in the dark of night. Not unless they were asking for trouble of one kind or another. And especially not on a night like this, when only a few hours ago, an invading army who had allied themselves with an aggressive and mutinous faction of our clan had infiltrated our keep. With the sole purpose of proving their domination of everything and everyone in their path.

The risks were daunting indeed. But I had no choice but to find Kade and to free him. If there was anything I could do to ease or end his agony, I would do it. No matter what it cost me.

So Maisie and I walked quietly, arm in arm, toward the blacksmith's hut. I feared for her safety as much as my own, yet I was glad of her stubbornness. I was grateful not to be alone.

The tradesmen's area was located at the near edge of the village, easily accessible by clan members from the manor and the fields, as well as by the soldiers. There were leatherworkers' huts, wood turners, inventors, weavers, agricultural equipment builders, stonecutters, glassblowers and metalworkers, among many others. We made sure to keep a comfortable distance from the soldiers' barracks, which was not far from the tradesmen's huts. Even from a distance, it was easy to see that the barracks were crowded, noisy and well lit.

Our journey was slightly longer than it should have been, because of this detour, but we found our way over uneven ground.

"I have a sleeping potion in my pocket," I told Maisie quietly. "And three weapons. If we find the dungeons, we can try to drug the guards."

Maisie glanced over at me as we walked. "'Tis a good plan, Stella. Once we find these elusive dungeons, which are in a top-secret location privy only to the highest-ranking officers in our fractured army, I'll hold down the guards while you pour the potion down their throats. And if they don't submit quietly, we'll wield our weapons, experts as we are, against the most feared, lethal, bloodthirsty rebels in all the Highlands. I don't see any problem with your plan whatsoever."

Of course she was right. I was daft to even be considering doing what we were about to attempt to do. "I have to try," I whispered.

"I know, sister. I would try, too, if it were me. That's why I'm here with you. I want to help you. I want to… make it up to you."

I'd always loved my sister, despite her complex and sometimes-exasperating character, but I had never loved her so much as at that moment. "You don't have to—"

"Aye. I do. But after this, consider us even." She laughed lightly and despite our situation, I couldn't help smiling back at her. "Besides, I have an idea."

"What idea?"

"Just leave it to me, when the time comes." She paused as we made our way over a small stream, stepping on dry, upraised rocks to get across. "What is it that changed your mind about him? About Kade?"

I thought about this. "I don't know. I realized I'm a better, happier, stronger person when I'm with him." It took me a moment to try to put it into words. "He makes me feel powerful…yet protected at the same time."

"I know what you mean." She fell quiet then, and I understood why.

"You'll find someone else, Maisie. I know you will. I'm going to help you."

"We'll see," she said. We needed to keep silent then as we drew closer to the buildings.

We had reached the village. At this time of night, few people were around. Most had gone back to their cabins in the residential areas, or to their farmhouses. The occasional window was lit from within by candlelight as we passed by, and we were able to reach the hut without being seen. It was clear long before we reached it that there were no candles burning in Caleb's windows. When we tried the door, it was locked.

"What do we do now, Stella?" Maisie whispered.

"We try to find the dungeon on our own," I replied, not at all sure how to go about doing that.

As if in an answer to my silent prayer, I heard laughter. A man's laughter. From somewhere afar, over the rise of a large, rounded hill. The sound of it was familiar to me. I knew who it was from the beatings I'd been subjected to at his hand, and Aleck's.

Hugh.

He'd found it amusing, my tears and my pleas. He'd enjoyed the small power it afforded him, to bully someone weaker than himself, and at his laird's orders no less. Something about the unbalanced hierarchy of it had satisfied him. It occurred to me then that he didn't know of Aleck's death yet. No one did, aside from me and my sisters. It also occurred to me that Hugh was Aleck's right-hand man; they always trained together, fought together, planned together: if Aleck was the cause of the division within our army, and the instigator of the Campbell alliance, then Hugh would no doubt be a part of it, as well. And if Aleck wasn't entertaining Campbell and his officers—he was occupied, they knew, with other pressing matters—then that task would have fallen into Hugh's hands.

Hugh would be with Campbell and his men. The very men who had taken my husband away.

There were other voices, too, and laughter.

I pulled Maisie along with me, cautiously. "This way," I whispered.

As we drew closer, the voices grew louder. There were many of them, maybe eight or ten. It would have been Campbell's senior officers, I guessed. Gathered, very possibly, around the entrance of the dungeons.

The area behind the hill, as we made our way around, was covered in shrubby bushes and tall grasses; the brushy fauna seemed overabundant in the open space of the grasslands, as though it might have been planted there to disguise a doorway. At least I hoped that to be true and I was looking for evidence that it might be. And I was glad of the shrubbery; it would allow us to stay hidden.

From our distance, we peeked through the shielding branches to see a number of men gathered. I counted them: eight in total. Seven of them were seated in an uneven semicircle around a small fire. They were talking and passing around a bottle of whiskey. The eighth was lying on the ground; he appeared to be asleep. I focused more carefully. I could identify Hugh, and I could see that the other men were Campbell's top-ranking officers. The sleeping man, I thought but couldn't be entirely sure, was Laird Campbell himself. Several hours, perhaps, had passed since my husband had been taken by these men. More than enough time to inflict very real damage on a prisoner. Campbell appeared to be taking a respite from his torturous pursuits, satisfied perhaps that he had made a good job of it for now.

Behind them, near where Campbell slept, was the unmistakable shine of metal.

Hinges. And the frame of a door.

The dungeons. Clever, I thought, to situate the prisons so close to the barracks, but underground, with a secret entrance, hidden from enemies who might try to retrieve their prisoners.

I knew we had found it. I knew that behind that door was my husband.

Somehow we needed to get past these men.

The bottle of whiskey was placed to the side and I could see that it was less than a quarter full. If I could somehow pour the sleeping drug into it, I thought the proportions would be right: enough to knock them out for an hour, maybe more.

But how?

Maisie offered me the answer, as though I had asked the question aloud. My sister, for all her faults, was well versed in the ways of clever feminine wiliness. And she had a plan.

"I'm going to distract these men, Stella," Maisie whispered. "And you're going to sneak around behind this row of bushes and pour your potion into that bottle of whiskey."

I looked at her in the semidarkness under a bold crescent moon and a myriad of bright stars. The black clouds were gone now. I prayed that this might be a good omen. "What are you going to do? You can't show yourself, Maisie. 'Tis far too dangerous. These are uncivilized men. There's no telling what they might do."

"I can handle them," she said. "I'll promise to return to them with food and more drink. And perhaps a little more than that. They'll allow me to leave. I can be quite convincing when I put my mind to it."

I hoped she was right, and I feared greatly for her safety. I refused to let go of her arm.

"We've little other choice, Stella," she said, prying my fingers loose. "Let's do what needs doing. Go." And with that, my sister unfastened the top two buttons of her gown and strode out into the clearing.

Galvanized with fear, for her, for me, for my husband most of all, I crept along behind the row of shrubbery, as quiet as I had ever been.

"Good evening, soldiers," Maisie said coyly, walking right into their circle as if she were a long-lost friend of Campbell and his rebellion. "Hugh," she greeted. "Campbells, welcome. I've been sent from the manor to offer our guests refreshments. Indeed you must be hungry."

Her intrusion, for a moment, was met with silence. Then, with leering chuckles, followed quickly by lewd, suggestive comments. "You've no idea, lass," said one of them, "and I know exactly what I intend to eat."

This inspired bawdy laughter.

Maisie giggled lightly at his comment. I was astounded by her bravery. She had the courage of all these soldiers put together. Either that or she was *that* sure of her feminine influence that she had no doubts whatsoever that she could manipulate these and any other men any way she chose. "That might be arranged, after

I bring you some meat from our kitchens. What do you prefer? Lamb? Or venison? Why don't I bring a bit of both?" She stood close to the soldier who had spoken to her directly, fingering the tufted horsehair of the helmet he still wore. "A big, strong warrior such as yourself needs sustenance."

"Aye," the man replied, somewhat less lecherously, as though he was, in fact, hungry.

She weaved her way through the men, describing some of the food the kitchens had to offer. She had the undivided attention of each and every one of them.

And I took my opportunity. I reached from behind the leafy branch I hid behind to grab the whiskey bottle, which was unstoppered. Carefully—and quickly—I poured the entire contents of the glass vial into it, swirling it to mix the contents. Then I placed the bottle back where it had been.

Maisie watched me out of the corner of her eye as she leaned over one of the men, granting him a privileged view of her abundant cleavage. "What a big sword you have," she commented, touching his shoulder. "I like strong warriors with big swords. Why don't I get you some more whiskey, as well? Have you run out?"

The soldier looked to his right, locating the bottle. And to our infinite luck, he took a large swig, then passed the whiskey around. The men drank all that was left. "Aye," said one of the men, to which the other men laughed.

"Stay a little longer," one of the soldiers said, touching Maisie's gown with his hand, but she skirted him coquettishly.

"I'll be back soon," Maisie told them, retreating into the darkness. "I'll feed you myself if you're good. If you let me play with your sword."

"Hurry," one of them called after her.

There was some murmured mirth in the aftermath of Maisie's interruption, which lulled into silence within a matter of minutes. By the time Maisie found her way back to me, several of the men were snoring loudly and all of them were sprawled on the ground, deeply asleep.

Our plan had worked.

Campbell still lay in front of the door, holding the keys loosely in his grasp.

It almost seemed too risky to tamper with him. The possibility of waking him would have unleashed too much consequence. But of course we needed the keys. I had no doubt Kade would be chained and worse. But as I reached with determined trepidation to extricate the keys from the sleeping warrior's grasp, a hand went over my mouth as I was grabbed roughly around the waist and pulled behind a bush.

My FIRST THOUGHT was that one of the men had awakened or had feigned sleep, suspecting our plan, thwarting it and avowing to kill us in retribution. I was so certain that my time had come that I almost gave into it. I went still, allowing myself to be dragged backward. Episodic images flickered across my consciousness. My mother's face, hazed by the distance of time; my sister Ann's kind eyes; the scent of the night garden; Kade's expression as we'd made our wedding vows. And in that flashing memory, I had a sudden and powerful realization: he'd loved me even then. I'd been too overcome on the day and knew too little about the manifestations of his emotion at that time to read him. But now, in hindsight, I understood. *He wants you.* And I wanted him. Desperately and acutely. More than my own life.

I thrashed against my aggressor, reaching for my knife and breaking free at the same moment he let go.

I turned on him, holding up my knife, ready to strike.

But I stopped myself, as I realized who it was. It was Caleb. His hands were held up in a defensive disclosure. Maisie stood behind him. Both of them looked at me with a mixture of shock and disbelief. "Stella, you're *armed?*" Caleb asked. "You're fighting back?" In his simple questions, I realized Caleb had summed up the changes in me that my marriage had, if not introduced, then at least *allowed.* I was empowered. And I had to admit, it felt remarkably good. I felt strong and wild-eyed. Defiant and bold. Here now, with a knife in my hand and a purpose to fight for, I felt a truer version of myself than ever before. I was going to get what I wanted—my husband—no matter what I had to do to find him, free him and keep him. Or I would die trying. "While I applaud your sentiments," Caleb said, "put it down. I'm here to help you. There's another way in. If Campbell wakes, he'll kill us all. Come. Hurry."

We crept farther around the base of the tall hill, following Caleb. "How did you find us?" I whispered.

"My brother heard that your husband was taken. I went to find you and your sisters told me where you were headed. Jamie's waiting for us at the back entrance. 'Tis used by the tradesmen," he explained. "I used it when I installed the chains."

Jamie was loyal to my husband, I knew that. And I was relieved by it, especially now, in this fraught and dangerous darkness. It made me feel as though our cause had numbers and hope. Campbell was here, but Aleck was dead. Campbell's small army was among us, but so were our own troops, many of which were against the mutiny, and fighting on our side.

Caleb spoke again. "Jamie has sent messengers to summon the Mackenzie army. Since they're our closest neighbor, they'll at least know of our plight. They may even have made it to Kinloch by now. They were dispatched some time ago."

If we didn't free Kade by the time the Mackenzies arrived, he would be used as a pawn against his family, and if they didn't agree to any—and every—request made of Campbell, Kade would be tortured, slowly and horribly, until his life bled away. And there were many, many requests Campbell could make of them, I knew. He wanted ultimate power of the Highlands, including Ossian Lochs and Kinloch, too. Kade's life was worth it all to me, and to his siblings, but how much would be sacrificed to save him?

I stopped in my tracks, remembering a crucial detail. "The *key,* Caleb. We still need the key."

Caleb smiled slyly, pulling something from the

pocket of his trews. He held up a large and intricately carved silver key, which shone white in the moonlight. "I always make an extra. It proves handy to possess the master key to every lock in the keep."

I almost threw my arms around him and kissed him. Out of gratitude and nothing more. My fondness for Caleb was there, in my memory and here now. Once I had thought of his face as an etching on my thoughts, and it was true still. If Caleb was a pleasant, comforting surface inscription, then Kade was a deep, gouging totality. My love for my husband had become so much a part of me that it felt like the very blood that coursed through my veins. Aye, his warrior's blood had mixed with my own, transforming my life, and me along with it.

We could see Jamie's silhouette now, against the night. But there was no door, nor bushes of any kind. And then, as we drew closer, I could see that a trapdoor had been opened, lined with sod and dirt. There was a small hole in the ground, just large enough for a man to fit through. The top rungs of a ladder leading down were just visible.

Wordlessly, Jamie began to climb into it, disappearing from sight. Caleb made a move to follow him, but I held his arm. "Caleb," I began, "you don't have to risk your life. You've done enough."

But Caleb gently removed my hand, as though remembering Kade's warning. "Your husband, Stella, is soon to be laird of our clan. Considering our past, my life will be a living hell if I don't prove to him that I am worthy and loyal. Let me do this."

Caleb began climbing down into the dungeons and I didn't bother to argue with him further. In truth, I was glad of his newfound bravery, and I understood it. We had both grown in this way and there seemed no point to deny him his right to prove himself.

I turned to face Maisie, and I held her hands. "Your debt is repaid, sister. There's no need for you to come farther. Go back to the manor and lock yourself away. As lady of this keep, I'm issuing you an order. I'll not take nay for an answer."

"Stella, are you certain—"

"*Go.*"

I wasn't sure if it was the manic resolution in my voice, the ominous and unfathomable black hole or the combination of the two, but to my intense relief, my sister, for perhaps the first time in her life, obeyed.

Maisie retreated toward the manor as I began my descent down the ladder into the dark abyss of the dungeons.

I MIGHT HAVE been descending into hell itself. The darkness was thick and total. I could see nothing, not even my own hands as I clutched the damp rungs of the wooden ladder, my feet feeling clumsily along the narrow, slippery surface for the next step. It was a long way down.

I thought of Kade. Alone. In pain. In the dark. Was his life draining away as he dreamed of the gentle hills of his home, wishing he had never seen me or met me or sacrificed himself as he had?

There were shuffling footsteps below me and a sudden, vibrant light. Jamie and Caleb had reached the bottom and had lit a small torch that illuminated an orange circle of brightness. They waited for me to climb down the last rungs of the ladder. "This way," said Jamie, leading us into a narrow dirt tunnel.

I listened for sounds, of groans or calls for help. But there was nothing but our almost-silent footsteps.

We didn't have far to travel. The tunnel soon opened up into a large, open chamber. Along one side of the corridor was a row of prison cells, carved into the dirt and clad with thick iron bars. We passed one, and another. Empty. And a third. Could it be that Campbell had taken my husband somewhere else? That he had tricked us into thinking that Kade would be kept here when, in fact, he'd hidden him somewhere else, somewhere we would never be able to find? Or had he killed him already and buried him in an unmarked grave? The thought caused me to choke back a sob. What had I done?

But my fears were, in part, allayed. There, in front of us, at the end of the oval room, lay a large, inclined slab. And a figure. A man, clad only in the shreds of his kilt.

Kade.

He lay so still. Too still.

It took me a moment to make out in the dim light that he had been laid on a bed of nails. As we drew closer, I could see that his wrists and ankles were bloodied by the chains that bound him. And he was being stretched, his arms pulled above his head, his legs pulled tight. His bare chest was cut and bruised, covered with dirt and stripes of dried blood.

Was he alive?

At that moment his head turned. His eyes were glazed and dull. He squinted against the small blaze and flinched at the sight of us. Hatred radiated from his beaten body and shone from his narrowed eyes, returning some life to him, at least. I realized he couldn't see who we were. He might have thought it was Campbell and his men, returning to beat him again, to tighten his bindings another notch.

"Release him," I said to Caleb. "Unlock the chains."

Caleb was already there, and Jamie moved with him, holding the light near Kade's ankles so Caleb could see.

I went to Kade, standing close to him, looking into his eyes. He recognized me, I could see that, but there was no joy in him at the realization. Behind the haze of his pain and delirium, the hatred lingered, a thread of fear, a brief glimmer of hope and, most of all, fury. I wanted to touch him, to somehow relieve him, but I hesitated. I didn't want to hurt him, or anger him further, and the look in his eyes unnerved me.

His gaze swerved to Caleb and Jamie, then back to me. He was clearly unsure of our agenda, of our loyalty, and I could read the doubts as they flickered across his face. *Have they been sent by Campbell? Or are they here of their own accord?*

"'Tis me, husband," I said. "We've come to free you. You're safe now. Your brother's army is on its way."

I was glad I had thought to tell him this, because it was the mention of his brother and his clan that speared through his fugue. His eyes became clearer and focused, just as Caleb unbound the last of his chains.

In one fluid, unexpectedly quick movement, Kade jumped off his torturous pyre and stood before us. He looked big, spooked, battered, yet entirely lethal. And it was a good thing, too, I thought. Because at that very moment, a second torch illuminated the night, emerging from the far tunnel that must have led to the entrance. A lone soldier, instantly recognizable.

In his other hand, Campbell held his sword.

IN AN INSTINCTUAL movement—and I could identify a small surge of pride at my newfound tendencies—I drew Kade's enormous sword from its scabbard, still slung across my shoulder, with some difficulty. I could barely lift it. Somehow I found the strength. I held it up. "Kade," I said.

If there was doubt in him, and if he questioned my motives in that moment, he didn't show it. He turned instantly, and seeing his salvation on offer, he walked over and grabbed it from my hands. His body, though beaten and bloodied, had lost none of its animal grace; he moved with an arrogant, fluent confidence that I could only hope and pray would see him through.

Kade was at a disadvantage, aye, since his strength had been depleted by agony and injury. But he had Jamie, who, although young and inexperienced, was at least armed. I handed Caleb the second of Kade's weapons I carried: the large bone-handled knife. Caleb contemplated me with a brief look of incredulity, but he took the knife. It looked awkward in his hands; he was as untrained in the art of warfare as I was, but something was better than nothing. And I had my small knife. Small, but still capable of killing a man: this I knew to be true. In fact, it was still carrying the blood of proof.

But my silent celebrations at our odds were decidedly short-lived. Hugh appeared in the arched doorway, menacing, armed and very much awake.

The battle was on.

Campbell struck at Kade first, a mighty blow that carried all the weight of his intention. And Kade answered the blow as his equal. My husband, bloodied or not, came to life with a sword in his hands, as though energized and healed by its familiar solidity, as though he absorbed strength from its steel. They circled each other, and I backed away, taking refuge behind the bed of nails, crawling under it, readying myself to lash out at Campbell's feet and legs if the opportunity arose.

Hugh went for Jamie, knocking his sword from his hands in a single swipe. Hugh was a seasoned warrior and outweighed Jamie by a considerable amount. But Jamie retrieved his sword and answered his charge, holding his own, but barely. Caleb could do little to help his brother. He held up the knife and clung to the periphery, desperately out of his depths. But he was here, and at the ready, and offering whatever assistance he could, and I was glad of it.

Campbell and Kade's fight was at fever pitch, blow

after blow, the echoing clang of metal against metal filling the room like brash, violent music. Kade was tiring, I could see; the torture and blood loss had taken their toll. I was desperate to intervene, and crept closer.

A howl punctuated the darkness. Jamie was hit. I couldn't see where. His leg, I thought. There was blood, and lots of it. And they were wrestling now, with Hugh pinning Jamie down. Caleb leaped on to him, stabbing with his knife. And Jamie's sword found purchase from below. Hugh growled in pain.

But my attention shifted. It was then that Kade stumbled. Just slightly, but it was a sign. Campbell was working his advantage. Their swords were blurred with the heat of their fight. And Campbell's back was to me. His feet moved closer to where I was crouched under the pyre.

I struck, slicing through the flesh of his calf.

Campbell howled, not expecting my attack. He lost concentration for a single moment, looking behind him. And it was all the opportunity Kade needed. It was the kind of invitation he trained each and every day of his life to exploit. Kade's sword struck at Campbell's throat, above the chainmail's edge, in a precise, fatal angle, sinking deep.

With a final, brittle choking sound, Campbell's body fell to the floor.

Campbell, whose family had led two generations of war throughout the Highlands, was dead.

Jamie, Hugh and Caleb all lay on the floor. There was movement, but I couldn't tell who it was; the torches, discarded nearby on the dirt floor of the dungeon, were now flickering and sparse.

Kade walked over to where they lay, surveying the damage.

Caleb stood, somewhat unsteadily. He stepped back from Kade, as though fearful that Kade might attack him next.

Jamie was groaning and writhing. His leg, I could now see, was badly injured.

Hugh's bulky form lay still, a spreading puddle of black underneath him. Kade, as though to make sure of it, stepped forward and cut his throat.

Kade pulled Jamie to his feet, supporting him. He looked once at Caleb, then once, in a lingering, intense glare, at me. Then he walked to the front entrance of the cave, dragging Jamie along with him.

I thought to tell him, *'Tis not safe! What if the soldiers have wakened, as Hugh did?* But I had a feeling my husband would neither listen to me nor be frightened by my warning. Either way, he was already gone. Caleb and I followed him.

Outside, the first hints of dawn were glowing along the horizon. The sleeping soldiers lay where we had left them, showing no signs of life. Kade took in the scene with alert contemplation. Kade lowered Jamie to the ground, where he sat quietly, his face pale with pain and blood loss. Kade found a discarded tunic on the ground and began shredding it into long strips. He said to Caleb, "Help me tie their wrists," which they then proceeded to do, and particularly securely. One or two of the men stirred, but none woke. When all of the sleeping soldiers' hands had been tied, Kade said to Caleb, "Assist your brother to the manor and see that he is looked at by a healer. Rally Tristan, Eion and Colin. Have them imprison these men and do their utmost to secure any other Campbells on the premises. Are we understood?"

"Aye," Caleb confirmed.

"I will join you momentarily," Kade added. "But first, I have some urgent business to discuss with my wife."

And with that, my husband picked me up and began to carry me down through the dense shrubbery and down toward the loch.

CHAPTER TWENTY

WE HAD WALKED some distance around the side of a small cliff, and were now out of sight from the fields and the manor, alone.

Kade set me down on my feet. He grabbed my arm and pulled me roughly alongside him. His grip was not at all gentle, and he clearly didn't care if he was hurting me. In fact, the dull pain as he dragged me into a secluded recess of rock had a very different effect on me than I might have expected. I did not shrug off his punishing grip, nor did I protest the stunning strength of his attack. My body was responding to him, as it always did, rising to his demands, opening to him, readying me for his onslaught. I felt brimming and supple, inexplicably. I could taste an otherworldly, unruly anticipation.

He pinned me against the hard rock wall, holding his sword to my neck. I went still, staring directly into his cold, vivid eyes. One of his eyes had a dark ring of a bruise around it and there was a cut along his cheekbone. His hair was a wild mane, matted with dirt and blood. He looked wilder and more enraged than I had ever seen him. This was how he must have appeared to his victims on the battlefield. Here was the ruthless warrior I had once feared beyond reason. Here was the beastly assailant who would take of me what he wanted without restraint or remorse.

Or he would kill me. I knew it was a very real possibility. He had been tested beyond his limits, and *I* was the cause of it. And, while I knew his ferocity was capable of melting without warning into something akin to devotion—I'd experienced it firsthand, after all—I knew his state of mind now was as far removed from benevolence as it was possible to be.

"'My husband is a brute and savage,'" he spat, repeating the words I had spoken. "I'll show you *savage,* wife. 'Tis who I am after all. You said it yourself." Kade's hands held the fastenings of my cape, his teeth bared; then he ripped the garment open, sending several bone buttons flying. My dress underneath had already been ripped, hours ago, and gaped open with his violence. My breasts were barely covered, and my nipples drew instantly tight at the rush of cold air and the feel of his stunningly hard body shoved up against mine.

I didn't care.

I didn't care that he might beat me and hurt me. He was considering it: I could read it in the shattered light of his eyes. The blade of his sword traced a line—very, very lightly—down one side of my throat, along thin, vulnerable skin. The slightest pressure would cut into my vein as he drew, if he chose to do it. I knew how sharp his weapons were kept.

"I love you," I said.

Deep within him, there was a buried, almost-undetectable recoil. He had not been expecting this.

His breath quickened, but he did not release his hold on me or remove his knife. He continued to quote my betrayal back to me, word for word. "'Tis well known this was an arranged marriage I wanted nothing to do with. Even Aleck knows it to be true.'"

"It was the only way I could keep you alive." My throat was parched. My voice was little more than a rasped whisper. I reached to touch my palm to his face but he flinched away from my touch angrily.

"You should have let me die," he seethed. "It would be a better fate than *this*."

"What *this?* We're *here*. We're alive. We're together."

"It matters not," he said with quiet fury, watching the trail of his blade's edge with some concentration.

"I want you, husband," I whispered. "Take me now. Take me before you kill me. Please."

"Do you not have a *new* husband? Have you not *already* been taken, as you wanted?" Somewhere beneath the rage of him, there was a gritty, graveled sorrow to his words that caused a hollow ache in my chest and a stinging burn behind my eyes.

"He is not and never will be my husband," I said. "He's dead." This did cause my eyes to fill, at the memory of what had *almost* happened, at the brutality and the horrific violence.

Still Kade's sword traced its thin line. He seemed so distracted by what he was doing that my statement barely registered. He didn't believe me. "Is that so?" he asked with an air of disengagement.

"Up and in," I breathed. "Twist and slice. It was easier than you said it would be. But there was much more blood than I ever could have imagined."

He paused, his regard walking up my face until he met my eyes. "What?"

"And then I slit his throat. Just in time."

His stillness unnerved me. His furious, caustic glare was not at all what I was hoping for. "Just in time?" he finally said.

I was losing some kind of edge. I was unraveling, for a thousand different reasons. "Aye, husband. *Just in time.* Just *after* I pretended to hate you so that Campbell would allow you to live. Just *before* Aleck *almost* claimed me as his own, *very nearly* violating everything about me, breaking me and destroying us, *just before* I slit his throat with your knife and watched as the light left his eyes and his blood spilled all over me in a sticky, horrible flood! *All right?* Could I spell it out any clearer for you?"

Kade's eyes narrowed and he gave me a look of cool disbelief. And it infuriated me down to the depths of my being that he could dismiss my loyalty to him so easily, even if I'd been convincing in the moment. Did he know nothing of me? Did nothing we'd shared in the past month and the distance we'd come even matter? Maybe it didn't. Maybe our connection had been only a purely physical, passing wave of lust—nothing more substantial, nothing more meaningful. Maybe the risks that I had taken and the lives I'd cut short to defend his own proved nothing to him, nothing at all.

"You…*intended* to kill him?" he said. "All along?"

The effects of this day had, at last, overwhelmed me. I was crying and seething all at once. "Of course I did, you daft fool! Is it really *that* easy for you to doubt me? Have I not shown you and told you and begged you to take me and possess me in every way because I desire you with my whole heart? And as for my *body,* I can hardly control the effect you have on me without even the slightest touch of your hell-raiser hand! Why, even now—" Here, I faltered, breathing heavily. I could not begin to tell him that even his threats and the sliding glide of his sword were not only causing my heart to break but also inspiring the most delicious, wicked necessity in my warming, secreted places that was so intense I thought the hidden sensation might very well drive me mad.

His sword just barely disengaged. Vexingly, I missed its promise. I wanted to feel the contact—*any* contact—with him and his wrath, his pain, his love.

"Go ahead," I said to him. "Kill me if that's your plan. Here." I lifted my chin, giving him a clean, exposed target. "Do it and get it over with. I've had enough of this, of you, of all of it!"

He seemed to be having difficulty grasping the meaning of my confession. "You mean your betrayal was all a…a *ruse?*"

"Are you an idiot as well as a brute?" I yelled. "*Aye!* I wasn't about to stand there and watch them carve your heart out with their razor-sharp meat cleavers! I knew they would allow you to live if they believed that I held no feelings for you, and that you were of value to them. I didn't think it would be so easy to fool *you,* however. Did I not just risk death—and worse, several times over—to free you? I *love* you, with everything I have! I dream of you and crave you and want you close to me and in my bed, always. And most of all I want you to keep your word to me—the one I *asked* you to keep, the one you'd *promised* you'd keep—and make love to me and seal this marriage once and for all, you... you *big man!*"

There was no humor in Kade this time as I blurted out the inane accusation. His emotion in his eyes was fiery and wrought. The blade at my throat was withdrawn, and I heard the heavy thud as it was dropped to the ground.

He kissed me.

I was so strung with the conflicting turmoil of my ordeal and my passion, I almost tried to push him away. His mouth caught at mine, opening me to his avid invasion. He kissed me as if he had already taken possession of me, as though he were already inside me. I could taste his hunger. This kiss was full of him, and full of all the promise of what he was about to do. His tongue drove deeper, articulate and unrelenting. And the more passionate his kiss became, the more I wanted of him. I felt his sweet, loaded aggression to my very core. Every lick and every drive sent a clenching awareness to my tender depths. He *was* going to ravage me, and I wanted all of it, every ounce of his force and his ruthlessness. In an incongruously gentle gesture, his fingers stroked back my hair. In his touch I could feel a light tremor, the hum and near restraint of his incredible power and his intense desire.

Kade's hands moved to my breasts, jerking aside the shredded covering of my gown and my cape, pushing the velvet fabric over my shoulders and letting it fall to the ground, baring my skin, which gleamed pale in the darkness. I was naked before him. His hands cupped my breasts and he leaned down, his mouth seeking the tip, stroking with his tongue, drawing the tight nub into wet heat. I almost wept as the firm, damp tugs sent jolts of pleasure to the low pit of my stomach, and lower still. He moved to my other breast, heightening the need with his ferocious, lush intent. I couldn't get enough of him. I was pinned against the mossy rock wall, and my hips writhed forward, tilting against him, cradling his hardness with the soft, rhythmic pressure of my plea. He felt the furtive invitation, and stood to take my mouth in another demanding kiss. Biting, licking, tasting. And it wasn't enough. I reached up to weave my fingers through his wild hair, pulling him closer. My breasts pressed against him, dragging sensually through the light pelt as his hands moved down my body, gripping me from behind, kneading into me. I knew I'd wear the bruised marks of his lust tomorrow, and I was glad of it. I had never been so wild with need, so desperate for something, anything. I moaned into his mouth as his fingers touched me, parting damp flesh so sensitive I could only cry out as he delved deeper, stretching me deliciously. His thumb found the delicately bundled nerves at my center, skating in a bold, fluid design, expertly coaxing the untamed pleasure. I was almost lost to it. I could have let myself succumb to his lush caresses. But I was determined to stave off my release until we were fully joined. I reached beneath his kilt, gasping at the sheer size of him, rigid and immense.

Kade's fingers slid from my body. He lifted me with shocking ease. I gripped his flexed arms, astounded by the raw strength of him, which excited me beyond belief. His power was primal and potent. I wanted him to use it on me. I wanted him to possess me with it unconditionally. My arms were wrapped around his neck and I was kissing his lips, slipping my tongue just between them. I felt him. The broad head of his shaft was pushing into my snug entrance, forcing entry, and the stretching burn of his invasion was simply the most profound sensation I had ever endured. I was so wet that his impossible thickness began to glide deeper despite my forbidding tightness, and I writhed at the unfamiliarly thrilling torment, which caused him to sigh with a spoken oath. He tore through my innocence with one forceful drive, and the sharp burn burst instantly into a sumptuous, pain-flicked pleasure. I knew this promise. He had imprinted my body with his compelling, stormy seduction. I understood that behind the notes of pain was a higher, fiercer pleasure. My body locked tightly around his hot, thrusting flesh, pulling him deeper.

"Stella, Stella," he was murmuring, *"So sweet, so soft. You feel too good, lass. I've wanted you for too long. I love you. I love you. Since that very first day. Oh, God, 'tis too much. I love you."*

He lowered my legs, holding my weight entirely but allowing my feet to lightly touch the ground, opening me to his erotic assault. This big, hard warrior husband was all around me, holding me, devouring me, plunging deeply and repeatedly into the slippery, tight constriction of my body. I gave myself over completely to his dominating demand. The pain was shaded and low-lying, upholding the pleasure, intensifying it relentlessly. I tried to hold it back, but the glow flared, rippling in a flowering surge, overwhelming me entirely. I gave in to it, unable to control myself, riding the overflowing, rippling torrent of pleasure. Kade's grip on my hips tightened, and he bucked upward, sinking himself deep within me, groaning as he gave in to his own deluge. My inner muscles clenched around him in welcoming pulls, calming gradually into a dreamy, lulling delirium.

We stood there for some time, both of us unwilling to disengage. He held my head against his shoulder in a protective, shielding embrace. Then he gently took my face between his hands and looked into my eyes. Behind his stoic relief, I could read there wonder and unbound elation. "I love you," he whispered, and I repeated his words over and over, kissing him, until the kisses grew in intensity once again. And my husband's expansive presence deep within me had not abated.

Kade seemed adamant about keeping himself thoroughly wedged inside me, and the light softening that had taken place after his release now gave way to a joyful, skewering revival. He lowered us to the ground, somehow maneuvering us so he lay on top of me. And he was still firmly rooted inside me. Now that the ecstasy had subsided, he felt larger even than he had before. His body seemed to vibrate with a warm, febrile animation that lurked just under the surface of his skin.

He kept himself still, touching his lips to my face in nibbling caresses. He pushed back the unruly strands of my hair, watching my half-closed eyes. Then he began to move again, just barely, with a subtle grind of his hips. "You're going to burn again for me and with me, wife," he said softly.

I was limp and fully, massively impaled. My hair was damp at the roots, my skin flushed. I shook my head back and forth. I couldn't find that level of pleasure again; I felt utterly shattered, beatifically used. I didn't think I could survive another round of such intensity, let alone aspire to it. "Nay. I can't," I told him, squirming against the fullness within me. I felt entirely occupied by him.

His body began to move more insistently within me. Controlled, coaxing thrusts. "Aye, you can. And you will." His movement gained momentum, spearing me with thick, persuasive heat.

Kade held my jaw in his large, warm hand, forcing me to look him in the eye. "Wrap your legs around me, lass." Almost too spent to find the energy, I obeyed him nonetheless. The edges of dawn were upon us, and his eyes were too blue, his face too severe in its beauty; the sight of him in all his turbulent glory caused a tightening in my chest that almost felt like faith. "You," he whis-

pered, looking deep into my eyes, "are the most exquisite creature that ever walked this earth. Now kiss me.
Open again to me, your husband. You are mine, and I
am yours. We are bound, irrevocably."

It was he who kissed me, with astounding adoration amid the passion; the kiss was hungry and sweet,
transformative in its urgent, connective desire. I kissed
him back, opening to him in every way it was possible
to do. My arms and legs were wrapped around him,
holding him as close as he could be. His obsession was
so complete, so extreme, that I felt as though the entire
center of me was only him, as though I were merely a
shell and all that was in me, from my pleasured, wanting flesh to my heavy-beating heart, was him, and his.
The wave began as a low, gentle current, stoked by his
tempo, fed by his thick, silky depth. My hands were in
his hair, my tongue playing his tongue, drawing him
deeper into me. The pleasure was molten and otherworldly. I was consumed, my body lit with seductive,
all-encompassing rapture. I cried out into his mouth as
he plunged into me, my body answering his, clamping
hotly around his deeply insinuated flesh, drawing out
another astounding, ecstatic deliverance. His groan
was a savage, animal sound, as though all his agonies
were being released. He shuddered from the force of
his own upheaval, his shaft pulsing vibrantly inside
me, flooding me with life-giving warmth as the tears
wet my cheeks.

'Twas done, I realized. This marriage was, at last,
sealed.

IN THE LIGHT of an amber-hued morning, Kade held me close to him for a time as the sun rose upon green hills swathed in heather blooming purple and pink. The bright sky was precisely the same color as my husband's eyes. "I'm going to take such good care of you," he whispered to me. "I'm never going to let you go." He led me down to the loch, where we swam together. The coolness of the water felt delicious against my sore, swollen flesh. He came to me, washing me with the enchanting, careful brush of his hands. His caresses continued, cleaning me, touching me with meticulous care. Such care, in fact, that the coolness warmed and the luscious rhythm spread. Warm fingers entered me, enticing the charmed heat, and I came again, in long, luxurious, abounding shivers that were teased and extended for endless, entranced moments.

We dried ourselves in the sun and dressed as best we could with the ripped and soiled clothing we carried.

Our fortune had taken a turn for the better, it seemed. The keep, as we walked back to it, was overrun. Not with Campbells; they had either fled or were likely being held captive. These visitors were many, huge, and clad head to toe in the now-familiar green and blue tartan that caused my husband to smile widely and sweep me into his arms.

The Mackenzies had arrived.

EPILOGUE

IT HAS BEEN exactly ten months since Kade and I made our marriage official. Between that day and this, my life has taken on an enchanted quality that astounds me each and every day with its beauty. Glenlochie is practically unrecognizable. Its refurbishment is an ongoing process, but the manor has never looked more magnificent. The gardens are gloriously lush, the fields bursting with crops that will soon be harvested.

The wider clan has enjoyed a startling transformation. Gone are the days of resentment and idleness. Now, as a people, we pride ourselves on hard work and endeavor, and we are, more than ever before, reaping the rewards of both our individual and collective industriousness. We are sought out by other clans for reasons of bartering and commerce, as our tradesmen are becoming newly recognized as some of the most productive and skilled in Scotland. Not only the manor but our village and the surrounding orchards and agricultural lands have benefitted from the new prosperity this trade brings. New shops and houses are being built, of bigger and more elaborate designs. Experts are taking on apprentices. Bartering stalls are everywhere, offering useful and innovative supplies that are not only necessary but increasingly grand and frivolous, from food to furs, from goats to gold. The walls of our keep are strong and well kept.

The army is becoming a well-oiled machine, and is more loyal to my husband with each passing day. In the end, my husband issued the men of the army who disputed his leadership a choice: exile or a challenged duel to the death against him. One man fled, and several others lost their lives. After that, there were no more protests about his leadership. We maintain ironclad alliances, of course, with both the Mackenzie clan and the Stuart clan, who possess the two strongest armies in all the Highlands. We also have close ties with the Munro, Buchanan and Macintosh clans. With the combined forces of the six armies, my husband feels confident we could win any war that might be waged.

Laird Campbell's rebellion died along with him. Without Campbell to rouse skirmishes across the Highlands, the landscape of our countryside has taken on—at least relative to what we had endured in recent years— a diplomatic, hospitable character. We are frequently invited to balls and gatherings at nearby keeps, and we entertain more visitors than ever before. An unprecedented number of interclan marriages have taken place in recent months, and our territories seem to have entered a time of peace and prosperity that is being celebrated far and wide. Kade and his brothers suspect that small rebellions are discussed and planned among the less-prosperous outliers, and they remain ever watchful, but their confidence and preparation have, for now, proved adequate.

My sisters, as I am, are happier than I have ever seen them. Clementine decided not to retreat to the nunnery after all. She has found great satisfaction in the kitchens, and runs them with a flair that I didn't even know she possessed. Cooking, and especially baking, has become her passion, and she spends every waking hour orchestrating our family's shared meals with great success. My husband even commented once that our menus are now rivaling those even of the Mackenzie cooks—his highest compliment.

Bonnie married Jamie as soon as his recovery allowed. He walks with a limp but has regained his strength almost entirely. He remains one of Kade's most dedicated soldiers.

Lottie renewed her romance with Aiden Buchanan, married him soon after and was swept away to the Buchanan keep in a flurry of festivity. Each month she writes us elaborate letters detailing the very boisterous and sometimes scandalous activities of the lively Buchanan clan. Her husband, she relays with obvious glee, entirely lives up to—and perhaps even surpasses—the Buchanans' well-known reputation for "exuberance."

Ann and Agnes have been inspired by the close friendship they have made with Kade's sister Ailie and have taken up dressmaking, with surprisingly creative and successful results. Their designs reflect both Ann's whimsy and Agnes's style, and they are overrun with requests for their skills, so much so that they now have a number of assistants. For this reason, and that of our newfound prosperity, the ladies of our clan are looking more refined and fashionable than ever before.

Maisie, of all my sisters, is the one who still lacks a certain calling, save one. I suspect, however, that the past several days have introduced new and pleasing possibilities. We have been entertaining a group of Mackenzie and Stuart clanspeople, including soldiers who have come for a special event. The first evening after their arrival, Maisie met a Mackenzie officer named Rory who just so happens to be Kade's—and Wilkie's—first cousin. The resemblance is somewhat remarkable. Late that evening, I noticed Maisie and Rory in a rather intimate embrace. I caught my sister's sparkling eye as she was being led, quite willingly, away. I haven't seen her since.

I still run into Caleb from time to time. He has become a respected sword maker. He and Kade have even formed a somewhat stilted working relationship that seems to have eased, especially after Caleb's betrothal to one of the village girls, a sweet, fair-haired weaver named Hazel. I wish them only joy.

My husband has been true to his word. His love for me infuses my life. He dedicates his every waking hour to my safety and my happiness. And now, in my delicate condition, he refuses to leave my side.

After our initial trials and tribulations smoothed out, I have found that the complex layers of Kade's personality, once peeled away through patience and gentle affection, expose astounding revelations. My husband is moody and volatile, aye. He is gruff and aggressive. These traits are natural by-products of his position and his overt masculinity. But underneath his strength, at the very heart of him, exists the kindest, gentlest and most loving person I have ever known. His love is unconditional and overwhelmingly heartfelt.

Over time, as I learned to trust him, Kade, too, has learned to trust me. He is highly tactile, and likes us to spend our private time together close, touching me and caring for me not only physically but emotionally, as well. He takes great interest in my innermost thoughts and my feelings, and each evening asks intricate questions about my activities during the day, when we have spent time apart. If there is something that bothers me, he'll address it directly and immediately, working through any problem until he is satisfied that I am no longer fearful or distraught. It is one of the most endearing qualities of him: he notices details, proving to me, time and time again, that he cares for me, and deeply. I have never felt more treasured or more loved.

In the past few months, however, my husband's care has become almost manic in its intensity. I have been appointed a team of not only healers and caregivers, but also guards and attendants. 'Tis not necessary, but I can hardly blame him. Both our mothers' deaths, after all, were the result of complications during childbirth. Kade's brother Knox, more recently, also lost his wife and child, and I can read the terror in Kade's expression, late at night as he lies next to me with his hands on my body, caressing and calming as though attempting to smooth away the dangers.

Three days ago, Wilkie and Roses arrived at Glenlochie with their two-month-old baby girl, named Mackenzie Rose Sophia Stuart, and a large entourage of protectors and attendants. Roses, despite her slender, somewhat waiflike appearance, gave birth without difficulty. Both she and her baby are strong and healthy: I know they must be or Wilkie would never have agreed to the travel. Roses's personal healer and closest friend, Ismay, is never far from her side, nor the baby's. And Roses herself is a talented healer. Both she and Ismay have offered to help me at the birth of my child, and although our clan has its own team of gifted healers, I am comforted to know that they will be on hand.

And Kade's other siblings are also visiting, Ailie with her betrothed, Magnus Munro, the tall and brooding copper-haired laird-in-waiting for the Munro clan. He is never far from her side. And Knox Mackenzie, much to his siblings' surprise, has taken an interest in a new arrival at Kinloch—a boisterous, red-headed city lass who, according to Christie, has caused some upheaval which I've yet to learn about. What is clear enough is that Knox Mackenzie seems to be sporting an entirely new personality. Gone is his stoic sternness; he is more quick to laugh and lighthearted than he's been, Kade says, since the death of his wife. Only Christie has yet to find a match as yet, but we have no doubt she will succumb eventually to one of the many men who pursue her. I don't believe Kade specifically asked any of them to come for the birth, but he readily agreed to it at their suggestion. I know my husband is not only relieved but calmed by their presence here, and so am I.

I am due any day. My belly is huge and I can feel our baby inside me, kicking and nudging; this baby is active and full of life. All in all, after a brief and early bout of morning sickness, I've had an easy, uneventful pregnancy. Kade and Clementine make sure I have only the most wholesome foods to eat, and my husband has, of late, forbidden me to work. I obey him without too much complaint; I feel wondrously alive, but I silently admit that the child does absorb much of my energy, and I am content to please my husband by taking care to relax and allow the baby to thrive and grow. My complexion is glowing and my hair is thick and glossy. My body feels healthily rounded and feminine. My husband finds my fertility something akin to a miracle. He is fascinated by the way I look, the way I feel and, it must be said, the way I taste. He cannot get enough of me, he says, and I believe him. He proves it to be so, and I have never felt the inclination to deny him whatever he wants of me.

I wake to his touch. He's nibbling on the lobe of my ear, playing with my fingers, whispering sweet words. "I love my wife," he's murmuring. "You're so warm, so sweet."

His mouth is kissing a line down my neck across my breast, and his hands are on my body. My eyes are still closed and I make a small sound of protest when he draws away. There's a stillness to him that gets my attention, and I open my eyes to the glittering brilliance of his blue contemplation. He's aghast at something, and I glance down to see what has given him pause. My breasts are leaking. Milk spills from me in glistening droplets. I'm shocked by this—although I shouldn't be, of course. The sight of the pale liquid seems so simultaneously lusty and life-giving, I am filled with heavy awe. Kade, holding my gaze with his own, leans over me. Instead of covering me or wiping me clean from an awkward distance, as I might have expected him to, he seems mesmerized. He teases me with his tongue, circling, licking the moisture, fastening his lips around the taut bud. I feel mortified by this, and I gasp aloud and try to push him away.

"Kade, you *mustn't.*"

"Aye, wife. I *must,*" he murmurs against my breast. He seems overcome. "I love you," he says. "I love everything about you. Everything, everything. You. Your face. Your hair. *I love you.* Your body. Your breasts. And *this,* most of all." He's holding me down with his hands, suckling me, pulling tenderly with his mouth. The sensation is indescribable. Needy and demanding. Potent and sublime. But then, without warning, a low pulse of pain blooms deep within my body, swelling uncontrollably. I cry out, my entire body clenching with this deep-rooted burn. I push at him. I sit up, moving to the side of the bed, and my husband stays with me, helping me stand. I don't know why, but I feel a restless need to stand, to walk, to get away from this discomfort. But as soon as I do, there's a momentous fluid shift inside me, and a torrent of liquid streams down my legs, wetting the stone floor. We both stare at it for a moment.

"'Tis time," I say, surprised at the calmness in my own voice. "The baby is coming."

Kade, for all his bravado, is frozen, his eyes affixed on the growing puddle on the floor. His face registers fear—it's an expression that rarely surfaces in him and looks strange and unnerving, wrong somehow. It clashes with him, but there it is.

And he is still frozen. He stands like that for a minute or more. I, meanwhile, am coming to terms with my own situation. I'm holding my swollen stomach and drawing in long lungfuls of air, exhaling, and again. Another deep-aching wave comes over me.

"Kade," I cry, and he instantly comes to life. He seems torn, hesitant to let go of me. But then he disengages, running for the door.

"I'll summon the healers."

"Wait," I say. "Kade."

"What, lass?"

I smile at him, despite the deep, lingering pain. "You're not clothed, husband."

He looks down at himself. Then he grabs his kilt and wraps it around his waist, not bothering with the sash or a shirt. Nor his weapons. It is the first time I have ever seen him willingly go anywhere without them. "I'll not be long, Stella. All right?"

I nod at him. Kade's eyes are full of worry, and he bolts from the room.

I wrap a sheet around myself, and I half sit on the

bed, waiting for the next contraction. Already, the waves seem close together.

And one does come, an unfathomably agonizing ache that rolls through my body with a force that stuns me. I can't suppress the moan, but I don't fight the pain. Behind it, there is life and promise. An instinctual impulse tells me to go with it, to ride the wave, that fighting against it will only prolong it and endanger my baby. And me.

My awareness shifts, as though veiling me in a protective trance, which gives me an odd comfort. Time takes on a dreamlike, elongated quality.

I am vaguely aware that Kade is with me again, and many others besides. Roses. Ismay. My own midwife named Bea. My husband is shouting orders at people as he lifts me and places me carefully on the bed. Another wave. And another.

There's arguing, and I'm covered with furs momentarily while Kade's brothers enter the chambers to gently but insistently guide my husband out of the room. I know he's not far, though; I know with certainty that he's outside the door, pacing and anxious and ranting. And probably being given a whiskey.

Roses is holding my hand, telling me to push the baby out. "'Tis time," she says. "This baby is ready to be born."

I focus on the white glow of her hair and the green light of her eyes, and I do it. I push. I have never known any pain equal to this; it is extreme and all-encompassing, but I let it come. After what feels like a very long time, finally, I feel the beautiful, slithery relief as my baby slides from my body. The relief of it is unspeakable but, inexplicably, short-lived.

"A boy," Ismay says, handing the baby to Bea, and I am overcome for two reasons. A boy. *A son.* I want him. I want to hold him. But there is more pain—*so much more*—and I can't understand it. *Why?* Is something wrong? Am I dying, as my mother died, and Kade's mother, and Knox's wife? Is this the tragic tradition of our lives and our deaths and our families? I want to call to Kade. I want to see him one more time. I moan, but the sound is primal and inarticulate. *I want him,* I try to say. *I need my husband. I want Kade.*

"Push again, Stella," Roses tells me, squeezing my hand. Her eyes don't look sad or frightened. "You're not finished yet. Push again."

I'm having trouble understanding how or why or what it means. My coherence seems swathed and clouded by a thick layer of pain. Where's my baby? But the urge to push overwhelms me, and I do as Roses says. I push again. And again.

This time the relief is more profound, more final. The pain is, quite suddenly, gone. It takes me a moment to adjust to its absence and to realize that a second child has been born. Two babies. *Twins.*

"A girl," Ismay says, beaming.

I am cleaned and covered, and the tiny wrapped babies are brought to me.

The door opens. My husband's vivid blue eyes are only on me, riveted and concerned. He looks at the tiny babies nestled against me. He comes to me, brushing my hair back from my face.

His face is close to mine, our gaze connective and real. He kisses me lightly and his touch returns me to myself. Even our words are joined. We say them together.

I love you.

* * * * *

The "First Lady of the West,"
#1 *New York Times* bestselling author

LINDA LAEL MILLER

welcomes you home to Parable, Montana—where love awaits

With his father's rodeo legacy to continue and a prosperous spread to run, Walker Parrish has no time to dwell on wrecked relationships. But country-and-western sweetheart Casey Elder is out of the spotlight and back in Parable, Montana. And Walker can't ignore that his "act now, think later" passion for Casey has had consequences. Two teenage consequences!

Keeping her children's paternity under wraps has always been part of Casey's plan to give them normal, uncomplicated lives. Now the best way to hold her family together seems to be to let Walker be a part of it—as her husband of convenience. Or will some secrets—like Casey's desire to be the rancher's wife in every way—unravel, with unforeseen results?

Available wherever books are sold!

Be sure to connect with us at:
Harlequin.com/Newsletters
Facebook.com/HarlequinBooks
Twitter.com/HarlequinBooks

H HARLEQUIN® HQN™
™ www.Harlequin.com

PHLM765

New York Times Bestselling Author

SUSAN MALLERY

He won't hesitate to put his life on the line...but will he ever risk his heart?

Falling for Justice Garrett was a high point in Patience McGraw's awkward adolescence. Even after he disappeared, Patience never forgot the boy who had captured her heart. Now he's back in Fool's Gold, California, and her passion for him is as strong as ever. But how can she trust that he won't abandon her again—and her daughter, too?

When bodyguard Justice Garrett was a young man, witness protection brought him to this idyllic town and he never forgot its warmth, or the sweet beauty of his childhood friend. He's returned to open a defense academy, and the Patience he once knew is all grown up. He can't resist her smile, or her curves. But Justice's past doesn't make him husband, or father, material.

Patience and Justice think they'll succumb to just one kiss.... Then one more.... Okay, just one night together. But they might learn that falling in love is beyond anyone's control.

Available wherever books are sold!

Be sure to connect with us at:
Harlequin.com/Newsletters
Facebook.com/HarlequinBooks
Twitter.com/HarlequinBooks

HARLEQUIN® HQN™
www.Harlequin.com

PHSM760

REQUEST YOUR FREE BOOKS!

2 FREE NOVELS
FROM THE ROMANCE COLLECTION
PLUS 2 FREE GIFTS!

YES! Please send me 2 FREE novels from the Romance Collection and my 2 FREE gifts (gifts are worth about $10). After receiving them, if I don't wish to receive any more books, I can return the shipping statement marked "cancel." If I don't cancel, I will receive 4 brand-new novels every month and be billed just $6.24 per book in the U.S. or $6.74 per book in Canada. That's a savings of at least 22% off the cover price. It's quite a bargain! Shipping and handling is just 50¢ per book in the U.S. and 75¢ per book in Canada.* I understand that accepting the 2 free books and gifts places me under no obligation to buy anything. I can always return a shipment and cancel at any time. Even if I never buy another book, the two free books and gifts are mine to keep forever.

194/394 MDN F4XY

Name _____ (PLEASE PRINT) _____

Address _____ Apt. # _____

City _____ State/Prov. _____ Zip/Postal Code _____

Signature (if under 18, a parent or guardian must sign)

Mail to the Harlequin® Reader Service:
IN U.S.A.: P.O. Box 1867, Buffalo, NY 14240-1867
IN CANADA: P.O. Box 609, Fort Erie, Ontario L2A 5X3

Want to try two free books from another line?
Call 1-800-873-8635 or visit www.ReaderService.com.

* Terms and prices subject to change without notice. Prices do not include applicable taxes. Sales tax applicable in N.Y. Canadian residents will be charged applicable taxes. Offer not valid in Quebec. This offer is limited to one order per household. Not valid for current subscribers to the Romance Collection or the Romance/Suspense Collection. All orders subject to credit approval. Credit or debit balances in a customer's account(s) may be offset by any other outstanding balance owed by or to the customer. Please allow 4 to 6 weeks for delivery. Offer available while quantities last.

Your Privacy—The Harlequin® Reader Service is committed to protecting your privacy. Our Privacy Policy is available online at www.ReaderService.com or upon request from the Harlequin Reader Service.

We make a portion of our mailing list available to reputable third parties that offer products we believe may interest you. If you prefer that we not exchange your name with third parties, or if you wish to clarify or modify your communication preferences, please visit us at www.ReaderService.com/consumerschoice or write to us at Harlequin Reader Service Preference Service, P.O. Box 9062, Buffalo, NY 14269. Include your complete name and address.

JILL SORENSON

He's her only hope...

Park ranger Hope Banning's plans for a little R & R are put on hold when a plane crashes at the top of a remote mountain. Hope will have to climb the summit and assess the situation. And the only climbing partner available is Sam Rutherford—the enigmatic man she spent a night with six months ago.

Ever since Sam lost his girlfriend in a falling accident, he insists on climbing solo. But Hope and any potential survivors need his help. As Sam and Hope set out on an emergency search-and-rescue mission, he realizes the sparks still sizzle between them. And when they learn a killer is among the survivors, they must place their trust in each other for a chance at happiness.

Available wherever books are sold!

Be sure to connect with us at:
Harlequin.com/Newsletters
Facebook.com/HarlequinBooks
Twitter.com/HarlequinBooks

HARLEQUIN® HQN™
www.Harlequin.com

PHJS795

PORTIA DA COSTA

When it comes to diamonds—like their men—some women prefer them rough

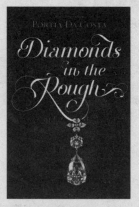

Thanks to her grandfather's complicated will, Miss Adela Ruffington, along with her mother and sisters, is about lose her home and income to a distant cousin, the closest male heir to the Millingford title. For Adela, nothing could be more insulting—being denied her rightful inheritance for a randy scoundrel like Wilson, the very man who broke her heart following a lusty youthful dalliance years ago.

Still smarting from the betrayal of his latest paramour, Wilson Ruffington never anticipates the intense desire Adela again stirs within him. Despite his wicked tongue and her haughty pride, their long-ago passion instantly reignites at a summer house party, the experience they've gained as adults only adding fuel to the flames.

Wilson and Adela are insatiable, but civility outside of the bedroom proves impossible. Determined to keep Adela in his bed, Wilson devises a ruse—a marriage of convenience that will provide her family with a generous settlement, as well as prevent scandalous whispers. Their plan works perfectly until family rivalries and intrigue threaten to destroy their arrangement…and the unspoken love blooming beneath it.

Available wherever books are sold!

Be sure to connect with us at:

Harlequin.com/Newsletters
Facebook.com/HarlequinBooks
Twitter.com/HarlequinBooks

www.Harlequin.com

PHPDC811